MOON JUICE STOMPER

RAY CASTLE

Copyright © 2019 Ray Castle

All rights reserved.

First Edition

This is a work of fiction. The names, characters and incidents portrayed in it either are the work of the author's imagination or are used fictitiously. Any resemblance to actual persons, living and dead, events and localities is entirely coincidental.

All rights reserved. No part of this publication may be reproduced, stored in a retrieval system, or transmitted in any form or by any means, electronic, mechanical, photocopying, recording or otherwise, with the prior permission of the publishers.

The author is especially indebted to Paul Chambers, Bruce McIntosh, Nick Taylor, Loui Ruijters, and Jeanette Lyons-McKinnon, for their help with this book.

Cover design by Alister Ferguson.

Paradise Precipice

FEBRUARY FULL MOON 1990

"Shiva shambho bolenath!"

JULES RAISED THE SMOOTH BARREL of the ceramic, ochre coloured chillum to his third eye, then lowered the safi-wrapped tapered end to his mouth with clasped air-tight fist as maestro DJ, Voltaire, struck two matches together igniting the ceremonial mix of Gold Flake tobacco and Manali charas. Jules, the organiser of today's party, took several locomotive starter puffs and one deep inhalation on the conical shaped pipe and passed it to Zane, an ex-anarcho punk, who passed it to Asta, a solo mum, who passed it to yogi Ananta, who passed it to Jaeger, a doyen of special Goa music, who finally, full circle, passed it to Voltaire together with a TDK cassette from out of his flax Bali bag.

It was early afternoon and they were sitting in Nirvana chai shack at the end of Spaghetti Beach, Little Vagator, where a party was about to start. Up until he'd smoked the chillum, Jules's mind had been wound tight with the fraught dealings of throwing the party, which was desperately needed. Gazing out of Nirvana chai shop at the shimmering Arabian sea he felt a weight lift off his mind as it drifted into a reverie upon an ether rainbow. *Tribeadelic nomads trekking the nadir bliss of a thousand-arm audio Buddha, dance or die, this is it...*

Large black speaker cabinets had been carried down a steep stony track from the cliff above the beach balanced on the heads of labourers, and set up on stands in a circle under fluoro painted palms. Seeing Danilo arrive, Jules stood up. "Let's get this party started!" Briskly, he headed to the dance floor.

"Fantastico!.. At last a beach party," Danilo effused with arms in the air greeting Jules at a palm leaf DJ hut.

"If we don't party now," declared Jules, "it's never going to happen. The sun's in Aquarius. The full moon in karma drama Leo. All going well, we'll be dancing through till tomorrow. We're tribes of the moon, aren't we?"

Together they inspected the dance floor where fringe fashionista, Zsu, was packing up packets of powder paint she'd been brushing on to palms to create hieroglyphic patterned decor. From out of a shoulder bag, Jules provided Danilo, an Italian DJ and regular on Spaghetti Beach, with two Sony Walkman Professional tape players decorated with dayglow OM stickers. The Walkmans were patched into an old battered mixer on a small wooden table. Into one of them, Danilo snapped a freshly recorded cassette he'd titled, TIME ENZYME, written in black marker pen. With headphones clipped to his head, he fast forwarded searching for 'Tune In (Turn On The Acid House)' by Psychic TV.

Jules lit sandalwood incense, placing it on the DJ table next to amethyst crystals clustered around a six-inch high brass Nataraja. To the side of the dance floor, on adjacent terraces, chai mummas were arriving with utensils and food packed in baskets balanced on top of their heads. They unrolled reed mats, which would become landing pads for sweaty dancers, and neatly arranged biscuits, cakes, fruits, cigarettes and kerosene cookers, glasses and spice ingredients for chai. Vassala, Jules's regular chai mumma, beamed him a large smile of approval. A bar wallah had arrived and was unloading bottles of Limca soft drink, soda water, Kingfisher beer, and a big block of ice in a sack, which had been delivered to the cliff of the beach on a bullock drawn cart.

The sound system owner, Vijay, informed Jules that everything was connected and signalled his assistant to kick over the generator recessed in a trench. Jules dug into a silver-studded leather bum bag for a wad of fifty rupee notes, which he put in the PA wallah's hand, it being the final payment for the PA hire and necessary inducement for authorities.

Danilo slid up the level on the mixer and the PA spluttered into life with muddy sounds, followed by coughing dull beats until, with Vijay's coaxing adjustments, full bandwidth took hold of the beach in which Timothy Leary's voice implored, "Tune in, turn on." Everyone who had been tanning, bathing, playing racket, reading paperbacks, backgammon gambling at Middle Vagator and Spaghetti Beach turned their attention to the audio-activated dance floor like homing pigeons being called back to their roost. Skimpy-clad, lean, bronzed bodies soon gravitated to the booming speakers to dance in the dappled afternoon shade of gaily painted palms.

Making his way up Vagator cliff track, Jules stopped half way to look down at the powering-up party. The sight of the rallying gaggle of first blush groovers getting down, put a sunny smile on his face that was much wider than the yellow smiley face on his singlet. It was testimony to a thorny paradise, the ultimate place to party, a place where he could truly step outside of his mind. Carrying a backpack of paints, brushes, string and some unused party banners, Zsu also trekked up the track. Together at the top of the cliff, they looked down at the party and congratulated themselves.

"I'm going home to freshen up," she said. "Put on something fitting for the occasion." Jules's eyes fell from her sweaty smiling face down to hip-hugging orange lycra hot pants and legs splashed with pink powder paint disappearing into faux snake-skin split-toe ninja boots.

"Don't be too long," he said.

"Ciao," she said straddling the sun-baked seat of her red Yamaha motorbike with her backpack, and suddenly let out a gasp as the searing heat of the seat burned her butt. Jules, light headed with idolatry glow, watched her dart off into a stream of motorbikes coming the opposite direction towards him. Their riders dismounted and descended the rocky track to join the party of dancers prancing in the space shower of music Danilo was spinning.

The palm grove swelled with more arrivals, including the cow man who joined in the techno, tribal chant with a series of blasts on his Rajasthan horn, followed by a backsheesh-soliciting hand fishing for rupees at the edge of the dance floor. Nonchalant holy cows splashed with fluoro powder paint meandered through the party not blinking an eye lid as dancers careered around them.

Nearby in Chapora fishing village motorbike taxi pilots at 'the big tree' were happy that a beach party was in full swing again. It meant more tourists. Hipster Harry, a rake-skinny American in his early sixties, was sipping a grape juice at Scarlet Juice Bar in the village. On hearing news of the party, he hoped to hitch a ride with thrill-seeker, Doc Silver, who's silver fox hair trailing in the air caught Harry's eye as Doc cruised through the village on his low-slung, silver, Enfield chopper.

Doc wore yellow leopard-skin patterned cotton leggings with a black leather codpiece, complemented by a lime green singlet screen-printed with a pink Ganesh and a turquoise stone necklace on his silver chest hair. This garb, and the glaze of Doc's kohl rimmed oceanic eyes was sure sign of party antics. Most likely, thought Harry, he'd been up since the night before?

"Hop on Harry," Doc said, and wound back the throttle of the souped-up Bullet Enfield, roaring it's non-muffled exhaust, rocketing the jocular couple up Chapora Hill, with Harry clinging on with white knuckles as they blasted past the kitsch Jesus statue next to the local Hindu temple heading towards sugar cane corner, where they slid to a grunting piston halt. Doc ordered two glasses from the hand-cranking sugar cane wallah. After he and Harry downed them, he ordered half a dozen bottles to be delivered to Spaghetti Beach, paid, and kicked over the fat banging motor of the Bullet. The back wheel spun in loose gravel, nearly throwing Harry off the back, who managed only to stay on by grabbing Doc's cod piece belt from behind. "Don't worry Harry," he said reassuringly, "I've never laid a bike down, we'll be on the dance floor in no time. With both wheels of the chopper gripping the melting seal of the pot hole riddled road, they hurtled towards Disco Valley.

In the early eighties, Doc Silver had led the charge of the reformation that saw a New Wave synth-electronica demimonde break away from the old school Anjuna Acid Rock jam band scene that had been the de rigueur of the seventies. Doc put on parties DJ-ing Electro, Disco and Industrial music. Indomitably, he and a posse of renegade DJs, with the assistance of locals, set up lights and speakers in the wildest of locations. Doc knew every motorbike track, and the one he was now blatting his Bullet motorbike down was over grown with jungle and sending pigs squealing in all directions. Once down on the flat at Vagator Beach, he deftly steered his chromed steed toward Spaghetti Beach, where the party was full kicking with obscene amounts of pleasure being had.

On seeing Doc and Harry arrive on the braying motorbike, Zane got up from a chai shop mumma's mat to greet them. They made their way to the side of a speaker stack to check out the heaving dance floor. Pent up frustration was being discharged from the tension that had built up from a crackdown and music curfew. Doc kicked off his cowboy boots and sashayed to yogi Ananta. Playfully they wove through the movements of the dance floor like it was a palpitating, synchronous, multi-headed creature. Soon, Doc and Zane found themselves in the sweet spot centre, odoriferous with body heat from a happiness explosion.

Zane spotted blotter baba Shazam, a purveyor of mind-altering goodness. He was holding court next to large rocks by a barely-trickling stream disappearing into Jungle Palace, a labyrinth of tropical flora to the right of Nirvana chai shack. Shazam was wearing a loud fractal-patterned jump suit that appeared to Zane like a chaos attractor in his field of vision, as he loped eagerly towards him.

"Crikey!" he blurted. "Shazam you've got me spinning and I ain't necked nout yet." Shazam looked up from dispensing tickets to a couple of English gals in fluoro spandex leggings, their arms wound with silver Rajasthani bangles, gold rings in their noses and silver anklets on their feet. "Superfrajalistaexpialidoceous," he said in a rhyming musical voice like it was a hocus pocus incantation. "See how happy the palms are today. Are you up for a Gorby? Are you a cosmonaut of the revolution?"

"Is that your top shelf?" quizzed Zane, pulling a sly grin.

"Aye," said the wizard with a sparkle in his eye as he placed a ticket of blotter in Zane's hand. Squinting at its graphic details, Zane saw it had a partial portrait of a vaguely familiar famous man in a suit and tie with bald head, which had a strange looking birth mark.

"This one brought the Berlin wall down. It's a double-dip Mikail Gorbachov," Shazam said proudly through a peep-hole mouth from which hung a long white beard. Zane looked the blotta baba wizard in the eye, smiled, and swigged down the perestroika paper with a gulp of bottled Bisleri mineral water, followed by a loud holler of, "Boom shankar!.. here's to the psychonaut revolution." Instantly his body reflexed with a nerve spasm, as the mind emulsifying elixir slid down his gullet.

The sweet sun-kissed melodies of the Goa morning techno on Danilo's tapes infectiously fired up tanned lithe bodies to perspire micro-deltas of sweat. Doc Silver's bottles of sugar cane juice arrived and were being devoured by the quenched dance floor. A local boy plied dancers with ice popsicle sticks from out of a polystyrene box he carried under his arm. The brother of the PA owner set up a bar where mineral water was the most popular drink with no one drinking alcohol.

From up on top of the cliff, Jules saw another bar arrive which immediately set off a high-pitched quarrel in Konkani that sounded like seagulls squabbling. Then another bar showed up. Jules didn't know whether to laugh or scream. A Goa dance floor was a place of serious action that was inhospitable to drunks. Bars made most rupees from selling bottled drinking water. Alcohol—not being part of Hindu tradition and a libidinal accelerant in a tight-laced culture—was strictly controlled in India, but not in post Portuguese colony, Goa, where it was liberally available and a sacrament for the weeping Christ. But hippies preferred Shiva's Himalayan sacrament of ganja and hash (charas). Chai tea served by Hindu village mummas was the favoured compliment to Shiva's sacred pipe.

There were no spectators nursing bar drinks. It was a smokers' club with a clan creed of—*safi…stone…string…matches…chillum…boom!* The ritual use of soma dating back 3,500 years ago in India's history of sacred plants (doctrine to sadhu ascetic religious culture) had been made illegal in Nepal and India after American political pressure in the seventies. And how poignant, Jules pondered, that it was the hundred dollar US greenback that the black market money exchangers loved the most, to the extent that no one went to banks to change foreign cash anymore. And how fantastic it was what black market dollars could buy you in a corrupt third world country steeped in mysticism. And how fantastic freak-friendly Goa had been up until the crackdown.

But not anymore. Party politics had become so dire, and the scene's need to dance so desperate, that it was now over a barrel being held to ransom to get something which, in the past, was a given, no permission necessary. This season dancers were grounded. No parties in Goa felt like riding a motorbike with flat tyres.

Jules and Zsu threw themselves into today's daytime party like their lives depended upon it. Like an irresistible techno itch of infected collective flesh that yearned to be scratched on a dance floor crying out to be rebooted, the days leading up to it had been tetchy and inflamed with acrid discontent that had hung heavy in the sticky tropical heat.

From up on the cliff looking down on the drama of the party, Jules lifted his gaze out to sea. A cineplex projection appeared on the horizon in the form of Greek pagan gods followed by androgynous Indian gods, then Portuguese galleon ships appeared with red crosses on their sails, followed by writhing bodies of Hindu witches being burnt at the stake in Panjim when Goa had been the Rome of the East. And suddenly, through all this, burst an Indian warship which fired upon the mainland. Then, the vision he was experiencing dissolved to hippies sitting in a circle on the beach with fishermen in outrigger boats putting out nets. *Oh, the glorious seas of faith. The anchors that have been dropped here.* He looked up to the clear blue sky firmament, like he was having discourse with invisible spiritual agencies, heavenly bodies, and alien intelligences; as if he might get an answer as to where the scene was at in the history of the universe and what was being played out today. The most troubling planetary deity was the ringed one—austere Saturn, which spun with gravitas like an old Devil, and which he regarded as the shadow of the scene's carefree fun in the sun. Saturn, the party pooper planet, intent on boxing in dreamy, nebulous, Neptune, the symbol of Shiva's trident, which ruled music, mysticism, eternity, soma and space cases.

Looking down at the party he asked himself. *Was this the lost tribe of the future?* His head spooled with fast rewind replays of how he came to be here making this party against all odds of exigency, which was testimony to his burning attachment to it. So much so, his whole life centred around being here every season. Today's highly compromised baksheesh-brokered deal was like grasping transactional lube to appease an obsession. To get a fix. To have a hit of proper amped-up paradise. Today saw him prostrating himself in acquiescence to the 'C' word, which seemed to trump everything in India, including (he cynically hated to admit) godly concerns and rabid addictions. The 'C' word was fine, as long as it worked in your favour. The 'C' word was testimony to black market forces, and if he believed the papers, the black arts of *the Devil's playground,* which the scene was accused of being worshippers of. Thus, besides corruption and compulsiveness, post-colonial Catholicism was very much in the mix.

In the past, you could pretty much butter any tight situation with rupees. But now it seemed to entail increasing degrees of valiance and defiance. The wheeling and dealings of the last twenty-four hours had brought Jules to this paradise precipice. His hippocampus clouded momentarily, he felt himself descending into a cellar of doubt. More moments stalled, cornering him in a state of vacillation which threatened to destabilise him in a tail spin with an undertow of worry worms. Nervous sweat seeped through the pores of his clammy skin. Was this really the last gasp? Did this nomadic, marginalised, lost tribe of the future really have any air of entitlement here? Oh, to dance in the palm grove of golden apples on winged feet one more time, which up until the music had just been turned on, seemed a bridge too far this season.

Niggling pinches of perturbation gripped his stomach. He wiped perspiration from his brow with his arm and considered the shifty lie of the land, the state of play, the politics of ecstasy, the love of the locals, the scene's fraternal aphorisms: *peace—unity—respect—openness—love and light.*

Being an organiser of play time brought with it politics on all fronts. Divisive vapours fumed in the passion play of pulling off a party. As evidenced ten minutes ago by the tantrum DJ Atma Blaze had dumped on him. Blaze wore tie-dyed nappies and dark sun glasses over which hung dark knotted dreads and waved a not-so-holy sacramental-pipe that was more intent on dissolving resistance to maintain one-upmanship.

Abruptly, Jules arrested his careering-off-a-cliff-edge train of thought before sharp spikes of anxiety could lock him up any further. *Get a grip. It's time to lance this festering boil. Make a stand here on beloved ragtag, safi beach.* His faltering mind and fluttering heart settled and gave way to triumphalism and a fleeting moment of martyrdom, like the saviour of a utopian dream. Then the anthem melody of 'Sundown' by The Overlords rallied the dance floor bringing an uplift, like a tribe once again on a cosmic crusade. The sight and sound of which, injected him with renewed ardour, his flesh rippling with goose bumps, the hairs on his arm standing up. The whole thrilling rush and rising excitement bringing home *the Goa experience,* making today's temerity worth it as he curled his toes over the edge of the paradise precipice he was standing on. Isn't it fascinating how bodies absorbed the characteristics of the frequencies they danced to? He watched a German girl, her blonde plaits flying as she spun non-stop like a top, aero-gyro omnidirectional egg-beating through the dance floor as though it were a wacky morphogenic soup. Like one body, made up of many frenzied bodies all pommelling the grass under the palms. Which was something that would normally be happening at three in the morning, not three in the afternoon. The big black speakers on stands under the palms represented a whole lot of love. Jules was now seeing them in wilderness settings all over the world. He thought he heard, "found myself in India," being whispered in his ear by the girl he'd met at the Mullumbimby flea market in Byron Bay, back in the seventies.

Gussied-up in iridescent purple spandex leggings, recharged and refreshed, Zsu rode her Yamaha back to the party along the gravel track between Vagator Hill and Hill Top Restaurant, whose owner, Bravan, she waved out to with her only getting an unenthused waggle of his head in reply. A couple of days earlier he'd pleaded to her and Jules to make a party with him, this would have been plan B if Vijay's connections for today's beach party had fallen through.

DJ Atma Blaze was coming the opposite direction from the beach and was steering his black Royal Enfield straight at her. Alarmed, she slammed on her brakes nearly capsizing herself on to the gritty track as the back wheel slid out leaving her teetering, holding the Yamaha at a forty-five-degree angle.

"Are you trying to kill me?" she lambasted him.

"Maybe I am!"

"What the fuck?"

"What's up with the party?" Blaze said, looking daggers. "Does Jules know who he's dealing with?"

"It's a party, that's what everyone wants. We've been given assurances."

"Is this your party?"

"No, it's everyone's party... For God's sake Atma get off your high horse—"

"Ha!.. You're a succubus," he sneered through dangling black dread locks that were like thick ropes made of dried ganja buds. His bullet hole eyes smouldered behind dark shades. Reflected in them, she saw herself mirrored resplendent like she was Minerva, goddess of war, wearing a glinting shield. She narrowed her eyes and fixed them on him like thin red laser beams penetrating his shrouded blackness.

"Wow!.. your such an imitation holy man. Do you know how horrendous it's been getting this party together? Come on Atma, it's not about me, it's not about Jules, it's not about you. This party is for everyone. It's greater than one—"

"Well, I wasn't invited," Atma whined like a petulant child.

"You mean DJ?—Oh dear!" she mocked him, but then rose above her rancour and softened her voice. "Hey don't take it personally, you played the last party. Come on, have some fun while we can."

Yet, in her eyes, he saw how repellent she found him. It made him crazy, it felt like poison in his veins. He wound the throttle of his beast-like motorcycle, spinning the rear wheel in the red dirt and blasted off leaving Zsu to eat black and blue clouds of exhaust fume.

Down on the beach at the bar, Jules clasped his hands steady around three glasses of lemon soda and took them to the DJ hut located under two coconut trees. Jaeger was there crumbling manala cream charas with his thumb nail into the palm of his hand and had slipped Danilo a cassette. He cued a track off of it pressing the pause and play buttons on one of the Sony Walkmans. At the perfect moment, as the current track tailed off, he released the pause button to unleash the rallying, rapturous, ascending synth riff of KLF's 'What Time Is Love.' It cascaded out over Little Vagator Beach sending limbs vaulting skyward like the wings of endangered, migrational rare birds riding thermal air currents essential to their habitat—now under threat.

Sipping tangy soda fizz, Jules looked up to the cliff top and thought he saw the goddess, Pallas Athena, descending down the cliff, her hair glistening with sparkling glitter and shinning silver armlets and shimmering holographic-patterned romper-stomper boots. He put on his aviator Ray Ban sunglasses to sharpen his vision and registered that his phantasm was the sun flashing off Zsu's sequinned halter neck top. She made her return to the party that was festooned with her vivid dayglow paintings, batiks and brushwork strokes on palms and rocks.

Still seated in Nirvana chai shop, Voltaire's multi-tracking Gemini mind was locked on to the quadrants of a backgammon board assessing checkers and numbers of his dice throw, as well as contemplating a dance floor afire with fierce dancing and wondering how it would be toward midnight when he was due to play. Secretly, he was hoping that the special Goa music he'd been given by music mafia connections hadn't been leaked and played by others before him. It was crucial to have fresh explosive tracks for when the moment was ripe to tip the group mind into modular expansive. He could always be relied upon to deliver spellbinding sets with deft timing. Some special mixes he'd dubbed tape to tape from A and B side versions, snipping out vocals. Being a technodelic tape jock sonically surfing a wormhole of altered states, on the edge of the East in the eighties, had been akin to dance floor psychodrama therapy in a split off bubble world of non-stop nirvanarama.

Zane danced robotico rejecto at the side of a speaker stack, his brain whirling like an unhinged flywheel. The oscillating bodies under the fluoro paintings in the late afternoon sea breeze appeared to him like amorphous amoeba. The precision of the tuned circuitry of the music—with its toe-twitching drum machine beats, and tickling hi-hats—micro-sliced gaps in space and time through the auric field of the dance floor. Like an umbilical loom patched into his vagus, the music mainlined Zane. Its annihilating rhythms propelling him feet first through a virtual reality portal. His body breech-birthed upon Spaghetti Beach, with him rummaging through porous membrane personality masks dissolving off his face. His central nervous system lit up meridians in his body electric, like his inner circuitry was pulsating fibre optics. Fractious feelings got smoothed over like a trowel rendering the plaster of paris of his brain. Burning coconut husks wafted, smelling like burning flesh. Wounded soldiers on a battlefield appeared, one of them was him, another, a colonel, his rejecting father whom he had never buried the hatchet with—a waring authority figure within.

He'd found a home in the black sheep travellers club of Goa. The softness of Asia had tenderised his nihilistic burred edges. He'd become a born-again Indo tribe pariah, subscribing to vegan-boom-shankarism. The beatific head land of Vagator allowed him to live another life, one that offered a remedial escape hatch from the ennui of the prison of the given. A self that felt ill-fitting from the day he was born. A gale force self, prone to self-sabotage in weathering the shit storms of life, which required daily dosages of head gear to bevel brain chemistry.

Danilo played 'Neue Dimensionen' by Techno Bert—it throbbed out of the sense-surround PA like an electronic rubber band upon which everyone on Spaghetti Beach bounced higher and higher up to the disco in the sky. Zane's synapses spazzed. He adrenalised. Large winged butterflies in the pit of his gut spiked him with nerve spasms that zapped his sphincter tight like a clenched fist. Urgently, he bolted towards jungle palace nearby in desperate need of an Asian squat. There, one lone protruding pink snout of a small, black haired pig was waiting. Zane looked the pig in the eye. It's bristly fecal-smeared face had a look of flighty paranoia, but also keen anticipation, as it patiently hovered salivating, ready to pounce. Zane did pranayana breathing to assist the muscular release of the sharp gripe of bowel tension. After cleaning off his ablution with his left hand using bottled drinking water, he felt purged, liberated from queasy constrictive memories of being stuck in the birth canal and the alienating feelings associated with authority figures. Now, with cabin pressure stabilised and historical ballast jettisoned, he was ready to get airborne. Take flight on the dance floor.

Spaghetti Beach was going-off like there was no tomorrow, swept up in nutty New Beat, vectoring free-form to wiggly, wobbly, Acid House, muscularly getting down to Electronic Body Music, Tribal House, synth-lush astral Eurobeat and hi-NRG Disco. Like hyper-spatial hypnosis in motion, love beach was sizzling with sci-fi electrofried exoticism. A perpetual, pureed time-stretched tape-to-tape techno tranzendentalism. A mandelbrot maze of fractal figures random synchronised in rhythmic abandon.

Zane found Zsu and Jules dancing near the cliff-side of the bubbling dance floor. "It's a belting, blinder," he screamed. "Fuck me!.. just what we needed—"

"Only when I'm dancing, do I feel fully alive," Zsu yelled back in a high-pitched voice through pneumatic breaths.

"Absolute satori!" Jules chimed in, ducking and diving about them.

A skinny, sweaty, dreadlocked dancer was cooling his over-heated head in front of the fan directed at the PA amplifier. Nearby, Danilo peered up from tape players to see, with the bat of an eye lid, and leap of a heartbeat, a retinue of khaki-uniformed police wielding bamboo sticks come down the cliff track. With chest crushing anxiety he slid down the fader, killing the music. Everything came to a halt on the dance floor. "Cops!.. Cops!.. Cops!.. voices screamed hysterically in a mass freak-out.

Gripped by the alarming upsurge of hard, cold, official reality, Jules darted straight to the DJ hut where Danilo was hastily gathering up his tapes. Grabbing both his Sony Walkmans, Jules tugged them free from their leads into the mixer and stuffed them in his bag and scampered with Danilo, leaving the mortified PA wallah, Vijay, shaking at the knees by his mixer. Five cops with peak caps had descended to the flat of the fiercely stomped dance floor.

Some dancers skittered in panic to the chai mummas, others became enraged shouting, "Piss off!" Such that the cops themselves became intimidated, edgy and vulnerable—like they were intruders on consecrated turf. Zane was one of the most vocal protestors. Every fibre of his being trembled as temper-tantrum rage welled-up bottlenecking his brainstem with competing fight-flee-fear signals overloading his adrenalised motor cortex receptors, bringing about a virtual synaptic shutdown, which had him collapsing distraught on a chai mat moaning ululations. Other freaks around him were shrieking and barking, "Fuck off!... Fuck off!... Fuck off!..." With a baby in one arm, a persistent solicitous beggar woman stood near the chai mat emotionless, indifferent to the escalating drama, her other arm outstretched, backsheesh-wheedling Zane; until Doc moved her aside.

Moving toward the centre of the empty dance floor, Zsu—in a hoodoo, high-banshee voice fed by deep fortifying breaths—commenced to recite an incantation sutra in Hindi. She took up a defensive pose like that of a dancing cobra snake, her aura and guise like Kali, the goddess of destruction. She pivoted from one foot to the other fixing a tai chi chuan, martial arts, mesmeric gaze upon the bedevilled cops clustered together at the centre of the dance floor. Then, she started to skip like a kick boxer, which rallied a rising chorus of enraged cussing from an amassed mob of fuming dancers with Zane flinging terse taunts and some picking up stones to throw.

Then, a gun shot rang out across Vagator Spaghetti Beach. Everyone looked up to see a policeman with a Lee-Enfield bolt-action .303 rifle, used by military forces of the British Raj, at the top of the cliff. Around his neck hung a gold chain with Jesus stick.

Beatific Head Land

A LOCAL TATA BUS from Mapusa to Chapora pulled into Starco Corner, North Anjuna, at noon on a Monday, the second week of January, nineteen eighty-seven. Jules Nightingale got off it shouldering a public transport-beaten backpack. Stepping onto the red dirt at the edge of the road he felt like he'd touched down on hallowed ground. Thrilled excitement resuscitated his travel-fatigued body, having arrived in Panjim deck class on the overnight ferry from Bombay and the previous night spent sleepless on a bed bug-ridden mattress in a flophouse hotel. The bus, belching fumes, turned right toward Vagator and he gazed at the ocean. On the side of the road next to a Catholic weeping cross on a cement plinth stood a local teenage boy wearing a faded T-shirt with holes printed with "Goa Is a State Of Mind."

"Mista, you want room?" the boy called out.

Eyeing the boy, "Yup, but first I want to murder a cold beer."

The boy walked over to him. "Mista come this way." They walked towards the beach. There were no waves to write home about on his next postcard to Sydney.

At the White Negro Restaurant the Kingfisher beer was refreshing, but tasted rough, yet was compensated by the not too bad fish and chips he washed down with it. All and all, amounting to a damned good Western style treat after endless spicy curries. Goa was not India, according to Zsu, who he'd met at a party in Bali two months earlier. Goa had magical allure in Jules's mind, as she'd told him it was her *home*.

Offering to show him a room, the boy led the way down a dirt lane to a house with a courtyard in which there were chooks and a yapping small, scrawny beige-coloured dog. Stepping out of the front door, a smiling middle aged Goan woman in a flower-patterned dress wearing thick horn-rimmed glasses and a cross tattooed on the underside of her left wrist, greeted him. She introduced herself as Anastasia and showed him a ten-rupees-a-night room.

"I'll take it," he said, too tired to look any further. He gave ten rupees backsheesh to the boy, unhitched his back pack and collapsed on to the single coconut fibre mattress that lay on a dried cow shit floor. After waking late in the afternoon, Anastasia provided him with a plastic bucket to take a shower at the local well. His shoulder-length flaxen hair dried fast in the heat of the day. Tying it into a ponytail, sharpened him up. The contents of his backpack, he exploded into the corner of the room. He pulled on a pair of board shorts, slipped on a singlet, strapped on a bum bag, donned Ray-Bans, bolt-locked the door with his own padlock and ventured out into soft, orange sunlight.

Wandering in flip flops he headed toward the beach through palm trees along a well-worn track that had been ground into fine red and brown dust. Exotic riders with wild hair, in skimpy, bright coloured patterned fabrics—like the prismatic plumage of a *neo tribe*— passed him on Rajdoot and Enfield motorbikes heading toward the dipping sun. The path ended in a nest of motorbikes by a palm frond pyramid structure, out the front of which was a brass trident, Shiva lingam and a dhuni. A lithe sadhu sat in lotus position wearing an orange g-string langoti, his body rubbed with ash, thick matted dreadlocks wound around the top of his head into which was stuck a silver Shiva moon and around his neck hung rosaries of aksha nuts. Scattered about were a gaggle of freaks on reed mats baton-passing chillums.

Walking past the holy smoke circle, Jules the traveller, heard French and Italian being spoken amidst volleys of jovial laughter. At the sea shore the sun was turning red as it commenced touchdown on the horizon. Down on the sand a naked Western yogi did a salute to the sun in a headstand lotus pose. At the moment, the sun kissed the Western horizon, a Tibetan prayer bowl rang in traveller Jules's head. It was the sound of eternity at the place Zsu called—*far out*. A mythic, beatific beachhead, that had beckoned in the traveller's imagination ever since enchantress, siren, Zsu had lured him here, like he'd been cast under a spell promising *paradise*. Gazing upon the sun's touchdown on the Arabian Sea felt heaven sent, its prescient landing an eternal returning beyond this lifetime.

For traveller Jules, hunkering down at the dhuni crumbling sacrament on the West-meets-East headland, not knowing a soul, felt like consummation of a pilgrimage with the *safi clan*. A cobra-headed chillum was passed to him from his left; he lifted it and tapped it on his forehead with a "boom bolenath" incantation—and took a pull. Lung sacs filled with jet streams of Himalayan rubbed cannabinoids riding a head rush of Gold Flake nicotine. Exhaling, his mind melted in an elevating uplift. Passing the chillum to his right, he gazed out to sea into the heart of the molten sun setting on the horizon and gradually sinking into a sea of infinity.

"Got a Gold Flake?" came a Mediterranean voice next to him.

"Nah—I got Panama fags."

"That'll do."

"Stunning sunset," Jules said.

"It's tops," said the chillum circle stranger, flicking dreadlocks off his face. "You just arrived?"

"Yeah, from Down Under."

"Under where?"

"Sydney. And you?"

"I'm from the land of Zeus."

"Zeus, the Greek god?"

"Yes, yes, I'm from there.

"Cool… the Greek gods talk to me… Hey g'day, I'm Jules."

"'Namaste!.. I'm Zikos," said the dark haired dreadhead taking a chillum out of a mauve Rajastani textile pouch. "When I came to India I met the goddess, Parvati. She looks over me."

The Greek looked like a gypsy with a dark goatee, ears pierced with chunky golden earrings swinging under his dreads and a strapping physique contained in a gilded Afghani vest. Around his neck he wore a Tibetan, mala choker made of amber. He prepared a mix with fingernails under which had lodged dark putty-like charas which he'd rubbed himself in Kulu Valley, Himachal Pradesh.

"Asia is intoxicating," Jules said, "I first met Hindu gods in Bali."

"Hmm, seductive place," Zikos said, licking the side of a cigarette. "It's horny, enticing…and yeah, deceptively mystical." He peeled away the paper releasing the orange and brown speckled tobacco into a small, polished, coconut mull bowl where he'd picked off black fragments of his personal charas. "Bali is also treacherous. Dangerous for smoke. Didn't used to be like that. Now screwed up by a Muslim government. India is madness. Heaven and hell are closer together here."

"Do you know a girl called Zsu?" Jules chanced to ask.

"Yup," the Greek said tipping a mix into the warm chillum, gently packing it with a forefinger.

"Have you seen her?"

"She's around." Zikos wrapped a damp safi cloth at the bottom of the chillum and passed it to Jules, then cocked two matches on the side of a matchbox. "Boom bolenath!" he ignited twin flames to the top of the pipe as Jules sucked and puffed billows of holy smoke, then passed it back. The Greek grasped the ceremonial chillum with both hands cupped together air-tight, took two puffs, then passed it to his right. When it arrived to the sadhu, with him taking a toke, he coughed as though he had iron lungs.

The swoosh of a reed broom scratching upon a sun-baked dirt courtyard, chooks cluck, cluck, clucking, the high-pitched yap of Anatasia Dalgado's dog, and her voice nattering with a neighbour in Konkani were the sounds that Jules woke up to on his second day in Goa. The local organic ablution system was comprised of an outdoor latrine squat toilet with concrete slide trough serviced by a couple of small black hairy pigs. Their psycho eyes, rapid convulsive jaw action and grunts, both fascinated and disturbed him whilst he crouched preparing to feed them with a dump, like it was an advance and retreat pleasure game.

Goa pigs were always ready, he quickly found out, their noses and eyes vigilant to the state of the bowel and butt being bared to them. Since being in Asia, he was of the opinion that squatting and cleaning off with water using the left hand was much more healthy and hygienic than using toilet paper. On a couple of horrendous bus trips, he'd had urgent excruciating experiences which he hastily sort relief of by getting down on his haunches, like the locals on the side of the road, to disgorge the discomfort of burning curry containing bacteria that had blitzed his bowel, pushing him over the edge into liquid, poop purgatory. It was hot going down, and sure burned like a hot poker coming out the other end. Reassuringly, he kept reminding himself that these were the kind of experiences that rewarded one with mettle in the land of the metaphysical. His tolerance for fiery gastronomy increased.

Zikos said that he hung at the south end of the beach and ate at Joe Banana. Jules pulled on Speedo swimmers, wrapped a Bali batik sarong around his waist, fixing it with a black leather bum bag containing Rizla papers, Swiss army knife, Instamatic camera, cigarettes, lighter, rupee notes and a finger of liquorice coloured charas. Donning shades and flip flops, he followed a path past St Anthony Chapel to a large dry paddy field where a couple of black buffalo mooched. Dung smells and fragrant jasmine wafted through the salty air. Palms curved upward into the clear blue sky, their spiky leaves rustling in a slight shore breeze that cooled mid-morning droplets of sweat on his forehead as he felt his body loosen into sultry tropical air.

Turning around, he looked back at the whitewashed St Anthony Chapel. It rose up grandiloquent, like a colonial white elephant, testimony to an imperious Portuguese era that was not so long ago. It featured a deity that looked plangent, compared to the fairy tale gaiety of the allegory of the animal deities inhabiting Hindu temples that had captivated him on his travels. Pressing on into the agrarian beach vista, he imagined the paddy a radiant green in monsoon. His rookie, Asia traveller defences loosened, he liberated his feet from rubber flip flops and carried them hooked under his fingers. The warm, red, earth mingled with sand and was soft on the soles of his feet. He was happy to be at a beach once again, away from the din and stench and hustle and bustle of densely populated cities. The wet oatmeal coloured sand of Anjuna cushioned his steps and gentle waves lapped his ankles as he padded his way toward the southern end of the beach where he could make out figures. There were no Indians in sight. It was as if he'd dropped into an oasis. A traveller safe haven from marauding touts. A naturalist habitat for European migrational birds.

The serene natural beauty of the empty beach felt like balm to his brain, after weeks of wading through fetid, clawing cities seething with a sea of black faces, many of whom were intent on engaging in rupee hustle. The features of these black faces had disappeared in the auto contrast setting of the snaps he took. Passing an outrigger fishing boat with nets draped over it on the sand, he drew closer to the end of the beach and saw that the figures were bronzed and naked. *Western weirdos who'd changed colour. Was this a dispossessed nomadic tribe?* Drawing closer. *A freaksville juxtaposed on the edge of the third world?* Drawing closer still. *Were these first world gypsies?* Drawing even closer. *What kind of fourth world is this troupe of tribalists?* Squinting his eyes in the morning sun, he beheld peanut brown lean bodies sun baking and bathing. Feeling like an outsider, he slowed his steps and walked shyly diagonally away to the back of the naked beach scene, all the while craning his neck with inquisitive eyes turned to the corner of their sockets hidden behind his shades.

There was no white bum or boob in sight. Male and female angularity and curvaceousness with dangly bits and triangular patches of furriness fused into primal, tribal, communal flesh. There was even a pet monkey hopping about. This all stacked up in Jules's bohemian-smitten brain like a romantic, Rousseau, hippie dreamscape. From behind, he scoped the troupe of tribalists hoping to spot Zikos, or maybe Zsu? *What kind of dreadlock holiday was this?* And then, to his relief, he spotted Zikos's dreadhead with telltale golden earrings. The Greek was sitting with a bunch of tribalists. Feeling less of an interloper, Jules went to join them.

"Namaste," Zikos warmly greeted him.

"Wow!.. What a chilled beach," Jules said, unknotting the sarong from his waist and spreading it out on the sand and pulling off his speedo briefs and sitting down.

"Nothin' like a beach to empty your mind," said an older freak with an American accent sitting next to Zikos.

"I've done heaps of beaches," Jules said, "mostly surfin'.. but this is wild."

"There's waves galore here, too, man," continued the freak, who was lanky limbed with olive skin looking like he'd seen a lifetime of daily sun. "Here there's wavelengths that are wild to ride," he said like a joker smoker, who might well be "the walrus" from the Beatles's Magical Mystery Tour.

"Harry," said Zikos, "meet—arrrh…sorry man, what's your name again?"

"Jules."

"It's a pleasure…man."

Looking at the spread of hairy sun worshippers laid out, Jules said. "Some cool, loose, dangly scene here."

"Family!" Harry said, his sun baked features aglow. "Ain't no other place I'd rather be. Mumma India took me in. We rolled in on the magic bus. Man… it was a velvet revolution, we just kept on rollin'… Back then, the only fashion was the colour sarong you were wearing. We got around naked all the time."

Harry struck Jules as a genuine dharma bum. A Haight Ashbury original. The reality shift of the boho-bon-vivant-ness whirled Jules's brain. He thought of Zsu. *Where might she be?* He imagined her nude on South Anjuna beach. Shaking off his newbie, interloper awkwardness he stood up starkers bearing a white arse and strolled down to the warm ocean to join other tribalists bathing. Diving in, it felt like a ritual dip, a baptism—like the Hindu devotees he'd witnessed bathing in the Ganges at Varanasi. Indians don't swim in the sea, Zikos had told him last night. Indians are afraid of the sea. The locals stay away from it, they are freaked by *The Evil Eye*. Local fishermen are superstitious, they believe the beach is full of ghosts at night. On the beach the freaks are free to do whatever they like.

Jules's floated on his back in the tepid ocean, his body slightly submerged, he observed his lingam and pubic hair swirling gently like squid in seaweed. Taking in the beach scene, he let go to an immeasurable feeling of relaxation and freedom like he'd never felt before. His mind drifted back to when he'd danced naked in the mid-seventies, in a drum circle with Bhangwan sanyasins in a lush rainbow forest in Nimbin, North New South Wales. Looking around, he exchanged smiles with fellow floaters, duckers, divers, swimmers, huggers, snoggers and felt accumulated travel stress drain out of him.

Returning to the sand to drip dry in the heat on his sarong, he toked on a passing joint which heightened the awe of the cool clan he was immersed in. His eyes surreptitiously observing every face and body in detail from behind mirror aviator shades. *How did they all end up here?*

"Hey dude, fancy some food at Joe's?" Zikos said, rising to his feet.

"Hell yeah!—I'm panging," Jules said, spaced-out stoned on an empty stomach, his mind cartwheeling the tribal sun worshippers of South Anjuna Beach.

With sarongs wrapped around their waist, they walked bare foot along a well-worn path that wound through coconut palms near the foot of South Anjuna Hill. "Harry is a trail blazer pioneer of the scene," Zikos explained. "We call him Hipster Harry cause he's an original beatnik. And man, he blows a mean sax and seriously gets down on the dance floor. He pretty much discovered this piece of paradise, right here." Zikos pointed to the ruins of a brick house. "Everybody used to eat together on his porch."

"Do you know where Zsu stays?" Jules asked.

"Badem. For sure you'll catch her at the flea market."

"We met in Bali," Jules explained. "Love what she makes."

"She also makes wicked parties," Zikos said.

"She told me about them, I can't wait."

"Did she tell you about the cobras?"

"No."

"She employs a snake charmer."

"Shikes!"

Arriving at Joe Banana Restaurant, a glistening silver Enfield chopper parked at the entrance, with the head of Shiva airbrushed onto its tank, caught Jules's eye. Inside a Belgium couple in their twenties were seated at a rickety table. They had lily white skin that was like a wearable art gallery of Jaipur gem stone jewellery, which they'd designed. Colette had bleached blonde hair. Jeroen, new wave razored hair and wore a black T-shirt with NEON JUDGEMENT written in red gothic font. They were looking forward to the flea market where they would sell their intricate designs presented in fold out wooden cases. Most exciting of all, they were brimming with anticipation as they'd just heard of a party tonight. Zikos greeted them and he and Jules joined them at their table. The menu, a few hand-written lines on a scrap of paper, was pinned to the wall.

"Joe's bhaji, thali and shakes are the best!" Zikos recommended.

After they ordered and a long wait, two bhajis were delivered by Joe on wrinkly bow legs wearing shorts and a well-beaten singlet with holes worn through, which Jules was coming to realise was the thread bare local dress code. After wolfing down his bhaji and papaya shake, he ordered a thali. Attentively, he pricked his ears to the banter of the coterie at Joe Banana's, which was made up of an eccentric array of colourful characters. Some riffling through a tattered cardboard community mail box checking for aerograms, letters and postcards. The loudest of all, Doc Silver, a silver fox in his mid-forties with a striking flurry of aluminium coloured hair who wore cut-off Levi's, out of which shot shaved legs with cowboy boots.

"Jeez, they're pack of fuckwits," hollered Doc waving his hands about from an adjacent table. "Everyone knew about tonight, how can they do that?" he complained in a sharp, rising, chain saw New York accent. "We'll have to find another system. Stuff those moron Krauts. How can they do that?"

"What's up Doc?" Zikos asked.

"You wouldn't believe it," the chain saw voice whined an octave higher. "The best sound system in Mapusa was booked for tonight on the beach, but they blew me out, rented it for an Indian wedding, and now I hear an idiot Kraut upstart in Vagator is jumping in to do another party tonight."

"That's stupid," Zikos said. "Your right Doc, we don't need two parties on the same night, it splits the energy."

"That dipstick Johnny-come-lately in Vagator," hissed Doc, "knew about tonight's Anjuna party. I hate it when dumb arses blow it—"

"So, the party this side is looking shaky?" Zikos said.

"No way, Jose!" Doc Silver said vehemently, and hastily exited Joe Banana's mounting his chopper, his cowboy boots ferociously kicking it over and loudly roaring off.

That night in Chapora Village a barber's blade glided smoothly through the lathered stubble on Jules's face and down to his Adam's apple. Reclining back in the barber chair relaxing into the drawn out vanity treatment, his eyes were entertained by the coiffure paraphernalia of Bengal razors, creams, brushes, scissors and altar of OM stickers and pictures of holy prophets on the cracked mirror. Next to it was a poster of Ganesh, the elephant god which had first enchanted him in Indonesia. Closing his eyes, he sunk into the worn, leather, barber chair. His mind replayed Bali, like holiday Super 8 footage in his head. He saw himself and Zsu sipping cocktails poolside surrounded by lush tropical plants with radiant bright flowers and the most fantastical deities he'd ever seen carved out of stone.

"It's island of the Gods," she said. "It's the sugar mountain jewel of Asia. Money and mysticism are well wedded in Hinduism, avarice is not a sin. Bali is drop dead gorgeous, but you can end up a target. We're like honey for marauding ants."

The barber, wearing grey polyester slacks and white short sleeved button shirt, massaged Jules's head, neck and shoulders, then said into Jules's ear, "Finished." Startled, he opened his eyes like being jarred out of a wet dream and was greeted by his clean shaven face in the mirror framed by garlands of flowers, holy men, animal gods and a little Shiva alter with a flickering light bulb. He dug into the bottom of his bum bag. It jangled with paise coins. He paid five rupees and strolled down to the general store glimpsing Chapora River through palm trees where canoes carved from logs sat on its tidal bank.

He bought candles, a couple of reed mats, and ordered fish curry rice at a local restaurant which he ate whilst observing the village's night life that was starting to swell with freaky foreigners. Local men in monotone attire smoked beedies. A Hindu woman zoomed past side-saddle on the back of a motor scooter sari-wrapped with a sweep of radiant colour flecked with silver and gold. At the next table, French was being spoken with the word—*party*— repeatedly punctuating the conversation. Jules interjected: "Excusez-moi!.. Do you know about parties tonight?"

"Yes, yes," said a girl with a mohawk, her scalp tattooed in sanskrit. "I heard of two parties—"

"That's what I heard," Jules confirmed. Then Doc Silver rumbled past on his Enfield chopper. "Hang on, I can check." He abandoned his half-eaten curry to chase down Doc, who had spun around and was heading back toward him. Jules waved his arms as the silver steed chopper swerved to miss him and slid to a growling halt.

"Hey!" Jules said. "I saw you at Joe Banana Restaurant earlier. Can you tell me what's up, party-wise, tonight?"

"It was sabotage!" declared the seasoned quicksilver maker of mischief. "But its back on," he said jiggling his eyebrows with a puck grin. "It's all on for South Anjuna, as planned." He revved his chopper and rumbled up to the big tree by the juice bars to drop the news on the boom shankar brigade puffing pipes and sipping juices.

Doc Silver's outlandish, avuncular clowning about was an esprit tonic for the Chapora chillum wheezers and bar flies. Some believed Doc was a struck-off shrink. Rambunctiously, he ranted and rollicked between the old guard of South Anjuna and the young Vagator techno anarchists, and was prone to ruffle the feathers of some of the South Anjuna gentry, whom the crusty Chapora party animals jokingly referred to as, "the Beverly Hills of Goa."

A French freak looking like a pirate, wearing black and red stripped tights, gave Jules a ride to Starco Corner on a TVS moped. Back in his room, Jules pimped himself into party mode donning zebra patterned shorts, Rajastan aladdin shoes and a T-shirt that said, EMBRACE THE CHAOS.

Stepping out into the night with a rising, sickle Shiva moon for his first Goa party, he was psyched with anticipation. The dirt track was dark, the Made-In-India torch in his hand, dim. The Baroque sacred heart grotto of St Anthony's Jesus was shrouded in shadows, the anarcho-Goth in Jules imagined gargoyles and bats lurking in them. In the distance, he could hear the flanged sound of electronic beats and smidgen snatches of synthesiser melodies. All sonically smudged and disembodied through the shifting sea breeze and rustle of palms. The tide was rising and the crest of the waves shimmered in the moonlight with phosphorescence. Gazing down the end of the beach, where he'd had a dip that morning with the naked nomads, he saw lanterns on the sand and flickering lights in the palms.

Passing Guru Bar, he came upon something washed up on the wet sand. Moving closer toward it, he stopped dead in his tracks with his head spinning as he realised it was the head of a goat with horns—most of it's flesh eaten away. The music suddenly took the form of a multi-headed hydra that spoke in technological tongues. A dissident urban reptile of the Sydney squat scene, and identifying with Industrial subculture, Jules found himself gobsmacked. His mind scrambled to decipher the strange sound pastiche he was walking towards.

South Anjuna Beach had been transformed into a chai shop encampment tendered by local mummas who stoked kerosene cookers making pots of steaming spice tea. Sojourners of a bewildering machinery of night sat on reed mats sipping small glass cups of tea, like East-West gypsies on magic carpets. Pungent plumes of charas rose above them from circulating chillums, the aroma infused with the perfume of burning incense sticks that chai mumma's had stuck into bananas next to plates of cake.

Walking through the gypsy camp, he was magnetically pulled toward the palm grove that had become a flickering enviroteque of fairy lights and pulsing with hypnotising computer beats. Standing on the edge of the dance floor gaping, he encountered a scene of cavorting bodies garbed in a hotchpotch masquerade of hybridised fashion. A fusion of ethnic and New Wave motifs screaming with colours, stripes and sparkling fabrics; accessorised with waist pouches, studded belts, a regalia of sculptured jewellery, talisman adornments and amulets.

The music sounded futuristic. Surgically, he attempted to decipher the idiosyncrasies of its granular synthesis, which could well be the circuitry of enigma machines from outer space. It pulsated out of four sound sources within palms that were Jackson Pollock splattered and dripped in a confetti of fluorescent eye-popping paint. Flabbergasted, he stood and gaped. *Psycho…troppo… dance bizarre…* He couldn't identify one track. It was the sound of an alien world in an ancient vase inside a palm grove. The sickle moon rising above South Anjuna beach looked like the silver one in the Sadhu's hair on his first sunset, the day he arrived in North Anjuna—which had been on a new moon in Aquarius. This he read as an ingress into escapades in counter culture. Tonight, the moon was in space case Pisces about to enter—new frontier—Aries.

Gazing up at the Shiva moon suspended in the gazillion-splatter-sweep of the milky way, its stellar vividness upon jet black darkness was like he'd never seen before. The vastness of its glister, so arresting that he experienced himself a conduit between its glittering grandeur and the earth and the sand and the grass and the smell of cow dung upon which frolicked the freaky farrago with its oddity of gyrating, convolving bodies. *What is this electric intoxicating exotica?*

Turning to walk back to the chai shop encampment, he came upon locals huddled around a lantern playing a card game and drinking feni (a local brew derived from coconut palm or cashew fruit), with rupee notes rapidly changing hands. Casting his eyes into the chai mumma camp, Jules spotted Hipster Harry and went over and hunkered down on the same magic carpet of reed mats, steaming tea and smouldering pipe.

"Hi Harry," Jules said sitting down in front of Vassala, Harry's regular chai mumma. A Hindu widow in her forties with three children who was assisted by her daughter. Utensils, urns, baskets, cigarettes, biscuits, cakes, fruits and small chai glasses were neatly arranged around them. Her deep, warm, brown, eyes steadfast with a dutifulness that was a solid anchorage for her tripped-out loyal customers, who would pit stop from dancing at her hurricane lantern. For the absolute lost-the-plot lot, she was a light house rock of Gibraltar. They would rummage through a large basket she oversaw containing their discarded, tangled clothes and bags.

"Howdy brother," Harry said.

"It's sure goin' off," Jules said, turning to gaze at the pulsing palms.

"That grove is a sacred site," Harry said. "It all started with acoustic guitars and candles in the sand. Later it got electric. Had a stage there." He pointed to a couple of large stones. "We set up Marshall amps. A gift from The Who. Some freaks knew 'em, bought their donated gear overland on the magic bus. They did a song about it."

"I remember it. 'Get on the magic bus'…"

Harry fielded a passing charas-aroma chillum in one hand, took a toke and ceremonially passed it on to Jules in one smooth swing of his arm.

"Overland, back then," he said, "was the only way to get here. We were smokin' the best all the way. Man!.. once you had arrived down from the mountains, India moved right through you, real easy. By the time you got here by train and overnight ferry, you'd been tumbled into a polished stone."

"Afghanistan must have been wild back in the day?"

"Oh, man!.. we jammed the panelling of the bus with the best smoke. Pulled out the air conditioning, loaded it full up and when the heat came on, it stunk!.. Here, check this primo Afghani." Harry put a piece of dark soft hash with a gold seal in Jules's hand. "This one I smoke pure, not in the chillum." From out of a shoulder Kulu bag he handed a brass and porcelain hookah to Jules. "Filler 'er up bud."

"Hey thanks, man." Jules felt its softness in his hand and enjoyed its fragrance as he crumbled it into a polished coconut mull bowl in front of his crossed legs on Vassala's reed mat, which was feeling more and more like a magic carpet.

"The muslim babas in Afganistan," Harry said, looking out into the blackness of the ocean, "they were a Sufi sect called Malang… were minstrels on horses, couriers of information, like the newspaper. They had free smoke. There were chai shops with hash water pipes called Mr Hababula. Kabul had silversmiths who looked Mongolian, like the old tribes of Asia. There's always been feuding tribes there. Then, the Russians moved in, Christmas seventy-nine. All the smack and hash coming out of Afghanistan now is funding the Mujahdeen resistance—"

"We're all rebels," said a wiry man, mid-forties with wavy dark hair, in an American accent sitting next to Harry. He was dressed in Escher patterned pants and a hand painted tank top that featured a Tibetan mandala out of which sprung well buffed biceps and toned arms. "Goa is a safe haven, always been a sanctuary for pirates."

"Michael is our resident tennis coach," Harry said, introducing his friend. "We've got a court out the back of Gregories Restaurant. There's some hot players, everyone is fit from marathon dancing at the parties."

"Man!..it's kickin' in those palms," Jules said.

"You betcha," Harry said, poised with a match. Jules tipped the rebel Afghani hash into the porcelain bowl of the hookah and held the pipe to his lips as Harry struck the match. Jules puffed several short breaths, followed by two long drags, then passed the hooker to Harry who puffed, and passed it to Michael. Vasella's Afghani magic carpet sailed skyward like a helium filled balloon rising above South Anjuna Beach, and soon became a space craft which hovered over the dance floor. The gyrating life forms under the palms below took on the appearance of mutant bacteria in a cyborganic petri dish viewed through a microscope. The magic carpet landed back in the chai shop camp, Jules alighted, put on his aladdin shoes, farewelled Harry and Michael, and headed for the dance floor.

"Who's been sleeping in my brain," said a gnarly voice on top of a pulsing bass and gated synthesiser. Jules's body braced against the palpitating tat ta tat ta tat tat tat of the unrelenting, mechanoid zap-zap beats. The atmosphere had changed since he first dipped his toe into the palm grove—it was now otherworldly, extraterrestrial-like. A muscular, cyberdelic riff gripped his body like a hydraulic limb of a robot with atavistic dalek-sounding vocoder. The music, resembling nothing like his band—The Telepathics.

A tenor voice over the beat was commanding, "Der Mussolini." Abdomen muscles tightened, as incessant bass gnawed at his body and tore his knees loose, like he was in the grip of a vibrating cling-on rhythm device. His mouth was wide open and his musical taste buds were being aurally mouth washed. The unrelenting bass had its way with him. Pivoting and swivelling at the knees, his body felt like it was in uncharted territory with something taking hold of him. He was a long way from home and over his head. He came upon a wizard, with long flowing white hair and Merlin beard, sitting cross legged on a mat next to candles with small Shiva altar. A hand maiden with a mane of black cork screw hair, a garland of fresh flowers around her neck, wearing a black leather lace-up bustier and crimson Rajasthani fabric mini skirt, stood next to the wizard. Revellers shuffled about the wizard while she presented them with small plastic cups of glowing potion.

Continuing around the edge of the party, Jules came upon a small palm frond hut at the base of the cliff, where there sat a stocky figure with tendrils of dark dreadlocks hunched over a dim table light shuffling stacks of cassettes. *Aha!.. The DJ.* Through dangling dreads, darting beady, black eyes searched hand written names on inner sleeves in tape boxes collaged with sparkling art work, some spread out like tarot cards. Squinting, Jules attempted to stickybeak the track names of this unheard-of music. *This must be the East edge? It ain't Rock 'n' Roll Kathmandu. For sure, not Buddha Cafe Bali.* What is this plunder phonics? Not regular disco? Not insipid handbag tunes he knew from gay arse bandit clubs.

A child of the groovy generation, Jules Nightingale wasn't born yesterday, his trainspotter antenna scrambled to tag this *disco mystic techno*. He was in awe of its arcane, anarchistic, maverick flavours. Its deus ex machina atmospheres, suggestive of something clandestine, like a new kind of sound sorcery. The dreadlock DJ shuffled cassettes. Hangers-on hovered about, thumbs and forefingers crumbling charas into their cupped palms—all oblivious to Jules's gawking at the intriguing goings-on in the DJ hut. He turned around and headed back to the Shiva altar, but the wizard had vanished. The hand maiden showed up extending a hand with a cup of elixir, and with large, round, seductive lips mouthed the words—"Lucy in the skies with diamonds." Receiving the cup with a grateful nod, he made his way back to the edge of the dance floor. Raising the cup to the moon, he spoke the evocation, "Om Shivaya," and took a deep breath and skulled the elixir. The potion immediately spiked a spasm through his nervous system, like an alert signal in anticipation of the alchemical, neural tinkering that he had embarked upon.

Returning to Vassala's chai mats, he found her pouring glasses of spicy brew for a new bunch of magic carpet riders who were speaking Scandinavian. Jules settled on a mat and started crumbling into his mull bowl. The procession of characters in hybrid fashion fictions was an entertaining spectacle of crossbreed creatures. By the time Vasella passed him his glass of chai, he was feeling altered. By the time, he'd sipped half of it he felt himself to be losing his shape. Then experienced himself as a survivor of a ship wreck with his reed mat, magic carpet becoming a life raft which he could not abandon as there were strange fish fins in the sea all around him. Then the magic carpet of the chai mat became an atoll. *Am I going to spend the whole party marooned here?*

He turned around and looked at Vasella, her warm reassuring eyes were comforting, she smiled at him and then he realised that he was the only one sitting on her mats. Words did not come, he was tongue tied. On his hands and knees, he crawled over to her lantern and fumbled with the zip of his bum bag to pay for the tea. "Good party," she said approvingly. Maintaining eye contact with her, Jules believed her unquestionably, he then got a grip and rose to his feet. He thanked her with a Buddhist bow with hands together, turned around and headed to the dance floor of a new paradigm of partying.

In the shadows on the edge, he crouched on his haunches into an Asian squat, like a yoga posture to recalibrate his mind and contemplate the enticement of the strange psychodrama that was the dance floor. Mongrel, East-West wildlife creatures of the night hopped about in a peculiar panoply of striking ad-hoc costumes; far removed from regular fashion codes, and standard night club body mapping. A melange of styles that was as much off the wall as the music was underground, edgy, technologically alien, synthetic and otherworldly.

"Through the never-ending mists of time people have waited upon their redemption," came a voice overdubbed in a quirky electro track, 'Rebirth of The Anti-Christ' by Ironic Remark. "Now through the smog of modern civilisation the true nature of human beings emerges like a monster to devour the earth."

Jules felt as though he was in a science fiction thriller. The sound track an eclectic selection of dance floor instrumentals with snippets of strange voices from space saying, "don't be afraid, don't be afraid...something coming from a strange realm." He could feel himself slipping into another dimension as sounds and visuals poured through his eyes and ears. At the edge of the dance floor he shed his alladin shoes. Up through his bare feet upon the grass and sand came a stream of earthy sensations that titillated his body, as though Gaia was embracing him. He side-stepped trepidation and traced the flickering fairy lights spiralling up the curving palms to the shifting, sickle, Shiva moon, backdropped by the twinkle of stars, which appeared like pin holes in the curtain of night. Closing his eyes, he got sucked into a sensoria of sounds, smells, sea air and eddy currents coursing up through the soles of his feet turning him into flow motion on the dance floor. The sound track smoothed out into a hypnotic arpeggio synth-driven disco track, which brought with it a familiar feeling, triggering a memory of once having had pants-on grind sex with his girlfriend to it at an Oxford St club. He then recalled a conversation he'd had with Zane Lovelock, the guitarist in his band.

Jules: You remember that, "I Feel Love" song by Donna Summer? I spun out to an unbelievable new version of that on the weekend, it was high-energy disco overdrive.

Zane: Mate!.. how can you get off to that cheesy shit? You might as well go and buy some Abba records.

Jules: The DJ was playing some kind of megamix of the original. There was all kinds of new spacey sounds goin' on, it wasn't the same version as that seventies single. It just went on forever. It spun me around and around like I was in a cosmic trance.

Zane: It's mindless.

Jules: That's what I like about it. The constant, repetitive, hypnotic pulse. It doesn't pretend to have insight into the meaning of life. I love how it's so driving and wickedly energising. Disco music was never meant to be listened to while staying at home alone stoned. It talks to your animal body, especially when you dance to it with others. The gay boys go forever to it on speed.

Zane: Disco shit is lame in the brain.

Jules: You're missing the point, it talks to your body electric.

Now on the dance floor of the palm grove, Jules observed his arms and legs. They seemed to have a mind of their own, having latched on to the familiar ascending hook of the arpeggio bass. Everyone appeared to be dancing differently. No couples. He felt transported on to an astral plane, like he was dancing on air. This, 'I Feel Love', he was experiencing, seemed different, or was it the elixir which was taking hold of his sensory receptors? Surrendering to it, with the grip of his mind letting go—and after a long tease foreplay intro— the mantra voice ("I feel love") wrapped itself around his auric body and pulled him up to its booty bumper with a gushing dopamine rush. The secretions in his brain creaming him hyperspacial, as he swam omni-directional with animated bodies all around in a united space commingling, where gender dissolved. He felt like he'd dived into an electrified, aquatic world with fluorescent painted rocks, and was now part of a fish shoal in jangling psychedelic colours moving as one.

Individual tracks blended into a continuum. His attempts to dissect its audio aggregate parts was like a twisting tunnel of quantum, Rubik cubes. Dancing was all that mattered. He marvelled at the moves his body was making, like it was amphibious in a plasma of sensoria. Then felt out of his body—yet weirdly buoyant. A security alert was despatched through his vagus. His intestines tightened and breath quickened. The nerve message was prehistoric, reptilian. He checked the firewall of his space capsule and tightened his money belt, bum bag. He dared not to stop dancing. Mind management was paramount. Staying locked to the incessant, pushy pulse of the music seemed to be the key. The sounds inside of it, like a depth charge to his body armour. Percussion and bass pounded his guts. Tom tom drums stroked his rib cage and the kick drum rump-thumped him and drove his loins. Then, it all stopped, like the rhythm of the music had thrown him and the party off South Anjuna cliff—communal coitus interruptus. All that remained was a lone, ascending, modulating synthesiser chord, coated with choral voices, which left him suspended in space like he and the party had become aerial candy floss.

After what seemed forever, the bass and drums came rushing back in so forcefully that there was no room left for thoughts, doubts—or anything. The irresistible surge of the beat now more emphatic and flesh-pounding than ever before—like being inside a giant beating heart. And then, quickly the conveyor belt of sound changed again, propelling him into a groove gear shift, which had him strapped into a roller coaster, like a

Disney Space Mountain ride that throttled him into Techno torrent rapids where he became both particle and wave form, with his muscles, tendons, ligaments, bio-mechanically combusting a million micro-cellular processes commandeered by frequencies and beats and bleeps which had him flying on his feet with agility and adrenalised torque.

Nearly spinning out of control, he found himself wobbling, swerving, vertiginously like a marionette being pulled by invisible currents coming at him from all directions. His pelvis, a fulcrum pivot, from which thighs became pistons and calves crank shafts and ankles hinges and the soles of his naked feet, terminal springs upon the Gaia goddess through which the cosmos pulsed and exited his body, as if he were a lightning rod—cum tuning fork. With feet locked to the beat, the automatic pilot of his body had a mind of its own. He observed how syncopated and add-lib his dance moves became as he shifted and twisted and pranced and danced with precision to the strict machine music.

The petri dish of the dance floor was now clad in an eerie, machine membrane. The air filled with reverb stratospheres that conjured (with eyes closed) visionary worlds through which whip-lash claps spanked (with eyes open) a menagerie of new-species lifeforms leaping about. The fierce dancing of free spirits in wild abandon all around was liberating. It was as if he'd been abducted into an alien world of silicon surf, his neuro-eroto-psycho-motor wiring meddled with. The machinery of night in the electrified palm grove brought perceptual shifts and unravelled memory spools of personal scripts, some of which he mentally wrestled with. But applied the maxim: *free your arse and the mind will follow,* which became his tripping mantra when psychic undercurrents got him in a jam. In fact, storming on his feet in the middle of a dance party would come to be his most cherished place for euphonic epiphanies in motion.

The dreadlocked DJ spun the wheel of the party into noire electronic escapements, that had hairy vein, engorged bass lines with lashings of synth stabs stitch-witched with hissy titillating hi-hats and jackboot snare snaps. The electrodelicised sounds in the popsicle palms becoming a spooky ectoplasmic aquarium. Acid frazzled, with salty sweat running down his face from his tremulous brow, he found himself caught up in Celtic knot subways of thought. At every entrance, sneered hellhound black dogs. Everyone around him was on horseback, percussive slave snare and skin-pricking hi-hats whipped heathen haunches. Some riders turning into horrific creatures like the Hieronymus Bosch painting, 'The Garden of Earthly Delights.' A vaguely familiar figure, half horse, half man, galloped across Jules's vision like a centaur. *Was it Doc Silver?* The centaur had a white pony tail and its head was gesturing at him. Jules replied with a wide smile.

Time ceased to exist, but he had the inkling that the dance-a-thon had come to a Tibetan Bardo phase, which felt like disembodiment, as though his ego had been shredded in the darkest hour. Just before dawn there appeared a masked sea sprite, whom he'd previously glimpsed darting through intersecting dancing figures, that leaped about with leggy body language which was frightfully familiar. Was this temptress, siren Zsu in another form? He looked down at his left-hand ring finger on which was a silver ring which featured a sigil Lucifer symbol. It had been placed there by her as a gift in Bali. She'd told him it symbolised the light bearer morning star, Venus. He gazed up, but the siren spectre had vanished in a tail flip through the churning lattice of dancers.

The air was loaded with suspense, the mood of the party—cum rite of passage—had changed. A faint trace of light appeared above the cliff of South Anjuna Beach. The music softened, became celestial, as though light was being transduced into sound. Richly layered cosmic synthesisers wrapped in orchestration airlifted the holy communion dance floor upward to the heavens, faces pasted with emotion from nocturnal journeying into the redemptive light of a new dawn. The dance floor wore a collective smile, the likes of which Jules had never seen before. A new morning of creation, like no other, with uplifting new sounds. Like a developing photograph revealing itself out of a darkroom umbra in gradients of alchemical light, that transformed faces out of shadowy ultraviolet rays into soft pink amber rays of golden light, stroking heart strings with audio visual delight.

One hour after sunrise, the cliff face of South Anjuna Beach took on the monumental appearance of a sonic temple. Jules felt as if he'd been picked up by the scruff of the neck, had the shit shaken out of him and shown the face of God. Two hours after sunrise, with a second wind surging the dance floor, Jules trance-danced like he was riding thermals of celestial frequencies ascending and descending on indefatigable legs, weightless on winged feet. And then he looked up to the side of the DJ hut and saw the siren creature de-masked, standing next to the dreadlock DJ. It was, indeed, Zsu. Just as he was about to fly up to her like Peter Pan, DJ Atma Blaze put his arm around her, and they turned and walked away from the party.

The Spice Must Flow

IN A WORK ROOM at the back of a Portuguese villa, in Badem, a foot-pedal driven Singer sewing machine whirred with a chattering needle. A local tailor twisted black leather through the foot of the machine to join the fine silver ribbing of a six-pack leather cassette case. On an adjacent oblong table, patchwork off-cut pieces were laid out next to a hand drawn stencil pattern for a jacket. In cane baskets were leather belts, bum bags, chillum cases and caps. On racks hung vests. One wall featured an ultraviolet painting of dancing figures on a planet made of cheese with spiral nebulas and quasar zooming by. This was where prototype leather craft and garments were created for *Tribes of The Moon* by Zsu Riviere, a fashion designer in her early thirties who'd been raised by a solo mother in Marseille. The villa was leased yearly, with a local woman, Bhakti—who was always neatly wrapped in colourful sari with jet black hair neatly tied—taking care of household chores and her husband attending to night watchman duties.

The Goa party season revved Zsu's heart and soul. The *special Goa music* fired her imagination. She lived to dance. The parties a cosplay, in which she got a kick out of seeing her creations on the dance floor. Her favourite postcard—*I love me in Goa*—a simple smiley, framed with funky palms, she liked to send to friends. When she first arrived in India in nineteen eighty-two, her "border-line personality" mum sent her an aerogram fretting about the dangers of cult gurus. This served only to pique her fascination even more, to the extent that she disappeared in Pune for several months where she immersed herself in group encounters at the ashram to get in touch with her inner self. The rays radiating from the charismatic guru were outrageously irresistible at the time. The screaming dynamic meditations, the crying, the loving, the sexual catharsis, the entrancing satsangs, the witty, profound humour of his words—all appeasing a fire inside her, a longing to get in touch with her core; and especially the reclamation of cut-off parts of herself that had occurred from the age of eleven.

Did she fall prey to spiritual platitudes? No. Did she prostrate herself in guru adulation? Initially yes, but ultimately. No. Was what she discovered with the guru and getting naked with sanyassins so enamouring, that she changed her name and publicly wore orange? No.

On reflection, in avowals to herself, she was adamant that during that maiden induction into India with "Punatics" at the ashram, she had discovered a—*self,* that she recognised, mostly because she had longed for it, for so long. Only to herself she could say that the ashram was like going back into her mother's body, devoid of all boundaries, but it required courage to look at the hostilities that it presented. And for this, she was grateful.

Albeit, much later, she did question a proclivity of falling for priestly type guys. One of the biggest break-throughs, though, was that she gave up trying to shake the black sheep tag, so much so that on subsequent pilgrimages to India, and the Goa black sheep club, she boldly turned around and embraced being a black sheep—turning it into a stylistic art form. A by-product of time spent with the Bhagwan was a nous for business. It rubbed off on her, too.

Electronic party music permeated the air of the Goa golden triangle of Baga, Chapora and Badem. Techno beats and squelchy frequencies sizzled from boom boxes, ghetto blasters, double-deck players, portable speakers wired to Walkmans and home systems with imported speakers. Ultrasound pictures of the *green womb* golden triangle revealed amniotic, piezoelectric nuclei encoded with illuminati geometries that was doing weird and wonderful things to the biochemical algorithms of those that exposed themselves to it.

Denizens of this *golden ratio* triangle experienced a participation mystique in dancing to electronic music. Curated and DJ-ed by interdenominational audio apostles on the edge of Asia, its beats were generated by bio-botanical drum machines quantised in new sound signatures encoded—like sonic scrolls of a new-age electribe gospel. Hunter and collector DJs and party organisers and star diver dancers drew psychic sustenance from its resonance; it becoming a rhizome spreading like cell division, replicating itself through a contagion of cassette copying, dubs of dubs, back pack to back pack on the Asia trail.

Just like pattern making and decorative motifs in fabric, Zsu identified patterns and themes in the music, that for her, were like the *electrical secrets of heaven*. The music impregnated itself into her designs: catchy synth riffs got embroidered into fabrics, bass lines embossed in leather, frequencies infused into filigree jewellery, harmonic codices made into buttons, zaps and bleeps into zips, pad sounds like screen prints of gods and goddesses, industrial-junk-funk force legato amulets, beat box cassette bags, pitch-bend techno tank tops, cyber punk ripped T-shirts, electro lightning-bolt vests, analogue arpeggio earrings, midi-quantised jackets, oscillator chokers, ring modulating mini-skirts, chord-hook jock straps, modulating psychonaut hats and caps…

Zsu couldn't help but believe that this techno, intellecto, sample-delic cut 'n' paste music was *a cosmic conspiracy*. A zeitgeist leap into the age of the *spiritual machine*. Like it was being channelled by an elite cabal of esoteric artists, and that certain DJs who conjured it were endowed with the powers of sorcery, like some kind of *digital occult*. The experiencing of it, in the right kind of party, had the capacity to change the course of lives.

Jaeger, a jeweller and DJ—whom the die-hard Reggae and Rock crowd in Anjuna in the early eighties had scorned, decrying him, "The Swiss techno witch"—was a regular visitor at Zsu's house. On hearing the distinctly customised sound of his Enfield pull up, she asked Bhakti to make chai. While the tailor continued at the back of the house, she sat with Jaeger in the lounge where a down-tempo tape she'd collated and titled, INTRA VENUS, was playing on the stereo.

On one wall of the spacious lounge hung a large painting featuring a geometric Sri Yantra overlaid with an opaque sigil pyramid with Horus's eye. On corner tables with hoof feet, sat bronze figures of Pagan god Pan and Tibetan goddess Tara. On a low wooden table, flower essence oils burned next to a brass bowl of water with a white lotus flower floating in it. The tranquil fragrances were being wafted gently by a slow rotating ceiling fan. Bhakti placed a plate of croissants on the table, freshly bought from Oxford's Store at Nelson's Corner. Drinking chai, Zsu and Jaeger sat opposite each other on thick bamboo couches nested with a toss of cushions made of Rajasthan fabrics.

"How was the Anjuna party?" quizzed Jaeger

"Atma dipped in the night. Would've been struggling even more had I not given him some of my latest tapes with guaranteed floor-fillers. Of course, the tapes he left with me had nothing fresh."

"Yeap!.. that's Atma," sourly scoffed Jaeger with pinched lips. "Doin' his steppin' stone manoeuvre-groover routine, as usual—"

"Finito!.. basta!.." sullenly declared Zsu. Then lapsed into silence, her face clouding up, the flower fragrances in the lounge not able to conceal an odiousness. She then let out a self-disliking snicker, like she'd been in a fantasy bubble that had burst sending her plummeting to the floor. Jaeger was a close friend, their mutual interests much less complicated then her torrid Jezebel dallying, which belied secrets of another kind.

"Oh, poor you," Jaeger sympathised. "Well, the real deal is coming for the full moon party," he said encouragingly.

"I can't wait," she said with an indomitable smile. It was one of her stock smiles which she employed impeccably to elicit favours. Through a window, shafts of morning sunlight warmed the lounge. "I'm so looking forward to this party. I've asked Doc Silver to start with his rarities. The impossible to find music that only he has, as he refuses to swop his tapes."

"Yay!.. Uncle funkle Doc Silver," Jaeger said. "For sure, he'll have his posse of Chapora angels in tow. Oh!.. I just remembered, I need some more cassette bags."

"A new collection is being made," she said. "Pass by tomorrow. How's it with the Manali connection?" she said in a hushed voice, holding her right forefinger firm above her upper lip looking at him with an air of cool calculation.

"Jhoti has suitcases ready to go," Jaeger reported, raising a cheek with a half-smile. "They're definitely stronger and looking less like they were made in India."

"That's good," she said, "because Shane is visiting and says Bali has dried up. Friends are ready to fly out after full moon.

"Any day now," Jaeger said, "there's product coming down from the mountains packed in speaker cabinets. I'm gonna talk with Alfonso in Mapusa, see what's available care of the cop slush fund. They're more than pleased for us to donate, you know, recycle seizures they have nabbed. Well, at least it's better than just forking out rupees to them for protection, recycling keeps everyone happy. And besides, we'll be getting it much less than wholesale price from the mountains and not having to transport it to the beach."

"That's all well and good," she pulled a long face, "so long as it's primo quality."

"Alfonso is on the level with me," Jaeger said, "he knows the difference, I road test everything he offers me. And besides, he's a closet sniffer, I look after him. Of course, he's not the only one double dealing with foreigners caught with their pants down. More worrying, I heard that a narcotics squad from Delhi might soon be nosing around. Cops pay heaps to land jobs here cause of the handsome harvest they are able to extort from stoners. And it's gonna skyrocket big time."

"What do you mean?" she said pensively.

"Haven't you heard?" His face paled, the air thickened. "Over a tola (ten grams) is gonna be a criminal offence."

"Oh, no!" she recoiled in shock.

Jaeger scowled. "It's across the front page of today's *Gomantak Times*."

"This sucks!" She sighed, like air rushing out of a deflated tyre.

"Since the seventies," he said, "the fucking Americans have been pushing for prohibition. It's gotten worse as a result of the Sikhs shooting Indira Ghandi last year. The Americans had already paid fifteen million to Nepal in an aid package in nineteen seventy-four and pressured them to make hash illegal, plus the Indian hemp act was made law. Indira had been best friends with the Russians, but the idiot son, Rajiv, not. The Americans gave fifty million to the Indian government."

"Oh fuck!" Zsu lamented with pinched eyes staring straight at Jaeger. "So, what they are saying is that Shiva's sacrament is now illegal in India?"

"Looks like it."

"Ha!.. so, they really want to turn us into criminals," she said mournfully.

Jaeger slumped into silence staring over Zsu's shoulder at Horus's all-knowing eye on the wall.

Bizarre Bazaar

BETWEEN A LARGE RICE PADDY and South Anjuna Beach, future artefacts of a nomadic neuro tribe glistened under languid palms. Artisans sat on reed mats next to wooden display cases. Hand-made hippie and ethnic wear and New Wave party gear was strung between palms on string. Refreshments were chai mumma tea, imported canned beer in buckets of ice, and expresso with cakes and brownies.

Selling was fun, shopping incidental to socialising, exchanging, sharing, trading and traveller networking. Hipster Harry told Jules that the Anjuna flea market started with a family of friends in the early seventies. Back then, hash and opium was openly sold, as well as highly prized Western items like electronics, watches and cameras, which were palmed off to Indians. The kind of restrictive items that customs officials would write in passports upon arrival, forbidden to be sold. Besides Levi jeans and Jap tech, foreign passports were also sold at the flea market. It was a happy-high communal experience which everyone used to attend on foot, as there were no roads.

Roaming randomly through the Wednesday market maze in the sweltering humidity of the afternoon heat, Jules became mesmerised and spun-out by the array of unique nick-knacks, tantalising mystical trinkets, adornments, jewellery, craft, sarongs and bright coloured garments on display—like a wanderlust feast for the eye. The flea market was the primary place of communication where everyone came together. After one in the morning at the party, the other night nearby in the palm grove on the beach, it had been impossible to talk. Body language on the dance floor said everything. In the market, Jules was fascinated to figure out who was who of the party people, eyes now hidden behind sunglasses and getting about in daywear under the shade of palms and rambling, flapping Rajastan textile hangings. Most vexing though, was the whereabouts of Zsu?

With eyes peeled, he did find the *Tribes of The Moon* stall with its distinctive style, which raised his hopes. Beholding her creations in the weirdo splendour of the Goan, bohemian bazaar was like a puzzle in his head coming together completing a picture. The jewellery, accessories, garments, sarongs and unique wearables appeared even more bewitching, and brought back memories of their time together. His eyes fell upon a silver and gold piece of jewellery, in the form of a bird, in a wooden display case. Rolling his eyes up from the bird he was greeted by a tall blonde Nordic hottie. He introduced himself as Zsu's friend and enquired whether she was here.

"She's already left," explained the girl, who wore hot pants with a black singlet blazoned with fluoro pink text—JACK THE TAB.

"That's a pity," Jules said, bowing his head in disappointment and gazing at the mysterious bird, its wings arched skyward.

Looking up he said. "This phoenix necklace is stunning."

The girl opened the case and put the bird in his hands. "It's one of her newest pieces. It's magical, isn't it?"

Holding the phoenix in his fingers he said, "It's marvellous. Zsu sure does have a special touch with mythic symbols. We met in Bali, she invited me here."

"Really!.. Hi—I'm Asta."

"I'm Jules—Nice to meet you."

"Oh, so this is your first time?"

He removed his shades. "Yeah!" He looked around and smiled. "It's quite something. This market is a hive of stunning stuff. Do you know where I can find her?"

"Try Chapora after sunset. Are you from Down Under?" she asked with a sparkle in her blue eyes.

"Yeah. How did you know?"

Asta blushed. "Your Mambo board shorts."

"Hmm... actually, I'm more a muso, than a surfer. Have a band, but at the last gig the guitarist broke his wrist—"

"Wow!—what happened?"

"He's a radical cat. It's a crazy story..."

He farewelled Zsu's attractive friend. Her friendliness felt like sweet compensation for Zsu's absence and the crush-shattering passing glance of her with the dark dreadlock DJ. Considering the apparent quality of hot chicks in the scene, he felt like he was falling in with a pack of pedigree pooches in a tropical paradise. He wondered what breed of dog they might consider him? He replayed the disheartening impression he'd had of Zsu when she'd left the Anjuna party. She looked like an Afghan hound on a tight leash.

Walking towards the beach his eye caught a tank top with imagery of jungle vines and galaxies. An Italian standing next to it said he painted it, and introduced himself as Lazzaro. Jules lavished him with praise and scored the psychedelic top. Continuing towards the refreshing sea breeze, he spotted Doc Silver in paisley bermuda shorts with a can of Tuborg beer in his hand. He was loudly laughing and animatedly moving about in conversation with a cool looking character in bright green and black striped, spandex leggings.

Jules walked straight up to Doc and said, "That was a mind-blowing party the other night."

Doc beamed with glee. "Sometimes you get tested, have to surmount obstacles, get Ganesh on board. He looked toward the palm grove where he'd set up the party. "It's one of my favourite spots to boogie this side of Starco Corner." Then narrowed his eyes at Jules. "Hey brother, you're looking a bit flushed."

"It's balmy," Jules said, wiping perspiration from his brow with his arm and turned to face the market, which was now in the process of dismantling itself. "I'm overloaded... amazed by the freak wear."

Doc chuckled. "Let me get you a drink," he said pointing at a bucket with canned beer in iced water.

"Thanks man."

The bar wallah extended a hand with an ice cold can of Becks. Doc flicked him some rupees and tapped his Tuborg on Jules's can and his friend's can toasting, "Cheers!.. Hey meet Danilo..."

"G'day—I'm Jules."

"Ciao."

"Danilo played the first Techno here," Doc said.

"Really!.. What did you play?"

"Kraftwerk," Danilo said, who wore shades wrapped around a high cheeked cherub face.

"How did that go down?"

"Not well at all. In fact, it was shocking. Way too strange for the Rasta, Rock 'N' Roll hippies. Back then, in the seventies, Steely Dan, Joe Cocker, Peter Frampton, the Stones, Bob Marley was being played on cassettes in between jam bands. That's when everyone started matting their heads into dreads—"

"It was smacked-out guitar jams," recalled Doc. "Amps were connected to a lead from a house. Brown sugar was gettin' fixed all over the place."

"*Techno dread* came at the beginning of the eighties," explained Danilo. "The old school Acid Rock hippies of Anjuna hated it." Danilo and Doc chuckled and swigged on their cans.

"I got called, The Techno Gestapo," Doc said, twisting his boots into the sandy grass. "I remember when the hippies started cutting their hair. It was the passage of Rock and Reggae giving way to New Wave. Back then, Bob Marley never got North of Starco Corner."

Jules, surprised, said, "That's where I arrived."

"Starco Corner was the border," Des said.

"Border?" queried Jules.

"It's the border between Vagator and Anjuna," Danilo said. "There was a civil war back then. It was old school Rock, American Funk and Reggae hippies versus Disco, New Wave, Electro, Techno renegades. Doc led the charge. Man, it was like *The Reformation*, like we were renegade priests. It got pretty hostile, we did fire cracker pranks. Put 'em in over-ripe papayas and exploded them at Reggae parties."

Doc took a last swig and crumpled his can in his hand. "We became whipping posts, took a lot of stick. It's amazing how square some of those hippies were, and still are."

Danilo put his hand on Doc's shoulder. "Some freaked big time. Bach Flowers Paul took a swing at Doc. Couldn't stand the music. We made our own parties. Eventually the scene got sick of boring jam bands and realised it was more fun tripping and dancing to electronic music DJ-ed by cassette jocks."

Jules relished this story, it paralleled with his post Punk Industrial allegiances and playing with tape loops and recording on a four-track reel to reel Teac.

"Vagator was the frontier of New Wave," Doc said, all wild-eyed. "It was like a religious war," he twisted his boots into the ground. "Atma Blaze kicked up the most stink cause we stole his fire, his band was playing parties, but it got so boring, they'd be nodding off on smack. But then there was a resurgence of acid and hippies got hip to the fun to be had dancing to continuous psychedelic computer music."

"I make music," Jules confessed, "It's experimental. I got fed up with the band thing, too. The worst was having to deal with arsehole publicans running hotel venues to get gigs. The booze barons—"

"Here, it's a smokers' scene," Danilo said devoutly, tipping a small coconut bowl full of tiny charas pickings into a Rizla, in which was laid a bed of tobacco. Many market sellers were packing up their gypsy camp wares and heading down to the beach where chillum circles gathered as the sun started to glow red hot and was about to touch down on the horizon.

"India is not about alcohol." Doc said. "It's Hindu. Charas rules. The Catholics brought booze to Goa."

"Ha!.." Jules said." I tried the local suds, Kingfisher. It's rough as guts."

Danilo passed Jules the rolled joint and flicked a lighter to fire it up. Jules puffed and passed it to Doc, whose eyes turned from blue to teal green after he exhaled.

"Indian drunks on the dance floor are a pain," Danilo said. "They try to grope the girls but don't last long. We blow them off the dance floor with heavy music."

Down on the beach, the flea market community was getting high on plumes of Kulu Valley smoke. When there was only a pink halo left on the horizon, after the sun had sunk, Danilo offered to give Jules a lift on the back of his Rajdoot motor bike to North Anjuna and suggested he come to Vagator. "I hang at Spaghetti Beach in the afternoon and Primrose in the evening."

Greenback On a Roll

NOT BEING MUCH OF A SKIER, escaping the chill of the Swiss alps in January of nineteen eighty-one, for Jaeger, was a bonus of adventuring to India to study Sanskrit as part of a module of his course in Asian studies at Basel University. But the discovery of a graffiti picture on the wall of his Bombay hotel room of a heart, out of which two palm trees arched up to the sun with *Goa* written underneath, was a godsend. At twenty years of age, the drawing had lured him to Chapora where he became possessed by an overwhelming passion that ignited an inextinguishable bonfire in his brain. This fire engulfed him with the raison d'être realisation that music was all that mattered. To the extent that he dropped out of Uni to embark upon the lifestyle of an Asian traveller, adaptive in survival skills he resourcefully acquired in Goa and Manali.

Riding a red, Thunderbird Enfield motorbike—that he'd bought, and travelled around India on—the fat boom, boom, boom of its cylinder under his arse put him in a zen mechanic nowness-of-the-moment, that only certain music under the influence was even more capable of delivering. Stripped off to his waist with no helmet, his shoulder length, dark brown hair and face blasted by the rush of velvety tropical air was like no condom sex on wheels. It turned him into Joe Machine, 'Follow the Rainbow' (the name of one of his favourite tracks). As a teenager, his imagination was ignited when he watched the sequence, 'Born to Be Wild' by Steppenwolf, in the movie *Easy Rider*. In Goa, bereft of rules and regulations, unlike the stiffness of Swiss society, he was able to get his Hermann Hesse on. Testimony to his induction into the *Indo tribe* of Goa, and calling on the path of an obsessive hunter and gatherer of mystical machine music, he got a tattoo on his forearm of Lord Shiva's trident with caduceus and orbiting symbols of planets, crotchets, quavers and bass clefs.

It was the day after the flea market and he was gunning his Enfield along the narrow road from the beach strip to the local town of Mapusa to see a man about a dog—and glue was on his mind. The bike rounded the corner of the towering white washed Basilica near the intersection of the road that led to Bobby's Bar and Badem. The road was never that busy, just the odd Ambassador taxi, some motor bikes and local Tata bus. By the time he got to the top of Mapusa hill, which was like a dividing curtain between two worlds, he coasted down into the swarming town. It's hustling and bustling and horn tooting immediately put him back on the planet of ceaseless car traffic (a striking reality check to chilled lotus eater beach life and itinerant fly-by-night party antics in la-la land). It almost felt like being back in India.

On the side of the main road, women in tar-sticky bright coloured saris carried gravel on top of their heads in buckets. Side streets reeked of spices and were draped with sagging power lines. Buildings were yellow and blotchy with aged cement, out of which jutted reinforcing rods skyward, like hopeful erect veins seeking the flesh of future bricks and mortar. Large bushy weeds hung off three-hundred-year old ruins of Portuguese merchant, noble, class mansions.

The Enfield turned into the central roundabout which dazzled with Bollywood hoardings. Trebly Hindi music squawked through the cheap petrol air. Men lolled in doorways smoking Panama cigarettes and bidis, while others spat red betel juice. Jaeger parked and ducked into a small fabric shop where he presented a crisp, brand new one-hundred US dollar bill to the black market money changer, who salivated over its perfect condition. It was exchanged for wads of fifty rupee notes tied with rubber bands, which Jaeger had to tediously count. After his lunch date, he needed to buy Araldite glue at the hardware store and pass Paradise Pharmacy.

Upon entering Malabar South Indian Restaurant, Jaeger was greeted with a smile by its pot-bellied owner, who was anchored to the till on a stool. At a private corner table sat an Indian with a trim moustache in white button down shirt and polyester trousers with black leather shoes. With a Rolex fastened to his wrist, he raised an expresso coffee to his lips, above which shifty eyes clocked Jaeger's arrival. The watch was a gift from a compromised tourist.

"Hello my friend," he greeted Jaeger, who sat down at the table with him.

"Hi Alfonso."

"The Anjuna party went well?" Inspector Alfonso asked.

"I believe so, unfortunately I couldn't make it. Doc told me you helped out."

"Of course… anytime. We're here to assist."

A barefoot waiter arrived, they ordered masala dosa and Jaeger asked for chai tea.

"It can get messy," Jaeger said, "with the bars meddling with the parties."

"They are a nuisance," Alfonso said. "The squabbling is a headache. They really should learn to share the cake. Better to make the parties at the beach—"

"Out of sight, out of mind," Jaeger said smiling.

"That's right," Alfonso said. "And we don't want the schools complaining."

Jaeger narrowed his eyes. "What's up with the new law? Ten grams is now a criminal offence."

A thin smile slid across the Inspector's face. "Don't you mind that," he said reassuringly. "It's scare mongering from Delhi, just more talk about *the war on drugs.*"

"Ha!.. Are you kidding me, or what?" Jaeger said with misgiving. "It's put everyone on edge."

The dosas and chai arrived on the table. Inspector Alfonso tore off a piece of his and dunked it in a sambar dip. Jaeger didn't eat. He sat with a glum face, rubbed the stubble on his chin and sipped his tea.

"Don't be troubled," the Inspector said. "Nothing has changed in Mapusa. Goa is not Delhi." Everything can be accommodated."

After Jaeger did manage to eat his dosa, the Rollex hand pressed three grams of charas into Jaeger's hand under the table.

"Three kilos," Alfsonso murmured.

"If it's as good as the last lot," Jaeger said, "I'll take it."

The Inspector paid lunch. Wading into the heavy heat of the Mapusa afternoon to buy glue, Jaeger thought, *better the devil you know than the devil you don't.* On the way, he dropped into Paradise Pharmacy to score Dexedrine and Mandrax and pondered the big Pharma industries of his home town, and the utility of the anonymity of his Swiss bank account, and the social welfare of Swiss junky parks. He regarded himself a disenfranchised East, West, intercontinental half-breed. In the general scheme of things, he was happy with his lifestyle as a romantic rogue hopping international date lines. Walking toward Mapsua General Hardware, he figured he was still well on top being the benefactor of a decent quota of fun—getting-by hook or by crook in the bent mind-field privileges that Goa was rich in. *Sure beats workin,'* he thought. And would later discover a track with that very name, by Beats Workin' which would turn his crank, big time.

After shopping at Mapusa General Hardware, and stepping back out on a crooked and cracked footpath, it occurred to him that it was here that he'd first met Alfonso, which was when the shady sleuth had cottoned on to the popularity of Araldite glue with foreigners.

ON THE EDGE OF VAGATOR JUNGLE a restaurant cum smokers' salon, crackled with synthesiser frequencies and computer beats. Freaky characters roosted inside and out. Every conversation was peppered with chatter gab of—"safi…matches… boom!… string…" It served as a night hitching post, providing lip service for party action. When there were no parties, those hanging at Primrose Restaurant took on a grim pose. It was nine o'clock and there was nothing grim about it. A motorbike taxi pilot pulled up and Jules alighted. The entrance was rammed with Enfield, Yamaha, Rajdoot motorbikes and TVS mopeds.

The music playing was, 'P-Machinery' by Propaganda. Threading his way through bikes and crowd milling in the courtyard, Jules was greeted by a thick social aroma of charas smoke that hung in the techno tinged air. The columns and fresco ceiling of the stoner saloon featured hand painted surreal, op art, which looked familiar and had a signature—'Lazzaro'. The same as the tank top he'd bought at the flea market. He made his way to the counter where there were bollocked-up orders, and took a chance on receiving a mango ice cream with fruit salad, then retreated to the courtyard where he heard a voice directed at him. "Hey man!" He turned and recognised a familiar face.

"Hi Zikos," Jules replied.

"Welcome to Primrose," said the tall Greek.

"What a menagerie?" Jules said.

"It's a staging post for the night," Zikos said. "A hub for heads. It's where you get the juice on what's goin'on? The lowdown on what the pigs are up to."

Jules looked at him perplexed. "The pigs?"

"Yeah—the ones that give you the shits," Zikos said, "not the ones that eat your shit."

Jules laughed, Goa pigs having become his pet fascination. He swore he'd seen them flying. He shared this hallucination with Zikos, who said, "Oh man, these pigs eat so much acid they sure do fly. But I'm talking about the pigs that hide behind trees with bamboo sticks. The fuckers that set up traps with ropes over the road."

"That must be scary in the dark."

"Especially," Zikos said, "when you're mashed. It's hell for the girls riding those crappy TVS mopeds, they ain't fast enough to escape nothin'. It's a cat and mouse game with the fucking cops. Here you find out the latest… which intersections are a sweet runner, which ones where the pigs are lurking. They want cash, try to search you lookin' for your stash. It's better not to stop. Us fearless Enfield Bullet riders, we just blast straight at em like bats out of hell and freak em right out. They have no choice but stand aside. Though, sometimes you get swiped with a stick."

Jules recounted a close shave at a Delhi Hotel in which cops searched his hotel room, but didn't find anything. "Luckily, I'm psychic, I was suspicious of the hotel manager." He then recalled another incident on a train trip to Jaipur when two cops entered his carriage and lit up a rollie of hooch and passed it to him.

Zikos chuckled. "Some cops you can have fun with, while others will bleed you for all they can get away with. It's theatre man. It's India. Goa is paradise, but vipers can bite you, cops can be at your door in the day, and thieves breaking in at night while you're out partying. In the past, it was remote, you could have a couple of kilo in the house, no problem. It was the junkies you had to worry about—they would steal from right under your nose."

"Oh no!" Jules said, appalled.

"Hey man," Zikos said, "I saw you having a right bouncy time in the palm grove at Anjuna the other night."

"It was gobsmacking nuts," Jules confessed. "Like a religious experience… that was some serious space time continuum—

"Meltdown!" Zikos said with a wide grin.

"Man, I got dismantled," Jules said. "At first I found the music strange. But once the punch had me, there was no resistance. I gave in…danced my head off."

"Right on, dude," Zikos said, and cast his eyes around the odyssey of characters at Primrose. "The night is young. The French gang are up to something in Chapora Fort. It'll be maximum lift-off up there. It's an alien landing pad."

Jules's body instantly became electrified by the prospect. He was indebted to the friendly Greek for his shepherding as he had detected an aloof coolness with some in the scene, particularly towards rookie newcomers. Of course, he could imagine there was plenty to be paranoid about. He smiled and said he'd better chase up his fruit salad.

"I'll be backside," Zikos said. "Just follow your nose."

Jules claimed a fruit salad from a muddle of orders at the counter. Leaning up against a column he spooned creamy curd and papaya and watermelon into his mouth. German synth electronica by 16 Bit came out of the speaker cabinet above him. "Where are you? I've lost you," said the unrequited vocal refrain of Sven Vath's voice in the music, which sounded Euro, post-modern, its neo-classical virtual strings got Jules feeling—all sappy. He'd heard it played in the party, and wondered at the time if Zsu was close by? Hearing it again filled him with a bitter sweetness. Spooning the last of the tropical fruit into his mouth, it felt like a palliative for femme fatale forlorn. Snapping himself out of the mushy, silly feelings that he found himself mired in, he distracted himself gaping at the tableau of wild night life all around him. Its non-stop smoking, its shifting faces, its pre-party twitching, its clashing garb of colours. There was no retreat into being a wall flower, as there were no walls in Primrose, just a charas haze.

Venturing backside, his social thermometer registered sub-clique. No one was speaking English. Outsider awkwardness threatened to maroon him. He teetered and stuttered on his feet, but was suddenly rescued by a voice in a cluster of shadowy figures.

"Ciao," called out Danilo, his legs iridescent in blue stretch tights with a black motorcycle jacket hanging off a shoulder. Jules had never seen men partying in spandex before. Well, not since glam rock days when he wore platform shoes. The sub-scene in the shadows, backside of Primrose, appeared mostly Mediterranean. Flickering beams of motorbike headlamps flashed upon the flamboyance of the silhouette of bodies which appeared androgynous. Heavy eyeliner faces of both sexes were illuminated by the coals of glowing chillums and matches that ignited them.

"Hi," Jules said to Danilo, feeling relieved to know someone.

"Welcome to Club Vagator," the Italian DJ said.

"Thanks," Jules said. "It's like an aviary of exotic night birds."

"This is where we roost," Danilo said, twitching in his tights. "It's the habitat of a thriving new species. Now it's time of the *season*."

Everyone appeared to be talking in French, Italian and Spanish, with the word, *party*, buzzing lips. Jules spotted Zikos with another bunch of shimmery, shady figures and joined him.

"Hi man. Want a sniff?" Zikos offered.

"Charlie?"

"Hundred percent Columbian."

"Muchas gracias."

Zikos plucked a plastic sachet from his pocket, plunged his motorbike key into it and presented it to Jules's nose coated with white crystals. Upon nostriling it, dopamine transporters blitzed his brain. The Italian being spoken around him became like a sped-up opera aria, with the buzz word—PARTY!—reaching high pitched falsetto. Jules was not much of a powder head, but Zane—the guitarist in his band—was a fiend. Now pinging on the Columbian rush, Jules heard one of Zane's ripping riffs volt right though his head, like he was standing next to him warping feedback through his Marshall amp.

"We are in for a big night," Zikos effused, shuffling on his feet, his face beaming with anticipation.

In the shadows all around Jules, jabbering jaws stoked the promise of the night's enticement. He felt like he was back stage at a drama about to unfold. Then, was struck by the need to retreat to his room and get ready. "How do I find it?" he asked Zikos.

"Tell the motorbike pilot—party Chapora Fort." The Greek once again offered his key to Jules coated in Columbian and said, "One for the road." After sniffing it, Jules felt like a second stage rocket had launched him into the circuitry of the nocturnal wildlife of Vagator. A motorbike pilot delivered him back to North Anjuna. He requested to be picked up again in one hour.

Standing outside Anatashia's house the sounds of howling, whining, whimpering, growling dogs could be heard in every direction. A piercing chorus of yelping and yipping came from the direction of St Anthony's Chapel, which brought on an increased barrage of jabbing, yapping barks throughout all of Anjuna, that stridently stabbed the dead of night in multiple part disharmony—like canine guardians had been taken possession by phantoms of the night.

In one corner of his room, Jules had exploded all his clothes out of a backpack, in another corner soiled ones lay for Anatashia to hand wash. The new tank top of planets and jungle, painted by Lazzaro, caught his eye. He discarded the T-shirt he was wearing and pulled on the new top. Immediately, he felt appropriately body mapped for the coordinates of the night flight he imagined he would embark upon up on Chapora Fort overlooking Vagator.

With Charlie zinging him, he was seized with suspense, his chest and head felt like it was gripped by a leather glove. Sitting on the floor, he consulted his ephemeris and saw that Venus was entering the cavalier sign of Sagittarius. He swigged on a bottle of mineral water and lay down on his mattress and shut his eyes. Neural transporters rifled filing cabinets in his head. A switch flipped. The interior of Jules's head became a passive screen on which was projected Super 8 film from a cartridge titled, PYRMONT SQUAT. Grungy scratched footage of his Sydney life rolled across his inner retinas. The sound track—The Telepathics.

A wide panning view of the derelict industrial wastelands of Pyrmont Pier wharves. A zoom into a squat comprised of grimy tenement worker's cottages.

An interior shot with a double mattress on the floor. Books by J G Ballard, William Burroughs and issues of Research Magazine. Cut-up photographs and polaroids pinned to hessian walls stripped of wallpaper. A trestle table, on top of it a Yamaha DX7 synth and a Brion Gysin dream machine comprised of a light bulb suspended in a rotating cylinder with cut out shapes on a Technics turntable.

Jules could hear his heart racing, he opened his eyes and recoiled from the Super 8 playing in his head. It was a leap of worlds from Pyrmont to North Anjuna. Both worlds were on a crusty edge. In both, it was the people that made it what it was. Unbranded types, deviant types, that thrived in fringe fermentations outside of regular boundaries. Places in between. He opened his eyes, took a swig of water, closed them. The Super 8 continued, this time in grainy black and white footage.

Cranes hovered over the grey landscape like industrial wetland stalks rebuilding nests. Miasmic gases steamed out of chimney stakes staining the air with industrial odours, and the earth thunked and screeched with heavy machinery. Subterranean subversive creatures with piercings, tattoos and sculptured spiky coloured hair slithered through it like camouflaged urban reptiles. (One was Jules, he wore black stove-pipe jeans.)

Distorted electric guitar played by Zane Lovelock reverberated in Jules's head. It brought with it an image of him leaping skyward to intercept a soccer ball, which marked the beginning of The Telepathics when, at that moment, Zane and Jules aerially cracked heads.

A wide angle shot of 16mm Bollex footage of a motley mob (Pyrmont squat versus Newtown squat) tearing up lawn in a kick-a-bout. A close up slow-mo shot of two boots thumping on a dirt smudged soccer ball. Zane sporting mohawk hair, dog collar choker, nose ring and T-shirt with sleeves hacked off stating—MEET EVERY SITUATION HEAD ON.

The barking of Anatasia's dog and a voice, "Hello mista, hello," brought the projector in Jules's head to a holt. He opened his eyes.

"OK, OK, I'm coming," he hollered to the motorbike pilot waiting at the gate. He laced on Reebok runners, strapped on a bum bag, snatched shades, grabbed a jacket, padlocked the door and adventured to Chapora Fort.

Mooching, moseying cows was the only life in Chapora when the motorbike pilot, with Jules on the back, slid through the village half an hour after mid night. Arriving at a knot of motorbikes parked-up near moored fishing boats at the mouth of Chapora River, he paid the pilot and headed up a stony track. Up above, the sound of electronic beats beckoned from the seventeenth century medieval stone fortress. Entering it through an arched entrance, he beheld a fast-forward-the-future-bacchanalia-technodelia. Two hundred dancers were prancing about on a stone-flattened dance floor. Along a rampart wall above Vagator Beach chai mummas had set up, plus one lone bar table.

An orientation orbit of the party revealed Danilo spinning cassettes in a small bamboo hut by the seaward rampart. Hanging about nearby were the same faces from backside Primrose, who bobbed to the music whilst attending to chillum chores of mulling, toasting cigarettes, loading, lighting, starting, passing, emptying ashes, pulling cleaning string through—and hollering, "boom bolenath!" Whilst a couple of shady characters sequestered racking-up on one of Danilo's cassette cases.

Jules found Zikos on a chai mat, sat down and ordered tea. The Greek extended a welcoming hand in which was a small folded square of foil, which he dropped into Jules's palm."

Opening it, Jules said, "What's this? It looks like an atomic particle."

"It is," Zikos said. "Don't be misled by size."

Inside the foil was a grey coloured Berlin microdot. Not much bigger than a pin head, it looked the tiniest of doses he'd ever seen. Wearing a faux leopard skin vest, like Lord Shiva, the strapping Greek vouched, "This dot is the ultimate—I've already dropped."

Jules looked him in the eye, took a deep breath and imbibed the minuscule pill with a sip of chai. Elevated high up in the Portuguese fort, with the aroma of charas in the air, he marvelled at the mystery of the universe as it blinked at him. The night sky sparkled like diamond dust as space junk, satellites, meteorites and comets criss-crossed—with every possibility that a UFO would soon come into view and land.

He soon got swept up in the infectious force fields of the dance floor, becoming saturated in the madness of its multifarious motion, as if experiencing himself in a new solar system. All around him, wacky weirdos were leaping into the air. A break beat track hooked him in. He cut loose with forty-five-degree body snaps, which got him hopping about like a spring-heeled jack. Then found himself inside a video game where he heard a chopped-up Indian female vocal wailing through the music, followed by a voice that said, "You're at the controls of a nuclear reactor twenty thousand leagues under the sea, it's overheating, global shut downtown. You have to proceed to the escape capsule."

The wailing returned, plus video game sounds. "Your fifteen billion light years away," the voice continued. "You fight with cyborgs, suddenly you find yourself in a fighter jet." Danilo was playing 'High Score' by 16 Bit. Jules looked up at the sprawling expanse of the cosmos. Though it appeared vast, it felt intimate and palpable, like he was made from it.

Techtronic robo-bleeps, 808 drum machine beats, and sibilant fizz and hiss of high hats bounced off stone ramparts tickling his hips. Sweating pure adrenalin, motor neurons rapid fired. Reflexing tendons, ligaments, his muscles stretched uncoiling a kundalini helix up his spine. "Sanctimonious rituals," said a voice in the music. "The duty of the beast." Peering over a rampart, he looked down over Vagator and wondered what nefarious wild life inhabited it and was up here tonight. Danilo was playing 'Flesh' by A Split Second. Jules turned his gaze seaward and looked down at the white water of waves crashing on rocks below. The kind that a mermaid siren might shipwreck a sailor on.

"Welcome to paradise," came a hauntingly familiar, soft voice from behind him.

He spun around and was met by glowing emerald eyes with long lashes.

"Zsu!.. Zsu!.. Oh, my God!.. It's you!.. It's you!.."

"Jules!.. Fabulous you are here," she said.

"Nice to see you," he said, spun out. "WOW!.. WOW!.. WOW!.."

The creator of *Tribes of The Moon* was dressed in animal skin patterned leggings and radiating drop dead allure. There was so much to talk about. But he was tripping balls, his mouth struggling to form words. Emotions overwhelming him, threatening to burst him apart as they exchanged belated greetings until she turned to the dance floor and said, "Let's dance." Weaving in and out of the dance floor action they snuck snapshot glances at each other which got his Berlin microdot mind musing, whilst his body let rip on the asteroid-like surface of the fort. Later at five in the morning, after techno trekking the night, he was at a comfortable cruising altitude in his head and spied her alone on a chai mat and landed and sat with her.

"Humble apologies," she said contritely, hating herself for being the person who'd teasingly skirted around him at the last party, and *not available* to greet him.

He looked at her, smiled, and second guessing her asked, "What?"

"That Anjuna party," she said. "I'm so sorry I didn't say hello. I was hung up."

"Oh, really?"

"Yeah, I was caught up in a story."

"What story?"

The emerald green eyes in front of him became overcast, her face pale and white. "Jules," she said, forcing a winsome smile. "Please… I don't really want to talk about it." She fluttered turquoise and gold-highlighted eyelids. "So, how do you like Goa?" she asked at pain to deflect the humiliating *story*.

"Love the crazies. Love the parties. Love your stall at the market." And with his eyes delighting in what dangled from her ears, "Love your Lilith jewellery—it's exquisite!"

"These are because of you," she said, raising a hand to touch silver and black onyx earrings, like they were a talisman. They were in the form of a cardinal cross with crescent moon, that bobbed about the nape of her slender neck. "I made them after what you told me in Bali."

"Lilith rocks!" he said. "Lilith the dark moon goddess, she is deeply mysterious."

"I feel Liliths's presence," she said.

He arched an eyebrow. "I'm sure Lilith speaks karmically to you." Holding her gaze, her mesmerising eyes turned into micro kaleidoscopes made up of multiple hues of green and gold.

"Would you like a bump of E for the dawn?" she offered in a soft chocolatey voice wrapped in a tantalising smile. The invitation was melting, sending blood rushing through his capillaries. He grinned and nodded. From out of a silver studded leather bum bag she produced a plastic sachet containing white crystals. She measured equal amounts on to two Rizla papers and folded them neatly.

"Here!.. a candy flip," she said, fastening her eyes on him and placing one of the MDMA sherbet bombs in his hand. They clicked chai glasses and she toasted, "Sante!" They swallowed, and returned to the dance floor where they felt aerated and elevated and alive and effervescently bubbly above Goa, fortified by chunky, pitted bricks and mortar from the depths of time.

When first light broke on a mountain range in the distance they shared a blue and gold-tinted chillum with a bunch of her friends, including the Italian ceramic artisan, Cosimo, the maker of the pipe. They soared like black kite birds that hovered and ducked and dived in air thermals off the ramparts and gazed inland at a Tolkienesque mist-layered vista. It was like he'd landed on a numinous head land where a femme fatale siren was greeting him, *"Hello sailor!"*—which tingled him to the bone, just like she'd done at his first port of call in Asia.

And now, reunited up high in the mists of time with the sound track of 'Flucht' by Zwischenfall in a medieval European fort with the siren turning into Dionysus, and the dawning realisation that his ship had not been wrecked, and feeling his dancing wings unfurl wider than they'd ever spanned. He felt his heart airborne, the party a quantum-quark-step leap beyond anywhere he'd been before. Up till now, relying only on telepathic instinct, he'd resisted peering into her horoscope. But the next day, he could not resist applying the metaphysical lens of his ephemeris to her planets. What he saw, entranced him even more.

Serpent in The Seed

TWO DAYS BEFORE the fort party, Zsu woke up with a yuckiness caking her heart. The emotional hangover was unshakeable since she crawled out of Atma Blaze's haunted house in Assagao in a bedraggled state. The back of her legs sore, as she'd thrown herself into advanced yoga sessions with Yogi Ananta on the upper reaches of Disco Valley to realign chakras—plus an all-juice detox and colonic to rid herself of rancid feelings.

Full-stretch unknotting emotions stored in her spine, on a drooping-palm terrace under a clear blue sky with ocean view, Ananta showed her a pranayama mula bandha exercise. It strengthened the base of the pelvic floor at the perineum, right between her yoni and anus. Pranayama breathing cross-legged with a heal tucked under her mula bandha muscles, allowed her to take control of her root knot, giving command of what she wished to have flow out and breath into her pleasure centres. Recently, she'd had a nightmare of sticky horror in which she became Kali, the goddess of death. She saw herself squatting over Atma, like he was Shiva, and lowering herself onto his lingam. At the moment of climax, she extracted his seed and plunged a dagger into his heart and ate his intestines just like the female black widow spider which cannibalises in the act.

And so, like in homeopathic laws of sympathetic resonance where suppression is avoided, she now viewed Atma as symptomatic of susceptibilities in her knotted pariah self, which she yearned for someone to rub their fingers through. She considered a final exorcism of yucky feelings bound up in their story. But unbeknown to her, he'd acquired a new story which was going to change everything.

Late in the afternoon after the colonic, she stood naked and embarked upon the ultimate purge, and fixed a silver pentacle star necklace, with an amethyst at its centre, around her neck. Then, stepped into a blood red g-string, pulled on lycra leggings, fastened a bra, and fixed a snake skin Aphrodite belt around her waist. Over a shoulder, she slung a leather bag containing Wicca craft accessories, which included a tube of lube, a small silk bag of Himalaya salt, and an Aphrodite Kali belt device, then headed to Atma Blaze's house.

Upon arrival at the medieval mansion in the late afternoon, she was met by the screeching craw, craw and carr, carr sound of crows in the large mango tree that arched over the path leading to the house. She parked her sleek, red, Yamaha motorbike next to his big black Royal Enfield. It was a chrome machine with heavy metal thunder, machismo, just like its promo manifesto—*Made like a gun. Goes like a bullet. A symbol of freedom.* He'd once ridden it up a plank into the lounge where they'd bucked raw hide on its blazing saddle to the tune of The Bollock Brother's 'Harley David (Son of A Bitch)' belting out of big black speakers with a vocal that preached, "Get stoned, fly like a witch."

Zsu leaned into the jaws of a heavy, cast iron gate that was guarded by sentinel stone lions. Shouldering through weeds up a crumbling path, she looked up at grotesque, reptilian gargoyles, which appeared to mock her with scabrous grins. In the twisted limbs of the sprawling mango tree, crows continued to craw, craw and carr, carr. She wandered what the gothic gargoyles had seen over the centuries, coming and going into this cavernous, eerie house? What kind of lives had been lived here during the Portuguese reign? She recalled the wild stories from the seventies she'd been told by Atma, when it had been an opium den and rampaging party house, as evidenced by his Polaroids of freaks wearing jangling face paint, love beads and bell bottoms and paisley.

A breeze suddenly rushed up the path and rustled the mango tree and cooled the perspiration on her beading brow, but did not appease the flutter of butterflies in her tummy.

"Are you sure you want to be here?" said a chorus of voices. The crows flapped their oily black wings and caw, cawed and carr, carred. Startled, looking up, she stopped dead on the path, her legs shuddered and her head turned in a frightened gaze.

"The serpent is in the seed," said the chorus of voices. Instantly she recalled what she'd been taught by a Balinese witch doctor about poltergeist. Trembling, she stood motionless in ninja boots on the cracked cement steps through which crawled prickly vines. She looked up at the large, battered, wooden front door, above which was a mottled orange tile roof that was scaly, with pieces broken off. Stricken with dread, she sighed. *Oh Gawwd!... S-h-e-e-i-t!...* And then thought, *Entrapment!*— which was the comment her bestie, Asta, had made about the bind Zsu found herself in. A deep chasm of vulnerability opened up, like an earthquake fault line. It was followed by a rush of wretched self-loathing that threatened to puddle her, like a dirty roiling drain that was spewing over the steps to Blaze's front door.

Desperately needing to shore herself up, she commenced pranayama breathing focusing on mula bandha, and got directly in touch with her perineum muscles to tap into the potent nerve centre at the axis of her base chakra. Clambering for composure, she walked half way up the crumbling cement steps of the house, it's jaded grand structure now taking on the appearance of a jaundiced mansion of a megalomania lord inflated with Goddedness.

Jeezus Christ what am I doing?

"You're in Goa, it's a groovy world of addictive behaviour," replied the chorus of voices.

Then, she heard the flap of wings and a loud craw, craw. A large crow had dropped from the mango tree onto a stained, stone, Catholic cross in the garden next to the stairs. It's beady black eyes at the top of its sharp beak locked onto Zsu. Then the chorus of voices spoke again, but this time more voices joined in like a choir reciting a mantra.

"Thy will be done in earth,
As it is in heaven.
And lead you not into temptation,
But deliver you from evil.
For thine is the kingdom cum
The power and the glory,
For ever and ever.
Amen."

The crow flapped its wings and splattered a creamy, greenish poop upon the pockmarked, archaic, stone cross. Zsu squinted her eyes, sucked in and bit the inner soft folds of her cheeks, whilst slowly inhaling through her nose and gazing at the crow on the cross. Unflappable, she stepped up to the large wooden doors and took out the small silk bag of Himalayan salt from her bag and sprinkled it about the entrance. Then, in glowing red letters, a neon sign flashed the word—BETRAYAL—in her face. She felt the combined gaseous fluids of outrage, and hurt, surge through the plumbing behind her eyes.

The intimidating bark of dogs could be heard behind the doors. Implacable, she steeled herself to knock. Just as she did, the doors swung open setting free, three snarling peanut butter coloured dogs that scampered about her feet and sniffed the salt. The dogs then turned into Cerberus, a three-headed hell hound guardian of the underworld—offspring of Echidna, a half-woman, half-serpent creature.

With a wry grin, and wearing a Shaivite orange sarong, Atma Blaze greeted her. "Wow!.. your back."

Stepping inside the hallway, she could feel her warrior priestess self, teeter, on the verge of caving in to her wanton, precocious, show girl, Lolita self. The fetid air inside the spooky, dimly lit rooms was masked with the burning of sandalwood. On previous late night visits, she'd seen vampire bats flying through it, and hanging in its high arches.

You are my poison. I want you, I want to possess you in this dark paradise.

They made their way to a spacious lounge with high wooden ceiling that was like the cloisters of Count Dracula, or the residence of Aleister Crowley. Diaphanous light filtered through baroque iron work on the windows. It was not enough to illuminate the vastness of the lounge, leaving it shrouded in a shadowy batman cloak that wrapped around its cob web corners. Candles burning at a central altar at the far end illuminated deities. One wall featured a Tibetan mandala, another, a large poster that was a skull with a third eye and Psychic TV arial crucifix symbol. The altar was framed by a grand, pyramid shaped shrine flanked by JBL speakers. On the tile floor were rugs from Afghanistan, at the centre of which was a low round table with the book, 'The Upanishads,' open. Either side of the table were two crimson coloured velvet chaise lounges.

The pyramid was ornately decorated with reflective stickers of holy symbols and prophets and silver and gold strips of holographic tape. The inside of the shrine was densely populated with a pantheon of idolatry Hindu and Buddhist effigies and strange primitive dolls and sacred objects, including a crystal skull head and head of a goat painted fluoro in dots of hundreds and thousands. Everything was arranged as if standing on ceremony around a central plinth on which was a Shiva lingam made out of black cryptocrystalline quartz from the holy Narmada River. The speakers had deep throats and emitted a ratta tat tat pulse of Industrial Goth sounds.

DJ Atma Blaze, a thick-set trustafarian in his late thirties with dark dreadlocks down below his bum, had metamorphosed from a guitar-skanking Rastafarian into an Industrial Electronic Body Music DJ—and declared himself a sadhu. In the seventies he'd played guitar at Goa parties, but after the computer music reformation of the eighties, he converted to *Techgnosis*. He loved ritual, and liked to get priestly doing daily puja where he'd thumb a third eye red tikka on his brow and make offerings to the Goddedness he had amassed at his altar. A mala of yak bone skull heads with precious stones and necklace of Rudraksha seeds hung from his neck. He had piercing jet black eyes and a holy man beard, which he liked to tug when he was grandstanding Sutra and Vedas knowledge. During the heat of the day, he wound his thick gunja bud-like dreadlocks into a large bun knot on top of his head, through which he stuck a miniature silver trident.

He first learned of the unifying tribal spell of music as a Deadhead, following the Grateful Dead around California, and graduated to a league known as, *The Brotherhood of Eternal Love*. The year of Woodstock, he embarked upon a spiritual odyssey to India with reams of blotter paper packed into the pages of dog eared paperbacks by Aldrous Huxley and Ram Dass. He further dharma-bum binged on the teachings of Rama-Krishnam Babaji, Paramahansa Yogananda and other prophets of Godhood. His evangelist grandfather had been a man of God, too. His Jewish princess mother, a descendent of the family tribe name—*Katz*. Atma's arrival in India was like a shamanic baptism, to the extent that he expunged his Christened name, Bruce Jones.

Zsu perched herself on a chaise lounge. Reluctant to allow herself to fully sink into its wrap-round allure, she crossed her legs with tenterhooks and tossed her pony tail like a fetching filly. The soft surfaces of the chaise spoke of seductive pleasures previously had on its velvety curves and soft clefts. Two ceiling fans slowly chopped the sultry air. Atma fetched drinks from the kitchen. She declined the beer he offered, choosing lemon water instead, but then changed her mind as she desperately needed to relax the tightness in her tummy that pulled unhappiness strings in her face, that were beyond redeeming.

Incense, in homage to the divinity of gods and goddesses and totem objects, spiralled up; the holy smoke making twisting dragons in the grandiosity of the hoodoo lounge. Like the gargoyles and lions and crows and hungry ghosts in the garden, the figures seemed to want to talk to her. Some even smiling, as if to congratulate her on her brazen stance in surmounting her consternation to return to the Lordy lounge. Her eyes fixed upon a statue of Kali. Outside the open windows, crows craw crawed and carr carred.

Returning with two Tuborg cans, Atma sat down on the chaise lounge opposite her. "So, you're back?" he said taking a sip. The crows, craw crawed and carr carred louder and she thought of their sharp, penetrating beaks.

"Seems I am," she said with a blank face maintaining a stony gaze at Kali, and raised the Tuborg to her lips. The cold suds excited her mouth and cooled and relaxed her as the beer slid down her insides. Upon arrival at her tummy, the alcohol set about anaesthetising butterflies and sluicing prickly furies into submission. The torrid feelings that were like pinched nerves of treachery to herself, bound up in the invidious, trespass trampling of her heart. Now with a tourniquet around it. A heart that had latched itself to a pedestal.

"Actually—Atma I came to get my tapes back and…" She choked and inhaled sharply—the baleful refrain of the music playing, sustaining the wrath she was not able to vent. She stared into the dome centre of one of the JBL speakers, as though it were a portal into a black hole. The guttural voice and quivering synthesiser coming out it was like that of a ghastly spectral spirit at a séance, or the visceral voice of a Japanese Butoh dancer who had survived the Hiroshima holocaust, and quite possibly, the voice of one of the gargoyles she met on the steps.

"What's playing?" she asked.

"'Addiction' by Skinny Puppy," Atma said, lighting a joint. "It's off the album, 'Cleanse, Fold and Manipulate.'

Manipulate!.. How fitting she thought, looking at Atma puffing on the Manali Rizla, his locomotive breath exhaling the sadhu smoke into the air between them.

She reversed her crossed legs. *I didn't fall for you, you tripped me over in a mystical smoke screen.*

Up until just recently, her lotus flower had been well floated by his highfalutin beardy, spiritual patter. An esoteric schmooze, in which he would paw the social air with a billowing butterfly net of colourful hip-priest blather, into which would fly gossamer-winged delightful things. Zsu, the brightest and vivacious catch of all. In fact, so avid had she been hooked that she became his shining bobbin on which to spin even more captivating yarn. Until her own yarn sowed him up and hemmed him in and over-laid him and they discarded thimbles and stitch-witched and warlocked and pricked each other over and over—until their fingers ran red.

In the middle of a yoga, sun salutation, asana sequence—while looking out to sea over Disco Valley two mornings ago in Vagator—a burning realisation ran up her spine: *Love has become a bruising battlefield. Sex, a power game of domination and submission.* The stretch and release of yoga had brought tranquillity to an inner tossed emotionscape that had quaked and pinned her down and penetrated her to her aching core. Which was like a trembling crucible beyond the boundaries of her skin and hard wiring of her steely nerves, all the way down to her black painted toe nails and the curdling of blood through its narrowest of passages.

Atma passed the smouldering, pacifying joint across the table, as though it were a white feather of peace in a gauzy haze of illusion. When their fingers touched, she almost looked at him, but instead her eyes traced the holy burning charas smoke as it rose up to be beaten by a crusty ceiling fan, where she had a vision of Michelangelo's fresco at the Sistine Chapel. Then, recalled that it had been painted under duress to the Pope. She loved to weave fantasies around lofty guru types. It was only now dawning on her that the magisterial pedestal she'd gullibly hoisted Atma up on to, was her retrieving her lost-at-sea fisher king father. Her susceptibilities to the glory of Goddedness, had her experiencing Atma's intense expresso-black eyes and long locks and wise knowledgeable words of *truth*—like he was a sage. Yet, another insanely dissociated part of herself—like a psychosis—was impassioned to merge with the inner magus constellated deep within her.

Wearing saffron robes with matted holy man hair, his sanctimonious spiritual cabaret was an enchanting hook. His espousal of having read Vedas, doing time sitting with sadhus and yogis and doing Vippassana, which Zsu had assumed meant meditating. But, in actual fact, what he did was smoke a lot of Himilayan dope with them, which gave him kudos as he trotted out a bravura of mystical aphorisms, espousing his calling as a hip priest revolutionary riding the Electronic Body Music wave. Captivating as the trope might be, it didn't ring true, as he'd never been seen to dance, nor done beginner level salutes to the sun on a yoga mat.

The dreamy-eyed artifice of her projections began to fall like darts hitting the wire around a bullseye. They quarrelled and clashed. An estranged divide opened up between them, like a swing bridge, its wire rope hack-sawed by embittered words.

Shouting, "Anger is holy," she'd served him an ace.

"Anger is corrosive," he replied.

She served for the match. "Anger is frustrated love and it's highly motivational." It was delivered with a twisting top spin that aced him right on the T of his third eye tilak. It was so blistering, that it pinged him right through to his pineal gland sending his spiritual antenna into white noise.

"Fuck head!" gutturally rasped the gargoyle voice in the legato staccato of the Industrial techno that electronically gurgled out of black speaker cones riding a dystopian, post-punk Goth drum machine. The gargoyle had glassy stoned eyes with inflamed lids. Zsu experienced the voice and splenetic frequency of the music as though she was tasting the dark green and yellowish brown acids of her bile, yet the disenfranchised refrain and melancholic melody of its noire synthesiser atmosphere was also delectable and elegant in an eloquent grotesque kind of way. Frankenstein-like, its existential gravitas was demoniacal and dripped and oozed with alienated blues. The apertures of her eyes opened so wide they bent around the corners giving her fish eye vision. She could feel her freshly, flushed entrails from the colonic squirming her spleen in sympathetic resonance with the rancour and disgust of the music.

"This music is pithy," she remarked. "I love it!.. I just love it the same as I adore the dark alien, erotic, sci-fi mechanical worlds of the artist HR Giger. You must have played some of it at the party, something sounding like this swallowed me up in the depth of the night, I became a protozoan cyborg inhabiting a pulpy chrysalis world."

Atma pulled his goatee, his black eyes widened. "I played 'Assimilate.' This is the psychedelic zeitgeist, it reflects the Kali Yuga prophecy of our age of darkness which will end in twenty twenty-five. It sure ain't lame kiddy disco the other DJs are playing," he said in a haughty tone of voice.

She puffed on the joint, surrendering to the spaciousness it brought to her mind and receptivity to uncontainable supernatural forces, and became transfixed on the shrine where her eyes fell upon the monkey god Hanuman. The ape deity sat cross legged with large pouting lips, deep brown eyes, jewelled crown, and hands that had ripped open his chest exposing the lovers Rama and Sita in the space of his heart. The tourniquet around Zsu's own heart loosened, she passed the joint to Atma, their eyes met fleetingly, and then her heart jumped violently, like a bat was in her face flapping wing claws, and then a shrieking sound came from the front garden. She and Atma leapt to their feet and went to the window and saw a troupe of monkeys with long question-mark-shaped tails swinging in the mango tree. One was sitting on the Catholic cross, which filled her with disquiet that something uncanny was going on.

"Hey poor!.. Hey poor!.. you don't have to be poor any more, Jesus is here!" said a voice in the music coming out of the shrine speakers. "Don't tell the Devil… feel like your life is going nowhere?" ('Welcome to Paradise' by Front 242 was playing.)

Atma laughed loudly. "Look at us, we're surrounded by crosses… we're heretics." He disappeared to the kitchen and returned with a stainless-steel container of fresh curd and a white porcelain dinner plate which he set on the round table. He lit a bunch of incense sticks placing them next to a large bronze statue of Tibetan Buddhist deities in a tantric embrace. The scented smoke spiralled around the figures like twisting snakes. Atma stopped the tape deck and commenced to chant a mantra. "Om namah shivaaya om namah shivaaya om namah shivaaya om namah shivaaya…." Continuing to chant, he slowly dribbled curd over the large black Shiva lingam at the centre of the altar around which was a golden yoni that had twin flared hooded cobras either side, like welcoming labia. The creamy curd that now ran down the erect stone lingam stirred hot and cold emotions in Zsu.

"Om namah shivaaya om namah shivaaya om namah shivaaya om namah shivaaya...."

She recalled last season when she first become smitten with Atma's mystic man aura, his wanderlust tales of pilgrimages to the Kumbh Mela, the biggest religious event in India. He'd hung out with naked ash-smudged holy men—the Nagas, and undertook initiations and was given admittance to a sect—*The Naga Sannyasis Order*. His words had been like magic wands that stroked her imagination and sent sensations through her body that tickled neural pathways to her crown chakra. But soon their dalliance became like that of a ouroboros sixty-niner yoked in a tumble rinse of soma solvents, that left their combined personality weave frayed, their merged masks abraded, the running colours of their dope revelling, unravelling on a slippery slope. The sheen of the spiritual veneer of the magus mask that Atma wore, which Zsu so ardently wished to see herself reflected in, had become scored, scratched, disfigured, warped—leaving her feeling like a splattered upon drop cloth. A drop cloth that she slashed holes in, and donned with bewitching seduction, like it was a trampled, vampish garment off of the floor of her temple harlot collection, which she would entrancingly peel off, like a high-gloss paint stripper. But, in her opinion, compared to him, such steely cajolery was nowhere near as diabolical as his ruthless expediency in eliciting allegiances inflicted with a honey coated razor blade.

Their torrid hook-ups had sweltered into an irksome stench, with the overarching feeling that everything about him had become a perjury to herself. But it was not that entirely clear whether it was him, or a deluded part of herself which she experienced in him, that she needed to purge. And so, not one to waist a crisis, she chose to rise to the occasion with the assistance of the Tuborg in her detoxed tummy and boom shankar in her lungs and gave herself permission to loosen into his domain, rather than pull out a dagger and stab it into his velvety scarlet chaise with retaliatory intention. Like self-sabotage, as if the soft rouge lips of the couch were her own body.

Atma stopped chanting and ejected a cassette titled, ATTRITION, and slotted another one titled, THE FAITH HEALER, which brought a New Wave track rocking out of the speakers with a voice that said, "She gets high on Edgar Alan Poe."

"What's your take on Samsara?" she asked him.

He fixed a gaze upon the black lingam. "The wheel of life, no?"

"Right!" she said. "As in karma," feeling like her heart was a reversed Hindu wheel of life, just like the Nazi Third Reich.

He stroked his goatee. "The eternal cycle of birth and death and rebirth."

Zsu's face took on the appearance of a she-wolf. "And don't forget pain. All the pain bound up in desire, no? There's suffering in Samsara, too."

"Right!" He looked up from the plate on the table between them where he'd tipped an ant hill of white powder from out of a plastic bag. "To incarnate is to take on suffering."

The voice in the music said, "If she had to take on a lover it would be Charles Manson, in that lady's eyes he is rather handsome."

Zsu sipped on her beer and said, "So if Samsara is our karmic inheritance on the eternal cycle of birth, suffering, death, and rebirth—how much of our personal suffering is coming from the collective soul? Surely, it is inseparable?"

"Whoa!" Atma said chopping at the ant hill. He stopped, hs neck tightened, he took a deep breath as if gasping for existential air. It was as though she'd monkey wrenched the machine head off of his metaphysical motor. He shifted on the chaise and released air from his charas coated lungs. "The damnation of humanity." And resumed chopping.

A voice in the music said, "The gateway to hell lies deep within her soul."

Zsu wondered if she was the daughter of the Devil? Lifting her upper lip bearing she-wolf teeth, she said, "Don't you think our personal shit, is collective shit. The scene here is full of experts escaping shit. The shit of society is inside all of us. Don't you think we're connected to the whole? If society is racist, sexist, violent, consumed by greed, these diseases live in our collective soul, too. The cells of these cancers are distributed among all of us because our lives are the tissues that make up the psychic organs of the species mind—"

This whirled Atma's brain, sending him into a spin. "Maya!" he snapped back, raking his fingers through the undergrowth of his weighty dreads to let in air to the sweating follicles of his tightening scalp. The result of the whiplash of her cosmological conjectures. He then replied with one of his catch-all standard sutras. "Oh, the clutches of Maya—that which is not."

With eye liner smeared, heightening the whites of her eyes, she snarled like a wolverine. "Maya is illusion." The word, *illusion*, piercing the non-stick Teflon coating of his self-righteousness like it was an incisor tooth. "The chaos of feelings isn't illusionary, everyone here will tell you they have something to rebel against, something they want to be rid of." She sucked in her cheeks with the bitter taste of yucky feelings. "Ha!...the system... a sick society... the screwed-up feelings of toxic families..."

A voice appeared in the music saying, "I'm free and easy, my life is my own, I come and go as I choose, just look me over, I take what I want."

For the umpteenth time, Atma reiterated his mystique of the East credentials. "I hung heaps with babas and sadhus, they're the rebels of the Hindu tradition, plus I hung out with Tibetans in Dharamsala—and man!.. they have something to rebel against. When I came to India, I was rebelling against everything."

She looked questioningly at Atma with burning eyes. "The paradise we are having here is by the grace of a cultural divide, and a good dose of providence. We are privileged, the Indians view us as barbarians, they see us as weird and different. So long as we keep paying them, no problem, do what you like—"

"The Goans don't judge us," he said with a smirk, blading off two lines from the ant hill. "They see us as happy, nutty people. India has so many celebratory festivals. Meditation, transcendence, devotion, multi-dimensional realities—it's all engrained in their culture. We came to it through the entheogen doorway, he said rolling up a hundred-dollar greenback. "The rule of karma never fails." He dropped his head to the plate and tooted up a line with a clean sweep of the big bill. He pushed the plate of blow and unfurling note over to her side of the table, she gave him a white-hot look of devilment. A voice in the music introduced the mistress of the black macabre. "The gateway to hell lies deep within her soul. Let's go and meet her."

Zsu leaned over the table to the plate, retightened the greenback, contemplated Atma's spiritual freebase, and bugled it up. Stretching out on the chaise, her brain ping-ponged with dopamine. Adrenaline flooded her blood. Her heart hammered the sides of her rib cage. Her jawed tightened. She felt an empowering upsurge in apparent—Goddedness.

"The faith healer," said a voice in the music by The Bollock Brothers that poured out of the altar speakers into the holy lounge. "Faith and hope and charity, everlasting sweet desire. Can I put my hands on you?"

Releasing her jaw, she said, "Don't you think blinding belief itself is a form of bondage?" Atma's brow creased. Zsu's tummy tightened and she said, "Unquestioning religious ritual oppresses free autonomous thinking."

He fiddled with his mala necklace. Her jaws picked up speed. "The immovable caste divisions in India are oppressive. It's savage, social discrimination."

The furrow in his brow deepened. He squeezed a Shiva trident stud on his ear lobe. She had no appetite, but her gnashing teeth wanted to bite something. "Indian society is sexually up tight, you would think that's to protect the woman, wouldn't you?"

He nodded and raised both hands to his bee hive dread bun on his head to secure an errant thick tendril of matted hair that had broken free. Her jaws had become like a Dobermann gnawing a bone. "You know what?" she glared. "The chaste, perverse sanctity of it is an insult to men. It leaves men with no self-control. It's fucked up!"

Not wishing to volley with Zsu on the lot of Indian society, Atma offered not one word of reply, but what she was saying was on the money. He chose to glide over caste divisions and discrimination, preferring to stay lofty in a spiritual romanticism. An appropriation of flowery ideologies with which to wreath himself a sadhu baba identity, serving a public image belief system. As for the relationship of freaks with locals, it allowed freedoms not possible anywhere else. Her ranting volley unsettled him, as much as it provocatively thrilled him.

He got up and fetched a decanter bottle of green liquid and a tin beggars cup, into which he poured the liquid, then ignited it with a lighter holding a sugar cube in a teaspoon over the devilish looking blue, yellow and green flame. After the cube dissolved and flame died down he poured absinthe into two ceremonial shot glasses and bladed two more parallel white lines.

The Maxell C90 cassette wound to an end leaving just the OO-OO-OOO-AAA-AAA-TCH-TCH-TCH sound of monkeys and caw, cawing and carr, carring of crows outside.

Zsu got up and slotted a tape of her own, which she'd titled, TRANCE ECSTASY EXPRESS. They snorkelled the lines and skulled the high-octane tipple, which instantly delivered a caramelising of cortex and stoking of her solar plexus and ameliorating of jittery jaw that wanted to jabber questions tugging her mind like, *What's our karmic pleasure quota? Are we Prometheus stealing fire from the Gods?*

What she liked about lines was how they neatly bundled messy, entangled feelings and intrusive thoughts into insignificance, by sending them back down into murky cubby holes of her mind. And how the utility of lines enhanced the omnipotent emboldening of libidinal lubricity. And how—right now—it was a snap to slip into temple harlot enchantress mode.

Peering into the constellation of Goddedness in the shrine, Zsu saw Kali rise up out of the charm effigies amassed there. It was as though Kali was a volcanic island giving birth to herself out of a chaos ocean of dark arts. The death, mother, lover, goddess, had horns and a large red tongue hanging down dripping with saliva, or was it blood? Kali kept rising in size until she subsumed the entire shrine. Zsu felt her own tongue curl out of her mouth and her eyes enlarge and burn with fiery acetylene intensity.

A voice in the track playing by DAF said, "The world is a mess. You get me on the floor. You make me want to dance. You put me in a trance. You make me want to have…"

Under the charm of Kali, Zsu got up and slithered and swayed to the music and ground her hips up close to Atma and pulled his holy man goatee and stroked his chest hair under his mala, like he was a tom cat. She untied her Aphrodite belt, spun it in the air, cracked it like a whip, removed her bra and boob swiped his body and swung spilling breasts into his face and rubbed his thigh and stroked his chest some more, then lowered her head and pressed her third eye into his tilak-ashed forehead. She then danced with her hands in the air above her head in a trance with eyes rolled back and hips gyrating, then slowly rolled her lycra pants down her hips to reveal a blood red, sheer g-string. Rushing flushes of heat coursed from her pelvic floor down her thighs and legs to her feet as her strip tease pulled her deeper into the root of her mula bandha muscles, that were now contracting and expanding with demon lust.

Outside in the garden the monkeys and crows and lions and gargoyles witnessed another visitor who did not ascend the steps to the front door, and was not detected by the three-headed hell hound Cerberus, as the music was too loud. The unannounced interloper from Mapusa crept to the side of the house and peered in a window on tippy toes, his chocolate brown eyes, large as saucers, taking in the cobra-like temple harlot seduction of the sadhu hip-priest seated on the chaise in front of the shrine of Goddedness. Atma's heart pounded like a kick drum and his lingam rose up under his sarong. Moving closer, Zsu pressed her blood red, netted, delta into the hip-priest's face and slowly ground her hips and plucked the silver shiva trident from his piled bun. Clawing his scalp, she mussed his dreads until they dropped down his shoulders and back and salaciously rubbed her body into his.

Goddessness seduction had become a ritual burlesque in which gaseous fantasy of flesh contorted into a tangential cabaret. Besides the stealth interloper at the window, the audience included cupid, gagged and bound in a corner chair, like a hostage surrounded by broken arrows. Atma's erect lingam had lifted his sarong off his thigh. Zsu discarded her g-string and sat on the chaise and removed the sarong and lowered her head to kiss the lingam's tip. The interloper at the window with straining calf muscles felt his own lingam firming inside his polyester slacks, as he maintained a racy view of the Kali karma sutra show.

Temple harlot Zsu commanded hip-priest Atma to get down on his hands and knees on an Afghan rug. Naked, she got astride him, riding him like a Royal Enfield. Then dismounted and took the tube of lube and Kali Aphrodite strap-on made of leather and silicon from out of her bag. After fastening it around her waist, she pinched his nipples and spanked his buttocks and squirted a dollop of lube into his smiling moon. Then slid a hand, like a blade, back and forth across his crevasse, and spanked him some more and circled a devilish finger around his back door several times before inserting it into him. With her other hand, she reached up to his knotted dreads hanging down and tugged them like reins on a haltered horse. She alternated a tight grip with release and spanked him and repeated and then got on her knees right behind him and wickedly inserted the strap-on lingam up to the hilt—and reached under and pulled on his jewels and squeezed his hardness.

"Every man and women is a star," said a voice in the music from the speakers at the altar. "The body is a universe." (A track by The Anti Group was playing.)

Atma moaned and groaned as Zsu lent her full weight into his jacksie, slamming home the Kali lingam right up to the leather mount of her Aphrodite belt. Slowly withdrawing until its head was just inside him, and then lunging hard her Kali self into his rear end again, and reversed and repeated, again and again while Atma howled and screamed like he was in labour giving birth in a crucible. Outside, Hanuman was hanging in the mango tree with the other monkeys. Rama and Sita had leapt out of his chest and embraced swinging in a hammock under it. The interloper had collapsed in a stupor of voyeuristic debauchery, his eyes ravaged, aghast.

The temple harlot unbuckled her strap-on and lay down on the chaise. Atma got up and slid a hand down an inner thigh and ducked her petals. He lifted up her legs and applied lube to her back door, then pressed his bowed lingam into her splayed flesh on the velvet mouth of the chaise. Zsu cried out an ululation of pain and pleasure, which she regulated with her mula bandha muscles and deep groaning breaths.

Insatiably, with clawed fingers on the window ledge and legs stretched and neck craned, the interloper got up once more and salivated a peeping Tom eye-full, as Atma impelled and pommelled Zsu's tender body. Wheezing and spluttering with twirling dreadlocks, the hip-priest sadhu felt apocalyptic fire about to surge through his lingam and his jewel sack tighten.

"Spirit in the serpent, serpent in the seed, excretion of the cows," a voice said in the music. Quickly Atma withdrew and straddled Zsu on the chaise and spasmed and roared like he'd bungee leaped into a weightless void. Warm serpent seed shot out of the eye of his lingam onto Kali's long extended tongue.

"Cosmogenesis," a voice in the music said.

Atma gasped, "Don't swallow!" and collapsed onto her. She marshalled all her Kali strength and rolled him over and mounted his chest, pincer gripping him with her thighs on the chaise. Levelling hot poker eyes to his bullet hole eyes, she pressed her forehead hard into his third eye red tilak, pulled back, and tongued his snowball into his open mouth. He gagged and gulped and gurgled and gagged and swallowed, but she was not able to clear her throat. She slid off him, their distinctly separated sticky bodies mangled in obscene disarray, like survivors of a train smash.

Outside, on shaky legs with sullied slacks, the interloper—Police Inspector Alfonso—checked his gold Rollex watch, and quietly retreated from the window making his way back down the path. Time had disappeared. The mango tree a gnarly silhouette bereft of devious life. The sun an afterglow with twilight fading to grey. The gothic mansion spooky, as shadows devoured the Goddedness within. There was a power outage. Atma groped for candles. Zsu remained silent. Now, more than ever, she was aware of how alone she'd been, beneath a wheel she thought was love. Though, what she did not know was that this last gasp purging, and his withholding, had signified Atma's serpent seed vows to a golden goat cult in Goa. She dressed, collected her tapes, gathered her devices, packed her bag and left.

The Nearest Phone

TWO DAYS AFTER the Chapora Fort party, Jules moved into a palm-thatched cabana to become a cliff dweller above middle Vagator Beach. He stored a bag and passport at Ram Dass chai shop nearby and rented a Rajdoot motorbike. The nearest phone was an hour ride away. He followed behind Zikos's Enfield which brought tricky close encounters with gritty terrain. The Rajdoot caught the attention of perilous gravel on the side of the road when he swerved to miss a pot hole, which sent the bike sliding out from beneath him, inflicting a graze to his knee, which—judging by similar wounds he noticed other newbie riders sporting—was the thrills and spills of coming to grips with wheels on Goa's loose surfaces.

After an hour-long wild, ride on narrow roads through rural Goa, they arrived at O' Coqueiro Restaurant on the outskirts of Panjim. Holding his ear hard to the receiver of the restaurant's Bakelite phone, he heard a crackling line. At the other end, an operator was switch boarding him to a Down Under phone number. The ring tone continued for some time with no one picking up. The operator rang a second time and a woman's voice came on the line:

"Ah-yeer-hallo".

"I have a Mr Jules Nightingale calling collect from India for Mr Zane Lovelock.

"Um…err…lemme see ef hez 'ere."

There was a long delay. Jules pressed his ear to the phone like he was listening into a nautilus shell and thought he could hear the faint roar of waves of Bondi Beach down the line.

"Hullo," said a coughing voice.

"Mr Jules Nightingale calling collect from India, will you accept the charges?"

"Yeah, yeah… sure, no worries—crikey!.. Jules.

"Hey Zane, it's me… Jules, I'm in Goa—"

"Brilliant to hear your voice matey." The line crackled, hummed and hissed. "I thought you were in India?"

"Still am. Well… Goa isn't exactly India."

"Oh, right. I got your post card…sounds mental—"

"Totally insane. The parties are nuts…How's your wrist?"

"I'm out of plaster. I'm back strumming the gat—"

"Great!… You gotta get your arse over here. The most vile fun is being had. The freshest sounds are being played. It's off the hook, mate!"

"In India?"

"Yes, I know, it's unbelievable. I shit you not. It's continuous crazy music. Parties full of freaks. DJ's playing cassettes…madcap dancing on the beach, in the jungle, in ruins, in a fort. Not a band thing—"

"Who's doin it?"

"It's a mystery. Freaky characters… trippers… masala teapot yogi back flippers…. God only knows, a bent traveller scene of fruity loopers. The vibe here is another dimension. Feels like a cosmic conspiracy… a world beyond… the music sounds like its coming from outer-space, like star-trekking into the future—"

"Strewth!"

"It's a mania. The wildest edge of experience I've every known. Tribal warriors. Galactic star divers. Cowgirls. Lazor cowboys. Absolute lawlessness. The head gear is outasight!"

"Core blimey!.. I heard Kathmandu is happening."

"Nah!.. not the same. This is beach. It's pumpin' with psycho disco and wacko electro tracks. I heard The Residents, Peter Shelly, Alien Sex Fiend, Test Department, Depeche Mode, Ministry. There's cosmic fairy tale melodies in the morning, I'm told it's Italo House. It's a musical melange. Total freaksville—all kinds of crazies gettin' down…"

On the return to Vagator, the Goan landscape of paddy fields, white cement houses and wedding cake Churches rushed by as Jules toed through gears of the Rajdoot. Palm trees flickered by in his peripheral vision like frames of an animation movie as he found himself replaying in his mind the belated, rekindled connection with Zsu up in the medieval fort. The moving and grooving on its asteroid-like surface. The melting cooing and laughing on the chai mat. The dancing upon astral frequencies in soft morning light, their bodies coated in pink and golden sun rays. The vision questing up high in the mists of time back dropped by a dreamy inland Tolkienesque vista. The soaring of their spirits like the kite birds that spiralled in the thermals above the ramparts. The watching together of fishing boats heading out to sea from the mouth of Chapora river. Her contrite apology about the story she'd been in and the chagrin it brought to her face and bitterness on her lips.

Zikos slowed down at the intersection for Calangute and Arpora. Locals were shopping at a corner store. Freaks, wearing shades, sat outside at a juice bar. Jules flashed on the shades that Zsu wore up above Vagator after the melting dawn, in which he saw the elation in his face reflected. Shades that concealed glinting emerald eyes around which smouldered soot black mascara. Itchy witchy eyes that appeared more bewitching on the wild side of the Starco Corner border than in Bali. Dreamy mysterious eyes befitting the dark moon goddess, Lilith. *Was she an old soul? What kind of gathering was that? Perhaps souls from another time in a medieval castle. A dejavu?*

Gripping the handle bars of the Rajdoot, he recalled Zsu's voice. It was liqueur coated in his ear over the party music that was still playing in his head. Following behind Zikos, it seemed as though the Rajdoot was being towed by the Enfield. The sun was dropping toward the sea and their shadows had grown long on the road when Zikos and Jules pulled up next to Ram Dass chai shop. Inside they met yogi Ananta. He was lean and tanned with light brown hair in a ponytail, and emanated a glow of a simple life lived outdoors on the Asia trail since the seventies. He also was camped out in a palm leaf cabana, two terraces down from Jules.

"Come to mine for sunset?" the yogi invited.

"Boom!" Zikos replied.

After buying Limca and mineral water from Ram Dass, Zikos and Jules made their way down Middle Vagator terraces of volcanic rock through cabanas inhabited by freaks. Halfway down they arrived to a flat area where Ananta was feeding scraps of banana and papaya to a cute black pig with a fluoro coloured collar. From out of a neighbouring cabana appeared a dreadlocked freak, who originally hailed from Munich and went by the name Rasta Jake. He wore a sarong, above which was a tattoo of Lord Shiva across his bare chest. Everyone sat down out front of Ananta's cabana on reed mats and pulled out pieces of smoke as the sun was about to touch down.

"Your pig?" Jules asked.

"Yup—Ditzy is her name," Ananta said, "Had her since she was a piglet, otherwise she'd be eating turds her whole life. She lives on the terraces and attends yoga class."

Most days, the American yogi taught beginners, intermediate and advanced levels of Ashtanga yoga on a shaded terrace, a stone's throw away. The rupees he earned, paid for a Goa season.

"It's nearly full moon," he said. "Where's the party?"

"I heard Disco Valley," Zikos said.

"Great!" Ananta said, "That'll get get all the flabby new arrivals into shape." The yogi thrived on pranayama, eight-hour dance marathons and coconut juice.

"Most here are vego," Zikos said. "Though the fish curry is great, but the meat crap—just piglets."

"Now that's recycling," Jules said gazing at Ditzy. "Your pet pig is cute."

"The other day," Ananta said, "Ditzy was off her rocker. She'd gotten into my Kerala buds. Goa pigs really do fly. You should see them when they're on acid pooh. It was pretty bad when there were lots of junkies gettin' around with hep C from sharing needles. Their smack waste was causing the pigs to cark it. Even used to be a freaks' magazine called, *The Stoned Pig*."

The yogi loaded up a brown glazed chillum with a mix of Panama tobacco and charas. He pressed the mix down with his finger, dribbled water out of a plastic bottle onto a ripped strip of cotton sarong serving as *safi material*, which he wrapped around the bottom of the chillum. He passed the pipe to Jules to start, which required Zikos and Rasta Jake to shroud Jules with a sarong as an on-shore breeze threatened to blow out the matches.

"Mahadeva Shiva Shambo," incanted Ananta firing the chillum behind the sarong, as Jules inhaled with bellowing lungs, then passed the pipe to Zikos, who passed it on to Rasta Jake. He was the owner of a brightly painted Mercedes van parked-up by Ram Dass. It had done several journeys from Greece through Turkey and Afghanistan to Goa, and back again, before the Russians invaded.

"Afghanistan was tops," Rasta Jake said. "We camped around fires, wild horsemen would show up, some were thieves. I lost a friend up there. One morning we found him not breathing, he over did it on opium. Then everything got really twisted. Can you believe it? The local cops stitched us up, threatened us with murder charges. We had to pay our way out of there."

"Back then," Ananta explained, "jet travel was expensive. Everyone came overland. When the first freaks arrived at South Anjuna beach, there was nothing. You just claimed your own palm tree, we lived in huts like this, real primitive. There were no motorbikes and roads, hardly any houses. We all cooked and ate together like a big family. Man!.. I was fleeing Viet Nam. Fuck that!.. I didn't want to be toting no machine gun, killing gooks. It was already enough, surviving redneck Texas. For us, India was a sanctuary. A soft asylum. The Indians loved us, no one judged the way you looked."

Rasta Jake took the last pull on the chillum, and then thumped the end of it down on the palm of his hand to loosen the wedged stone inside, and emptied the ash and hot stone into a coconut shell. "I was living naked in Arambol," he said, "up the jungle back side of the lake in the seventies."

He threaded a string, made from a torn piece of sarong, into the chillum barrel. "We used to walk the beach from Arambol to Morjim and pay a few paise to cross the river by canoe to come to the parties." Ananta grabbed the string when it appeared at the end of the pipe, and pulled it tight for Jake to rub the pipe clean. After which, he wiped the stone and placed it inside the chillum to complete the cleaning ritual. The orange red disk of the sun kissed the horizon. Everyone fell silent, all mesmerized by the sun being swallowed by the ocean, which left a trailing fiery afterglow.

"It's a wonder I'm even here," Ananta said. "It's a wonder I'm here to share this melting moment with you." Everyone pricked their ears to what he'd just said. "In Nam, we really got fucked up, man…we had to medicate ourselves on junk. It was gruesome and horrifying. Lucky I didn't get to kill no one. I parachuted into a jungle clearing, broke my ankle on landing and took a round in the leg," he pointed to a scar. "Buddies were getting shot up, dying all around me. I lay down like I was dead. I was spared, retrieved, hospitalised, thank God I escaped that hell. Shiva was looking out for me."

That night, after Primrose, laying in his cabana with the rhythmic wash of Vagator waves down below and chillum cannabinoid transporters heightening his brain, a Super 8 cartridge titled, LIQUEFACTION, projected images inside his head of him staring into a dream machine, the sound track was by The Telepathics with him singing.

> *From collapsing structures we're form reborn*
> *Grazed societal skin bleeding urban blight*
> *Liquafaction life forms ooze up towards the light*
> *Primitive ghosts dancing resplendent in delight*

It was the last track The Telepathics recorded in their studio, a dilapidated corroded cooler shed at Pyremont squat, known as—*The Lab*. Jules recalled a mishap that occurred during sessions leading up to its completion with Zane not showing up. Tracking him down, Jules found him passed out together with his S & M dominatrix girlfriend, Evangeline, in her lair. On the night stand was a spent needle. Later, contrite, Zane confessed that he'd scraped the deep end and had a visionary near-death experience.

Elephant Tree

"DISCO VALLEY is one my favourite places," Zsu told Jules three nights after the fort party, as they dined on prawn curry by candle light at an outside table of Pascal's Restaurant in Vagator jungle, at the top of the valley. "It's alive with animate energies and nature spirits," she said gazing into dense trees.

A power outage occurred, which made her cheeks glow in the naked flame. Her face filled with little girl joy as she peered into the wilderness that had become more luminescent in moon light. The candle flickered, changing the contour of her lips, her emerald eyes glistening like a cat with pupils widening like she had prey in her sights and ready to pounce. The metamorphosis of her face charmed Jules like peekaboo through a seductive veil.

As they ate strawberries and ice cream, Jules felt his heartstrings being strummed. Unhesitatingly, he reached over and held her hand. A hush fell upon them. With pupils glistening in candlelight, they dissolved into the lustre of each other's eyes. Eyes that now had become wishing wells, neither of them blinking. They felt a current zap them and were transported into a sepia tone silent movie in soft focus. When the lights came back on and background music returned, they found themselves in a vivid technicolour world with full effects.

"Wow!.. where were we?" Jules gestured with raised eyebrows, his face filled with joy like he'd stepped back on earth having had a foretaste of the rush of tenderness that he anticipated would soon be on offer.

"Oh, my God!" she gasped. "That was some ice cream melt. Shall we go for a wonder down yonder?"

"You mean Disco Valley?"

"Yes!.. Yes!.. I want to take you there," she said seductively—her pheromones invisibly pulling on him. He paid, and she led the way down through a garden that soon narrowed to a track which snaked into thick jungle illuminated in silvery moon light.

After navigating through a dense leafy maze of branches and vines she said, "We're getting close."

"Close to what?"

"You'll see."

Making their way through big, spindly, spook trees, she padded lightly twitching her ears like a cheetah until they arrived at a clearing where they were greeted by an elephant.

Astonished, Jules wondered whether he was hallucinating. "Is that what I think it is?"

"It's Ganesh," she said.

"Wow!.. Far out!.. So it is."

"Isn't it fantastic," she said. "The spirit of Ganesh resides in Disco Valley. Ganesh is the remover of all obstacles."

Jules walked toward the elephant. "How is it possible?" He moved closer. "Oh, I see... This is un-fucking-believable."

Thick vines had grown over some of the brickwork of the ruins transmogrifying it into the form of an elephant. Holding hands, they walked around Ganesh and looked up at the rising moon through a lattice of branches from a Bodhi tree. They embraced, their hearts raced, the earth fell from beneath them. They floated in space. The elephant knelt down, they mounted Ganesh, the elephant then carried them down Disco Valley through the jungle towards the beach. At a flat clearing the elephant bent down and they alighted. Taking a deep breath, she looked into Jules's eyes and said. "I'd like it, if you would wish to kiss me."

The proposition short circuited his brain. Lapsing into silence, they melted into each other's eyes with his lips meeting hers. She pressed her third eye to his. Jules went into free fall as time stood still in a lingering kiss in shimmering lunar light. Then she announced, "This is where I'm going to make the full moon party."

Astounded, he said, "It's such a magical place."

"Ganesh has blessed us," she said. An electrical charge coursed through her body, the same kind of electric zap she felt when dancing. Jules was speechless, he nodded his head in awe of what he was feeling and she was proposing.

"Ganesh is the guardian of Disco Valley," she said. "It's a sacred place."

Disco Valley Party

MAESTRO VOLTAIRE had the physique of a jockey and an acute ear for music. He hadn't been back to the West in a long time. No one really knew where he came from: France, Belgium, Luxembourg, Switzerland? He lived minimally on a cow shit floor up Chapora River. Only occasionally did he venture out of Goa, which would be during monsoon when he'd head up to the mountains of Manali. Chameleon-like, he thrived in the transitory fashion foliage of the shifting bohemian milieu of a Goa party *season*. All the while, maintaining a clandestine lifestyle within its undergrowth, peopled with crusty survivalists, pirates, outcastes, trustafarians, run-aways, healers, dealers, fringe fugitives, dilettante tape-jocks, bare foot dancers, toasters, jokers, tokers, mystical maniacs, music fanatics, monkey biz movers 'n' groovers, spandex-stretch aerial-asana levitators...

Nirvana chai shack, at the end of Spaghetti Beach, Little Vagator, was Voltaire's hangout. It was where he revved on circulating chillums and its crosstalk in Italian, French, German, English, Konkani—and the roll of a backgammon dice, which he gambled on, and typically won. Like a piazza, out front of the palm frond, shaded, tables of Nirvana chai shack was where friends and friends of friends languidly sat and lay sun-tanning and down at the seashore played beach racket.

When DJ Voltaire wasn't at Spaghetti Beach, everyone knew a fresh batch of dance cuts had arrived on tapes from Europe. He wore a poker face and kept his ace cassettes close to his chest, especially a straight flush, i.e.— a C90 chrome cassette of crème de la crème he'd collated, courtesy of the *Goa music mafia,* after winding through miles and miles of tape of latest releases. This *special Goa music,* mixed tape to tape with no pitch control, he could be relied upon to drop at the right moment to unite an eccentric dance floor of dissidents under a groove. The only time you would see him at parties was when he chose to accept a request to DJ, which he liked to do in the shadows tucked away, sometimes on a chair, done for the love of it, as the parties were always free.

On Friday the thirteenth, March nineteen eighty-seven, minds were prey to superstitions. However, theologians would tell you it was the day Eve bit the apple from the Tree of Knowledge. That afternoon—wearing a T-shirt on which was printed FAD GADGET in block text over a collage of machinery and dolls—Voltaire was not at the beach. He'd become a spectral-analysis tape worm loading Akai and Tascam cassette decks, winding and assiduously scrutinising and dubbing fresh '*Tekno*' (the uber informed spelling of the new sound) from stacks of TDK, Sony and Maxell chrome cassette tapes.

According to his picky criteria, the calibre of tracks today yielded only a few exceptional stand-out discoveries. The rest, mostly unsuitable fizzers. This season's collection had been acquired by exchanges with other collectors and DJs. Many of which were 12 inch vinyl that Jaeger had hunted down and recorded with his three-head Nakamichi in Switzerland. With nimble fingers on the Akai deck, Voltaire fast forwarded two minutes into each track, assessing—*yes/no/maybe?* The music exploded to life intermittently in bursts of sonic tease through Kenwood speakers on book shelves, as he evaluated whether to record it. Some boarder line tracks he took, as he wished to reconsider them with further listening.

Today's session was being done in a white washed brick house tucked away in Gummal Vaddo, leased by a friend, Sofia. A petite Italian in her early thirties, she wore faux lizard skin patterned lycra leggings with Bali batik bikini top exposing an OM symbol tattooed on a nut-brown shoulder blade. A gracious host, she relished close proximity to the musings of mavens of the new musica in her stylish pad, where friends would pass and only the best Malana cream charas was smoked.

Like all houses in Goa, Sofia's home had a voltage regular box, as the electricity was strange with wild fluctuations. Likewise, many in the scene were wary of dosing up if there wasn't reliable voltage control on "way too strange" strains of music in the party. For many, only a handful of DJs could be trusted for heroic dosing-up to. Voltaire's voltage control was prestigious, his approval rating high.

The fat putt-putt-putt sound of an approaching Enfield could be heard in between stop and play of the current track under Voltaire's musical scrutiny. "Jaeger's arrived," Sofia cheerfully announced. Voltaire smiled looking up from scribbling track names with a blue biro on the inner sleeve of a new TDK C90 cassette.

"Boom!" Jaeger said, walking through the door, his shades pushed up onto his forehead. Sofia poured glasses of chilled lemon water.

"What's playing?" Jaeger said.

"New Beat," Voltaire said, passing him a tape titled, MENTAL OVERDRIVE. "It's like a whole new hallucination generation. Techno has now become a gateway drug."

Everyone laughed.

"Who's tape?" Jaeger asked.

"Bam Bam's. The stuff he recorded in Amsterdam. There's some plush Frankfurter cuts from *Suck My Plasma* label. Plus, different mixes of what you found in Ghent."

"Love the Music Man shop there," Jaeger said. "It's stacked to the ceiling with white label vinyl." It was his favourite shop to forage, which was like searching for gemstones in Jaipur."

Voltaire picked up a cassette titled, MASTERHIT. "This is a game changer."

Jaeger eyed the tracks on it. "Front 242 are so on—"

"Psychological thriller material" Voltaire said. "Well machined—"

"Front are power-packed," Jaeger agreed. "More cyber punk than the Teutonic techno of the Germans. I wonder if these geeks, all dressed in black, know what kind of life their music is having under the influence in fluoro palms. I wonder if they have any idea how explosively it moves the colours here?"

Voltaire pulled a sly grin and mentioned the track, 'Pleasure and Crime,' by Signal Aout 42 and said, "The politics of ecstasy. Crises of belief system—"

"Yeah—and big bang theory," Jaeger said. "It's like there's a planet voice in the electronics of the music. Cold War. Armageddon. World at the brink of destruction."

The technogeist of the new music, for Jaeger and Voltaire, represented a revolutionary medium. Libertine partying to the prototype, intellecto Techno tracks they cherry-picked and played in the psychedelic rinse of the parties in tropical India, was like the spell of a utopian romanticism. An ideal seduced by virtual realities made possible by computers and designer drugs. As if, in curating the tuning of circuits, their compelling sets created a participatory narrative that evoked a wanderlust in travellers to re-envision *an illuminati*. Some believing they were the *chosen ones*. Like stumbling upon a serendipitous experience that was evanescent— which they wished would go on forever, just like the art of addiction.

A Frankfurt, synth, techno track skipped out of the speakers with a catchy melody on top of which a sour voice in the music said, "Money, fame, success. Producers and artists overflow the market, consumers don't know what to buy. All these artists and new sounds conspire only one purpose, they wish to get one thing: money, fame, success. Because of this they turn vain, greedy, slimy and conceited, arrogant and decadent, slippery and eager, randy and corrupt, spineless and impotent. Where will it lead to if it goes on like that? The poor, poor, people they only get exploited."

Jaeger cracked up in laughter at its snide tone. "This is super! Who is it?"

"'Ugly World' by Zong," Voltaire said with a cynical jaw, who regarded himself a free agent and a nihilist. For them, the parties were subversive, an anti-fashion, beyond commerce. They were wary of adulation, i.e.—cult of personality (maybe true spiritual gurus exempt). DJs should be heard and not seen.

Jaeger and Voltaire were hooked on collecting a certain kind of music for its art-rageous buzz. The freedom of the kick of playing it in the metaphysical collective head space, that only could be had in Goa. In the mid-eighties, New Wave and Electro synth tracks worked well on the dance floor, but Voltaire was allergic to insipid vocals. Dub instrumental versions of club 12-inch vinyl allowed dancers to voyage, free-association in their imagination. Using two tape decks at Jaeger's house in Badem, Voltaire snipped the vocals out of tracks and combined A and B side versions into a modified edit to play in the party. Hi-NRG and Italo Disco tracks were energising to fly to, but the gelato vocal way too cheesy for trippers. Then one season, Jaeger brought something from Zurich that was utterly blinding—*Wowee!* An astounding music that was so surreal in its compositional fusion and theatricality that they termed it, *Dada Disco*. The absurd, cinematic, musical genius of Yello tipped palm tree dance floors on their ear lug, opening up wild shifting groovescapes for gallivanting. 'Goldrush' and 'La Habanera' were big hits at the last party the two DJs played in stone ruins of a house in North Anjuna.

On her veranda that looked out onto a rice paddy with water buffalo, Sofia and her two favourite DJs smoked a chillum. Exhaling, Jaeger smiled with the realisation that he could feel a revolution coming from two small countries: Belgium and Switzerland. He passed the pipe to Voltaire. "Has Zsu talked to you about Disco Valley next week?"

"Yes!—full moon…these fresh sounds are inspiring."

"I can't wait," Jaeger said. "It's gonna sound great through big speakers."

Hunters and collectors and DJs were highly protective of the special Goa music they'd bought, ferreted, and acquired through exchanges with special connections. The music, leather cassette bags, custom jewellery, stash belts, artisan chillums, were all a fungible currency, like premium quality substances. DJs with special Goa tracks did not wish that it's potency be diluted by it being indiscriminately copied around. It should only be heard first time in the party, in a group ritual experience, where neural receptors were in sympathetic resonance, where dancing to it collectively evoked a participatory mystique.

The rarest of special Goa music tracks were traded by a core, nexus, literati of collectors. Such transactions came with an implicit swapping caveat: the understanding that certain tracks were akin to sacred scrolls of an arcane cabal. Such highly prized hard-to-find music should not to be passed on to others (well at least not until the end of the season) via the Goa grapevine of dance, data, dubbing and contra-swaps for soma, or gifting, or favours, or trading. Fetishistically, such music would take on a life of its own, like the frequency wavelength of a sonic sect, with it being in the possession of only a few.

At the end of the season, it was fine for it to be given out on mixtapes, like musical mementos of magical party experiences. Its rarified sounds and melodies reactivating emotions and body rushes, that only a party in Goa could deliver. Some obsessed hunters and collectors and DJs were of the belief that the real *special Goa music* was akin to secret spells, or magical incantations for hypnotising dancers. And heaven forbid, should the freshest of new season music be leaked casually, and heard in chai shops and restaurants. Although, previous season's music was more forgivable, which would end up as degraded dubs, like photocopies of photocopies.

Jaeger rummaged in his leather shoulder bag and passed a cassette with a colourful collaged inner sleeve to Voltaire. "You might find something on this."

"Who's it from?"

"Remo."

Fishing around further in his bag, he felt tubes of Araldite glue and realised he'd better split. "I have to be off. Gotta see a man about a dog."

Chooks cluck, cluck, clucked, scratching for food outside a house made of large brown stone bricks with orange terracotta tiles, in Assagao, tucked away behind trees on the back road to Mapusa. The Hindu owners did not fill out forms normally required by police if renting to foreigners. Zikos was inside removing the inner casing of a Samsonite suitcase using a screw driver and pliers. A red Enfield showed up scattering the chooks. Zikos greeted Jaeger. Inside the house, Jaeger took tubes of Araldite out of his bag and gave them to the Greek and told a story about a friend of his up Kulu valley.

"My friend, a circus escape artist, he was stopped on the road by local police in Himachal Pradesh. They searched his backpack and found a Maglite torch, pack of cards and three kilos of Malana charas. After playing cards with the cops for an hour, he left with his bag, the cards and two kilos."

Jaeger swopped his motorbike for Zikos's Enfield, and headed to the beach. After midnight, Zikos dismantled the crash protector pipes from Jaeger's Enfield, and took them inside the house and removed three kilos of fingers of charas. Laying them out on a table, he used a Kingfisher beer bottle filled with hot water to roll them flat into a thin laminate, which he would cling wrap and carefully insert into the inner wall of the Samsonlite suitcase and glue the casing back together.

In the late afternoon on a Sunday in the middle of March, with a full moon about to rise, Indian tourists dressed in beige and white button down shirts and shimmering saris, had alighted from a Bombay Tata tourist bus. It was parked at the end of the road overlooking Disco Valley at middle Vagator Beach. As they gingerly made their way down the narrow gravel track that led to the valley and beach, an Enfield Bullet chopper loudly coughed and spluttered impatiently in low gear behind them. It was under the command of Doc Silver, who wore a tank top with the face of Japanese novelist, Yukio Mishima, printed on it. Doc restrained the descent of his steel steed by toeing his right cowboy boot on the back-brake pedal, but gave the Bombay saris and button down shirts a hurry-up by squeezing the clutch handle and loudly revving the throttle of the chopper to shoo them out of the way.

Once the Enfield Bullet hit the flat of Disco Valley, for Doc, it was like returning to an Elysian field. Kicking it into a higher gear, he galloped the chopper up the valley towards the jungle, passing through historical dance floors which brought back rushing memories of swashbuckling parties. Many of which, he'd set up and DJ-ed. Up one side of the valley were various size terraces and plateaus which lent themselves to small and medium size parties. He was so well acquainted with the terrain, he'd trained his chopper to equestrian jump from level to level without throwing him off. Riding through a patch work of chai shop mats, he arrived at the edge of the jungle, half way up Disco Valley. Seeing bar tables being set up, he shot their owners a disdainful sneer. He hitched his steed in the middle of the dance floor where Zsu and friends were stringing up large paintings between trees and applying lurid, fluoro colour on their trunks and branches. Goa was a place where there was always something to mix: charas, tobacco, paint, fabrics, accessories, music, cross-cultural romantic infatuations—all coming together on wilderness dance floors.

"Hi Doc!" Zsu said, looking up from mixing water with bright yellow powder paint in a cut-off mineral water bottle. The paint was from Chapora general store where it had been weighed into small plastic bags and fastened with cotton thread.

"It's stunning," Doc said, casting an approving eye over the set-up.

"Thanks. Are you still fine to start the party?" she confirmed.

"My oath, I'll be here to kick start."

Zsu then turned her head sharply toward the entrance of the chai shop area, "Oh no!" she cried out. Two bars were setting up tables there.

"Goddamn!" Doc glared, "those pesky bar assholes are at it again," his face contorted with annoyance. "They just don't get it."

"I did ask them politely," she said. "They've moved their tables forward. By the time you start they'll be on the edge of the dance floor."

"Over my dead body," Doc fumed, staring down the local barmen through the double barrel of his narrowed eyes that were burning. Picking up a roll of string, he paced in tight circles and confronted the bar shemozzle. "Looky here fellas," Doc hollered in a loud New York chainsaw accent at three Indians squabbling amongst themselves, setting up blocks of ice, crates of Limca, soda and Kingfisher beer.

"No further! No further!" He reprimanded and flounced about tying the string between two palm trees across the path to the dance floor clearing. "Off limits!" he barked sternly and dug a boot heal into the ground. Then dragged it to make a line from palm tree to palm tree, like a referee of a scrappy football game. "Don't pass—or else!"

Downcast, dark faces with white errant eyes looked at him like a pack of infant terrible hounds. Once he turned his back, they resumed arguing in Konkani. Labourers under the direction of PA owner, Antonio from Mapusa, were placing speakers on metal stands. Rama, the lighting man from Chapora, was up a bamboo ladder. Zsu gave instructions on the wrapping of trees with fairy lights and positioning of ultra violet tube lights. Local boys splashed buckets of water on the dance floor. A bamboo and palm frond DJ hut had been constructed by a coconut farmer just inside the jungle out of sight. Zsu dressed the DJ table with a garland of marigold flowers and later would add large quartz and amethyst crystals and brass miniature effigies of Shiva, Ganesh, and the Tibetan goddess, Tara.

"Chalo!.. moosh!.. scoot!.." ranted Doc Silver, his chain saw voice rising like an evacuation siren. Zsu looked up from inside the DJ hut to see Doc's flailing arms making large, sweeping movements in the face of a prospective beggar. Zsu didn't know whether to laugh or cry, it was an all too familiar hustle, in which Doc set himself up to bat curved balls, to clear loaded bases to get a home run boogie on a gritty ballpark.

Badem Hill overlooking Chapora River was prime spot to view the sun setting over the fort. Jules was taken there by a couple whom he'd had a juice with at the big tree in the village. Nils, a hansom Swede, with a tattoo on his arm of a snake eating itself, and his Spanish girlfriend, Elvita, split their time between a jungle hut by the lake at Arambol Beach and a house in Chapora. Jules followed them on his Rajdoot motorbike along the river road and up a hill track to the church where clusters of motorbikes were parked up. Their riders sat on sarongs toking and gazing glassy-eyed at the sun slowly slipping off the horizon behind Chapora Fort. Jules and his new friends joined in with friends of theirs. The softening light of dusk imbued the atmosphere with suspense, as they held their breath for what was about to rise due east. Then the sacredness was ruptured by a heated discussion that broke out.

"To waste seed, is to waste DNA," asserted a Nordic looking man in his thirties with shaved head, goatee beard, and a red clay tilak on his fore head.

"You mean, like in—jerking off?" said a middle-aged dude in cargo pants with unbuttoned shirt exposing dark shag-a-delic chest hair.

"Exactly!" declared the shaved head. "Men suck seed and women drink 'sav'—or sap."

"But aren't the Hindus obsessed with semen, too?" said a woman with henna coloured hair and unshaven armpits in a broad German accent. "Don't they refer to Atman as the cosmic seed? And of course, the Hebrew god was down on the waste of the seed, no?"

"Correct," said the shaved head. "All our sex laws come from the Hebrew god."

"Oh, man!" reacted the shaggy chest. "It ain't nothing but a jizz cult sucking on Satan's knob."

"No!—seriously," the shaved head said. "The mens' 'i' is phallic, or pole, and the dot on top symbolises the sperm. The ladies' 'i' is inverted, or 'i' inside, so their sap is their dot on the 'i' which is also the North Star, symbol for knowledge."

"This is complete mens' wank," the henna hair sharply retorted in a stern feminist tone of voice. "You're pulling my leg."

"No he's not," the shaggy chest said. "He's pulling cock."

"No!.. No!.." retorted the shaved head. "Women should drink their sap. In root language, 'mun' means mouth, and by drinking sperm and sap every cell in the body becomes the information of its original source—"

"And Odin is the source!" Nils said in a devout tone of voice.

Jules, sitting next to Elvita, whispered into her ear, "What's this all about?

"It's *The Saga*. You haven't heard of the O.O.O.?"

"No."

"It's a story from Norway told by a mystic called Osser. It's about Pagan times in paradise before the ice age. He rolls his tongue in an ancient Nordic language that was passed down by his mother. Some say he was conceived by his grandfather."

Jules sat astounded, his mouth agape. The heated discussion calmed down on the agreed probability that Scandinavians were the first Europeans. When the full moon popped-up above Badem Hill, it was bulbous and beckoning, its colour like that of papaya. It loomed so large and close, he felt as though he could reach up and touch it. A chorus of "boom shankar" hollers could be heard from smoking circles as ceremonial chillums were ignited, producing puffs of holy smoke. All eyes were upon the moon's voluptuous incandescence as it commenced its luminescent ascent over the night to usher in full moon lunar-tech follies.

SEQUESTERED IN THE REPOSE of her home, Zsu unwound from the exertion of the party set-up and execution of exacting brush work spells. Lunar rays glistened on her body as she sat in a ferny roofless bathroom and poured heated well water from a copper urn over her Chandrika soaped skin. Relaxing, she contemplated which combination of garment accoutrements and accessories from her collection to wear to the party. The entrancing arrangement of adornments on her body, she regarded, not just beauty enhancements, but hex juju. She dried herself off with a sarong and entered her boudoir of scent strategies and shining things. Pre-party stress gave way to a rising glow of omnipotence, as she contemplated the social slalom ride to come: the flow motion in group pleasure, the frolicking in the jungle filigree of moon shadows in Disco Valley's flora; and most speculative of all—the charms of the spells of her fluorescent, powder paint, ring of fire.

She glided outside into the courtyard where she did a tai chi chuan dance, which included Taekwondo, that enabled her to harness turbo emotions into a laser-like sword, cum wand. After a gentle half hour session, she fetched crystals from her bedroom and placed them with other crystals at a court yard altar. It comprised of minerals, effigies and sacred objects, including skulls from Tibet carved from yak bone—all to be purified by the Virgo lunar light.

    A snake charmer arrived. Zsu lit whole packets of incense and recited a Buddhist sutra. The snake charmer performed music on his pungi instrument in front of a basket that he'd taken the top off. Zsu chanted a mantra she'd been given by a Javanese witch doctor. Two hooded serpents rose up out of the basket in a kundalini trance. Returning to her sanctum, she picked through a regalia of itchy-witchy wear. Assisted by hidden hands, she applied scents and jewellery. On a finger, she placed a ring that was an eight-pointed star of Ishtar. On each point was a silver star with a tiny skull. It had been given to her by Jaeger, after she'd made him a leather jacket into which she'd sown, shed cobra skin. Obsessively, she took care not to wear the same combination of accoutrements more than once during the party season. Party was ritual, a sacred space in which to experience *Tribes of The Moon* refracted in the group mind. Party was where boundaries dissolved. Party, in Goa, was where Zsu Riviere experienced the most love.

    Kerosene lanterns from chai shops lit up Disco Valley from the edge of the bar area down to the beach. The sound of a distant petrol generator and swarming motorbikes could be heard in the background of conversations in a multitude of languages on chai shop mats. Half an hour before midnight, Doc Silver snapped a cassette into a Sony Walkman to start the party with, "I'm Tired of Getting Pushed Around" by Two Men, A Drum Machine and A Trumpet. Dancers jettisoned bags and jackets with chai mummas, and headed to the dance floor, like sonic moths homing in on ultraviolet frequencies.

    Prior to dropping down to Disco Valley from his hut on an upper terrace overlooking middle Vagator Beach, Jules had peeped into his ephemeris to scope what was happening in the heavens. The astrological weather spoke of chaos and transfiguration—Venus very much in the mix. *What kind of person threw a party like this?* He snubbed the disquiet of inner voices. *Take heed, all is not what you see. What went down with the dark dreadlock DJ?* Grappling with notions of emotional intelligence in deciphering the symbols of Zsu's horoscope, he felt himself being pulled deeper into the intoxicating mystery of her allure, and wishing to savour it, like willingly falling prey under a tantalising wicked spell. And so, just let himself float down the terraced slopes of the valley into the party surrendering to what the mistress of ceremonies had install. The air in

Disco Valley was suffused with aromas of steaming spicy chai, incense, charas, and salty wafts from the Arabian sea, together with odour traces of cow shit and sweat and flatulence from the loosening of muscular retention in the combustion of the dance floor. After mid-night, vividly patterned creatures of the night energetically hopped and jumped and pranced and cavorted hyperspatially throughout its electrified Elysian zones.

Teetering on a decision, and not seeing Zsu in the party, Jules committed to a Berlin microdot. Doc Silver's novel selection of music was intriguing and highly engaging to dance to. Jules barely recognised one track. Dreadheads were getting down, flinging their rope hair about to mental House Music and esoteric Techno and weird, hybrid, fusion styles he couldn't get a handle on. The solid-state circuitry of midi mavericks was tickling Jules's skin. It felt like sonic shiatsu triggering meridians in his body making it move in new ways. Vocoders teased him like the utterances of cyborg creatures imparting mysterious codexes.

In the midst of altered-state dancing in the sound shower's escalating elasticity, the microdot snuck up on him like a serpentine bullet train mainlining his vagus, putting him in a fugue. He glanced into a warping visage of faces attached to shimmying and shaking bodies swinging with arms and legs. The non-pentatonic tunings of the psy-harmonics in passages of the music transported him to foreign topographies of emotion, where voices of an unknown dialect appeared. *Had primitive ghosts become spirits in the machine?* Textures in the fabric of the sound were both dirty and digital. Then, the music changed. Angels appeared with blood stained white wings, their halos tinged in minor chord dirge. Thoughts atomised, taking on the form of three-dimensional molecular geometry.

The microdot turned the brain secretions of worrisome thoughts into floating shuttlecocks, easily batted way by a flutter of an eyelid on his dashboard. As the hallucinogen took hold he became acutely aware of multiple parts of himself. The different subpersonalities that lived inside of him, all clawing at him, wanting to have their say. He was seeing green LCD crawler text running over squirming, gyrating bodies on the dance floor that said, WE GIVE YOU A PLACE OF REFUGE. He wondered who, *We,* were? He spun three-sixty degrees and threw errant sub-personalities up against the ropes of his inner vision, summoning the overlord of his sentient super conscious mind to iron out the splitzer-frantic mentasm which the hallucinogen was magnifying.

Then, suddenly from out of a frenzy of bodies all around him, an agile-limbed figure appeared wearing glaring face paint with Thai Hill Tribe vest open at the chest. The figure turned into a gymnast performing sped-up yoga asana salute to the moon, moves—then stopped dead, motionless, in front of Jules, and smiled. *Ananta!..* Further afield, a bald-headed Caucasian Buddhist monk danced in a golden robe and a majestic carnivalesque female creature flapped diaphanous, butterfly wings. The hilarity of the splendour erupting all around him, set Jules free from being held captive by squabbling, schizo subpersonalities. What were those parts of himself attempting to defend? How did those parts set-up shop in his head in the first place? How much ram memory had they hogged in his hippocampus in the course of his life up till now? Wasn't it about time he reconfigured his memory board? Could this party be a silver bullet in snuffing out the hard-wiring of prenatal code written way back in time? Like back when he was zygote beta testing the waters that would spew him into this life, user permissions granted, no matter how buggy the predestined OS (operating system) of his family psychological inheritance. Its P ram zapped in world-shattering labour of birth contractions, just like the pummelling rhythms of the technodelic music he now found himself surrendering to. (The music playing was 'Push' by The Invincible Spirit.)

What did cosmos and psyche have in mind with the unique constellation of stars at the moment of his first breath? How much of this other *self,* had colluded in the fate of the blueprint of the heavens? Jules was experiencing himself as a mysterious traveller beyond the vehicle of his body. The hallucinogen was unlocking chambers in his brain—depositories of residues of memories. Sounds in the music were opening secret vaults of cryptic feelings embedded in fuzzy logic scripts. Strands of genome formed eons ago passed down through the quagmire of ancestral blood. *Ensouled into what?..* His brain spuzzed. Axons on the spinning platter of its infinitely vast hard drive threaded him all the way back down to the first memory of a homosapian ancestor.

Finding himself at the centre of the dance floor, it felt like the safest place. He got swept up in the engulfing abandon of—*Right here!.. Right now!..* Spinning pirouettes and arabesques next to him, appeared a Rudolf Nureyev doppelganger dancer in stretch tight leggings. He had long dark hair down to his waist, which he swung about like a head-whip to the music, that had now become like a dervish ballet.

The hallucinogen ran down the loom of Jules's spine, electrifying its circuitry. Piston-like percussion drove him to pound his legs harder and harder down on Disco Valley dirt. In the morphogenetic field of the bodies at its centre, he felt himself lifting off doing moves he never thought possible. *Oh, the wisdom of the body.* He over rode *out of control* alert alarms and tumbled in the flurry of eddies of aurally excited air. His distended third eye, like a guardian, thalamus, gyrus feeler, was in synch with the beat. His feet maintained traction with terra firma as the rising intensity of the lunar-tech full moon beamed down on the acid disco inferno.

Vivid costumed dancers bio-mechanically oscillated like night glow ingredients in a gurgling stew of sound. Surrounding them was the brushwork spells of Zsu's ring of fluorescent fire, that looked like flaming mother-in-law's tongues. Hieroglyphic symboled paintings hung off branches through which leapt a unicorn. The sound coming out of the black speakers of the PA at the edge of the jungle whisked everything like an egg beater. Electromagnetically, neutrons and protons inside particles of audio unhinged themselves from their sound-byte husks, turning Disco Valley into torrents of plasmatic electricity. Dancing bodies became a collective pulmonary, hyperventilating vast amounts of cubic air infused with Disco Valley dust. Jules microscoped into multi-cellular form where free radicals zoomed every which way. Pneumatically pedalling, his body became an automata buggy. Sub personalities of his split-off self, laughed at him from the plasmatic soup on the other side of the fish eye lens he was viewing them through. Shuttlecocks of thought appeared, he turned them into ping pong balls and flicked them away. Gravity was glutinous, he felt like rhubarb pudding, yet his automatic pilot had him phase-locked in a rhythmnism, reflexively synched in soma-saturated sound waves stretching brain plasticity in the swirling gyrosity of a supra-conscious telepathic, group mind.

The woozy dissolving of the interior lattices of his rhubarb-stalk self had been scary. Cognitive dissonance jack-knifed him. Fear defences had been scrambled when waves of anxiety hit like turbulence, as the microdot peeled him down through meatus to axon dendrites, where medulla oblongata merged with the transpersonal, where DNA matrices micro-binary spun inside chthonic corpuscles of plasmatic soup. It was there, in the realm of mystical drug tech, that he was hit with a transfiguring thunderbolt to the centre of his cerebellum, that was like an apotheosis deliverance cracking the epistemological sump of a solipsistic self.

Then, an elephant appeared. Lord Ganesh glowed with a cheerful aura that brought calm to Jules's psychonaut beaten brow. He felt his heartstrings plucked like a harp, and was struck by the realisation that he was at the exact same spot of his last encounter with the elephant god, the exact same spot where he'd melted in a lingering kiss with pillowy lips after he'd dismounted the elephant on the half-moon with the Disco

Valley mistress of ceremonies. Then, mistress Zsu appeared in a hallucination presenting him a chalice, inside which he couldn't tell whether it was wine, or blood. He wondered about the complex Scorpio waters he saw in her horoscope, the extremes of which he could imagine her a nun, a temple harlot, a high priestess. He pondered her dalliance with the dark dreadlock DJ, the apogee of which she was evidently in rebound of, with himself now seemingly on track to be the recipient of.

Fresh into the psycho-troppo kaleidoscopic world of a Goa party season, Jules was bombarded with fractal impressions—but wasn't wearing blinders. He trusted the sixth sense that looked out for him. He wondered about the machinations to pull off such a party. It was though he was being initiated into a secret society that resided beneath the surface of bohemian tourism, a secret scene that only showed its true colours and plumage and intentions after midnight. Time had telescoped on the dance floor, and once again he wondered where the mistress of grand ceremonies was? Was she doing her disappearing act thing? He looked over to the DJ hut in the jungle, its shadowy comings and goings of what he supposed was a sub-scene cognoscenti. He pondered the *special Goa music*, which was working wonders on him, filling him with bewildering fascination of the mystique of something rare, something veiled, esoteric—as though the music was coming from another planet—with sound, a bridge between worlds.

Suddenly—as if the valley had dropped beneath him like a huge trapdoor—he slid off the edge of his mind and tumbled into free fall, but then felt a whisker on the back of his neck. Pulling the focus on his sound and vision sensors, he turned around to be greeted by the swing of a long tail mini skirt. Cut up the thigh, it was made of strips of leather and lace with feather frills, at its centre was an Aphrodite belt pinched at the waist. Its bold, burnished buckle featured the symbol of Lilith. His starry glazed eyes met emerald eyes, that were offset with peacock eye shadow and star dust glitter. Libidinal voltage buzzed. Metabolic circuitry raced. Skin shimmered and glowed and glistened. Bodies briefly bumped. Trembling hands touched. All around them in Disco Valley the lost tribe of the future galloped full trot as Jules and Zsu—her less and less a siren, now more like a mesmerising minx—had a conversation of dance moves. Doc was playing 'Communicate' (Razormaid Mix) by Microchip League.

At half past one, a blue Yamaha motorbike pulled up on an upper terrace. Voltaire dismounted. He was barefoot, wore aquamarine spandex and sleeveless leather jacket, its zipped pockets packed with cassettes. He perused the psychic discharge below. The chai mumma lantern-lit valley snaked all the way down to the beach. Like a stealth bat, he zig-zag descended the terraces to the jungle below and slipped discreetly into the DJ hut, where Jaeger had his tapes out and was holding a loaded chillum. Doc was on fire with Chapora Angels (two Japanese cuties seen as a threesome on his lowrider in the village early in the evening) at his side. He mixed in the next track. It turned the dance floor into a feeding frenzy. Jaeger passed the chillum to Voltaire and struck two matches. After a couple of pulls, he handed it back, Jaeger took a hit and passed it to Doc. Jaeger reported to Voltaire that none of their new tracks had been played. Doc gleefully eyed them with a triumphant smile holding up a forefinger, indicating one more track, which he was cueing on a Toshiba boom box next to a rose stone miniature of Ganesh.

 Voltaire shuffled his cassettes and handed a TDK tape to Jaeger. The set was going to be eight hours, there was a lot of new music to play through the big speaker hyperspatialness in Disco Valley. Holding the tape in bejewelled fingers, Jaeger squinted down the list on the inner sleeve. The first track of the set should be a signifier, like a tuning fork to start the story. Hearing the new music, for the first time through big speakers, was going to be as much of a discovery for the DJs as it was for the dancers. Snap decisions, connecting tracks on the fly, were required to channel in-the-moment flow to make a journey, all the while gauging body antenna response on the dance floor, which spurred what should come next.

 Bent over the cueing boom box with head phones clamped to his head, Doc Silver punched its fast forward button. Voltaire changed his mind and picked out another cassette and scanned its hand-written list, contemplating a starter. Doc ejected the tape from the boom box and slotted it into a Sony player. One of Doc's Chapora Angels dancing exuberantly, almost bouncing out of her loud, lime-coloured boob tube, tripped on the tangled knot of bags and jackets spilling from the pile under the DJ table, and knocked one of Jaeger's cassettes off a chair to the ground. This drew a peeved look from the Swiss doyen. The cute Chapora Angel picked up the tape and apologised with a sweet smile, then shimmied over to Doc Silver's side as he released the pause button on the next track.

 'Killer Machine' by Laser Cowboys rocketed out of the speakers. Jaeger and Voltaire looked at each other blankly—one of their many aces was out of the hat, driving the dance floor ballistic. With six minutes to go, Voltaire had still not decided on a starting track. The middle of the dance floor was now molten, it was being rubbed raw in anima mundi mojo, as social skin shed itself in a jungle charge of pleasured flesh.

From the outer ring of fire of her fluorescent, flaming tongues art, Zsu weaved and orbited through dancers until she was in the nucleus blue flame centre of the dance floor, where Jules was incandescent. Together they teleported out of their exoskeletal form. Aloft, their avatar's spiralled up above the molecular orgy of the party. Voltaire launched, 'Future Generation' by Space Dance. Sweeping, majestic, melodies swooned the valley into a symphonic space waltz. The party heaved like a clipper ship, cutting through huge ocean swells turbo-charged with supersonic bass propulsion.

"Oh, my God!" Zsu screamed, as she and Jules soared on epiphanous wings, beneath them Ganesh floated above the masts of the main sails of the party clipper ship. It was tacking in huge troughs as waves of sound scrambled stampeding feet in the valley below. Ganesh smiled and waved his trunk in the air like a magic wand.

"Wow!" gasped Jules, zooming with Zsu like flying trapeze artists over the party. Then, Ganesh became a large hologram suspended over the party, which they swung through as the clipper ship below keeled to and fro. Their exoskeletal selves, all the while, egg-beaten in the moon juice stomping down on the dance floor.

Voltaire monitored the bleeping pulse of the party like an intensive care unit surgeon. Cabin pressure of the starship clipper was holding fine at warp speed. The all-important first track was eliciting an energetic response flinging the party further out into space from where Doc Silver's rocket had landed. Doc sat in the DJ hut smoking a joint with the Chapora Angels. Jaeger stood next to Voltaire as they plotted possible selections. Cassette cases on the DJ table were spread like cards. Voltaire selected a cassette titled, SPACE OPERA, and passed it to Jaeger for cueing whilst he made EQ adjustments on the mixer. The cassette was cued precisely on the first beat and snapped into the empty Walkman and cocked by pressing both the pause and play button. Space Opera would be the second in a series of sci-fi galactica cuts that were guaranteed to generate stellar flux. It was a track suited for both night and day, one which he'd had in mind for the morning, but hastily decided that the rising surge, which Doc had whipped up, was opportune for springboarding further into outer space. Besides, Voltaire had an arsenal of space age Disco in reserve. Jaeger passed him a Maxell metal tape titled, LASER DANCE, cued at 'Humanoid Invasion.'

Dust on the dance floor was being dampened by local boys with buckets of water. Bars were moving closer to capitalise on parched, dehydrated bodies. Doc Silver didn't want to know about it, he was having too much fun. Ten seconds after releasing the pause button on Laser Dance, Voltaire's decision was rewarded by seeing the party lurch, with bodies lunging upwards, as if trying to touch the huge moon above. The party clipper ship accelerated like it now had a fluorescent coloured spinnaker, sending the dance floor airborne, skimming wave to wave. Space station, Disco Valley, was further warp speed excited by Voltaire's selection of 'Outer Space Odyssey' by Voltage Control, followed by the Italo Disco of 'Space Trouble' by Why Not, at the end of which, Jules and Zsu returned to earth and docked back into their exoskeletal forms that were rocking in the oceanus of the party.

A loaded chillum was passed to Voltaire to start. It was fired up. He puffed, and handed it to Jaeger, then they both got busy shuffling cassettes as they sensed it was time to ride turbo charged camels on silk roads to Persia. Searching for tracks, they scanned tape sleeves to line up a bracket of exotic Arabesque electronica in which wisps of Indian and middle Eastern female voice wailed a devotional refrain. Psychedelic world music for the imagination to travel, infused with tantric tabla, abdominal serpentine darbuka drums and Linn synth drums to hitch gyrating hips to. Disco Valley became a gypsy tribe in a reverie of imaginings from another time in ancient India. The erotic figures from the sun temple of Konark appeared in amongst the cavorting bodies writhing in the oriental dreamscape, that would tail off with 'Walk Like An Egyptian' by The Bangles.

The DJs knocked heads together and figured that everyone was half way past coming up to the peak of not so normal. It was time to cranial massage the corpus gyrus. Tinker subterranean truths. Navigate darker soundscapes. Conjure machine elves and trickster androids. Voltaire threw caution to the wind, spinning the wheel of the helm, hard left into the radical buzz of edgy electronica. The kind of music you might cut or graze yourself on, in rubbing up against its gnarly textures in deep swells. Chunky grooves with visceral oomph that burned rubber on romper-stomper runners and pressed pebbles sharply into bare foot dancers. But not too much, wary of capsizing the party, or become laden in plodding hard-work techno that had dancers feeling like boulders were strapped to their backs and desperately needing to retreat to chai mats because the music was too heavy. Pushing the barometer of taste was a critical call. Knowing when to ease up, bring relief to the faint hearted by playing guaranteed floor filler anthems with hand-rails to hold onto, but not gut-out the psy-chaos that the depth of a spectral night demanded. DJ-ing, for Voltaire, was not done lightly, it had the weight of expectation, it came with pressure, like holding an Excalibur with magical powers. An art form serving a romantic ideal. The thrill seeker kick of an obsessive, compulsive urge. The fanatical need to scratch an insatiable itch of an underground scene in the psycho tropics of crazy-meets-mad India—the most off-the-clock permissible place.

Perspicaciously, Voltaire peered into his tapes cogitating combo possibilities. The arrangement of cassettes on the DJ table in front of him now morphing into the appearance of a scrabble board. Blinking his eyes rapidly, the cassettes turned into a jigsaw puzzle. Each cassette a dove-tailing tile containing pieces of music, ready like characters in the wings for the right moment. He looked up and gazed at the dance floor, a conveyor belt of beat freakery time-tunnelling a wormhole in the fabric of multivalent realities. Each jigsaw puzzle piece a hallucinogenic spell, an imaginal theme park ride, an aural-gasm rush, a mini drama in a nusical-neural weave. Which, when viewed from the Ganesh hologram floating over the party, might look like a moire mosaic made up of oscillating pixels, like dancing DNA around a helix. Something which, in the fullness of time, stem cell humanities of the future might graft into popular culture.

At four in the morning, the synapses of the three hundred dancers, in full trot, were rewriting neurotransmitter code in a cosmo-kinetic ultra-world, when suddenly everything went dead. All bodies came to an arresting halt. All sound shockingly ceased. Black lights snuffed out. The dance floor coated in silvery moonlight, collectively gasped. Stunned mullet dumbfoundedness gave way to full throat hullabaloo ululations. Animal sounds. Wailing. Howling. Above the freak-out, the chain saw voice of Doc Silver could be heard. "Antonio!.. Antonio!.."

Zsu raced to the DJ hut and was met with deflated looks from Voltaire and Jaeger. Doc—bare foot, looking bedraggled like he'd been crawling through the jungle on his hands and knees and bushwhacked—arrived yelling with wild-eyed urgency, "Generator!.. generator!.. generator!.."

Zsu, distraught, cried out, "Where's Antonio?'

Doc's face ran with mascara, giving him ringed racoon eyes. He shot her a look of—*seen it all before*. Screwing up a cheek, half bemused, half be-buggered, he said, "Probably drunk somewhere." He dashed out of the DJ hut into the jungle like a bush pig. On finding the location of the generator, he barked like a scolding wolf mother, "Gas!.. Gas!.. Gas!.."

Antonio's assistant, in a dhoti with tail between his legs, was filling the generator from a jerry can. Doc had had parties stop in the middle of the night on other occasions when, to his utter disgust, it was discovered that the generator had been stolen.

Once the generator spluttered back into life, the music appeared to have multiplied in strength, like a quadrophonia igniting intensified flex of the spandex. Voltaire gripped the rains of the party like it was a chariot storming skyward hitched to a bolting band of Pegasus horses on 'The Ride of The Valkyries.' Later, in the darkest hour, before a hyper dawn, a voice in a track ('The Latest Idea' by Indicate) said, "It's only been a few hours since I translated and spoken aloud the first of the demon resurrection passages from the Tibetan Book of the Dead." It was the time when the music became a psychopomp, a messenger of the gods, a medium for spirits to step into another world. A ghostly spooky world beyond form. There were some who were too afraid of the night in the jungle of Disco Valley, who'd only come to bop in the morning.

Danish Asta wore Viking boots. Like her bestie, Zsu, she had a flair for fashion. Sporting a sequinned outfit with her blonde locks wrapped in a headband made of reflective foil, she shimmered in sublunar light. Both were purveyors of haute hippie culture. Party for them was a fantasy play ground to splore. Their getup swung from being gussied-up Alices in dirty disco wonderland to crusading eco Amazons. They liked to blast in tandem between speaker stacks where they would become twin super-booster forces of nature, contagious to all around them.

After ascending aerial with Jules, Zsu darted and dived through aqua currents of the party in her fish tail skirt, later resurfacing with Asta. The party had gone through different phases. The two Alices hit full velocity jumping and jacking to Brutus beats, the kind of titanium techno Jaeger referred to as, *Electronic Body Music*. The musculature of these gargantuan grooves hurtled the two Alices into action-packed drama, in which they became warrior priestesses in a Star Wars epic.

Half an hour into the darkest hour, Zsu and Asta needed to pee. Like chattering canaries over the thumping music, they held hands and strolled up a path into the dense jungle of Disco Valley past the DJ hut. The shadowy branches, vines, trunks, dense leaves and thorny thickets of Vagator jungle reeked potential treachery for Goa gals alone in wilderness outskirts of parties. Zsu stood body guard for Asta while she crouched and squatted in bush, just off the path that led up to the elephant tree. Zsu gripped a thick hay baling needle in her hand that she had unsheathed from a hidden seam in her bum bag. Should they get jumped, she was prepared to unflinchingly jab it into the predator. They swapped positions with Asta keeping a steely needle eye.

"My name is Alfred Hitchcock, and this is music to be murdered by," came a voice from the the party back down the path. Voltaire was playing Fatal Error.

"Whew!" Zsu deeply exhaled crawling out from the bushes. "That was a relief, I had so much premenstrual tension. My lower chakra feels released, my mind has got some ballast back."

"Well done," Asta said. "It's a witches' brew occasion. Good to spill some blood in Disco Valley."

"My God!" Zsu said. "Full moons are so overwhelming. This one is Virgo, it does feel purifying, but not so virginal, not like the snake and Eve. More like Lilith, more like Kali."

Asta kissed Zsu hard on the lips. "What an amazing party. I love you, Zsu," she said handing back the needle. "There's nowhere else I'd rather be then here. How about we chill a bit at the Ganesh tree?"

They walked up the narrow path deeper into the dense jungle that looked like the moon had spray painted it silver. They smelled incense. At the elephant tree, they discovered a bouquet of freshly cut flowers with rose incense burning in the ruin.

"Someone's offered puja," Asta said, as they sat down. Under the influence of mushroom extract, they delighted in the dappled luminescence through twisting vines and spindly branches.

"I had a visitation with Ganesh tonight," Zsu said looking around. "It also happened when I brought Jules here."

"He's a sweet guy," Asta remarked.

"Um, yeah—I like him alot."

"A far cry from Atma," Asta said pointedly.

On hearing the dreadlock DJ's name, Zsu recoiled. She felt like vomiting. "I really don't understand myself," she gasped for air, as if choking. "I'm a deluded klutz... I've even been called a hussy. Gawd!...romance is like quick sand—"

"Oh hun!.. It's ok?" Asta said in a consoling voice. "Don't beat yourself up."

Zsu stared into the jungle. It was as though Disco Valley had gone silent. The distant thud of the music having vaporised into the ether. Her face clouded over in sadness. "I'm such a fuck-up with men," she said in a faltering voice.

"No, you're not," her bestie said. "This party is fantastic. You are adored.

"Yes, that's right, it's true, party is my ultimate love affair."

Asta put her arm around Zsu. "You do it so well."

The two girls had instantly bonded in the early eighties at their first parties where they met. Zsu had saved Asta's arse on numerous occasions. She'd once sprung her bestie from Mapusa Police station, which required persuasive powers beyond cash. And Asta had done the same for Zsu, too, in episodes when she'd crashed and burned.

"Jules is cute," Asta said. Zus's face brightened. She poked the tip of her tongue cheekily at her bestie through beguiling pouting lips. "It's his first season, there's something about him, we met in Bali." She punched the side of her head with the heal of her hand. "I'm such a sucker. You know what I'm like," she said with anguish in her voice. "I get seduced into believing my fantasies are real—"

"That's a gift of being creative."

"Imagination is reality for me."

"Love is like a tidal wave," Asta said. "It's out of control. Nothing rational about it."

"Ha!.." Zsu sighed and gazed up at the radiance of the moon like the earth's most intimate satellite was an orb that knew the mysteries of the heart. "Romance is an emotional affliction. A yearning to fill up a hole of loneliness. This party has the intensity of a dream, but we know it's not a dream. Thank goodness for the dance floor…" Then suddenly, "Oh, my God!"

"What?" Asta said.

Zsu's face had turned white. "There's a creepy feeling crawling up the back of my neck. There's something here. I feel a presence."

"I wonder who lit this incense?" Asta said, looking at the incense sticks which had nearly burnt down.

Zsu felt her body tense. "Maybe, whoever it was is still around?"

The distant thrum of the party faded. Zsu closed her eyes and breathed deeply. Asta composed herself and kept her eyes peeled, she sensed that Zsu was going into a trance, she'd seen her do it before. Zsu rose slowly to her feet opening her eyes and gracefully flowed into martial art movements chanting a Javanese mantra. Ceasing to chant, she closed her eyes and her face began to glow with a nimbus above her head.

Asta became anxious. "Zsu are you OK?"

Her bestie did not reply, her eyes remained closed. Zsu continued breathing deeply making slow circular movements. Dread began to pour through Asta. "Zsu, I'm getting the heebie-jeebies. Let's get out of here. Please Zsu!.. Talk to me!.."

Still her bestie did not say a word. She was in a trance, spirited away. Asta began to freak, she saw flames engulf Zsu, she didn't know whether it was a hallucination or if it was really happening.

"Zsu!.. Zsu!.." she shrieked at the top of her voice.

Then an Indian with a rattly little moustache, roguish smile, slight build, neatly dressed in black slacks, appeared on the path.

"Madame do you need help?" he enquired in a polite voice, which belied his black leering eyes that burned straight through Asta. Her body tightened like a guitar string about to snap.

Zsu suddenly opened her eyes. They were fiendishly ablaze. She looked around wildly as though possessed.

"Fuck!... Oh, my God!... Asta!—let's split!"

Zsu pulled out her peeing needle and raced straight toward the Indian with arm outstretched like a matador. The Indian bolted into the jungle. Zsu and Asta tore back down the path to the party.

Underworld Afterglow

LOOKING FOR HER HOUSE, Jules's Rajdoot motorbike missed one turn. He was trying to recall the directions she'd given him yesterday morning after the Disco Valley party, but his head had been spinning like a centrifugal juicer at the time. Now roaming motorbike tracks in Badem, his Rajdoot appeared to know where it should go, and took him to a large villa with white cement fence crawling with hot pink bougainvillea. Next to its cast iron rococo gate was written, *Casa Serendip*, which brought the sound of her voice saying those words. The titillating fragrance of the bougainvillea filled him with anticipation as he parked, but did not dismount. Instead, he just sat on the motorbike taking in the grandness of the Portuguese house, which spoke of colonial Europe at the peak of its powers in Asia. Its ornate, palatial solid brick was in striking contrast to the primitive palm thatch cabanas of the European hippie cliff-dwellers at Vagator beach. Which was where he'd crashed out after floating naked in the sea after the party with cryptic fragments of music and visuals swishing about in the sponginess of his jelly fish brain.

And later, finally decompressing horizontal in his cabana, he'd marvelled at the plasticity of a late twentieth century homosapian brain. Its capacity to reboot and defragment itself. Its resetting of errant file directories. Its repair of data cluttered program scripts. Its updating of faulty family firmware. Its deciphering adaptations of hand-me-down genes. Its quantum capacity to consider the idea of karma, the gift of free will in the cause of—*Self becoming*. The quest for *freedom* in whatever form, substance, place, person, scene—and feeling, it could be had. Freedom from what? The gift of the prerogatives of the first world, its opportunities, its greater rewards and quality of life, plus its neuroses of more, more, more—never being enough. Was being here the antidote? The mystique of the East under the firmament of milky way, cosmic confetti living a life of *otherness*. A seeker on a path of lightness-of-being dancing out of his body. *This must be as good as it gets?*

Sailor Jules continued to sit outside siren Zsu's Casa Serendip iron gate in the afterglow of his first full moon stomp. His circadian rhythm was pleasantly askew. His dopamine level slowly replenishing. System recharge and reboot would not be complete until after a second sleep. Peering at the gate, he got a grip, flicked the stand of the Rajdoot and legged off it. Wearing flip flops and a day backpack on his shoulder, he pushed on the curling filigree iron work of the gate. It let out a deep croaking sound, finishing with a squeak. Walking up steps to a pillared porch with large wooden front doors open, he stood at its entrance and felt like he'd arrived at a star gate portal of antiquity.

Taking a deep breath, he called out, "Hiiiiiiee!" His voice sounding like a cockatoo that rose to a falsetto and dropped an octave at the end.

"Jules," came a distant soft voice, soon followed by long tanned legs gliding towards him draped in a gaping magenta and maroon sarong with glints of gold thread that was pinched trim at the waist by a Rajastan silver string belt. The legs poured through his eyes and wrapped themselves around his chest. Their eyes met. Hers turquoise green.

"Namaste," Zsu greeted him with a warm welcoming smile. Freshly towelled, damp, auburn locks curled about her neck and collarbone, filling the air with a lavender shampoo fragrance. She led him down the hall past a small rococo table with a bust statue of Minerva, goddess of handicrafts and war. He caught a glimpse of her bedroom draped in sheer, filmy, fabrics and lounge with high wooden lattice ceilings that was adorned with art and spiritual objects. Everything about her home and its contents tantalised him with burning curiosity. He surrendered to the feeling of having been netted, hook, line and sinker. From out of his backpack he presented her with grapes. She placed them in a bowl and fetched a pitcher of cold lemon water and glasses from the kitchen, its surfaces decorated with blue azulejos tiles.

They sat on leather patch-work cushions in an interior courtyard dhuni with shrine, around which was assembled crystals and precious stones, with rosemary incense burning and two cobras coiled in a cage nearby in the garden. She popped a grape in her mouth and leaned towards him and said, "How are you?"

He looked her in the eye. "I'm feeling like that grape you just put in your mouth."

She smiled and applied pressure to the grape with her teeth. Its skin broke and released its sweet fleshy succulence—delivering pleasure, both to her and him, as he watched her chew gently on it.

"Well," he said. "I'm feeling rebirthed. Somewhat altered, rearranged. That party was not just a regular party, was it?"

"I don't do regular."

He lathered her with admiration, the awe of the Disco Valley experience. "It was transfiguring... I'm still processing it."

Zsu smiled and adjusted her posture into a lotus position with feet folded upwards, hands resting on her knees with deep-space blue nail polish, thumb and forefingers touching in a Buddhist meditation pose. A hush fell over them as they held eye contact alone in her home, all forks in the road and astral travel having led to this. The spark of their encounter in balmy Bali. The soaring on technodelic thermals on an alien landing pad in Chapora Fort. The giddy heights above the holographic clipper ship with Ganesh in the disco mystique of the Vagator valley, where a Pandora's box had sprung open. To what degree, for Zsu, she could hardly bring herself to share, least she scare him off, burst his first blush bubble of bliss in rites of passage in paradise. But what kind of paradise?

"Chaos magic," he heard himself say to her.

"Communing with the ancients," he heard her reply. "Like pagans, goths, huns dancing around the bonfire."

He felt like he might be still in some kind of virtual reality. And couldn't quite believe that he was now siting at her altar. But—*Yes!*... Here he was. He lolled his tongue out of the corner of his mouth and shot her a glinting eye and baited her. "Like heathens high on hedonism."

She laughed and raised her chin defiant. "Ha!—Let us not be lazy with the pleasures of sin," she snickered. "What is sin?.. Ha!—guilt!.. Damned religious bullshit." She twirled her hair with a flirtatious forefinger. "Let's take heaven by storm, let's experience pleasure on earth. It's healing to do so—no?" This she said with round lips and popped a grape into her mouth.

"Some would say, it's escapist," he said.

"There's a lot to escape," she said, her molars crushing the grape. "Escape society, escape being someone you feel you aren't." Her face grimaced. "Escape suffering."

Jules held her gaze and said, "You sure get to see gaping humanity and spiritual ritual of life in India. There's magic here. It's like it's either la-la land, or baba land. I felt transcendence in the party. In that transcendence, I absorbed a lot."

He wondered about what he experienced with her at the elephant tree, and in the party at Disco Valley. What kind of mind-melding was that? A mutual imagination projection, or what? Hardly just a hallucination? Whatever it was, it felt real, it felt like a consummation of the attraction. She was not a siren after all. There was no doubting the sensations radiating from his heart as they sat at the foot of the vivid constellation of magical stones making up her shrine with coiled serpents near by, his gaze fixating upon a peculiar, erotic looking alien-like purple plant.

"It's a voodoo lily," she explained. "Gives off a strange odour that's a charm for ghosts from a previous paradise."

Jules raised an eyebrow, not phased that she might be alluding to necromancy. Maintaining his gaze at the evocative lily he said, "Plant medicines and hallucinogens open psychic fields to invisible energies. It's not exactly escaping, it's more like vision questing—"

"Clairaudience!" she said, her eyes widening. "Hallucinogens are enhancing, but can be terrifying. These sacred substances ultimately expose you to your hidden self and the invisible spirit world and other intelligences." She lowered her voice as if confiding something even more secretive. "The full moon was alchemical. What we casually call—*party*, was in fact, a ritual. Everyone there, knowingly or not, were participants in a gyroscopic ceremony with music and soma and…" Her voice trailed off and she sucked in her lips. "A psychodrama with other entities."

He wondered what *other entities*, and recalled the LCD crawler text he believed he saw running over the dance floor saying, "We give you a place of refuge." He contemplatively pressed a forefinger up to his right temple. "There're no bad trips. Just fear of the power of the mind. It's scary having your ego shredded. It takes courage to look under the hood, see what you are made of. Perhaps we are born with everything we need to know. But the thing is, gaining access to it. Yeah, gyroscopic, I can dig that, like lunar electric bodies which, in the morning, become heliocentric, like planet bodies spinning around the sun at the centre of the dance floor." He confessed that he'd never danced so intensely. Never journeyed in such a wonderland of delight, horror and shock. She said that she'd experienced all of that, too. But did not tell him what happened in the darkest hour when moon shadows were holding back the dawn at the elephant tree.

She reached out and held both his hands. "I loved it when you told me you felt rearranged."

Gazing into her eyes he felt a flutter in his chest. "It's like self-remembering from the inside out," he said. "Psychedelic appears to be the mantra here—"

"Yes, it's why I love India," she said with a smile. "Goa can only exist here. It's the people that make a place, we've been drawn here from all over the world to this magical place. The music is like a magnet. We are drawn to it like fire flies."

"It's sure got its own frequency" he said. "It's like there's a harmonic OM in the music. Like something is being reanimated. Like technicians of the sacred using modern tools in electronic alchemy labs."

"Yes!.. Yes!.." Her body quivered with excitement.

Jules's telepathic antennae picked up a signal, "I'm getting a voice from space," he said. "It's saying, 'don't be afraid, don't be afraid, something coming from a strange realm."

"That's Jabdah," she said. "It's the friendly alien that visits the party every morning in the track by Koto, which all the DJs play. It's the number one tune this season."

"Wow!" he said astounded. "Perhaps these parties are an extraterrestrial test tube experiment—"

"I believe it!" Zsu said. "It's a freak culture, like a fungus in between cultures."

"Perhaps it's a fluoro conspiracy?" he said.

She burst into laughter. "It's a cosmic connection. Like the music and soma is a conduit. It just turns me on. The brilliance of the colours everyone wears here reflects the sounds in the music and drama and ritual of life in India. You go back to Europe, everyone gets around in a uniform of blue jeans and black T-shirts. What's that?.. sheep programming."

"Hm," Jules said. "India strikes me as the ultimate in escapology. The ultimate for drop outs, misfits, weirdos, seekers of quests out of the ordinary. The ultimate for swinging doors of expanded consciousness. The last bus stop for Neptunians. Those wanting something more than the material world—"

"People aren't trees," she said. "Society is obsessed about putting down roots, everyone here lives on planes, they're nomadic jetset hippies cum techno zippies who live in the ether. The locals are fabulous, they love us, they allow us to be. I feel more accepted here than I do anywhere. I feel a sense of belonging here."

He pondered the rural landscape in which holy cows wondered freely. "It's timeless, as though under the right conditions dormant star seeds have sprouted, and are now reaching up into the heavens nourished by this music. Maybe space rock crashed here eons ago, and microbes of alien intelligence are in this red dust. I'm seeing a Mars landscape—"

"Wow!—Jules, that's really something, because I have the same weird inkling." She thrilled at his theory about galactica electronica and alien intelligences at the parties. She unfurled her lotus locked legs, as if he'd struck a major G fifth chord, with all fingers of both hands spread across a Roland Juno synthesiser, the keyboard—her body, and the entire major G key—her mind. If laughter and crying is God's music, Jules was feeling like he was hitting the bullseye of her heart.

"India has to be the ultimate holy grail of metaphysical adventure," he said, transposing the ontological octave further up the G scale. "Seeking higher, in whatever form higher comes: Gurus, mysticism, meditation, magic, the occult, substances, music, trance-dancing—"

"Oh yeahhh!.." she said with a groan of longing. "Love supreme!—dharma heads find home in mother India. The dance floor in Disco Valley was full of dissenters. Dissenters of dominant reality consensus. I have to tell you…one of the most confronting immersions for me outside of regular society was Pune."

"Oh, so you were an orange person?"

"No!—I don't need a devotee robe or guru badge around my neck. But I respect the guru's provocative ideas and therapies. He's been more dangerous to up-tight society than all the sex, drugs and rock 'n' roll that you could ever throw at any institution based on fear and control."

"I can dig that," he said. "I did my own dynamic meditations, some of which included being regressed back to an angry young punk—like an infant terrible. Then I discovered the planets."

"Right!" She said. "You turned me onto them in Bali."

Jules looked at Zsu with penetrating eyes and grinned. "I dipped into your horoscope. I see Pluto, the dark lord, is your ruling planet. How do you relate to power—intensity—control?" Those words were like hefty beats on a large taiko drum that shuddered and shook through her bones.

"Oh, my God!.. that's rather full on." She recoiled taking a deep breath and looked away to the incense smoke spiralling upwards, like the cobras were out of their cage entwined up the brass Shiva Shakti trident at the centre of her shrine. Shifting her posture, she sat upright in lotus position and felt tantric fire shoot up her spine. Fastening her eyes on his, they gazed into each other's pupils without blinking.

"You're quite something," she said, her face becoming flushed. "There's no escape. Who sent you? It's not like your too nice to be unreal…um well… I know you know." She paused and took a long deep fortifying breath and reached over and held his hand. Then took another deep breath and said, "I like you."

Jules fell speechless. She wooed him with a wrap round smile, which engulfed both of them. It was like they were caught in a tidal rush at the mouth of an estuary. Hazel and green irises blurring in a lagoon sanctuary in dreamy slow motion. Secretly, she was ready to believe that they may have known each other in a past life.

"Watch out," he said teasingly as he reached over and kissed her. The temperature rose and sweat glands seeped. "You never know," he said, "I just might be the man in the moon." She swallowed a giggle. Eyes remained macro close, going in and out of focus—so much so that an additional third eye did appear for both of them. They kissed again, pulled back, and kissed and kissed continuing a conversation of kisses until they remained in one long kiss locked together like crabs with pincers and legs and arms wrapped round each other's hips and necks, with serotonin and oxytocin coursing through them.

"Zsu!"—called out a voice at the front door.

"Oh!" she said startled. "Someone's arrived. Who is it?" she hollered.

"Jaeger," said the voice

"Come through. I'm backside."

By the time Zsu and Jules had disentangled themselves, Jaeger appeared at the entrance of the courtyard. He wore zig-zag patterned shorts and a singlet emblazoned with FRONT 242 in red block letters on black. Jules remembered him as one of the DJs in the jungle hut at the party.

"Boom!" he greeted them and kissed Zsu on the cheeks. Sitting down, he pulled out a small coconut mull bowl and a leather sheathed chillum from a bag which Zsu had custom made for him.

"Disco Valley was amazing," he trumpeted and stuck his hand down his jocks to retrieve a finger of charas.

"The music was spot on," she said.

"It all connected," Jaeger agreed with a grin of satisfaction. "Voltaire stitched it brilliantly."

"Have you met Jules?"

"No, I don't believe so"

"Hi"

"It's a pleasure, man."

"Have you seen Zikos?" Jaeger asked, his face contorting with consternation.

"Not recently," she said. "That's right, he wasn't at the party? Would you like something to drink?"

"A coffee would be great?"

"Sure," she said, and went to the kitchen with Jaeger jumping up and joining her.

"Listen," he murmured as she filled an Italian coffee maker. "I'm worried about Zikos"

"What's up?"

"Someone has been popped at Bombay airport. Zikos was on his way out."

"Oh shit! Do you really think it's him?"

"Not sure, but it's possible, and if it isn't him, it's still not good."

She winced. "I've got someone about to go to Denpasar."

"I'll talk to Alfonso, see what he knows."

Returning to Jules in the courtyard Jaeger prepared a chillum. They smoked and talked about music. When Jaeger got up to leave, Jules offered him a tape of The Telepathics tracks from out of his bag. The Swiss DJ thanked him and offered to make him a tape. After dusk, Zsu and Jules sat together, their faces aglow in candle light, the garden softly illuminated by the moon in Scorpio, a sign ruled by Mars. They ate a curry prepared by her housekeeper and drank Merlot wine from Bordeaux—a present from a customer.

"So, you know Zikos?" he asked sipping the deep red.

"Yes, yes, he's a dear friend."

"He took me under his wing," Jules said. "He's been a guardian angel, showed me around."

"Zikos is a sweetheart," she said, knowing him not to be snooty, like some in the scene to new arrivals.

"What's up with him?" Jules ventured to ask.

"What do you mean?" she said guardedly.

"He wasn't at the party? Your friend Jaeger seemed concerned."

"Um… yeah…well…" she said hesitantly. "He must have been attending to something."

"Something risky?" Jules said pointedly.

Zsu's body stiffened. She grimaced. Her eyes became red like a rodent. She refilled their glasses. Took a hearty sip, waited for the wine's soothing warmth to hit her tummy and said, "Many here have secret lives. Straight society has made us criminals. It means nothing, except you can get locked up if you are not professional. Here, cash can get you out of a squeeze. But paranoia can screw with your head. It's a bummer if you let it get the better of you. You have to stay sharp. There's some here that are mercenaries, like Kamikazes. Too reckless for their own good. But hey, it's everyone's own call. It's survival. No one tells anyone what to do. There's a code of the jungle.—"

"Is Zikos in trouble?" he asked, point-blank.

Zsu fell silent.

"Monkey business?" Jules said bluntly.

She pinched her lips together. "I really don't know… Look Jules—you have to understand there are risks when you live outside the margins. You gotta go with your instincts. Sadly, the risks have become more severe."

"Like what?"

"Like a tola, which is only ten grams of charas, is now a criminal offence. Paranoia has risen, and so has corruption." A frown creased between her eyebrows. "Just pay they say and you'll be fine. Of course, now it will be more than before, but sometimes that doesn't work. Anyhow, I'm gonna find out what's up with Zikos." Abruptly she changed the subject. "So, you said you had something to tell me about my planets for this part of the world?"

"Right—your astrocartography," he said. "Your horoscope is ruled by Pluto. And can you believe it? Pluto, the planet of transformation, is rising right here in Goa for you?"

"Tell me, tell me, what's Pluto all about?"

"Pluto's the Lord of the Underworld," Jules delighted in telling her. "His other name is Hades"

"Oh, my God!.. That's insane," she gasped, and turned white as a ghost.

"You're in touch with hidden, powerful forces here," he said. "I saw that phoenix jewellery in your stall at the flea market. That mystical bird must be you. A symbol of resurrection."

"Holy shit!" Her jungle cat ears shot up into high alert. The word— *Underworld*, raced her pulse. Tipsy from the wine, and feeling exposed as a consort of Hades, she delivered Jules a devilish kiss which ignited them in flaming lips.

Party Brinkmanship

A BLACK AND WHITE INK-SPLAT patterned cow with large horns foraged through a pile of plastic straws out the back of Scarlet Juice Bar in Chapora village. It was mid-morning and it opportunistically ambled over to impose its wet black nose into a conversation at an outside table. Shazam, an illustrious blotta baba, was ranting. The Tibetan amber and silver woven into two plaits in his white beard jiggled under his chin from his jaw action. Suddenly, Scarlet intercepted the intrusive ink-splat cow, shouting in Konkani and landing a slap with a bamboo stick on a rear flank sending the cow into reverse. Shazam, dressed in a jumpsuit screen printed with cartoon strips by R Crumb, grabbed his plate of fruit salad and mango lassi and stood clear. Danilo, also at the table, remained seated clutching his papaya lassi.

"As I was saying," Shazam said, sitting back down, "lots of brown was going around in the seventies. It was cheap, people were carrying it in hand language from Bangkok. But man, that shit is such a downer."

Numerous blotta babas got about the scene, but Shazam was the most scintillating. The goodness of his brain ticket was direct from San Francisco. Sheets of it would arrive poste restante, Panjim. Once again, the ink-splat cow attempted to push its nose into the conversation, this time with a long pink tongue curling towards Shazam's fruit salad, who swiftly elbowed the determined, horned marauder in the head. Scarlet immediately appeared out of the door with a bamboo stick, delivering several sharp whacks on the culprit's hide, sending the ink-splat hoofing up the road past local ladies in saris with black umbrella's sitting on stools next to cane baskets with local prawns and small fish.

Shazam slurped his lassi and continued, "It was Rock and Reggae back then—".

"Then came fag Disco and New Wave," Danilo said. "That's when we cut our hair."

"God almighty!" Shazam said, thumping the table with his hand that was accessorised with a yak bone amulet. "The beginning of the eighties was like the French fucking revolution, short of beheadings." He turned to Danilo. "You were one of the perpetrators." The Italian DJ shifted in his chair and smirked through a half smile."

"The Anjuna crowd hated Techno," Danilo recalled. "If you played it, you were accused of being a heretic of hippiedom. It was bedlam DJ-ing electronic music."

Fractious divisions did tear the tight knit scene apart. It was hard for Danilo to believe that the acid guru sitting in front of him used to hate his guts, so much so that Shazam had been part of a wrathful mob from Anjuna who wanted ony Rock and Reggae at parties. On one desperate occasion, Danilo had the DJ table turned over on him while he was playing, "God awful computer music," because the Anjuna crowd were severely challenged by it, and didn't regard it as happy hippie high vibes. Danilo was part of a tear-away bunch of party pranksters playing the new sound. That included DJs from France, Italy, Switzerland, Germany and Canada, who rankled the American and English rock 'n' rollers of Anjuna. Danilo had been told by irate Anjuna hippies, including Shazam at the time, that his late night noire techno was a demimonde, and that he and other DJs like him were not real hippies and were hi-jacking the scene with their edginess and hokey cokeyness.

"The defining moment for me," Shazam confessed, "was when Hipster Harry got down on the dance floor to computer music. He convinced me. I tipped, and discovered how much fun it was."

Danilo laughed, and recounted how it all started with his first season in seventy-eight. "I got off the bus in Chapora and didn't know anyone, I had a Sharp double deck boom box and started dubbing tapes from people I met. The vibe was Joy Division, Talking Heads, Art of Noise. I met up with the French connection and we started a club called, The Flying Dragon, in a big house up the top of the road here in Chapora. Later, we did themed parties. You must remember the medical party?" he said eye-balling Shazam. "That was crazy, you were dressed up like a mad chemist waltzing around the party with a couple of syringes without needles loaded with liquid crystal."

Shazam's face lit up. "Tongues were laid before me all night."

Danilo poked his tongue at the blotta baba. "We made decor from bed sheets," he recalled. "Splashed them with red paint, like blood. Everyone in fancy dress, some were dancing test tubes. I wore a surgeon's mask. You never saw the DJ."

A silver chopper rumbled round the big tree of Chapora village, the fat pat-pat-pat of its chunky cylinder thumped past Scarlet's trailing exhaust fumes. Doc Silver pulled in, and joined them at the table.

"You were one of the perpetrators of the coup d'etat, too," Shazam said pointing a finger at Doc, who slyly peered over his aviator sunglasses and ordered red grape juice.

"Viva la techno revolution" Danilo said. "The nouveau wave computer music that freaked the Anjuna crowd. Back when they called us infidels."

"What a raging battle that was," Doc said. "What idiots. They just didn't get it. It was time to get down to the beat of a different drummer. Ha!.. how disturbing for them—the drummer happened to be a drum machine."

"Acid Disco was the bomb," Shazam said, "It's time had come, right on time for the acid revival. On a thousand micrograms, I fully got it," he said twisting a plait of white beard with a finger.

"Hey it's a freaks' place," Danilo declared. "It's about experimenting. We wanna be free, we wanna be free to do what we wanna do. The Portuguese turned Goa into a Christian state, when they left, it became altered state." Everyone laughed.

Doc's juice arrived and he instantly drained half of it and released the straw from his mouth and let his aviator sunglasses slide all the way down his nose to reveal searing eyes. Locking his fingers together he said, "Underneath the trippy palms, the dirt and the dust and the lust and the grit, there is a maw, like bacteria. Like when you fall off your bike, you have to take care, or else pus will get ya. You have to know with which hand to wipe your arse, and which to feed yourself and others. There's a food chain. And there's low life feeders who can become bleeders. Pigs can only eat so much shit here. There is plenty left over for slinging, and when it comes slung, wrapped in a long blade, then you have to take stock of the patch you are squatting on, or your bare boogie arse has to learn a new dance."

On hearing mention of a long blade, Danilo's scalp tightened, and blotta baba Shazam felt the thud of blood through his veins to his feet. All at the table had the inextinguishable memory of machete murders by a deranged freak on a datura bender, back in the early eighties.

Doc's forehead was steaming. "This morning I woke up in a sweat, like I'd been pinned down in a nightmare. But it wasn't a dream. Around midnight a couple of local arseholes showed up at my door flashing a blade."

"What!" Shazam gasped.

"Seems a turf grievance," hissed Doc. "I figure they are affiliates of the Calangute gang."

"It happened to me once," Danilo said.

"These thugs want a party put on for their pal who runs a bar." Doc said. "They missed out when the party got switched back to Anjuna three weeks ago. The thing is, this pesky lowlife is a gambling racket that has attached itself to our parties for which we are paying the cops to stay away."

Shadow Dance

AFTER CHECKING HER TAILOR'S work, Zsu refreshed herself from the afternoon heat with a bucket of well water and Chandrika soap. She dried off, put on a bikini top, cut-off jeans and hitched a flax Bali bag to her back. Riding her Yamaha, she took the back road to Mapusa until she came to an overgrown chapel. Next to it, she followed a track through cashew bushes to a simple secluded house made of large, rough-hewn, unplastered, dark brown bricks. She hopped off her bike and walked around the back. "Zikos!.. are you there?" she called out. No reply. "Zikos!" No reply.

Then, "Boom," faintly breathed a voice from inside. The back door slowly opened followed by a familiar figure wrapped in a sarong.

"Thank goodness you're here" she cried out, and ran to Zikos. They hugged, a weepy gladness filled her eyes. "I'm glad to see you." They sat on his porch. "What happened?"

"I returned on the night bus from Bombay," he said.

"We heard someone got done at the airport," she said.

"Some idiot with a shonky job. A Made-In-India suitcase cracked open. Stash apparently haemorrhaging. Customs all over it. Everyone in

Lakshmi Juice Bar who were about to do runs got the shits. There was talk they're now using an x-ray machine. I was due to fly the next day. It was too dicey."

"That's disastrous," Zsu said. "Who got screwed?"

"Someone on an Irish passport."

"Have you talked to Shane?" she said.

"No."

"What to do?" she said, dismayed.

Zikos sighed. "Swallow."

The Greek went back inside and crashed out. Zsu rode to the beach with sunglasses and face pressed into the rushing air cooling her brow that was overheated from Zikos's story. Driving past Hill Top Restaurant, the sight of the sea with the sun beating down was balm for the thoughts racing through her head. Arriving at Ramdass chai shop, she leaned the bike on its stand and made her way down a pebbly path to middle Vagator Beach where nude sun worshippers were tanning. Others, in g-strings, played beach racket, while some bathed in small waves. Middle Vagator—with Disco Valley and Spaghetti Beach on either side—was for Zsu, the centre of Shiva's seashore trident. The lotus eaters that hung here were like rare, seasonal, migration birds—friends of a common feather—unlike any other beach roost in Asia.

Zsu found Asta and friends and laid out her batik sarong on the sand. Sitting down, she slid off her cut-offs and released her bikini top. She was immediately wheedled with endearments on how smashing the full moon party had been. A long Rizla joint with cardboard filter, packed with Panama tobacco and charas, was passed to her. It was like a burning magic wand. Smoking it brought a much-needed mood adjustment and sensory enhancement, that rendered the sunny vista of sea, sand, rocks and bodies into an airbrushed dreamscape with heightened contrast and infinite depth of field. She felt the worrisome, interlocking weave around the casing of her mind loosen from its tightness, since hearing about the alarming Bombay airport incident. Relaxing with a muted sigh, she gazed out into the shimmering ripples of the sea in which bodies were bobbing about in play. The ripples became foam in which she imagined herself diving in to meet a winking trickster dolphin.

The blazing afternoon sun baked hot on her skin. She sauntered to the ocean to cool off. Sea spume gathered about her feet and swirled up her knees and frothed between her legs and ebbed about her hips. Wading deeper, gentle waves caressed her breasts and lapped about her shoulders and purled up her neck. She breast-stroked a little, then floated weightless out over her head feeling unshackled from her mind. She stopped and tread water, and spun around using arms and feet to feel fluid and free. A head with a familiar face flashed in front of her, then ducked under and a body torpedoed towards her. Her legs and heart pounded faster. From below, she felt arms wrap around her waist. The head of the torpedo rose up out of the water to meet hers. Eyes flickered and blinked and winked. Wet open mouths sucked for breath. Pearls of ocean dripped from tousles of hair, earlobes, nose and face, which had been freshly blade shaved in Chapora.

"Dolphin Jules!.. Oh, my God!.. Before she could say anything more, his mouth pressed upon hers and they submerged, fused in oceania.

That night in her house, Zsu burned lavender, sage and cedar frankincense. The dolphin play continued on a bed with satin sheets with silk pillows in her boudoir with walls draped in chiffon and charmeuse. All around were fluffy feathery things and leather and gauzy lace and twinkling things in candle light. Eyes melted. Avid lips pressed into each other and quickly turned into heated necking and kissing. Bodies bounced, laughter ran through them like the trickling delight of a forest stream. The whites of eyes pulsed like filaments wired to syncopating heart beats. His cheek on the nape of her swan-like tender neck, her fingers clawing the fur of his chest. Chemically electrified, they mashed into each other like mortar and pestle creating merged emotion that had not existed in this combination before.

A slow ceiling fan cooled the secretions of caramel, glowing, skin, flushed and fused in candle light—as if coated in almond liqueur ready for curling, cocked tongues to lick all over. Their naked, palpable togetherness with her purring in his embrace, transported them to a place beyond the mind, a place where pleasure brought transcendence, a place where flesh became molten feeling, a place far removed from the dance floor. The place of the angel attractor. The most inner sanctum place of temple harlot Zsu Riviere. No longer a vexing, chaos attractor teasing windmills of Jules Nightingale's mind.

He'd brought a pomegranate. Cutting it open, he told her to hold out a hand. Flipping one half of the fruit, he spanked its bottom with the flat of his hand and shiny crimson capsule seeds dropped into hers. She did the same for him, and they ate the jewel looking seeds. The boudoir contained Aphrodite belts with chunky shinning buckles, lacy leather bodices, an array of spandex, faux snake skin mini skirt, lace up stitch-witch goth boots, gypsy wear, silver studded cyber-punk bum bags, wristbands and dangling gemstone necklaces, priestess amulets and Wicca talismanic jewellery laid out on a dressing table. All testimony to crusades in fashion fiction, mythic role play, dance floor ritual; and, he suspected—femme fatale follies. He dared not over think the matter of DJ Atma Blaze, here now laying with her at this most melting moment of nascent thresholds, the fate of the die that had been cast in Bali

A batik sarong—depicting an alien space craft scene—was draped over an open window to a garden through which came the sounds of crickets, distant howls of dogs, and scents of jasmine and gardenia that mingled with essential oils in her inner sanctum. Candle flames danced up the wall and played upon her skin. Looking into Jules's smoky, hypnotising hazel eyes she saw herself reflected back like she had never seen before, as though he was an ophthalmologist peering through her emerald iris veils to a vitreous wishing well deep within her. She adored the way he appeared to devotionally woo and worship her, rather than the other way around, the way it had been with Atma Blaze.

Clutching at the reins of desire, tongues slipped through lips and lunged into mouths and twisted and teased. Arms and legs entwined in sweat gland skinship. They breathed in each other's body. Hair became mussed, mouths avid, pleasure ran over them like sweet papaya flesh. They rolled and caressed, bouncing off each other's body topography. Jules's lingam arched up. His hand glided across a soft, silky, inner thigh toward her delta. He slid his fingers ever so slightly through slippery curls and subtly pulled into her wet readiness. She trembled and nuzzled her head on his chest. With eyes gazing in and out of focus, she observed the rouge tip of his angled lingam pointing towards her from below his navel. He ran his fingers through her hair and softly raked up her neck to her scalp and pawed her. His belly and hips undulated, her head slid down to greet his quivering lingam. She was mesmerised by its bobbing crowned beauty, its cheerful firm friskiness, as though it had a mind of its own, like it was a third party in the room. She reached over to a bedside table and dipped two fingers into a small bowl of almond oil and gently squished and squeezed the fleshy stretchy sacks containing its seed pods. Jules's body throbbed, his lingam bobbed bulbous skywards. She opened her lips, in a whisper she spoke in tongues, a Kali hoochie coochie sex magic mantra.

Jules's cocked-up lingam had turned into an erect cobra snake that swayed about in front of Zsu's face like it was under her hypnotic spell. She teased it with short pokes of her tongue, until she made contact with the snake's darting tongue, all the while maintaining a droning mantra as oily fingers fondled Jules's jewels. The charmed cobra stood upright, engorged, quivering. She kissed its smooth round snout, then opened her lips and took the reptile's head inside her mouth and twirled her tongue around its smooth round hardness. Saliva spuzzed over the mammalian serpent's throbbing heat, its forked tongue titillating her throat, mainlining pleasure to the accumbens nucleus at the centre of her brain and down her spine to her base chakra where it flash-flooded her yoni.

A symphony of cells in the auditory flesh of heinous groove glands engaged in Saturnalian sex. Jules rolled his eyes in abandon, surrendering to the will of Kali as he felt explosive forces bring him close to the point of no return delivering a jet stream hurtling him out of control. The tantric threshold of which, was like he was about to burst out of his skin. Sensing this, Kali released the saliva coated snake from her enflamed slash-red mouth and shuffled up Jules's aroused body and rubbed her pooling delta in his face. He sucked in air through his nose and blew air out through closed vibrating lips, then opened his mouth and let his tongue twist and probe its way through mossy folds, until he found himself at a fountain head of labia around a mouth abyss of pure pink bliss.

After soft-tissue nectar imbibing, to a state of near asphyxiation, he resurfaced gasping for air, like he was drowning and given mouth to mouth, then tongue kissing, after which she gently blew heated breath into his ear and murmured in a low voice, "I am H.I.V. negative, my cycle is fine." He smiled and mounted her, gathering breasts in his hands and ardently nibbled softly on her pert rose buds.

Rock hard, he holy and boldly engaged her distended, palpitating pudendum, as she clawed his back with her nails and pincer gripped him with legs spurring him into her. Coital rocking, with his fullness inside her, they shook in undulating waves of pleasure. Then, he went totally still, and continued to breathe deeply. They kissed, tongues lunging into each other, her lurching. Headless, they shuddered and quaked, riding eddies—hips to hips, ribs to ribs, solar plexus to solar plexus—to a rising seismic tremor that seized them in tender, tissue, fission. Jules gulped for air, letting out a roar as he peaked, but she remained silent, as if gagged, not swept away in the rush of undifferentiated ecstasy, where dissolved selves merge into nether regions of oblivion.

On regaining consciousness and re-inhabiting his discharged body, Jules observed her silence. It was a self-contained silence tinged with sappy melancholy. A missed-the-boat intangibleness? In the silence, his eyes met her eyes. She blushed, a tear came to an eye, and then the other, as if something concealed was seeping out, the laying bare of an inviolable, impregnable feeling. Like an archaic, igneous emotion become obsidian at the magma of her core. The self-admonishment of plutonic body memory pushing down and rage boiling up. A passion that was ambiguous enough to suggest a lustful anticipation of subterranean pain.

With her face clouded over and her body about to crack, Zsu shivered and cried. His pleasure inside of her seemed to have stirred more consternation than it had delivered joy to her. No loud paroxysm and vocalisations. Perhaps a series of openings to different levels? A tear rolled down a cheek. He asked her softly what she was feeling?

"Please hold me," she replied.

Consoling her, he hugged crumpled, little girl Zsu, who belied external versions of her: The itchy-witchy vivacious vamp. The fashion provocateur. The party mover and shaker.

"Do you know about the goddess Persephone?" he said.

"She nodded. "Greek, isn't she?"

"Yes, she's Queen of the Underworld," he said. "Persephone was abducted from her mother Ceres by Hades to live an erotic life during the winter months—"

"My mother was difficult," she said with teary eyes. "I was happy to get away from her. My father, I don't know, I had step fathers." She sighed. "Family for me has been like poison in the blood."

"So, Goa has been your runaway home?" he said. "Goa is your family?"

She brightened. "Yes!.. here I discovered myself. Nobody is from here. The scene is made up of outsiders, no one was born here, we are all visitors, time travellers from all over the world. The Goans allow us to be as free as we like, it's the freest place I know."

Looking into her flushed face he said, "Perhaps you are Persephone in a tropical underworld?" He thought about the scene, and that it was Europeans escaping the darkness and winter chill of the world, and Goa—the domain of Hades?

"Jules, please stop, you're blowing my mind. Oh, my God!.. Perhaps you're right. Perhaps I am Persephone." She looked up at him through reddened eyes, a half smile breaking through. "Goa is a colourful underworld. But there are long shadows," she admitted. "Long shadows beyond all the bright colours."

"Hm," Jules said. "The brightest flame casts the darkest shadow. You can't run from the shadow. Wow!..so maybe you are Queen of the Underworld?"

"Oh, bloody hell!" she said pensively, narrowing her eyes.

"God knows, maybe I'm King of the Gutter." He said, self-deprecatingly. What Jules felt in their embrace said otherwise. "I love all your colours and shades," he reassured her. Yet there was something cat-like about her, in the way cats don't allow themselves to be owned, the way dogs do. There was something else cat-like about her, the way she could see in the dark when she led him through the moon shadows of Disco Valley jungle to the elephant tree.

"You see in the dark," he said.

Her face became pensive. She got up off the bed, wrapped a sarong around her waist and went to the window. Jules lay on the bed taking pleasure in the silhouette of the curvature of her figure and play of moon light on her face.

"The moon is an enchantress," he said. "The moon is our nearest and most intimate celestial body. The moon talks to the emotional body. The moon reflects the sun's light, softens it. The moon is moody, the moon is always changing shape, always changing sign."

She turned to him. Her face melancholic, her skin sticky with the emotional humidity of the air between them. "Oh, that's so me, the moon cycle," she said. "The moon is female. I bleed with the moon. It's beyond my control, it's like my body is yoked to the moon."

"How is it possible not to believe the power of astral bodies," he said. "We are astral beings. We are connected to what is going on above us. We are the psyche of the cosmos. The sun is life force. The moon is the emotional body. The mother—"

"Oh no!" she said with choked breath. "I loathe my mother." Her face became lunar-like, one side amber from candle light, the other concealed in the shadowy umbra of night. Gazing at moon shadows in the garden, she fessed up. "I think my Scorpio sun loves crawling around in the shady underworld of Goa moon light."

"You are enchanting in these shadows," he verbally stroked her as he peered at her rack of fetching garments. "Your style is dazzling."

"You're so kind," she said. "Well, I just love to play dress-ups. Jules I'm sorry I got bummed out." Her eyebrows crinkled into a frown.

"Please don't be sorry," he murmured. A piteous shroud lifted from her face. "There's no light without darkness," he said wriggling playfully on her bed, as if to whisk away the humidity of the disclosures that her boudoir had become suffused in. She felt an electrical current run up the back of her neck. It was as if his words were acupuncture needles he'd inserted into the tissue of her body memory, setting off circuit breakers protecting a fragile inner core. The trust at her centre longing to connect. The lifting of an invisible veil on a most delicious, fashion, seduction oozing bewitching allure—but which belied a wound.

Pushing a hand through tussled hair that had fallen about her furrowed brow and flushed face, Zsu sighed. "Well, this is something that is hard for me to talk about. She returned to the silky pillows on the bed with a lump in her throat. He put his arm around her. "This is deeply personal and private," she said with a solemn gaze. "I trust you. I need to share these feelings." Emotion engulfed her. The perimeters of the space they held together became porous. She broke down. "There were incidents…" her voice stuttered. "One of my mother's boyfriends…" She became shrouded in mournful silence, then sobbed. He pulled her face to his chest, cradled her head in the valley between his pectoral major muscles, her head rising and falling with his breath and heartbeat. Seamstress Zsu felt all the stitching and overlocking of the hussy hems and lustrous fabrics of her body mapping, come unravelled, and her most closeted drawers emptied out all over the bedroom floor. It was as if something private and complex, something madly secretive was being traded away for safety and comfort and closeness. A need for intimate disclosure of a kind of treachery to herself, a betrayal to love, a dull thud from the shadows of another time. A family curse more murky than any shady deal that had ever gone down in Goa, or any cover up by Popes involved in Satanic ritual sacrifices of new-born children in which their blood had been drunk.

Tear-streaked, she raised her head from his chest—their eyes met and she inhaled deeply and said, "I was fucked by my mother's boyfriend when I was eleven. His name was Hades." The sharing of her secret brought a bond of trust. It gratified a longing to be understood. A longing to break down a barrier. A longing to be truly loved.

"The fact that I was born, and still alive, will forever remind my mother that she was gang raped. The disgust and shame and abuse—like a wound, which I'm the product of. This feeling lives in my bones. And so, with every new relationship I struggle with this feeling. Am I good enough? Am I loveable? Not just to be fucked!.. The feelings disconnect… I blank out…I go numb."

The air in the boudoir became still born—silent. It was a loaded silence crawling with ponderous disquiet. He contemplated the strings and folded wings of the casing of her body clinging to him. It's plucked sounds and social butterfly flights into the imaginal artifice of wearable art, fantasy and bewitching myth. Yet, in the sanctum of their silky, satin, intimacy, the open tunings of her strings could not mask a drone cadence that rung with the reverb of a basement struck minor seventh chord. She turned away wanting to hide. She worried that what she'd confided had repulsed him. Did he now regard this most unlovable part of herself strange and damaged?

"Pluto!" he said, flashing on her horoscope. "The planet diety of the under soul, the domain of ghosts, demons, skeletons in the closet—"

"Oh, my God!" She gasped. "You're unnervingly psychic." She wistfully looked into a candle flame, her eyes glistening with tears. But there was no switching Jules off in his decrypting of her blue flame. She could feel the cylinders of inner combination locks clicking. His mysterious insight brought release. She felt penetrated. Deeply touched, less alone with her secret self. Then, she was struck by an image. Jules was holding a psychic blow torch, or was it a laser? Was he doing paranormal surgery on her?

"Something creepy happened," she revealed. "Just before dawn at the party I had a visitation by a disembodied spirit. I'd gone for a pee with Asta near the Ganesh tree. The apparition appeared in the doorway of the ruin. It was mysterious with a powerful presence. It said it was the ghost of Donna Ferreira, an eighteenth-century lady in waiting to the wife of the Viceroy in Panjim. She said, she'd charmed him and they had it off. But the wife found out. Enraged, she had Donna stripped and bound and rolled off the cliff at Fort Aguada onto the rocks below, but allowed her to keep the string of pearls that he'd given her. She told me that I had been a witch in the sixteenth century and burned at the stake. She warned me of looming trouble in paradise."

"What kind of trouble?"

"She didn't say."

"Look Jules," she said, wiping tears from her eyes with her sarong. "It's mind blowing, it's rapturous, it's no accident you showing up in my life. But hey, as you are finding out, this is a far out place, and it attracts extreme people. You could say it's a refuge for seekers, an asylum for misfits, spiritual wonderers, sufferers of world discontent. For most of us, there is no other place to be. For me, the happiest times and maximum pleasure—much more than romance—have been on the dance floor here." She gazed at a black effigy of Kali standing on a corner table. It was illuminated by a flickering candle, its wick spluttering and expiring in a crater of pooling hot wax.

Psychic Debris

EQUINOX, IN MARCH, the sun entered the head-strong sign of Aries. The season cooked hotter. The maddening heat scorching the earth, with brains inside bone boxes of Goa heads becoming fried, as the red dust of Bardez appeared, more and more like Mars—the ruling planet of Aries.

The maniacal end of season would tip into overheated delirium. The most crusty and resilient of first world refugees partied on in its swelter. The nuttier the techno troppo music—the better. The more wigged-out experimental, edgy—the better. Zsu and Asta got a kick out of hearing a track in the party with a voice stating, "Mars needs more women."

It was possible to disappear off the face of the earth in India. The terminally hooked had no intention of leaving the party paradise bubble, even if money and visa's ran out. Counterfeit ones were easily attainable. The most hardcore would stay through monsoon, that included a community of families with kids attending the local school.

By the time the season tailed off in the searing heat of April, two thirds of Goa heads would have discharged themselves from the cocoon of the paradise bubble through swarming Bombay. Its high-density extremes requiring a reality check after the out-space asylum of the psychotropics of Goa's jungle and beaches.

End of season was known as—"dread dregs," in which flip-out loonies would waywardly wander Bardez. The loose units, whose neurological circuit boards had popped, dopamine transporters derailed, synapses fused out. Those who'd dosed and danced into delirium with overcooked noggins, like golf balls shedding their casing with rubber band ganglia breaking out. End of season was like a cuckoo's nest taking flight.

Enter Doc Silver. He and other Mother Teresa's in the scene would rescue and take care of lost-the-plot flip outs. Even though Doc had an allergy to staged beggary, he wore his heart on his sleeve and would attend to the psychic debris of casualties from the season who roamed befuddled in the dread dregs heat of the parched, Bardez, Mars landscape. They'd be shepherded to a recovery ashram called, 'The Sanctuary,' between big Vagator Beach and Chapora Fort, where a couple of Buddhist monks from Bhutan would take care of them. The more acute lost-the-plot lot, were attended to by Dr Singh at his small St Anthony hospital in Badem. The most far-gone would end up in the psychiatric ward of Mapusa Hospital, which would require dealings with the authorities and cash inducements to repatriate them, care of embassies.

By the end of March, Doc was keeping an eye on several lost-the-plot cases, the most problematic was Nelsuk, a young man from Finland who was a member of the mystical O.O.O. (Osser Ouroboros of Odin) saga circle. Nelsuk was found by locals down a well where he was singing opera as he treaded water. Not wanting to come out, he believed he was escaping the demon god Thor and Ragnarok destruction of the world in nuclear war. Doc made out that he was Master of the Universe, and was able to coax Nelsuk up a bamboo ladder. The monks at the Sanctuary got him chanting and counting bead mantras at the ashram, but Nelsuk remained antsy. St Anthony hospital was full with motorbike casualties, so Doc got him on Valium and chaperoned him for a few days. After Primrose one night, he was picked up by police who could not make any sense of him when he became recalcitrant and cursed at them in Finnish and was taken to Mapusa Police Station. And then, there was the Greek woman who'd overdosed on Mandrax, after she'd gone up Anjuna hill, crashed out, and woke up with ants in every orifice. She freaked, had a psychotic episode and ended up in Mapusa Hospital.

Besides flip outs, all manner of misadventure was possible: snake bites, rabies from dogs, thefts (not necessarily by Indians), drug busts, motorbike spills, infections, diarrhoea, overdoses and sexual attack. Gratuitous violence was rare, but when it happened it was moonstruck nutso.

"The worst freak out was eighty-two," explained Doc, whilst sitting on a chai mumma mat with a couple of butterscotch blonde Swedish girls, the morning of a late March party at Jungle Palace, the backside of Spaghetti Beach. "It happened the day after a party, right here," he said. "It was the most loco affair with bamboozling search lights all through the jungle sending everyone bonkers. A weird static hung in the air after that party."

The girls, clad in bright colours, sipped chai and smoked a spliff. They'd just bopped ten hours non-stop inside Jungle Palace's fluoro-dripping-lifeforms and were bedazzled by the exhilarating experience. It was their first party. They were gaga, having discovered Goa's dirty little secret—the seemingly, limitless, free, mind-boggling fun and frivolity possible, unlike anywhere else.

"I don't want to ruin your day," Doc said, like he'd turned into Alice Cooper. "Three heads got decapitated up the coast on Arambol beach after a crazy party here in Jungle Palace."

"Oh, no!" gasped one of the girls recoiling in horror. The other, put her hands to her face.

"A dude got badly bent on datura," Doc said. "He ran amok with a machete killing his girlfriend and two randoms. Did a runner, never got caught. After that, they chopped down all the datura growing everywhere. You can't blame nature's plants though, can you? But don't worry," he reassured the girls. "It's an extended family here, everyone looks out for each other. But basically, its lawless. The cops are a joke. It's been a safe haven for extremists hiding out amongst peace loving freaks. I'm not just talking contraband. Members of the German terrorist gang, Baader-Meinhof, even camped out here in the seventies, and a few years back, the militant IRA. The most sinister cretin to infiltrate the scene was a French serial killer, who would torch to death drug smugglers."

The girls froze with a look of discomfort on hearing these macabre tales, like Doc was holding them captive, having hooked them under his protective wing, least they fall prey to the treacheries of the spell of the Asia trail. "This evil piece of work was known as, *The Serpent*. A deadly, psycho killer up there with Charles Manson. Even has the same name." The blue eyes of the Swedish darlings widened with every word coming out of Doc's mouth. "That mother fucker preyed upon hippies. Have you heard of Charles Sobhraj?"

The girls shook their heads with perturbed curiosity. "He murdered twelve people and was hiding out here. The cops caught him while dinning at O'Coqueiro Restaurant. He pulled off scams by drugging backpackers, robbing them and murdering them. Self-righteously accusing them of being drug pushers."

The girls clutched each other. "Why serpent?"

"Because he was a slippery bastard, he could get out of any jam. Typically, by charm and deception and drugging his victims. He got locked up twice and escaped by drugging the prison guards."

The music stopped and one of Doc's cute friends, Aki, joined them on the mat.

"Where are you from?" asked one of the Swedes.

"Osaka."

"What do you do there?"

"Making line on the road."

Doc cracked up, explaining that she did road gang work. And on cue, with a generous grin, invited all the girls back to his place for some lines.

"Hahaha!" The dishy Swedes laughed. They all made their way up the craggy cliff track to the tangled cluster of motorbikes at the top, where the girls on flimsy TVS mopeds tagged along behind Doc Silver's chopper.

Superstition had a fearful hold on the minds of Goans—especially snakes for the Catholics. But it was *The Evil Eye* they feared most. Clusters of chilli pods hung above front doors of houses and dangled off the grille of vehicles for protection. Clumps of the blazing red fiery spice hung above Doc's front door and off the chassis of his chopper. Two days after the Jungle Palace party, he woke up in a malaise. It was more than just a standard, post late-night endorphin-drained hokey cokey, scratchy, hangover—but rather the wroth in being extortionately had. Like sneaky, nasty, Ninjas creeping up the back of his mind, which got him thinking about *The Serpent*. The con-artist's ability to dupe and dope his way out of any jam.

Since the seventies, Doc had enjoyed a libertarian freedom to party, where ever, and whenever, but an insidious opportunistic undercurrent was conspiring to call the shots, which threatened to spoil the fun, and could not be fixed by blindly throwing cash at the situation. The dark nimbus of the Ninjas stumping his head prompted him to consult other powers than the immunity of chilli and tackling the situation head-on. Kicking over his chopper, he headed to Joe Banana for a pow wow breakfast with his Jewish American buddies, most of whom were trustafarians, like Doc, who kept permanent houses in South Anjuna. Some had been in the first wave of counter culture colonists to arrive at Candolim and Calangute, who got off with acoustic guitars with candles in the sand and boogied down at the first disco at the Rose Garden Restaurant by Anjuna Post Office.

For those drinking coffee shakes and passing around a spliff at Joe's, it was a downer to hear about the knife threat Doc had been subjected to by, "low level, huckster sharks feeding off the party food chain." Together, like a hedge fund syndicate, the trustafarians would gift a cash Christmas present to the Mapusa Police slush fund, ostensibly securing them individual protection for the season from house searches and impunity should they be caught with their pants down and stash bags open. Doc gurgled out the last of his shake from the bottom of his glass and farewelled them saying, "I'm on a good Samaritan mission to Mapusa and will drop in on the head shark to address the fact that we aren't on a level playing field anymore, as the tumbling dice has become a nasty vice."

The sun blazed like a lion's head in a blue, blue sky as Doc's chopper ascended Mapusa Hill. The descent down to the town was cooling on Doc's sweating brow, but didn't alleviate the overcast gusty squalls whiplashing behind his frontal lobes. The mildew, decayed, concrete cancer of the exterior of the Mapusa Police Station reeked of warped

Indian officialdom. Within its corroded, corrupt corridors varying degrees of compassion and *paradise tax* could be brokered with grubby, bent-cornered, rubber-band-bound rupees and shiny large-note green backs. The rusty bars of its cell windows were in tact enough to be custodial. The haggling of inducements for leniency required deft pussyfooting, which Doc had become shrewd at. He even regarded the mottled efflorescence of the concrete stains at the head cop shop as a kind of entropic psychedelia on the eye, but those unlucky enough to end up in a cell there, didn't see it like that.

The roasting April, Mapusa heat was being beaten by whirling tarnished ceiling fans when Doc strode through the arched entrance with blemished paintwork of the station, like he was an inside trader—virtually on the payroll himself. Parlaying with Indian officialdom, for Doc, was like a snakes and ladders game. Over the past decade, he'd dealt with various police chiefs. All regarded him, an affable representative of the scallywag party scene in the maintenance of mutual benefits. Doc was convincing in whoever he needed to be: Good times enabler. Boogie wonderland groover. Avuncular shepherd. Matey ally. Wisecrack opener of wallets, legs, hearts, and today—locked cells, and much more pressing far-reaching concerns.

In recent years, being posted to Goa Police had become one of the most coveted jobs in the Indian Police force—even more so than customs at Bombay Airport where foreign cash was slipped sleight of hand to turn a blind eye to the black market. More so than career examinations and performance, it was common knowledge that large sums of lakh rupees were involved in getting posted to the ranks of Goa Police. The three-star Chief Inspector of Police in Panjim was taking orders from the Goa Government and Delhi. Under him, the two-star Chief Inspector in Mapusa had jurisdiction of Calangute and Anjuna police stations.

With playful pluck, Doc enjoyed the constantly shifting charade game of calling the bluff with Indian officialdom. Now anti-hippie lobby groups in Panjim expected Goa Police to enforce the new drug laws. How this panned out in reality, with the scene religiously, recreationally, habitually flouting them—with actual prosecutions and cases reaching court—another matter. Well-seasoned boom shankar tribalists in the scene knew there were margins that were negotiable, but these margins, many feared, were becoming an arm and a leg, as the pungent smell of charas hanging in the air over Bardez became more and more odious and sticky with paranoia.

Two star, Augusto Fernandese, Chief Inspector of Mapusa sat in a neat fawn coloured uniform at an oak desk with glass paper weights on top of piles of paper and brown manila folders stacked high behind him. He was of bulky build with grizzled, regulation hair and fleshy, pitted-skin cheeks rising above unctuous lips. A constable knocked on his door advising him that a foreigner by the name of Doctor Silver was wishing to see him.

"Show him in," Fernandese said.

"Hello Inspector," Doc said with his silver hair piled high in a Shiva bun with an ebony chop stick and silver sickle moon spiked through it."

"Doctor Silver," the Chief Inspector greeted him with an oily, convivial smile, as he rose from his crinkled leather chair and shook Doc's hand.

"Nice to see you Inspector," Doc said, cheerfully plonking himself in a chair like he was dropping in on an old friend.

"Life is good at the beach?" Fernandese said with a wry grin.

"It's mostly been a fun season."

The Chief Inspector smiled. "Tourist numbers are up this year. So are parties, I believe—"

"I'm always happy," Doc said, "when there's music in the air. Parties are my church. Parties are good for the local economy. But now it's hot, end of season, only the diehards are left—the true lovers of Goa."

"My boys have gotten to know a few of them," Fernandese said.

"So, I gather," Doc smirked. "As you know, I try to make your job easy. I've been rounding up some casualties who've come off the rails—"

"They do get themselves in a dreadful state," the Inspector said.

"Too much of a good thing," Doc said. "For some, more is never enough—"

"It's a troubling situation," the Inspector said. "They roam about like zombies."

"Heaven forbid, we can't have that," Doc said with a deadpan face. "I do my damnedest. Some are a handful—"

"What's wrong with these people?" the Inspector said, waggling his head. "I can understand some of them want to be mystics—"

"Yes," Doc said in a pious voice, "Religious experiences can make some renounce the world."

"That's all well and good," the Inspector said," but we don't want scathing headlines like last year—"

"No, no, we don't want that."

Doc had promised the Chief Inspector he'd do his upmost to shepherd lost-the-plot cases after a sacrilegious act occurred last year in a chapel, resulting in locals giving the offending foreigner a bamboo massage beating. Within shifting latitudes of pliability, the Inspector was prone to turning a blind eye to dope vacationers who had fallen prey to a bust, which landed them in the watch house of Mapusa Police Station. Where possible, he'd prefer cash then send them to court. This might not always be the case with Panjim. Rule of thumb for dope vacationers, where there was threat of arrest, the situation needed to be negotiated swiftly, least they find themselves in the foreboding confines of medieval, Fort Aguado, that now served as a prison. Given the paltry salaries of regular police, it was pretty much mandatory that they jump on any opportunity to extort baksheesh from hapless foreigners. In previous times, the gifting of imported cigarettes and whiskey went a long way.

"I believe you are accommodating a young man from Finland?" Doc said.

Fernandese picked up a folder on his desk, pulled out a document and scanned its details.

"Hm… We have a Nelsuk Torvalds."

"That's my boy," Doc said. "I was taking care of him."

"The notes say, "Disturbed and abusive."

"He's actually quite sweet," Doc said, "when you get to know him. He's not well. We need to have him sent back to Finland with the assistance of the embassy in Delhi. Also, there's a Greek woman at the hospital who requires embassy support."

"It's that time of year," Inspector Fernandese said. "No shortage of stray, mad people in the lost and found—"

"I thank you for your understanding," Doc said in a kindly voice. "I appreciate you are a man of compassion," and gazed at the small cross tattooed on the underside of the Inspector's wrist. "I'm just doing Jesus's teaching." And then, in a formal tone of voice said, "There's something else, something troubling I need to share with you Inspector. Something you need to know." Fernandese shifted in his chair.

"A Devil's playground has infiltrated our parties," Doc said. "Gambling is a sinful, immoral and illegal vice, but I don't believe smoking charas is. It has been a sacrament in Hindu sadhu spiritual practices. But then it became a problem when your government did a deal with my country. And, of course, I'm sure you value our charitable contributions to the admirable services of the Mapusa Police, so that we can enjoy our time in Goa. But now a nefarious, parasite gambling mob, which is in cohorts with some bars and a local gang, want to coerce us with violence to make parties with them so they can continue to run their gambling racket. Whenever we have a party they set up a card game on the edge of it, where sizeable amounts of rupees change hands. We are paying you so that we can dance and partake in Shiva's sacrament, but they are not paying, and are now threatening us if we don't make parties with their bar pals."

Chief Inspector August Fernandese's round, fleshy cheeks became long and pensive. He leaned back in his chair, raised his chin, shot Doc a jovial grin, shook his head and said, "That's not cricket."

"Cricket!" said Doc, who came from a New York Jewish family with investments in Las Vegas. "I grew up with baseball. In the mean streets of my home town if you pull that kind of game you are likely to end up with a bat wrapped around your head, or a bullet in it. Why I love India is because it's the opposite. It's shanty!"

"Peace country," the Inspector said.

"A couple of nasty fellas," Doc said with a grimace, "I'm guessing the Calangute gang… They came to my house and flashed a long blade."

"The Calangute boys," the Inspector said. "We do have troubles with them. But nothing we can't deal with."

What the Chief Inspector did not want to admit, was that India was ruled by family gangs, who fell under the spell of rupee extortion, just like himself.

Doc leaned forward in his seat. "Inspector Fernandese let's get off to a good start next year. Let's iron out this problem, keep the peace. The Christmas presents from South Anjuna will be generous and sparkle much brighter. Of course, we have to keep the Chapora and Starco Corner and Nelson Corner boys happy, too."

The dirty boulevards of New York, in the seventies and eighties, had equipped Doc with a hang-tough kind of love. A trenchant, modus operandi wrench with which to deal with the grittiness of a big Babylonian city, where hustlers were likely to proposition you on corners in a concrete jungle stench of dry piss and street hassle. In seething, squalid Calcutta—where Doc first landed in India and encountered extremes of wealth and poverty, not dissimilar to the U.S.—he taxied about on barefoot human rickshaws in a sea of black faces, and was taken to a rat temple where he had an epiphany. And at the burning ghats of the Ganges in Varanasi, the sight of corpses burning on pyres sent shudders through his bones. Asia shattered any notions of an American jingoistic, first world view. The happiest people he ever saw were some of the poorest he encountered in Burma, Nepal and India whilst living simply out of a backpack.

Riding his chopper at night in Goa, Doc would don an anti-hippie-dippy Ramones black leather jacket, like it was an outer protective skin shielding a mushy soft centre that was charitable. He would wear a histrionic heart on cut-off sleeves, making him vulnerable, easy pickings for beggars and destitute freaks when his tough love wrench was out of reach. Beggars stirred conflicting emotions that quarrelled inside of him, wherein impatience overwhelmed sympathy, capsizing him in the melodramas of a three-year old in a middle-aged body. Sometimes he wanted to scream and shout, but mostly, he gave rupees to rid himself of the uncomfortableness that pricked him from under his skin like a flaring allergy.

In his late teens, railing against family pressure, a hip "outsider uncle," urged him to travel. Mystical India, with its contrasting extremes and social castes, pushed his buttons. Mad India, the place of high contrast. The place to atone for the weight of being born into a gilded family cage—the inheritance of privilege with its abstruse binding obligations. India, the place to be slagged and slurried. The place of high drama and placable surrender. India, the visceral place to embrace human existence, to tandoori roast in a rich masala of emotions. The earthy place to witness the resolve of human spirit through ritual of life, in all its vast array of survival and decrepitude and devotion and theatre of business haggle and enlightenment industry. All pin pricking a sacrosanct experience in pursuit of kicks, adventure and happiness—the kind that could not be had anywhere else.

Sometimes, when he let his guard down, the distressful aspects of India aggravated Doc, causing him to break out in a hot-under-the-collar rash. He did carry prickly heat powder, which he always scored going through Bangkok. A Thai rub 'n' tug had turned him on to it after having had it sprinkled on his nut sack, delivering a prickly heat chilly rush for a happy ending. Though, he was less prone to a rash in Mapusa, as it was not as extreme as *real India*. Mapusa was more well off, thanks to foreigners. After all, Goa was once the *Rome of Asia* with noble ruling class—hub port of the spice trade, heavily defended by Portuguese forts with cannons.

Walking along a grimy back street behind the police station to the corner of the main street, Doc passed the ruin of a Portuguese colonial mansion that was overgrown with weeds, its Roman Tuscan columns covered with a grassy skin, propped up by rotted ceiling joists. It's once grand structure, the residence of mercantile Portuguese overlords. He pondered the post Colonial masala mix of what had come to pass. The Catholic constabulary of Panjim. The black market. The maligned banking system. The share market. All that nourished his accounts. The choices wealth bestows, and its moral hazards. The water money of his family's business investments and offshore tax havens. The grief inherent in the pursuit of wealth and the curse and toll of gambling. It occurred to him that to make a party now in Goa, he too was a gambler. That the party scene—which he held dear to his heart, and represented freedom—had become a hot potato with a price on its lotus eating head.

At the corner, where his glistening silver chopper was parked, there lay a barely clothed beggar sprawled upon the dirty pavement with gaping sores. There would be no scraping this wretched soul off the infected loathsomeness of his lot on main street Mapusa. The beggar half opened one eye, and Doc dropped a twenty rupee note into the beggar's bowl. Then straddled the sun-baked seat of his chopper and savoured the softened sting of its heat through the crutch of his leggings. Tilting the heavy metal steed upright, he flicked the stand back and kicked over its fat cylinder. The grunting motor throbbed up his groin to his rib cage, chest and through his arms to the throttle. Just before he fed it with juice, he reassured himself, considered certainties: *Shiva's spice would continue to flow. Goa cops love hippies because they'd figured out how to get them to pay for what they used to have for free.*

BLACK BULLETS. VINYL FETISH. MIXTAPES.

After midnight, the night after the Jungle Palace party, Jaeger was at Zikos's house sitting around a candle breaking down a kilo slab of charas into black bullet-size pieces and binding them with cling wrap which he sealed in the flame of the candle. He'd already packed up his house and stored his stereo system in a locked chest with his Goa family for safe keeping until his return in November.

Quality smoke, music, and the finery of wearable things is what rocked Jaeger's world. His father had been a watch maker in Basel, the home of the LSD chemist Albert Hoffman. After dropping out of University on his return from his first trip to India, in nineteen eighty-one, he not only became obsessed about collecting Goa music, but also commenced collecting precious stones and miniatures of Asian gods. It was then that he embraced a talent for jewellery design, and set about producing it in Kathmandu, and selling it at the Anjuna flea market and Europe in summer. Not only was the jewellery well crafted, but also vested with talismanic charms derived from his knowledge of gemstones sourced in Rajastan, as well as sacred geometry which he identified in the harmonics of the synthesiser music he was collecting.

Jewellery design, and his addiction to music, was underwritten by boom shankar spice trade. This was achieved by concealing it inside laminated beach rackets and other items manufactured and shipped out of India. Returning to Europe in spring, through Amsterdam, he carried personal, crème de la crème charas from Kulu Valley, Himachal Pradesh, some of which he'd rubbed himself. This stash, he would normally meticulously imbed into the lining of his suitcase. But after the Bombay Airport incident and rising concern about the growing use of X-Ray machines by customs, many contemplating export runs got the jitters. Plus, someone had just been popped in Paris at the Charles De Gaulle airport.

Having premium grade smoke from the mountains of India, and the kudos of supplying it to friends, was paramount. On his many visits to Amsterdam (a boom shankar oasis in Europe), he enjoyed the Goa head camaraderie of chillum circles in Vondelpark, all the while networking black market connections. Besides moving smoke, he'd sell his jewellery at summer markets and constantly forage record shops for *special Goa music*.

Who is making this music? It was the same kind of question newcomers to Goa would ask. *Who are making these parties?* Goa parties were always free. Put on in the spirit of—*gifting*. Like an illicit new silk road, boom shankar spice trade funded the scoring of psy-disco-electro-house-*tekno*, in service to Shiva-Shakti shaking under the stars, in the jungle and on the beach. The emerging technology in the music was telling Jaeger that something revolutionary was happening—not just unheard of sounds, but something mysterious like a codified belief system, like a truth inside the music.

Record cover and label art seduced him, as much as his auditory nerve hearing the sounds through AKG headphones, whilst appraising tracks for functionality in Goa. Like fetish objects, the smell of freshly pressed new vinyl in bins of record shops turned him on. It was as gratifying to touch and smell as soft charas. He adored its shiny blackness, the patterns of the grooves and mastering engineer's signature; and especially thrilled over clear and colour pressings.

The staff at his favourite shop—Music Man in Ghent, Belgium—got hip to his taste for instrumental dub versions of club cuts, and would keep records aside for him, bestowing upon him the esteem of knowledgeable respect, befitting a big-spending obsessive, compulsive DJ collector that doggedly hunted down must-have tracks. And then he'd attend warehouse raves where some names on his tapes (Psychic Warriors of Gaia, The Young Gods, The Shamen, Greater Than One) would make appearances doing live fiddling on new-fangled synth gizmoes. At a warehouse squat rave, it occurred to him that when the music was played off of his tapes in Goa, it was transplanted into a tropical ultra-world, where it took on another life. Its sound sorcery, a data flux for a recontexturalised *psyche-out* dance floor, inhabited by a frequency fraternity finding transpersonal fellowship within it, camped out on the edge of Asia.

Upon returning to his Bern apartment from Amsterdam, in a Mercedes station wagon with secret stash compartments, he'd slide the vinyl out of its sleeves and place it on the slip mats of Technics SL-1200 turntables and watch it spin. Then light up a joint and drop the needle on the virginal record and enjoy every particle of sound that his Ortofon cartridge delivered to his Bang & Olufsen speakers. Later, he'd make mixes, recording them onto cassettes, which he would later dub, tape to tape, and give out to his music mafia connections. But first, he'd make master tapes of his bounty of tracks, including all versions, especially non-vocal instrumental mixes.

When the chilly northern hemisphere air arrived in October, like a homing pigeon, he'd take flight to roost back home in the tropics and a budding Goa season. His metal and chrome cassette tapes would be snug in protective leather six pack bags, custom made by Zsu, with secret stitch-witch stash pocket lining in case of police encounters at home, or on the road. Larger kilo-quantities of product were discreetly buried in the compound of his house.

It wouldn't be until he shared his new collection with Voltaire in the boom shankar ozone of Goa and road tested it in the psychotropic stomp of a full-tilt party, that the true gems of *Goa gold* would be revealed and its capacity to fire-up a dance floor. High on hash, the music transported Jaeger beyond the perimeters of his mainframe. The sensual pleasure of high tech synthesis in the rawness of a lush rural landscape, with cows and oxen and monkeys and goats and dogs and chooks and snakes and large ants, under the vivid twinkle of the mystique of a time immemorial metaverse.

Once danced to, in a party, the music became a deviant catalyser. The matrix of a world beat language that transcended mother tongues within which a cosmic-ensouled luminosity was experienced. A shared euphoria, like heavenly food of the gods. Music—like a lover, which never let Jaeger down, unlike the hazards of romance, riddled with entangled emotions.

The new language of the spacey, futuristic music—when made into a mix—became an entrancing meta-narrative for a neo tribe to vision quest upon. The music metabolically massaging muscle and cerebellum, like that of a commingling flow-motion emulsifying agent. The gathering of a party, not just a chemical heaven, but serving as a container of a loved-up-ness which he wished could be aerosol-sprayed around the world. Tape swopping with an inner circle of DJs and collectors, this season, had reaped Jaeger a bumper load of ten TDK chrome cassettes, most of which he earmarked as *special Goa music,* which he did not have on vinyl and was a world-beat melting pot fusion of genres: i.e.—Electronic Body Music, Chicago House, Detroit Acid, Italo Disco, Belgium New Beat, Afro Beats, Latino, New Wave, Electro, Techno, and even Hip Hop (Eric B. & Rakim 'Paid in Full' Coldcut Remix). These he carried in two of Zsu's special leather bags as cabin luggage.

The night prior to his and Zikos's flights to Amsterdam, they sat together in a Colaba hotel room of Bombay partaking in their last Indian supper for the season. Piece by piece, they swallowed the charas bullets they'd prepared. With eight hundred grams down, Jaeger's stomach protested and vomited bullets back up, which required him to re-swallow with dollops of lubricating curd to get all of his kilo payload down.

Down Under

MORE THAN ANY ENTHEOGEN or lab substance, the vicissitudes of the heart had gotten Jules in a tail spin on the roller coaster rhapsodies of Goa. Group Eros ignited him on the dance floor and Zsu bedazzlement had him hooked in a skein of bewildering infatuation. At the end of their time together, his impressions were in need of rearrangement so he could stay hectically in love with her. It wasn't until he was on the ferry sailing to Bombay up the coast past Vagator Beach that he was sure that she hadn't been a mirage.

"You can't lose your heart on the dance floor," he heard her voice in his head say when his plane lifted off from Bombay. When it reached a cruising altitude, he released his seatbelt and gaped out of the window at cloud forms, in which, to his amazement, appeared Michelangelo's La Pieta. He'd seen a reproduction of it inside St Anthony's Chapel one Sunday morning in Anjuna. It spoke to him like the wound of love. *The Catholic heaven.*

Before he jumped into the taxi to catch the ferry, Zsu slung an arm around his neck and pressed her hips into his and said, "What we shared was precious." This was followed by lingering bye, bye, kisses and an invitation to visit her in Bali. Now sinking into his seat on the plane, he put on his Walkman headphones and listened to a mixtape she'd made for him titled, GODS & GODDESSES. He wondered about the versions of herself she played out in Goa, and weighed up which version he might fit into.

She loved 'Liquefaction,' The Telepathics track on the tape he'd given her. It was remarkable how she did, indeed, experience a liquescence through him. A melting that she'd not known before, telling him how he'd turned her inside out, her heart strings having been struck in new ways. Jules heart had soared high like helium. It did get scratched on thistly branches. It did pick itself up from the red dust contained in an ancient timeless vase. It did pursue a magnolia artifice of enchanting confections, frosted with Venus flytrap icing on a vanity cake of longing. Beneath the beguiling, haute-hippie plumage of her glamazon fashion, he gained entry into alluring complexities where there was rapture, laughter and tears.

Six months ago, he'd not known Zsu and *Tribes of The Moon.* He'd not adventured solo-traveller through seething Asian streets with holy smoke rituals. He'd not danced ten hours straight in intergalactic palms to futuristic music that had Shiva as its deity. He'd not known the kind of freedom possible as a nomad on the Asia trail. It was both liberating and unravelling the way it now rendered just about everything obsolete about his previous life of art-punk squatocracy in the wastelands of Pyrmont Pier.

Returning Down Under, he'd stopped over in Bangkok, spending a couple of nights in Khao San Road where all the travellers sat around watching Hollywood videos, which struck him as mind-numbing, compared to journeying with the *Indo tribe* in Goa. Prior to boarding his flight, he poked a tola of charas up his jacksie. Stepping out of Sydney Airport, the sun was harsh, the taxi driver brash, the radio whinging with talkback. His Ray-Bans were inadequate in mollifying the oblique coldness of the mirror-glass CBD towers that loomed up to the sky in a shrunken reality. He no longer identified as an urban reptile. He'd become an extraterrestrial butterfly.

A large cockroach flying through the curry-spiced air of Jules's kitchen at Pyrmont squat collided with a slap from a New Musical Express magazine that Zane Lovelock swung at it. The dark, shiny, rotund insect hit the floor and spun on its back with all legs thrashing in the air. A Dr Marten jackboot at the end of black stove pipe jeans slammed down on it, turning the roach into insectoid mash. A cassette titled, STELLAR FLUX—Goa '87, which Jules had copied from Danilo, was playing through the stereo. Zane, the guitarist in Jules's band, The Telepathics, rotated his ears like a fox terrier hearing new sounds for the first time, but his tail was not wagging. Hailing from Manchester, England, he had bleached-blond chainsaw-chopped hair, a spiky choker around his neck and sported a black T-shirt blazoned with a red 'A' anarchy symbol.

"Sounds like these parties are fair dinkum sh-sh-shenanigans," Zane said with his mouth suddenly catching on fire. "Sh-sh-shit matey this curry ain't half bloody ho-ho-hot. Jeez me fu-fu-fucken lips are burning." Desperately he grabbed a bottle of Coopers Ale and took a swig.

"Sorry for the chilli overdose," Jules said looking up from his plate of steaming curry and rice that he was fingering into his mouth with his right hand, which was the custom of India. "I need my spice fix. It puts me right back in masala madness. The food, like everything in India, is pungent. It gives you a kick."

Zane poked at the inhospitable curry with his fork to see if he might find a piece of it that would not sting his mouth. "Sounds like you stepped into another world mate. Shed the shitdippery of this one." He then dropped the fork. "I'll have to conk on the curry," he gasped with stinging lips and desperately gulped his beer.

"Sorry!" Jules said. "Let me fix you some baked beans." He got up and rummaged in the dank kitchen looking for a can opener while Zane thumbed through Jules's Instamatic snaps of Goa and said, "Blimey!..the fashion ain't half blinding, innit?"

"Goa is anti-fashion, mate," Jules explained. "It's whacked out. I sneaked some party pics. Cameras are taboo. Privacy is respected. Shanti babba party freaks turn into snarling monster trolls if they catch you taking photos. There's clandestine characters galore. On the whole, it's pretty friendly. The authorities are bent as fuck. It's India, the place thrives on corrupt skulduggery. Everything is crooked, there ain't no straight edges in sight. The ultimate contraband is gold. Drives Indians crazy. That, and imported electronics, which freaks have heaps of. And of course, the freaks live in a thriving black economy moving hash, which trickles down into the local economy."

Zane's eyes lit up. "Fucking brilliant!.. So, you found sex, drugs and nefarious tunes in Asia?"

"You betcha!.. And it ain't rock 'n' roll—"

"What? So, it's disco?"

"A mix-up. Plenty dosages of *Cyber Punk*— all kinds of electronic flavours.

"Oh!— like what's on these tapes you've had on high rotation in the stereo since you got back?"

"Yup, I can't get enough of it. You won't hear this music on the radio. You won't find this music at local records shop," he boasted like he'd returned from a new frontier. "That NME mag of yours has no idea about this music or these parties. They call it, "faceless techno bollocks.""

Jules's felt like he'd returned from a voyage of discovery where new species of lifeforms had been encountered, back when the world had been proven not to be flat. Like he'd returned from a place which was much more colourful than anywhere he'd previously known, and where the milky way above had beamed him up, and where moon magic reigned over a neo tribe, who gathered from all over the world to dance to futuristic music in the most unlikely of places."

"So, it's tapes?" Zane said, as he opened a pouch of Champion Ruby tobacco and fingered for Tally Ho papers.

"Ain't no records. Too dusty. Its cassette DJs in the jungle. It's bootlegging, pirating to the max. It's a musical virus spread by travellers… there ain't no antidote," Jules said laughing. "*Gonzo Goa* is its own gospel, with its own sonic sermons and rhythm hymns," he mock preached. "It ain't no night club. It ain't bands on a stage. The word, *band*, is scoffed at. It's not entertainment. Goa tape jocks are modest, they play cassettes on Walkmans in palm huts out of sight. It's all about dancing and crazy fun. Tracks are copied tape to tape by a music mafia of travellers. It's underground—um, well… actually no it's not. It's overground in wild nature, under the stars and sunrise. It's a radical buzz and it's coming from the darkest mysteries of voodoo technology and propagating on moonlit beaches and ruins where I danced my head off with loonies in black light goin' ape shit all around me. I swear the ancients were talking to me through a chorus of angels and devils and extraterrestrials and phantoms. I was at the wildest edge, man… *Gonzo Goa* shouldn't exist, but it does. And now it's changed everything."

With hang dog eyes, Zane licked his rollie, looked up and shot Jules a sideways glance up and down. "Matey, you sure look different. You look like a paint bomb that's been thrown at a circus." Jules was dressed in vibrant dayglow colours and zany patterns.

"How's your wrist?" Jules asked. "Judging by how you swung at that cockroach its mended good—"

"After the plaster came off," Zane said, "I got meddling with me pedals and squealin' the axe again. You know, same old, same old, keepin' the rat mangle sodomy of life at bay, least I fall prey to some new form of headache." He sighed, and lit the rollie.

"Here!" Jules said, "this will make you feel better." He tossed Zane a piece of charas. "Stitch up a fair dinkum spliff."

Zane Lovelock, the son of a hard-drinking factory unionist from grim-up-North, England, had the disaffected demeanour of a man who'd seen trouble, and at risk to a firebrand chip on his shoulder. He'd gotten aggravated at The Telepathic's last gig, six months ago at The Brickworks—a venue in Newtown, Sydney—whilst supporting industrial artists, SPK and Severed Heads. The gig had commenced with the band breaking out of statuesque poses in fog strobe light to the sound of swarming insects as Jules delivered the bittersweet vocal of 'Liquafaction' on top of Zane's slash guitar and tape loops. Projected behind them was a mash up of Super 8 footage and cibachrome slideshow that included images of cyclops, reptiles, porn and collapsing buildings.

Severed Heads followed with whimsical synth ditties that galvanised the fringe crowd. Jules and The Telepathic's drummer, Ronnie, were drinking beers by the mixing desk while Zane snorted speed back stage when SPK commenced their outlandish, pyrotechnical performance—which they proclaimed to be, "Inorganic Unconsciousness." The atmosphere in The Brickworks became like flaming coils of hot copper wire as SPK unleashed an incendiary performance, that included whirling chains and spark-spitting metal grinder, against a seething backdrop of vehement imagery, including abattoir scenes, all drenched in scorching sounds.

The onslaught of sensory overload spewed over when a skinhead boot boy rushed the stage, which immediately got Zane seeing red and racing to the band's defence, where he got smacked with a fist and thrown off stage onto the stone floor. Other skins joined in, scuffling with roadies and punters. SPK stopped. The house lights came on and so did a deafening, disorientating fire alarm. Like jump-up baboons, the skinheads bailed. Jules rushed to check on Zane who was recoiling in pain screaming at the top of his voice. "FUCKEN CUNTS!"

"Are you OK?" Jules said anxiously.

"Nahh!" he screeched, "My hand's numb...its painful."

Jules glared at the arm that Zane had fallen on after being tossed off stage by the skin. "It doesn't look good. Let's get you to A and E."

An X-ray revealed a fractured wrist. All music making ceased. So, Jules headed north to Mullumbimby where he ran into a girl who told him, "I found myself in India." He'd already had a fascination in Vedic astrology and learned that he had Neptune in his astrocartography chart running straight through the subcontinent. The following week, he booked a flight to India via Bali.

Returning to the Sydney squat scene after Asia, it now felt like the husk of a chrysalis out of which he'd been transformed by travel into a new species of bright coloured butterfly—no longer an urban reptile. Acrid whiffs from a nearby brewery and a meat processing plant, battled with the musk incense he burned at his Pyrmont dockland pad. Pinned-up post cards of Indian gods and poster of Shiva, affirmed the mystical connection with the boom shankar *techno tribe* he'd met in Goa. Crimson coloured, mirrored fabrics from Rajastan now hung from the ceiling of his living space which he blasted non-stop with the spacey sounds on his Goa mixtapes. He gyrated in fluoro spandex and asana-stretched postures to it, which he'd picked up from Ananta's beginner classes on a flat terrace above Disco Valley. No one at the squat had heard this new weird computer music before. No one had heard of the word, *yoga,* before.

"What is it?" Ronnie, The Telepathic's drummer, dared to ask.

"It's getting high on prana," Jules explained.

"What's that?"

"Life force in the chakras."

"What are they?"

"Spiritual centres, like tuning meridians in the body, like tweaking circuits in the brain. It's asana flow-motion synchronised to heart beats per minute. It ain't aerobics, it sure ain't Jane Fonda on acid. It's a whole other thing. Techno and yoga are the metaphysics of cybernetics. It's postmodern, man! It's cut-up tribal trance, revisioned through technology."

Ronnie's jaw dropped. He nodded his head as he attempted to imagine the kind of party that the music on the Goa tapes was a sound track for.

"It's like a Fellini movie," Jules explained. "Except there's no director, cameraman, actors—just extras, who are frolicking in their own personal drama, within the grand drama of a wild party that has themed music—which functions as sound tracks, rich with multiple plots. It's the best fun I've ever had in my entire life. It just feels like the wave of the future…" He ranted like an anthropological beat professor. "We gotta tool up Ronnie. We gotta get busy with this musical science. We gotta make mind expanding dance music…"

Previously, The Telepathics had recorded their songs on a Teac A-3440 four track, reel to reel, in a dilapidated cooler shed that they'd named, The Lab—which was next to a reclaimed industrial space that screen print artists, Fetus Productions, also used.

Inspired by Jules's Goa tapes, Ronnie—the most cashed-up of The Telepathics—immediately saw the light, and went out and bought a Roland TR-909 drum machine and an Atari computer. And by chance, a revolutionary recording instrument—a Fairlight sampler, invented locally and ridiculously expensive—they were able to have use of.

Inside the Telepathics' newly equipped studio—now renamed, The Spice Lab—Jules installed a Nataraja he'd spray painted silver, around which he clustered crystals, the same as he'd seen at Zsu's house, and pinned a sarong with sacred geometry Sri Yantra on the wall behind Yamaha studio monitor speakers. In The Spice Lab, the Telepathics gathered around the black and white screen of the Atari computer, like it was a sci-fi portal, where sound and beats got composed on a grid timeline. It required a learning curve of understanding menus and endless mouse fiddling and frustrating crashes from buggy Cubase crack software, which required constant data backups on floppy disks. Reading manuals for midi was like a course in rocket science.

Zane's axe—his beaten-up black Fender Stratocaster guitar—represented revolt. It was the thunder of his punk days. His guitar travelled Down Under with him from Manchester when, like an outcast exile, he escaped the misery of the Iron Lady—Maggie Thatcher. He wondered what it must have been like to be sentenced on a long voyage on a convict ship Down Under to Van Dieman's Land (Tasmania) just like one of his Irish ancestors in 1860. It may well have been him, he thought, banished for inciting seditious behaviour by the swinging of his axe in Old Blighty.

Music brought shelter from the shit storms of life, it turned his crank. Music represented a revolt against ill-fitting, conventional reality. Music ameliorated splintered interior selves. Playing guitar in squatsville Sydney relieved an enflamed nerve, squeezed and compressed in cubic corporate structures standing on crushed Victorian bricks and mortar, built with criminal labour. There was a piezoelectric charge to Zane and Jules's relationship: Zane, the astringent, acerbic, transducer. Jules, the crystal radio Pollyanna. If it were a sexual relationship, they would be the couple that would fight, and then fuck, with Zane having the characteristics of a peculiar Australian beetle that could only get it on in the cinders after a rampaging bushfire.

Piquancy in The Spice Lab sharpened when Jules proclaimed, "Guitars are old school! The wave of the future is synths and samplers." On hearing this, the levels on the master channel of Zane's limbic brain clipped into the red, with him becoming all shirty and unloading a volley of splenetic cussing. Jules acquiesced with a compromise, but Zane stormed out of The Spice Lab to the palliative care of his girlfriend.

The next day, Jules visited the Newtown tenement digs of belladonna, Evangeline, Zane's "night nurse" girlfriend, who worked as a S & M dominatrix. Jules knocked. There was no response.

"Evangeline! Are you there?" No reply.

"Zane!" No reply.

Jules tried the handle. The door opened. "Evangeline!" he hollered as he stepped inside and walked down the hallway past the lounge. In the bedroom, he found two bodies at odd angles and needle paraphernalia. Alarm bells rang loud in his head. He yelled, "EVANGELINE!.. ZANE!…" There was slight movement. He rushed to the bed. "Are you OK?"

Zane half opened one eye. "ZANE!…ZANE!…" Jules desperately said, pulling back his mate's eye lids to reveal pinpointed pupils on a face that was torpid. But thankfully, he was breathing. Jules turned to Evangeline, she looked blueish. He touched her face, it was cold, he held her wrist feeling for a pulse. There was none. He shuddered with mortal fear and desperately massaged her chest and attempted mouth to mouth. Then panicked. "Oh, fuck!" He dashed to the bathroom and turned on the cold water tap. Picking up Evangeline's limp body, he carried her to the bath and lowered her into it. There was no response. "Oh, my God!... fucking hell!"

A week later, on a grey wet day in May, Zane teary-eyed, unplugged, strummed a requiem song at Evangeline's funeral. Dead autumn leaves were being whipped from the branches of plane trees by a cold biting wind that wailed mournfully. The days that followed were a black dog downer. Taking Zane with him, Jules headed north on the Pacific Highway in a Holden Sandman panel van to Byron Bay. Ronnie stayed on at The Spice Lab to get his head around midi controllers.

At the most eastern tip, Down Under, just south of the red neck border of Queensland, Byron Bay was a remote, unspoiled sweep of Pacific blue paradise. Like a lush green bubble, its rainforest microclimate was a haven for hippies, surfers, sanyassins, travellers, healers and dealers. Once a sacred place for Aborigines, who only visited to give birth, it had been a magical place for Jules in the past. When he was a teenager he'd attended Nimbin Aquarius Festival, which was the Down Under, *Summer of Love*. Later in the seventies, he'd had an inner journey spurred by a reading from San Francisco astrologer, Celeste Star.

Out front of Byron Beach under an awning extended from her parked-up VW Combi, she'd applied her mystical art to Jules's horoscope, which she'd hand drawn with a fountain pen. On the day of the reading, mutant-looking bush turkeys pecked at fish and chips scraps while the fins of a pod of dolphins could be seen in clear blue waves.

Dressed in a rainbow-coloured gingham dress, with long black hair, Celeste Star sat at a table draped in purple velvet with an amethyst orb placed next to Jules's horoscope. Referring to an almanac ephemeris, she indicated significant dates and said there would be "*a second Summer of Love,*" and that this would be the time when there would be "a confluence of your kind of people." Jules recorded Celeste Star's reading on cassette, in which she talked about Uranus and Neptune joining up at the end of the eighties that would bring another revolution and pointed out that Neptune was at the top of his chart. Enchanted by planet symbols, he bought books on astrology and discovered that Neptune ruled art, music, spirituality, religion, mysticism, healing, the ocean, the unconscious—and alternated states. Listening to Celeste's insightful voice, over and over on tape he heard: "Transits are cycles of becoming…you have free will… planet patterns indicate karma and transformation… a horoscope is a cosmic blueprint… astrology is the psychology of astronomy… symbols are mythical archetypes, imagine them as sub-personalities incarnate…" He then took to exploring past lives with a hypnotherapist.

When The Telepathics reunited back in The Spice Lab, Ronnie and Jules presented Zane with a band aid, in the form of a midi guitar. The band threw themselves into a whole new process of music making, huddled around the flickering screen of the Atari—which became like a cyber womb with umbilical cabling. Ronnie did the mouse work, while Zane and Jules played in riffs on midi guitar and keyboard. The first track they called, 'Karma Drama.' It was soon followed by 'Goa Goat Head,' based on what Jules had experienced on Anjuna Beach at his first party.

Jules and Zsu talked once on the phone. In Bali, she produced a new *Tribes of the Moon* collection and continued training with a shaman. He nearly flew up to Bali after Evangeline's funeral, but was cash-strapped having bought gear for the The Spice Lab. Like fading kisses, romance was feeling as though it was tortuously being crushed by time and distance apart, and the over-riding passion for creative priorities. With his eyes on the flickering Atari screen, Jules was afraid not to have his head in the music, least he suffer thinking about her.

After returning to Sydney from Byron Bay with the panel van full with Mullumbimby bud, Jules converted the stash into cash to buy, not only a Mackie mixing desk, but also a Dr Who looking EMS 'Synthi'-siser that emitted wiggly, eerie sounds and looked like an old telephone operator patch board with leads and sockets. Zane was off powder and managing to modulate brain chemistry with weed, tipples of ginger wine, and getting lost in a whole new world of sounds with his techno axe. But one band night, he showed up glowering. Most likely on crystal meth, Jules suspected. Zane set about badgering the band to join in a solidarity demo to protest the eviction of a Redfern squat. "We gotta mobilise! Make some bleeding noise!" he fumed. "Developers have brought in the cops. We could be next."

Jules sympathised. "It sucks them gettin' the shove, but bashing it out with cops is not necessarily the way to go. Diplomacy is smarter. Consider Gandhi's approach. Better to get the media involved."

"Nah!" Zane steamed. "Passive resistance won't cut it. The Council pumps out propaganda saying we are filth. It's information war. Don't watch TV. Forget mainstream media. We're self-sufficient cooperatives with gardens. For fuck's sake!.. we gotta stand up to ruthless corporations and property greed."

"There's squatter rights," Jules said in a calm voice.

"It don't amount to nout," Zane ranted, his eyes bulging out of a contorted face. "It's nobby cronyism. Ya gotta confront 'em if you want to change society."

Neither of the other Telepathics joined Zane in Redfern for the show down with cops, where he nearly got arrested. By November, they'd finished four tracks, in which Zane ardently contributed break-through musical hooks with his techno axe. Its creative utility enabling him to rise above the snags of sticky mind-sets he was prone to. Jules figured that India would stretch the canvas of Zane's inner, and outer world view, and that they should meet up in Goa. Jules had set aside bucks, but Zane struggled to be flush. Miraculously, a timely windfall occurred by way of a theatre company licensing some of his songs and paying him an advance.

In Ya Face

EYEBALLS STRETCHED OUT OF HIS HEAD looking down on an ancient new world through golden light. Ornate multi-tiered pyramid-shaped Hindu temples rose up out of palm trees, behind them a serrated high-rise sky line. Approaching touch down, he could make out oxen carts on roads. Exiting the Boeing, Zane felt the heat of the subcontinent hug him. A bearded customs officer with a turban asked him whether he'd anything to declare.

"Nah."

The officer pointed at the Walkman strapped across Zane's chest. It was itemised in hand writing in his passport. A large stamp—*Indian Bureau of Immigration Bombay 07 Feb 1988 single entry*—was slammed down on his visa, which took up a whole page. The arrivals gate spewed him into a swarming whirlpool of brown and black bodies in spiritual garb: Hindu, Muslim, Christian, Buddhist, Animist, Jain—wearing skull caps, white gowns, robes, holy beads, arms crammed with bright coloured bracelets, shimmering bejewelled, colourful saris, veils, dhotis, longhis and neat business slacks.

This must be the land of God, he thought. The Sisters of Mercy T-shirt he was wearing stuck to his skin under his backpack in the clammy air. As taxi drivers scrummed about him, he dug for his money belt buried in his pubis and pulled from it a hotel card Jules had given him. Thrusting it in their faces and bellowing loudly like an auctioneer, he asked, "How much to go there?" A haggling din of competing voices bombarded him. Then the voices frenzied upon other tourists like sprats feeding frantically on dissolving bread. Settling on a price to Colaba became high pitched drama that spiked his adrenals. The drive through the smoggy, humid air of bustling streets thick with traffic churning bicycles, rickshaws, buses, scooters, people and cows took him through a sprawling, shabby, patchwork of decrepit slums reeking with squalor. All rippling with daily existence.

Stepping out of the taxi, he was hit by a steamy olfactory that attacked his nasal passages with spices, incense, low grade petrol fumes and cow shit. On the dirty footpath, he was surrounded by a street huddle of marauding touts. "Chill the fuck out!" he snapped, clutching his backpack as he pushed through them B-lining to the entrance of a building with hotels on every floor to look for one called, 'Shanti Hotel.'

Arriving at a small foyer reception desk, after four flights of steps, he felt his sweaty jeans pasted to his legs. A smiling round face, with bristling black moustache, on top of a neat button-down white shirt behind the desk, greeted him. Discussion on the price abruptly halted with, "Fixed room rates only Sir." Which came as a relief, as he was too frazzled to haggle. After inspecting the room and signing the register, he lay down on a hard bed. A ceiling fan chopped the air above him, his body loosened, his mind unravelled. With a heavy sigh, he congratulated himself on having made it to India, his first trip to a third world country. His encounter with its most populated city left him reeling from it like a torrential onslaught. Everything about it rattled him. Yet, the thrill of culture shock and acclimatisation of being in a foreign country brought a new sense of freedom and autonomy from the shitdippery of the life he'd left behind. Jules had given him tips and told anecdotal tales, but nothing could prepare Zane for the heart-rendering hands-on initiation into India's sensory assault. It's open sewers of seething humanity stewing him in a vat of blistering first impressions.

After squat toilet and shower, he donned cargo shorts, singlet, flip-flops, and headed out into the human zoo of Bombay to eat and score. The streets clamoured and clanged with a hive of enterprise, Hindi voices, rickshaw horns, trebly Bollywood pop and sacred music. Everything imaginable was being sold in street stalls that cramped footpaths bustling with hustlers. He was like fly paper for hucksters and hawkers who all seemed to want to fix their opportunistic sights on him, sticking their tongues in his ears—"Hello mister, my friend…" to extract rupees.

Spicy aromas spilling from restaurants and street vendors inundated his sinuses through the thick sultry air. The writhing, toiling streets were flagrant and filthy and incessant with wheeling and dealing in which well-rubbed, creased, dog-eared rupees relentlessly changed hands. The atrocity parade of the ill, malformed and maimed on the street minced his heart. The insufferable, sickening sight of pleading beggars and cripples despairingly showcasing their deformities and hapless handicaps was like sharp shards of dirty glass being jabbed into his woozy stomach, causing him to buckle with distress and forced to look away. Compassion welled up, grief overwhelmed him, flooding him with discomforting pity behind a steely, street-savvy shield of instinctive defences—his vulnerable eyes hidden behind dark shades.

Distress sunk in, quickly turning to boiling anger and disgust at how this society dealt with hardship and suffering, which made him desperately want to flee from the desolate sorrow seeping through him. If only he could find a comfortably numb place behind what his eyes were exposing him too. But he could not shut them, he was forced to look, there was no escape. Each poor suffering sod that invaded his skin with eyes pleading, hands extended, filled him with abject despair. What is the salvation of such misery in need? Should he simply rid himself of the disturbing anguish by dishing out rupees to every afflicted, plight, plying him?—*No!*

But the point blank, insurmountable sorrow he became filled with, strikingly confronted him in contrast to the life he'd been living in a squat in the first world. He was hit with a whole new view of himself. His personal struggles, now seemed minute and petty and insignificant. Yet another part of him—his most crusty, cynical self, suspected that this spectacle of beggars thrusting handicap and deformed afflictions at him, evidently devoid of social welfare—was being staged in the heart of the tourist district, Colaba—dare he say it? *To maximum Bollywood tear-jerking sympathetic effect for the eliciting of charity.* Should he feel guilty for thinking this? Should he feel OK about deflecting the uncomfortable feelings that were now sickening him?—*No!*

Yet there was a timelessness in this eyesore of seeming woeful wretchedness, with India living up to its eminence as the place where the aperture of God was as wide-angled and harrowing with depth of field as it possibly gets. The vivid visceral place where the transparent membrane of the mortal coil was in glaring display. The place of gaping extremes of wealth and poverty. The place of survival and fortitude and mettle. The place that tore at the fabric of his notions of egalitarianism. Then, like some kind of ideological compensation, he reminded himself that India was the world's most populated democracy, with Bombay, its New York, its Babylon zoo. A Rolls Royce passed as he stood on a stained curb of footpath. He walked bristly along the street, his mind whirling from the high-impact sensory bombardment of first impressions in a new country. The kind of exhilarating buzz that travellers live for, like drug fiends experiencing the first rush of a new substance in their blood, or the first argument in a budding new relationship, followed by intense love making that takes the connection into a deeper level of engagement, having gotten in touch with something hot and complex inside one's self through the external agency of another, or a place.

Exploring narrow lanes en route to Dipty's, a juice bar hang-out for travellers, Zane's dart board forehead was constantly pin pricked with, "Hello my friend, want something? Afghan hash, Kerala grass, brown sugar, coke. You want girl?" As soon as he glimpsed the street pushers, he felt himself getting sucked into iniquitous currents that excited the monkey on his back. All of a sudden, every vice was clawing at him to be scored in Bombay Babylon at a quarter of the price of street value in Sydney. Rookie traveller defences gripped him with cautionary foreboding as he weighed up the situation of scoring a packet in a very dodgy foreign back alley. But then was saved by the realisation he first needed to change money.

"Dollar change? Big note, good rate," came a pesky street hustle voice.

"Nah!—not now," he hastily replied, breaking eye contact and strode briskly ahead where he soon encountered more predatory street snipes, whom he struggled to shrug off, before reaching a main road where he asked for directions to Dipti's. Along the way, he took up the challenge of eating spicy local food. Gulping mouthfuls of mineral water to cool off his mouth, he managed to get a curry down. Wandering further, he found a sign: 'Dipti's House of Pure Drinks' and ordered a mango lassi and sat down at an outside table where French was being spoken and a long Rizla was filling the air with a familiar distinctive aroma. It was the same as the Himalayan hash that Jules had laid on him, which was now truly heralding his arrival in India.

A waiter delivered his lassi. A Frenchman, wearing a silk shirt patterned with Egyptian hieroglyphs, was seated next to him smoking the joint. Zane asked him where he could change money for the best rate. The Frenchman pointed to a fabric shop across the road and lent into Zane's ear and slyly whispered. "Travellers cheques best. You can double your money."

"I only got cash," Zane said.

The Frenchman explained the scam of selling cheques unsigned and reporting them stolen. He passed the fuming joint to Zane, who shot him a shrewd grin and said, "Shit, wish I'd known. Yeah, way to go…rip off American Express."

"I don't suppose," Zane chanced to ask, "do you know where I can score some smoke?" The Frenchman grinned and twisted his dark Dali-like moustache with a thumb and forefinger. "Oui, oui, maybe possible." He turned to chat in French with his friend, whom it turned out was a purveyor of Parvati charas and, after further chatting, was happy to oblige.

Cashed up with rupees and a tola of quality smoke in his pocket, Zane farewelled the French connection and sauntered back to Shanti Hotel stoned off his chops. Retina stabs of vivid colour hit him with every blink of an eye lid, as he passed through a masala of Asian street life that got him swerving and reeling. Historical buildings were oddly familiar, like a waking dream of his mother country. Along Bombay's teeming streets ran red double decker buses. He was in an off-the-wall U.K. simulacrum surrounded by the monumental, ornate grandeur of stately Victorian Raj architecture. Within this waking dream, an inner landscape of memory was triggered, transporting him back to his childhood in Manchester, his trade unionist, Marxist father, the struggles of the proletariat and sepia photographs of distant relatives his mother kept in an album.

Like his stick-in-the-mud punk mates, who'd ridiculed him for making "bloody techno," telling him, "that ain't real music," his ancestors had been luddites who'd protested the introduction of machinery in the textile industry. He recalled the appalling sights of rag-clad slum dwellers in the hovels he'd seen in the taxi from the airport. *No workers' rights? Exploitation of the poor? Capitalism amok? Class system? No!... No!... No!...* His mind boggled. *What are the riches of the poor? Faith? Freedom from the weight of material possessions. Ha!.. If there is a God, and bejeez there's lots of 'em here, what's the bleeding meaning of this hardship?*

Seizing upon the encounter with drug dealers and the temptation in the alley, he wrestled further with dangerous feelings clawing his mind as a propositioning voice inside his head badgered him. "C'mon!.. score some stronger gear, why don't ya?—C'mon!.." The bombardment of street life intensified and he broke out in a sweat. "No!.. No!.. No!.." another voice slapped him inside his head. He hastened his walking pace, attempting to take control of the tug of war going on inside of him and elude being mired in the Bombay street life he was being pelted with. Then found calmness on a clear clean piece of footpath, convincing himself that the French charas connection (which was delivering a peppy uplift) was all he needed for now.

Strolling further through raw, thronging streets, he was sledgehammered with arresting impressions of a very old world, and a confronting third world interlaced with grand colonial remnants that teased him like an odd time warp. Plus, the usage of funny Indish English in signage. Taking a different lane back to Shanti Hotel, his eyeballs got even more stretched further out of their sockets at the sight of large revolting rats scurrying into a small park in which there was a temple where people were offering puja and feeding the infestation of red-eyed rodents coconut. The mangy, grubby, grey creatures were in circle formations drinking curd out of large metal bowls. Navigating back to cosmopolitan Colaba he ogled at a bunch of young Indian women in tradition-defying tight blue jeans. Sidling up to them on the sidewalk to pass, he was mesmerised by their smouldering kohl-encased onyx-like eyes and tripped over a legless beggar on a trolley.

Having hit sensory overload—with jet lag dragging, and the high of the Parvati smoke now on the downward slope—it was a relief to get back to Shanti Hotel. After climbing the stairs and retreating to his room and turning on the fan, he crashed out. He woke at dusk with his skin raging on fire and the sound of techno pounding through the wall. His legs screamed, *ITCH!* He scratched with his nails, which further intensified the fury of the irritation. In a highly-agitated state, he inspected the sheet. *Bed bugs?* "Fucking hell!.." He dived under the shower. Half drying himself, he pulled on jocks and stormed out of his room with the infested sheets bunched in his hand and threw them at the bushy moustache behind reception, then proceeded to shoot off a stream of expletives. After the bedding and mattress were replaced, a caramel blonde wearing a concerned smile, appeared at his open door.

"Hey!... did you get bombed by mites?" she said in a sympathetic voice.

Zane looked up, his face anguished from inspecting the rash on his raging legs, which he still couldn't stop scratching, but needed to, least his nails draw blood. "Yeah!" he said. "These blighters did me bad. Jeez, this hotel is the pits, innit? My friend recommended it—"

"This place is cool for other reasons," she said in a Scandinavian accent. "Hey, let me get you something for your skin." She disappeared and returned with a tube of cream.

"Drop it back when you're finished," she said, "I'm right next door."

"Thanks... you're an angel." He then urgently applied the cream to his inflamed, skinny, white legs. Drum machine-driven electronic sounds poured through the thin wall. "Is that your music?" he asked. His pained face turning into a grin as the antihistamine cream brought relief from the torment of the itchiness, which had got him in a right hissy fit.

"Yes, it's my tape."

"Love to dance do ya?"

"Yeah!" the girl said, wiggling her hips. "Especially what's on my mix tapes."

Zane's head tilted, an ear tipped to the wall attempting to identify the music. "I know this...It's Goa music?"

Her glistening eyes widened. "It's a party tape from last season. Were you there?"

"No, but my mate was. I'm heading there to meet him."

"Really!—we're going there, too. Hi!—my name is Kirsten."

"Howdy. I'm Zane. Thanks for the rescue with this cream."

"You're welcome."

After the itchiness chilled, he got up and knocked on Kirsten's door. She opened it and invited him in. The room he stepped into was thick with charas and tobacco smoke and the percussive zaps and bleeps of techno, which pulsed out of a Panasonic ghetto blaster. Next to it, on a table, was a miniature brass effigy of Shiva with nag champa incense burning.

A Viking looking man in his early thirties sitting on the bed said, "Hello—I'm Agar." He had broad shoulders with thick wavy golden hair in a ponytail and was cleaning a chillum.

"Do you fancy a pipe?" Kirsten asked.

"Don't mind if I do," Zane said, tickled pink. "I just scored some smoke from the French connection at Dipti's. Do you know that place?"

"Sure—it's a regular hang out."

Zane learned that they were from Copenhagen. "I went there once," he said. "Christiania rocks! "

"Actually, we live there," Agar proudly said.

"No kidding? Your privileged," Zane said. "That's my kind of place. Free as!.."

"Smoke is no problem there," Kirsten said, prizing a cigarette out of a packet of Dunhill, toasting it lightly with a Bic lighter and licking its side to fillet out the tobacco into a small polished coconut mull bowl. "No hard stuff at Christiania, just smoke. We even have a rehab for junkies."

Zane scowled, screwed up his face and sighed, as the memory of the loss of Evangeline came flooding back.

"Are you OK?" Kirsten said, seeing him looking downcast.

"Hey thanks for asking. "It's just… um…I had a junky girlfriend. She pinned out on me. Fucken shot through… R—I—P."

"Oh no!" The Danes consoled him. "Sorry to hear that, man." Agar extended a hand to him with a chillum to start.

"I'm a virgin at this," Zane confessed, holding the pipe and attempting to lift his spirits. "I haven't sucked on one of these before," making out like it was a phallus. "I'm first time India, you know."

"Welcome mate," Agar said. "It's time to burst your cherry." Then showed him how to cup and hold the chillum with both hands whilst keeping the wet safi material firmly in position, which Agar had torn from a sarong.

"Shiva bolenath!" bellowed Agar, igniting two matches.

"This is for you, Angeline," Zane said holding the pipe upright, sucking in several short breaths, firing it up so that it glowed red hot, then took two deep breaths and passed the pipe to Agar, who touched it to his forehead before smoking.

A head rush of Dunhill and holy smoke, whammed Zane. A jet stream of Himilayan cannabinoids shot serotonin up into his crown chakra delivering a happification high, that came on like a coiled serpent rising up his spine and neck to his head. He saw gilded doors opening to a temple pantheon of gods. His head bubbled with visions, one was him wearing a Cobra headed hoodie like the cover of Hendrix's 'Axis Bold As Love.'

Kirsten passed him the chillum. Further lungfuls lifted the lid entirely off of his skullcap. Prismatic petals floated about the room. The textures and colours of every surface in it tessellated to the bleeps, beats and zaps pulsating out of the ghetto blaster. Zane's cranium detached and spun and bounced off the walls like a whirling frisbee drone untethered from its remote control. Closing his eyes, he felt as though he'd been abducted by the music under the influence of the holy smoke and arrived at an unchained, happy place. A state of mind that Jules had spoken of. *An OM-ness. A bonding in a circle. The ceremony of a cyber tribe of Shiva.*

"We export this!" came a booming voice in the room over the music. Zane opened his eyes.

"We're in the spice trade," Agar said with a devious smile.

"What?" Zane said startled, not sure he understood.

"You remember *Pusher Street*?" Kirsten said, jolting his memory. "The main drag of Christiania—"

"Yeah!.. Yeah!.." Zane said, getting her drift. "I remember it. All the world's best smoke laid out like produce at a farmers' market. Yeah!.. Yeah!.. I remember thinking at time when I was there, it was like a gourmet smorgasbord for stoners. Fucken oath!.. I remember *Pusher Street*. I did some wicked gear there."

"We sell there," Agar said candidly.

"That's tops!" Zane said, his face mashed in happification, stoked to have landed on his feet—and now well off his head again, courtesy of up-for-it kindred travellers.

"I'm happy to be out of the darkness of winter and into the colour and heat of India," Kirsten said, selecting a tape from a six-pack cassette bag she'd painted in fluoro colours. "I just wanna dance all night under palms." She removed the tape from its case and slotted it into the second deck of the Panasonic and pressed the play button. A driving disco track powered out the ghetto blaster with an enchanting melody through which soared ethereal, angelic voices. Zane twitched and jacked about the room, energised by the incessant fluidity of the astral-glide of its groove. Then an ascending, electric guitar riff of chords suddenly appeared, whisking the track higher, like the upswing of a Himalayan alpine chair lift. The music got him pumped. He felt a force burn inside of him. A feeling that he lived for, in which he experienced himself most alive.

"What's playing?" he asked, burning to know.

"Tantra!" Kirsten said, passing him a cassette case, which she'd decorated with glitter nail polish and reflective foil tape. Peering at the top of the 'A side,' he saw written in fluoro highlight pen, TANTRA The Hills of Katmandu (Patrick Cowley Megamix).

"This is the bee's knees innit?" he said, nodding his head in time to the beat.

"Trippy disco gets me off," Agar said.

"Sure ain't vanilla, handbag, night club shite," Zane quipped. "My mate came back from Goa with tapes. Had his lights turned on. Gave me the bug. Got me infected with this *go-a-head* dance music."

The Danes laughed. "This music puts me right back in the zone," Kirsten said. "Goa changed my life."

"I can believe it," Zane said, "and I ain't even been there yet. Music has saved my life."

He then told them about The Spice Lab and ducked back to his room to fetch a tape with the new Telepathics tracks. After returning and the 'Goa Goat Head' track bounding out of the ghetto blaster, the Dane's gaped into its speakers whilst a chillum of the French connection's Parvati did some rounds. They recoiled, spellbound by what they were hearing. Agar's mouth dropped. "Man!.. this shit is another level. Are you serious, or what? Wow!.. Totally out there!"

This buoyed Zane. 'Goa Goat Head' sounded completely different coming out of a ghetto blaster in a Bombay hotel room loaded on high altitude head gear than it did through the studio speakers in The Spice Lab. What was it going to be like on big speakers with a horde of loaded dancers in Goa? With a wry grin he said, "Doof-a-delic is what we call this flavour."

Agar looked at him perplexed. "Doof what?"

"It ain't rock 'n' roll," Zane said. "It's machine tweak. Fiddling with vectors. Noodling parameters. Its knobbing around to get some throb on. Get some thumpin' doof—doof—doof—doof—on. Like in, four-to-the-floor—you know, as in, kangaroo kick-drum."

The Danes stared at him dumbfounded. "Down Under we have this special sound," he said. "It's a kangaroo kick drum… got a constant thump that kicks you in the arse. And you better watch out," he jiggled his eyebrows humorously taking the piss. "Those feisty big red kangaroos will smack you about if you become a wallflower and stop dancing."

"That's crazy shit," Agar said, taking the bait.

"Down Under is a hilarious place," Zane explained. "Things are done different, especially music. It's upside down, complete opposite to you guys. I tell ya. It's total bi-polar. People walk around on their heads. You are polar north, we're polar south. In my case, it's mongrel Mancunian meets Mad Max." He stood up. "I was born antsy, the stupidity of society does my head in. Makes my skin crawl." Then, he felt the irritation on his legs, the rash demanding to be scratched. He resisted the urge and went to the window and fixed a gaze on the Gateway of India, a grand monument on the harbour. Then wheeled around abruptly. "Bombay is fucking bonkers. Jeez!..the sight of those beggars was doin' me melon no favours, the poor blighters, all that grief on the street—"

"It's in ya face," Agar said in a hard tone of voice. "Poverty is timeless. It requires a mental tool set, encountering it," his lip curling to reveal a canine-like incisor tooth, which got Zane hallucinating him as an arctic wolf.

"Bombay is a hub of trade and trafficking," Agar took pleasure in telling him whilst cleaning the chillum, which, to Zane's fascination, entailed pulling the pipe's barrel back and forth on a string wound round a chop stick.

"Indians are mercantile addicts," Agar said. "Indians and Chinese, they're the ants and cockroaches of commerce. Bombay is dog eat dog. You got your bums and beggars in the gutter. You got high-class upper castes in luxurious high rise apartments with swimming pools. You got a gangster underworld that laundry through Bollywood. Its fucking insane, but I love it. Indians speak English, thanks to your Raj ancestors. You can have fun with them. The big cities are overwhelming. You need a safe haven hotel from the mind fuck on the streets. A room where management won't do the dirty on you. This hotel is cool. Some places are in cahoots with the cops, they come knocking on your door looking for your stash so they can put you over a barrel to extract cash." Agar slotted the warm chillum into a snug fitting leather pouch and suggested a tour of Chor Bazaar.

"It's a hunters and collectors market," explained Kirsten buckling up a multi-pocket bum bag, like she was going into a combat zone. Zane got all jaunty at the prospect of another bout down on the dirty, squirming streets of Babylon Bombay, now that he was rested and supercharged— stoned out of his gourd, the likes of which his hammered brain had never known before. But now under the protective wing of a seasoned Viking guide who knew the ropes.

Slicing through densely populated street stalls of Chor Bazaar, the tall frame of Agar was like an icebreaker cutting through swaths of skinny, bustling, Bombayites peeling away in his wake, as Kirsten and Zane clung to his stern. "Yell out if you want to stop anywhere," he shouted over the trader din of the market hustle. They soon got jammed in a hive of shoppers with Agar commanding that they keep a hand on wallets. Wading through the sea of brown and black faces, they came to a treasure trove of vendors displaying colonial vintage items: gramophones, Brownie camera's, Corona typewriters, ship bells and camel saddles. In a side lane hung a hand-painted sign: 'The Spring Man.' Underneath which was a small shop, chock-full with a viscera of Victorian metal springs and suspension mechanisms. Out the front of it stood the diminutive Spring Man. He had a white beard to his chest and wore a fawn Nehru cap.

"Stop!.. stop!.. stop!.." Zane yelled, eyeing the spring man and the shop next door with signage saying, 'Old Is Gold: Film Sets, Decorators & Costumes.' He struck upon the idea, *Steampunk goes Bollywood Raj*, and requested a group photo with the Spring Man, which entailed Kirsten's assistance haggling with the, 'Old Is Gold,' shop owner to borrow safari pith helmets and bugle for a photo with the Spring Man in a dense tangle of suspension mechanisms. This concluded with Zane coughing up backsheesh and performing a theatrical bow. Kirsten suggested they visit Crawford Market. Along the way, they ducked into a South Indian restaurant.

"The ferry is the best way to go to Goa," she said dining on a Biryani dish. "I wouldn't recommend the bus or train. Victoria Terminus railway station is swarming chaos. The overnight bus is a hell trip. I once got groped, but I sure gave that sucker a kick in the balls. Tomorrow morning we're taking the ferry."

Back on the street, Zane saw Indian cops in olive green uniforms with bamboo batons walking hand-in-hand. Standing at the busy cross road in front of the Flemish architecture of Crawford Market, she informed Zane that it was designed by the father of the English novelist, Rudyard Kipling. Looking up at the strangely familiar Gothic building, he was transported in his imagination to imperial England, when India had been the crown jewel of the British Raj. He thought of his Irish convict ancestor banished to the fatal shore Down Under in Van Diemen's Land, incarcerated into forced labour. Some days, Zane felt like an inmate in his own skin. Full time employment was impossible. The rock 'n' roll dole a stop gap. The witnessing of abject poverty in Bombay, where there was no sign of a safety net, really did get him feeling like he ought to count his blessings and reframe his disposition to the things that got his strop on.

In the first isle of the sprawling Crawford Market, he encountered sari-wrapped women with rolls of exposed midriff grazing on a vivid field of Indian sweets laid out by vendors. Other stalls in the massive maze of the market displayed patch works of spangled, embroidered, fabrics, and caged puppies and birds. Quickly it all became too overwhelming, his nerves jangled.

"I've had enough!" he snarled.

"OK—let's chalo!" agreed Agar,

"Chalo?" Zane queried.

"Like in, split—fuck off!' Agar explained. "Chalo is a very handy word in India."

The next morning, they taxied together to Bombay Port to join jostling locals and fellow travellers queuing to buy tickets and board the Konkan Shakti for the twenty-four-hour trip to Goa. When the gangplank opened, it was a scramble to claim a spot on the upper and lower decks with a sarong bed sheet. Agar and Kirsten settled into a pre-booked cabin, while Zane found a spot to camp in deck class with crusty, Western, weirdo travellers—including Japanese. The camaraderie of it all, loosened the casing of his pasty skin.

After the Konkan Shakti sounded her foghorn and steamed out of the harbour, heading down the coast on the Arabian sea, Kirsten retrieved him and took him back to her and Agar's cabin where he met, Om Tom, a seasoned traveller in his fifties. Tom had sandy grey hair and a wizened face, wore a Keith Haring T-shirt that featured dancing figures being zapped by a flying saucer, and was gluing up a joint. He'd left Wales in the sixties to travel overland and was amongst the first wave of hippies at Colva beach. Later, in nineteen-seventy, he crossed Baga River to hang out on Hipster Harry's porch in South Anjuna. The sun-weathered lines carved into Tom's leathery face appeared to Zane like a historical landscape of life lived outdoors on the road. The joint, the first of many, got passed around and Tom poured nips of duty free Johnny Walker. Before long, Om Tom was on a roll recounting tales of the call of the East.

"It was nineteen sixty-eight, I was at Uni. Met this German chick, dropped out," Tom said with a smoker's wheeze. "We hitched out of London, via Amsterdam, to Istanbul, then onto Kabul. We heard a whisper, 'Goa for Christmas.' All we had was Bartholomew's map of India and travellers' tales. The Beatles had already been to Rishikesh. We took the boat from Karachi to Bombay. Ended up at Calangute Tourist Hostel, headed south to Colva Beach where we slept in a fishermen's hut and discovered a scene. Well—it was more like a family of travellers in one big house. Freaks with pet monkeys. Harry was there. There was no restaurant. He invited us to stay. Everyone was trippin'. Someone was flippin'—you know, usual story, took acid thought he was Jesus Christ. I'd never dropped. My girlfriend had, she helped the Jesus flippo. I freaked. Maybe I got jealous, I couldn't cope and gathered my blanket, chillum, map and rucksack. I just started walking, hitching out of Goa. I got as far as Kerala, was even sleeping in police stations. The cops would give you a room for the night, or you could stay at any Sikh temple or ashram. They'd never seen white people, let alone hippies—"

"Excuse me Tom," Zane interjected. "Weren't they subject to the Raj."

"No!.. No!.." Tom said. "The Raj only hobnobbed with high class Maharajas, not commoners." He coughed heavily and took a swig of whisky. "Where was I? Oh yeah, there I was, I'd hopped off a bus in a small Muslim village, must have been one of the few white people they'd seen, they were mortified. The locals gathered around me insisting that I get out of town. I felt like an oddity from another planet. When I got down to Sci Lanka there was an anti-hippie campaign. A black cloud hangs over that island. Then I went up the East Coast to Puri, Orissa, to the Jagga temple, it was there that I met, *The Brotherhood of Eternal Love*—Leary's boys from Laguna Beach. They had bags of tickets and said, 'Open your mouth brother.' Bingo!.. that was my first acid."

That night Zane and Tom returned to the deck of the Konka Shakti to kip down, but neither were sleepy. Zane was impressed with Tom's tales of his halcyon days on the road, and wanted to know more, so they leaned on the railing and flushed their lungs in the salty air.

"Hash used to be legal," Tom said. "It had been smoked freely in Nepal, India and Afghanistan. Opium and marijuana was sold openly in Hindu temples in India and much of Asia, it was widely cultivated for use in food, medicine and cloth."

Tom wore silver amulets inscribed with Sanskrit, which he assigned as accreditations to holy Hindu soma lore. "You could have an audience with the Nepal King to buy a dope dealing license off him. There were hash shops everywhere, my favourite was called, *Eden*. I watched the first man on the moon on TV at the American Embassy there. They had a party. The Warhol connection was there and spiked the punch with acid. Night time was wild in Kathmandu, it was controlled by packs of dogs, I couldn't get back to where I was staying. I ran out of dosh and ended up in hospital with hepatitis. My family rescued me with a ticket out. Back in London, someone sent me a kilo, I sold it, and by late nineteen sixty-nine I headed back to India. January, nineteen-seventy, I was in Kabul, then went to Colva beach looking for Harry, but the locals said he'd gone north to Anjuna. When I arrived to South Anjuna Beach for the first time, there he was living on a porch of ruins.

Later in seventy-three, Nixon declared *War on Drugs,*" Tom said, his voice pitched like a CNN anchor-man. "Yeap!.. that motherfucker sent Spiro Agnew to do foreign aid deals with India and Nepal with the mandate that hashish and marijuana be thrown in with heroin, all decreed illegal. That immediately turned us into criminals and created a huge black market. I resorted to packing Nepali fingers into false floors of VW vans returning to Europe. A big-time exporter friend got smart flying out rare Mastiff."

Zane looked puzzled. "Mastiff?"

"Tibetan dogs," Tom explained. "They were air freighted in wooden cages inside which was concealed 'Nepali black.' This was the same syndicate that was supplying Warhol's crowd in New York." These illicit tales enthralled Zane, and Tom enjoyed telling them, especially to a younger renegade, which he saw in Zane.

After a couple of hours sleep, with dawn revealing a seam of Goan coastline, Zane pulled himself up off the slumbering deck of the Konkan Shakti that was full with dozing bodies and luggage. Leaning on the port rail, he kick-started himself with sugary chai and a fag and squinted and could make out strips of sandy beach. An Italian couple standing next to him pointed out Arambol, and as the Konkan Shakti chugged south, continued with a running commentary: "Chapora Fort… Anjuna hill…the white sands of Baga, Calangute and Candolim," until the Konkan Shakti turned into Panjim harbour guarded by Fort Aguada.

Om Tom joined Zane. Gazing up at the stone sentinel of the fort converted into a prison, Tom told him it was where freaks, who weren't able to weasel themselves out of busts, languished. Some imagining in their darkest hours, whilst locked up within its stone walls, that they'd been ensnared in a psychic wormhole in which the meting out of penance was required to appease a post-colonial karmic debt for the abuses of missionaries. The fort had been built to keep out the Dutch East India Trading Company, although all manner of spice, gold booty, and contraband had been smuggled past it. As Panjim harbour opened its lush mouth of verdant palms, the Konkan Shakti slowed. Zane was struck by the idea that he, too, was just another pirate arriving from outside of life's shipping lanes. The rising intensity of the heat of the morning sun made his skin clammy, yet he felt a strange shiver run through his body, like an electric current down to his rubber flip flops. Perhaps it was Portuguese maritime ghosts, or the disembodied spirit of Donna Ferreira, the party girl mistress of the Viceroy, who'd been rolled off the cliff naked in a barrel to these very rocks below. Closer to shore, the sight of white wedding cake-like churches and ornate colonial European buildings, with Corinthian and Tuscan arches, gave him the impression that he was arriving at a Mediterranean port.

Disembarking onto a gangplank through which Indians pushed, Zane, Tom, Agar and Kirsten regrouped on Panjim wharf. The Danish couple piled into a yellow and black Ambassador taxi to deliver them to their rented house in Arpora. Zane and Tom took a taxi together to Anjuna, where Tom would be dropped, and Zane to Chapora village.

Standing with his backpack at the fork intersection in front of the big tree, in the village, Zane looked at his Casio watch—it had stopped, as though he'd entered a twilight zone. Was this backwater river village it? Was this party HQ? Young cows meandered down the narrow unsealed main road lined with small cement houses and ramshackle shop fronts. Some looking like a bunch of closets strapped together with tarps.

Beneath the big tree was a small Hindu shrine. Freaky foreigners garbed in bright colours got about in flamboyant, flashy styles that were in striking contrast to the drab attire of the local men, a bunch of whom, sat playing cards and speaking Konkini. Zane spotted a sign, 'Scarlet Juice Bar.' It was where Jules had told him to go. Kooky, cool cats on motorbikes whizzed through the big tree fork from all directions. The plethora of psych-out wear they wore, broadcast attitudinal amped-up loudness, which got Zane feeling like he was a lepidopterist encountering a new species of butterfly that got about on wheels.

Like a screeching big cat pouncing, a Yamaha motorbike accelerated towards him at the fork, then swiftly veered left. It's rider—cheetah-like, with aviator goggled shades and animal skin-pattern-bikini top—gobsmacked him in auric vapours that left him gasping, "What the fuck!"

It was the kind of happenchance fork in the road where paths crossed, the same kind that had bowled Jules over in Bali. Kindred spirits drawn together by fate. The rider was Zsu. She'd been shopping at Gopal Provisions, one of the tiny shops that was like a bunch of open closets in which its cheerful owner, like a jack-in-a-box, proudly stocked a diverse range of imported munchies.

Zane ordered a papaya lassi, sat down, mulled up, and drank everything in.

Party Animal

Unlike the crusty party animals north of Starco Corner, who loved to get messy, grinding with frivolity to filthy, fibrous techno all through the night, the chic freaks who stayed in white-washed fisherman cottages in Baga, would typically only venture to Vagator at first light when the music was sweeter. For them, the edgy night time electronica heard north of Starco Corner, was liable to tear holes in the finery of their white clothes and soil the sheen of their gold jewellery.

As the Konkan Shakti steamed down the Goa coast last night, Doc Silver and Danilo rabble roused mischief, putting on a party that rollicked with prickly techno and tricky disco and naughty-boy pranks in the palms of middle Vagator Beach. During the night, water had seeped onto the dance floor from a trickling spring that fleet footed dancers turned into mud. At dawn, the Baga would-be groovers stood cautiously under palms contemplating the mucky, slimy, state of the of the party as sound-to-light morning music beckoned.

To their horror, they were greeted by a mud puppy, then another, and another, and another. The first to have gone down and wallow in the mud was yogi Ananta. This was done from a back somersault into gymnastic splits bounce on the mucky dance floor. Contagiously, more and more dancers succumbed, and quickly everyone became mud puppies—the party merging as one, like amoeba returning to the source.

Then, like a Holi festival, coloured dye powder bombed the white clad Baga brigade from above. Bags of it had been suspended in the palms and released by strings. Some tried to flee the mud and colour mayhem, but were hit by mud missiles tossed at them. Others were dragged into the mud screaming. Head-to-toe, the mud puppy party writhed into the morning. It would be Ananta's last dance this season. From then on, Baga people committed earlier to take-no-prisoners, Vagator parties.

Spaghetti Beach

ALCOHOL IN INDIA was strictly controlled, except Goa, where its availability quickly wreaked havoc upon the rampaging testosterone of out of state Indians. Tour companies from Karnataka and Maharashtra would promote the scenic delights of nude hippie girls. From out of tour buses parked up at middle Vagator, Indians wearing white dhoties would waddle along the beach like penguins, drink cheap beer at chai shacks and seek out ogle opportunities.

Spaghetti Beach, at the south end of Vagator, was where a predominantly Italian clique of freaks hung out lollygagging, lotus eating, back gammoning, beach racketing and bathing. Asta liked to play there, too. On several occasions, she and her girlfriends fell prey to lecherous Indians from tour buses. They would waddle up in groups of three or four to openly gawk and point cameras at them. Recently, Asta had been lying naked, sun baking on a sarong with her feisty Dutch friend, Esther, when they fell prey to eyes that ran all over them. Furious, Asta propped herself up on her elbows and confronted the prying interlopers. "Fuck off!" she yelled. "Go stare at your own women." But the Indian gawkers persisted. Feeling violated, Esther got up and grabbed a camera and tossed it in the sea.

The fierce individuals who hung at Spaghetti Beach were passionately attached to their patch, like it was their very own beach. Rebukes verbally hurled at interloping Indian tourists typically sent them scurrying. But this season a terrible incident occurred after unwanted Indians showed up and were shooed away.

"You can't come here!" lambasted infuriated Italians one week ago. "This is not your beach! This is our beach!" They'd been sitting in a group on Spaghetti Beach, which included the master chillum maker, Cosimo. The scolded Indians retreated, but had had their nose put out of joint, having been told that this part of Vagator beach was off limits to Indians. The following week in the afternoon, Ananta was playing beach racket on Spaghetti Beach and was approached by an Indian saying, "You want to have fight?"

Looking perplexed, he replied, "No thank you, why don't you ask somebody else." Soon after, he heard Danilo's voice yelling, "Ananta get out of there NOW!" Turning around, Ananta saw fifteen people scrapping, involving Indians and Italians. Together with Asta, they fled to the palm trees and watched the fracas quickly escalate to thirty people punching and kicking. With alarmed distress, she tapped Ananta on the shoulder and pointed. "Look!.. he needs help." Three Indians were on top of someone. Gripped by the exigency of the moment, Ananta rushed into the fray calling out, "Stop!.. Stop!.. Stop!.." He managed to pull two of them off, but the third had a blade in his hand, which he held two centimetres from the throat of Cosimo.

"What the fuck are you doing?" Ananta yelled, lunging and grabbing the hand with the knife and managing to wrestle it away. But then another Indian came running at him like a knight jousting on a horse with a thirty-centimetre machete. In a split second, Ananta flashed, *Oh shit! I've been cut.* On seeing the yogi lanced and clutching his abdomen, Asta gasped, "Oh, no!" and hysterically shrieked at the top of her voice, "STOP!.. STOP!.. STOP!.. ANANTA HAS BEEN STABBED!" The high-pitched wrenching intensity of her shrill voice immediately brought all the brawling on Spaghetti Beach to a halt, as friends rushed to his assistance and the attacking Indians fled.

Surprisingly, just a trickle of blood came from the wound. Ananta tried to make light of it, telling himself, *Oh no! I won't be able to go in the sea for a few weeks. This is going to take a few days to heal. Oh damn!.. No dancing.* But then, Danilo turned to him with a look of horror. "Ananta, hold yourself."

Gazing down, Ananta saw green omentum coming out of his stomach. Asta hastily wrapped her sarong around his abdomen. Then, he felt himself going into shock, on the verge of fainting. Friends assisted him up Vagator cliff where he was sandwiched into a threesome between Asta and Danilo on the Italian DJ's motorbike and taken to Chapora Village.

The Juice bars next to the Chapora big tree at the fork, where motor bike taxi wallahs hung and chillums smoked, served as a gossip hub, buzzing with the latest information. So, when Danilo's motorbike came down the hill past the Hindu temple (which had a statue of Jesus bare chested, in a lunghi, sitting with legs crossed) and into the village carrying Ananta in acute agony, the big tree learned of the shocking incident and word spread fast. At the Pharmacy, Ananta was bandaged up. But no taxi could be found to take him to Mapusa hospital, instead, he and Asta took a rickety, three-wheeler motor rickshaw, in which every pot hole delivered sharp pain.

That evening, Jules and Zane dined at Fatima Restaurant near the house Jules rented for four hundred rupees a month in the Vagator jungle, which he now shared with Zane, who kipped down on a mattress on the floor in a spartan room. A local family lived at the back half of the house, which was essential for security of cash, passport—and especially, Jules's Sony Walkmans, portable speakers, and most precious of all, a rapidly growing collection of dubbed tapes. Each Maxell cassette he'd titled in block letters with a black felt tip sharpie: VOODOO NIPPLE FIELD, ASTRAL ATTACHE, BODY ANTENNA, SOFT SHOE SATELLITE, PSYCHO CANDY CLUB, SPACID SPIRAL VOID, BLEEPING THE HERTZ, NADAR BLISS, HYSTERIC ODYSEY, AJAX TO THE MAX, ERASE YOUR MIND, PSYCHIC FLUSH, HOLY NOISE.

Jules had become an addict of the music. The music had taken possession of him with the same passion that the parties and siren Zsu had infatuated him in his first season. He now regarded the music, with its codices of sound signatures, like the scientia of a mysterious musical muse. He embraced it like a lover. Through obsessively collecting and swopping tapes, he struck up many new friendships, but only gave out the new Telepathics tracks to Zsu, Jaeger and Danilo. Judging by the response to the stand out track, 'Goa Goat Head,' being played in a party by Jaeger, Jules was astounded by the response. It had tour de force clout in its capacity to fire up a dance floor to gallop galactic with ferocious horsepower.

Mesmerised by the zeitgeist of revolutionary techno, Jules was impelled to apply it to the mobilising of bodies and uplifting of minds. He did not know it now, but would come to see himself as a *dance floor techno therapist.*

At Fatima Restaurant, Jules introduced his new friends to Zane, who was impressed by the multinational (Finland, Austria, Brazil, Spain, Canada) makeup of the scene. A copy-of-a-copy-of-a-copy of a last season mixtape was playing out of Fatima's crappy speakers. Zane identified the track playing as 'Paranoimia' by Art of Noise.

Ghastly accounts of the stabbing on the beach consumed dinner conversations. Most disturbing, the victim, Ananta, a peace-loving yoga teacher, was apparently in critical condition, which deeply distressed those who attended his classes, and the many who affectionately loved his moves on the dance floor. The shocking violence was unconscionable. Surely, it couldn't have been Indian tourists? Someone was saying it was local hoods from across Baga river. But at some terror-crazed moment of the mayhem of the attack, the hardcore at Spaghetti Beach would have realised who was behind the malicious attack, and were now praying that it would not result in fatal tragedy.

"Strewth!" Zane said, after Jules explained what had happened. "That's nasty, is he gonna be all right?"

"I hope so, he's such a love tonic guy."

They finished their fish and chips and salad and ordered mango ice cream, with Zane pleased by the plenitude of non-Indian dishes on the menu. "So, how's the parties?" he asked.

"Heaps!" Jules said. "At least two a week, sometimes three. There's immense stamina here. For a couple of weeks, I was totally nocturnal, like a fire fly buzzing in frequencies in wired wilderness. Every party in a new setting. Different beaches, ruins, jungles, all dripping in black light, all installed with blasting black speakers. In the day, I just crashed out under a fan. There are no half measures here. Man, I'm so glad you got here."

Zane's eyes roamed, taking in a potpourri of faces at the restaurant, mentally dissecting fashion, hair, jewellery, tattoos, accents. It was as though everyone belonged here, like they were at a rare breed, recreational, counter-culture camp. A slinky Japanese girl, whose sun-baked features gave her the look of a native American Indian, entered the restaurant. She was wearing suede tasselled boots out of which tanned legs disappeared up into butt-hugging orange hotpants complemented by a top with images of Devas, Devis and Lakshmis. Gliding past Zane radiating sexy vapours, her mystique of the East left him breathless.

"That's Machiko," Jules said. "She makes stunning stuff, sells it at the flea market. Lots of talent gets about here—"

"I'm getting the picture," Zane said. "How about that babe you met in Bali last year?"

That question was like a needle jab into a toe, prior to ingrown nail surgery. Of course, Jules had done the same to Zane in asking about the status of his girlfriend, prior to Angeline passing, which had proven to be a sore point, also.

"Um, yeah...well, Zsu," Jules said with a look of dismay. "Matey—you know how it is," he sighed and averted his eyes. "If you don't maintain contact, and you stop shagging, it goes off the boil."

"It's over?"

"Not exactly," Jules said in a wary tone of voice. "We still have a connection. But man!.." he grimaced. "It appears the thing we had was a whole new deal for her. And now, seemingly, it's not happening, according to doubts, like in, she can't explain. Like in, long distance love is tough—feelings become marooned. Us not getting together in Bali. That's chicks for ya. God knows?.. I kinda of suspected complications, saw some murky stuff in her horoscope. I'm just rolling with it. Seems like the horse play of a Goa season. I suppose it's hard for old fashion romance to endure the intensity of the psychotropic weather here."

There was no denying it. Jules had fallen hard for Zsu. When they met up again in December in Goa, he did have high hopes of resuscitating the bleeps of his curious, pinning heart on a radar of love that had faded since their tortuous time apart. But Zsu was giving off veiled, mixed messages, which required Jules to pull back, least he become spurned and sodden in lovesickness. It appeared as though their end of season story had petered out. Perhaps he'd plumbed too far, breeched blockades, exposed vulnerabilities she wasn't fully done with. Come what may, he wanted to cling onto his impression of her, their togetherness from last season, but she was now impressing upon him something entirely different, another version of herself that was signalling something had changed, with her needing to hide behind the words she said to him.

It was not as if there was an inalienable feeling of flat-out rejection. But rather a kind of unclear stasis, an emotional aloofness, like she was in need of protecting herself from feelings that stalked her body. A body memory, perhaps beyond the one she was living in, the one which had ensnaring prowess in party playland Goa. They did kiss briefly, not too dangerously, least he find himself having to restrain from running his hands over her body, setting off an outpouring of uncontainable feelings, leaving him bathed in sweet agony. The sorrow of abstaining from attempting to rekindle a deoxygenated flame. As if compensatory, he threw himself into collecting the music, embracing its vibrational turn-on, with the same ardour that he'd embraced her last season. From out of his shoulder bag he gifted her a cassette of the Telepathics' latest tracks. She hugged him. Her heart hammered. She pulled back, spun around and offered him her entire new season collection of tapes, which included guaranteed floor fillers (except for the confidential 'No Copy' tracks she'd been given) and presented him with a leather six-pack cassette bag that featured design motifs of mystical glyphs, comets, planets, stars, asteroids, eclipses, suns and moons.

Luchiano and Savina exported faux Baroque furniture and made beach rackets that were popular on Spaghetti Beach. Prior to the brawl this afternoon, in which Luchiano was involved, they'd invited friends to a dinner party at their home in Gumal Vaddo. It was a palatial Portuguese house which the Italian couple rented annually from a Catholic family who worked in Dubai. A local girl was hired to cook, do laundry, and nanny the couple's three-year-old son, plus a night security man. The interior decor featured art made by friends. A vivid painting by Lazzaro, the artist who'd frescoed the walls of Primrose Restaurant, had turned the lounge into a time tunnel of infolding, three dimensional painted surfaces.

The success of the modish couple's export business was testimony to Luchiano's craftsmanship. A cabinet maker from Milan, he ingeniously devised decorative inlays that concealed cavities compacted with high grade smoking nuggets, as well as thin laminates inside book covers. Many of those attending the dinner party played soccer on the field out front of the Anjuna Post Office. The team also included the Panchayat Mayor of Anjuna, Sylvester de Souza, who also liked to smoke Shiva's sacrament.

The cloying evening air on the veranda cackled with conversation, guests predominantly speaking Italian. Background chillout techno played on a stereo in the lounge. Mineral water, chai, beer and wine was wetting raspy throats from the chillums going around, including a couple made by artisan, Cosimo, who was there. Zsu sat with Shane, a friend from Bali, and Felix, a Berlin DJ, who was informing them of a party he was planning in a bamboo forest. The conversation soon turned to fretful concern about the gravitas of Ananta's condition and the shock of what happened on the beach. Asta was also supposed to be here, but was still at the hospital.

Cosimo, slight of build with short dark wavy hair, was still shaken by the life-threatening peril he'd been pinned down in on his beloved Spaghetti Beach. But, as numerous accounts attested, he'd been miraculously saved by Ananta's gallant act. It had been just over a week ago that Cosimo had been sitting with a group of friends when the unwelcome, pesky, interloper Indians showed up and promptly were told to piss off. It was Luchiano who'd stood up and proclaimed staunchly. "This is our beach!"

The pasta and salad that Savina prepared was about to be served. But Luchiano and Cosimo, and some of the others involved with the Spaghetti Beach fracas, had lost their appetite. They could not rid themselves of haunting distress about Ananta's critical stomach wound. A very Catholic part of them almost got them down on their knees praying. More than a suspicion, it was now becoming apparent that the violent raid on, "our beach," was a vendetta grudge by a ruffian gang from Calangute, who were irate about being told by foreigners that they weren't allowed on a Goa beach.

The sound of a Rajdoot motorcycle was heard pulling into the compound of the house. Savina looked to see who had arrived. "It's Asta!" she announced. Everyone stopped talking and gasped in anticipation of Asta's news. She'd come directly from the hospital by pilot motorbike taxi.

Luchiano rushed to meet her. "How's Ananta?" he urgently asked.

"He's been stitched up. Hopefully, he'll be OK," she said, alighting the motorbike taxi and paying the pilot. Luchiano breathed a dramatic sigh of relief. Asta looked drained as she walked up the steps and sat down. Savina offered her a drink. The cassette ran out on the tape player. There was a hushed silence as everyone gathered around to hear the painful details of Ananta's ordeal.

"At the hospital, they put him on a concrete slab," Asta recounted. "When the doctor unwrapped the sarong and took the bandage off, we thought his guts were going to spew out," she said with a squeamish look in her face. "The Doctor shoots us a look, as if to say, 'this is bad.' Ananta and I both freak, and then we just think—*yoga,* and start breathing together. The Doctor says he can't treat him and sends us to St Mary's Hospital. We go there and the surgeon says he would only treat him if we say it was an accident, not a criminal offence, as he didn't want to be a witness in a court case. I couldn't believe what I was hearing. Then, Doc Silver shows up and drills the surgeon, making sure of quality stitching, not cat gut. Doc insists on scrubbing up and donning a mask to oversee the procedure, in which they pulled out Ananta's intestine and, according to Doc, did a decent job."

Cosimo sighed with relief, stood up and hollered, "Bravo!.. bravo!.. brave heart Ananta." He bowed to a brass Nataraja at an altar with clasped hands raised to his forehead to give thanks to Lord Shiva.

Electron Bending Bamboo

NAUTILUS SHAPED BOTANICAL BLEEPS... goosepimpler quarkfarks...aero gyro spiral void...warp speed binary beats...syzygy dust motes...bedlam dharma projector...psychometric motor bass throbbing bone marrow...odyssey of noise...sine wave sound sausage...architectronic star merkabas...

The above were snippets of hallucinations participants in the sensoria of the bamboo forest, backside of Anjuna, were having. Tucked away in fluorostani foliage, DJ Felix stood at a small wooden table pushing buttons powering tape across magnetic heads, sending oscillating wiggly frequencies into the leafy labyrinth, where dancers moved to it like a quantum, quick step. Sacred geometric sculpture, assembled by Lazzaro, constructed of strings, wire, bamboo and gauze fabric, was suspended over the dance floor. Its arabesque interlacings—comprised of Pythagorean, golden ratio, star hexahedron, tetrahedron, octahedron matrices—had the mental cube appearance of giving form to the fractal-like frequencies of the harmonics pulsing throughout the daze maze of the party.

At the centre of it all, sat a large amethyst crystal on top of a central maple pole from which fairy lights spoked. Further afield, on bamboo poles, hung a three-dimensional Sri Yantra painting that flickered in the sonic wind of the music like an infinity matrix. Away from the thumping, hyperspatial holophonics coming out of speaker stacks, chai ladies poured steaming spice tea. Around them, cake, biscuits and bananas were neatly displayed.

Playtime rules for partying had changed this year, and prone to more foul play then the football on the field out front of Anjuna Post Office. Doc Silver advised Felix to have the Nelson Corner boys do a deal with local cops. After the blackmail intimidation he'd been subject to, "The Boys" (as Doc referred to them) were allies in dealing with the Calangute gambling mob, who now, it was believed, were culpable for the Spaghetti Beach attack. The Panchayat, Sylvester de Souza, reckoned that the threat of a criminal investigation had severely crimped the bolshiness of louts south of Baga River. Although beach strip parties were territorially public domain, at which gambling mobs could set up on the periphery taking advantage of cops being paid off by party freaks. Sylvester even suggested that the Baga party people should do more parties, which would ease "the evil worm of jealousy." The bamboo forest was spared of bickering bar politics, as it was on private property.

Thunderclap drum machines turned the bamboo forest into a technopolis. Within it, Jules romped and frolicked and gazed up through sacred geometric forms above the dance floor to heavenly spheres back lit by the moon rising in the astrology sign, Cancer, significator of family cum tribe. Sweeping synthesiser chords sideswiped him, careening his body on a trajectory toward the thicket of bamboo concealing the DJ table. Sideway glancing from out of the corner of his eye, he glimpsed Zsu standing next to Felix in a beguiling outfit radiating a charm offensive, that was all too familiar, as it had once cast a spell on him. She flapped diaphanous wings like a flyby lover, which he'd needed to inoculate himself from. He saw multiple images of previous versions of her, shatter into pieces like fairy dust.

"Behold, here cometh the dreamer," announced a voice in the music. A gear shift of freshly milled Frankfurt techno by 'Out of The Ordinary' surged the bamboo forest, its liquid analogue polyrhythms swirl-pooling Jules into the centre of the dance floor. Then, the music became dark, Wagneresque, evoking a formidable dystopian refrain like it was the last night of the world before a nuclear holocaust. He heard the sound of marching jackboots, saw swastikas—or was it the Hindu wheel of life? The allegory of the electronic wizardry in the music spoke to him like a providence, as if encoded by soothsayers (the DJ merely a heraldic intermediary). Foreboding, prophetic voices speaking German appeared in the music. It occurred to him he'd only met one Israeli in Goa, who told him that he could only enter India using a US passport. His head filled with thoughts of genocide and the Cold War that now threatened the world.

Before the party, Jules overheard a conversation in which Felix was regaled—"A techno saint." And how he'd opened hearts with cosmic symphonies as sweet as an angel's breath at dawn with the world rebirthing itself. But, as in the track by Psyche, 'The Saint Becomes a Lush' (which Felix liked to play), he was also an inveterate caner. Jules wondered where the Berlin DJ fit into the scheme of things, as he couldn't recall him playing last season.

Felix had boyish German good looks with wide hoover nose, his head a halo of blond curls. From off it he removed Sennheiser headphones and bent his tall frame down to the table with a chopped straw between his fingers. A moment later he stood erect, all animated, his op-art T-shirt luminous, and passed the straw to Zsu. Jules watched Felix survey dance floor action from behind a camouflage of bamboo leaves until the DJ's smokey blue grey eyes returned to alight upon Zsu. Her face now appeared electrofried, having just detonated her nose.

The sight of them together got Jules pondering, but it was necessary to move on. What mattered now was the music. Yet another part of him wished he could join them and ask the names of tracks. Torsten Fenslau was Felix's favourite producer. Some tracks had dual citizenship, functioning well also in Ibiza where he sometimes visited but never liked to spin tunes as that scene was not off-the-planet enough. Unlike Goa, where freaks of nature truly salivated heady, quirky sounds. For tonight's party, he'd prepared six hours of fresh techno from Germany and Holland and New Beat from Belgium, which was packed with dark humour; all recorded from vinyl onto BASF chrome cassettes in his Kreuzberg apartment.

Besides the thrill of finding it, there was the vainglory of playing the latest batch of explosive tracks to a dosed-up going-off dance floor far removed from Europe. Although, uncommandeeringly, Felix would also sit out of sight on a chair whilst manipulating tape decks. Generously, after airing his new season collection, he would share his music with DJ friends and collectors. The nights when there were no parties, all night recording sessions occurred in which bootleg tape-swopping of the latest "special Goa music" was selectively shared. The producers of this faceless music having no idea of the life that their music was having in the psycho tropics of Asia. By the end of the season, high impact tracks had been distilled down to a hit list of *Goa Gold* that had been optimum flux road tested.

Relinquishing the weights and pulleys of the surface struggle of mundane existence, Zane found himself less a border line personality off the spectrum, and more a dancing fool gushing in a bamboo rush of first-blush impressions. Immersed in another world with midnight tokers, he laughed out loud and busted a gut to never-heard-before music. The party was laid on for free. (Felix paid a hundred bucks, all-up, for sound system and lights from Rama in Chapora, and "thank you backsheesh" rupees to Erol, the owner of the bamboo forest. Plus, the Deutsche Marks he'd shelled out for the arsenal of new season vinyl he'd scored, all underwritten by hush, hush, ventures.)

If gut bacteria were a reflection of emotional history, then in India, Zane's historical microbes had run riot. The day of the party, he felt his infected entrails claw their way into his throat and run out his rear end, but managed to get down chiku (a sweet tasting brown fruit pulp) which worked a treat in plugging him up. Though, his stomach had no qualms about the free acid punch that his psychonaunt compass navigated him to. It was being dispensed by a Merlin looking character with long white flowing beard, who was just one of a multitude of crackpot figures, wispy-limbed galactic gypsies, oddball cyborg-like creatures, and space lizards he encountered as he bounced joie de vivre, fabulously altered in the diorama of the bamboo forest. What made drugs perpetually so sexy was the opportunity to be other, in an augmented reality, in which he could surmount the intermittent twitching of his neurology. Before long, he found himself in a gelatinous state, like swimming in time lapse moon jelly. Managing to get a grip on terra firma, he attempted to take charge of his exoskeletal vehicle, grabbing its joy stick like he was in a virtual reality game.

Then, Felix put the peddle to the metal, unleashing titanic techno drums that pounded bodies with thunderous typhoon beats, triggering cathartic chaos. Switches flipped the collective central nervous system into hyperventilation overdrive. The gung-ho Berlin DJ launched a troika of trenchant Electronic Body Music that roared through the bamboo like man-eating, hydraulic-hissing, machines on steroids.

(1) 'Out of Control' by Frontline Assembly, synapsed receptors in Zane's bio-mechanical circuitry, setting off convulsive spasms like a seizure. His flaying arms and hands deflecting rapid fire shards of sonic shrapnel.

(2) 'Commando' by Front 242, propelled him ballistic into an adrenalin-driven salvo psychodrama.

(3) 'Let Your Body Learn' by Nitzer Ebb, had him jettisoning his body, leaving him floating above it watching it move in ways he never dreamed possible.

He redocked into his exoskeletal vehicle and rode it through twisting torrents until cognitive circuits fried, and the rivets on personality masks popped, and thudded him into the bedrock of a crystalline self. A protozoan self, that crumbled into sediments of archaic memory in a carboniferous swamp. Feeling like a tadpole, he had a mutagenesis vision of his conception and was struck by the conceivability of a genetic predisposition to the curse of scowling ancestors.

Then, like electro-shock therapy, electrodes of jabbing zaps and spanking, slapping claps in the music, snapped him back on his feet electron-bending in bamboo with euphoria pervading every fibre of his being, as he jumped, jumped, jumped, higher, higher, higher in defiance of the pressure drop of the gravity of an inherited given.

Sometime after four, a three-dimensional Sri Yantra wire sculpture, bound with accelerant soaked material, suspended high to the side of the dance floor, was ignited. Towards dawn, Zane got his goat on with goat-headed seahorses. He found himself breathing through gills, wriggling in an aquatic world of sea anemone that sucked him into a translucent cocoon. Looking up to the surface through galactic geometries, he saw a zodiac goat with a fish tail. Felix spun the steering wheel of the party and pushed the play button. A new hot piece de resistance by The Telepathics leaped out of the speaker stacks. Bucking with horns, the music hooked the dance floor, aurally exciting its collective cochlea, igniting cosmo-kinetic bodies skyward with Zane becoming every particle of sound in the 'Goa Goat Head' track he'd made in late night sessions in The Spice Lab at Pyrmont squat.

After techno saint, Felix, delivered transcendence in a pink dawn, post-punk Zane Lovelock relived historical 'Unknown Pleasures' in 'The Beach' (a vocoder remix of 'Blue Monday') by New Order. Its anthem melody, an epiphany of Northern Soul disaffection. It brought with it the recollection of his life when, 'She's Lost Control' by Joy Division was his swan song in nineteen eighty, the year he left the UK. His face twisted into a pained grin as he recalled the moment he heard of Ian Curtis's death. It could have been him, he'd felt at the time. He thought of Evangeline, and how close he'd come to stepping through the veil with her, and what kind of damnation might have awaited him in the afterlife for having bailed too soon. Defiant thoughts pounded on the backdoor of his mind. *A terminal overdose will not be an option without my consent.*

The party finished at ten o'clock in the morning with lopsided faces dripping in sound-saturated emotion. Zane gathered up the reconfigured pieces of his new self, in a rearranged reality, and attempted to ground himself by joining a raspy-throat-coughing, chillum circle in the shade of the bamboo on a chai mat. With reality looking very different, he managed to find his TVS moped on the edge of the forest maze. He hoped it knew its way back to the house in Vagator jungle. Like a lost dog, it did meanderingly deliver him home where he headed straight to the squat latrine out the back. A black hairy pig with bristly pink snout greeted him. Squatting on his haunches, he bared his white scrawny arse to the pig, but all that came out was acid gas.

With his head still swimming from the deluge of electron bending in the bamboo, he poured well water over his rung-out body caked in blissful exhaustion from non-stop-modular-expansion-dancing. Laying down, the last lingering image he had before surrendering to sleep was of a bloke with a holy man goatee stripped off to a sarong. From out of it, swung his sizeable tackle as he danced under a large amethyst crystal, which had turned into an ouroboros snake eating itself.

Undercover In Subculture

THE HIPPIE HAPPENINGS OF THE BEACH strips north of Calangute were mostly off the Panjim radar, except for the odd rumour which would waft across the harbour, half spanned by an incomplete bridge. Rumours such as hippie girls suckling baby monkeys, indecent acts with goats, Devil worship and naked dancing in an inferno of drug-addled hell.

Since liberation from the Portuguese up until nineteen eighty-eight, when Goa became the twenty seventh state of India, there was stable governance. But now it teetered with instability as nascent Goan nationalism was on the rise. A new political party, *Save Goa*, principally funded by the Catholic diocese, was gaining political traction and was championed by *The Goa Voice* newspaper. "Hippies are an amoral scourge," stated one of its recent editorials. "This low life pest should be exterminated."

A sometime Bollywood actor, who aspired to be a script writer, palmed himself off as a freelance correspondent to *The Goa Voice*. Agreeing to go undercover as an investigative reporter, his assignment was to mingle with hippies, snoop, and get the dirt on a "Satan cult" and compile a vilifying expose on "The Devil's playground."

Naresh Kumar, in his late twenties, tall, broad chested, handsome, with dashing sweet caramel face, had once been support actor in a film, *Disco Dancer*, shot in nineteen eighty-one with scenes in Goa. The set featured hippie extras sitting around smoking a chillum on the beach, whilst he and his buxom belle canoodled soft focus under palms, back-dropped with a romantic sunset. Naresh was thrilled to be back in Goa, now cast as a spy, in which he imagined himself a Bollywood James Bond in disguise on a mission to chase down the Devil of iniquity.

A tailor in Mapusa made him Harem pants from star patterned material, which he donned together with a tie-dyed singlet, sourced from the Friday market. Around his neck, he fastened a mala of beads and wore a silver tree-of-life pendent that he bought at the Anjuna flea market. *The Goa Voice* paid him an advance, which he spent on accommodation at the

Vagator Tourist Resort, where he would secretly compile a report on Satan worshippers.

Slipping into the milling, smoking crowd at Primrose, he made his way to the counter to buy a Limca soft drink. With apprehensive dark brown eyes darting about the restaurant, it occurred to him that it was like an aviary of foreign birds. *Was it possible that other Indians might be here?* He felt nervous and awkward. A chillum came his way, he passed it on. Then became worrisome, thinking he might be detected as an imposter, having not toked on it. Unbeknown to *The Goa Voice*, he did enjoy the odd toke. Besides, behind the scenes in Bollywood all manner of vice was rife. *Better not get stoned on the job first day*, he thought, least he got too out of character and blow his cover. He was already getting stoned from second hand smoke from the many chillums curling charas-infused air throughout Primrose. It was further aerated with synthesised computer beats coming out of speakers attached to columns supporting the roof under which there were no walls.

His ulterior motive in taking on the undercover reporter gig was that it afforded him an opportunity to do research for a script he'd been longing to pen, ever since his last acting stint in Goa. He wondered what kind of Satanic party he might find? Seventies Goa was infamous for sex, drugs and Rock 'n' Roll, and now, from what was coming out of the Primrose speakers, it seemed like Disco had become devilish.

Pushing back trepidation at being the only Indian at a hot spot of very colourful foreigners—some prone to abject paranoia that could trigger psychotic outbursts—he stole glances at clusters of wigged-out looking characters. Then, a striking dark figure in tight jeans with a sweep of jet black hair caught his eye. *An Indian, no?* He peered hard, locking onto the curvy figure and got snatch glimpses of her face. The figure exited to the courtyard and stood alone. *Probably not a local.* But an Indian, nonetheless. He mustered courage, slipped outside, and ventured to stand near her. Still standing alone, she put a Benson & Hedges cigarette between her lips and felt about in her bag, but couldn't find matches. He moved toward her, his hand extended with a lighter.

"Oh, thanks," she said, startled, and lit up and took a couple of puffs.

"Your welcome," he said. "You're from here?"

"No," she said exhaling. "Well, um… originally, but I don't live here anymore. Just visiting. How about you?"

"I'm from Bombay. My name is Naresh."

"Hi, I'm Sheila. My family is from Candolim. We moved to the Gulf when I was young. As a teenager I hated it, but fortunately I could escape

Dubai and marriage, by way of a scholarship in England. Last year I graduated with a business degree. My father died, now my mother and aunty run a restaurant in Calangute. They were hoping that I might live back here. But it's just not possible."

"It must be a leap of worlds," Naresh said. "I visited England once, I have relatives who immigrated, they run a grocery in Essex. I must say, you do have a cute English accent."

"Oh, thanks," she said in a friendly tone of voice. "I live in London, it's a salad bowl of multiculturalism. India is a mono culture. Its traditions suffocate me. Primrose is not India—its Goa. It's something else. It's naughty!" This she said flicking her black mane of hair with a wicked gesture. Naresh felt his pulse race. He wondered what this attractive, English-Indian woman implied by, *naughty*.

"That leaves a lot to the imagination," he said.

She teased him with a smile and exhaled smoke into the air of the buzzing courtyard into which more gaily clad night hawks were arriving. "Goa is a crazy party place," she said. "People here know how to have fun. I returned here for a visit last year. I was at the flea market and heard about a party in the ruins of an old house in North Anjuna. It was hilarious. Everyone dressed in strange outfits, like a masquerade, some like circus characters, all crazy dancing to computer music. The likes, of which, I'd never heard…not even in London."

Naresh pulled a wide smile. "Yes, the parties really are something." He lied through his teeth with beaming warm eyes, making out that he'd already attended a few.

"It's kind of funny," she said, "how comfortable I feel here. I guess that's because I'm an outsider. You know, like someone in between two different cultures."

"In between?" he said, rolling his eyes.

"Yes!" she said. "Like a crossbreed. The way Asia and Europe come together here. Perhaps it's my own quest for identity. The way my Indian self, had to bend with my English self. How about you?" she asked, feeling like she'd overdone telling about herself to this, not so typical Indian chap.

"I'm on holiday," he said, "I did an English literature paper at The University of Bombay and worked in publishing. Right now, I'm in need of time out from the opinions of my family." (He privately congratulated himself on delivering his lines like the pro-actor, he regarded himself to be.)

"Not married?" she candidly asked, like it was a big deal. And it was a big deal in India, so much so, the bulk of lusty Bollywood stories hinged on romantic hang-ups involving family complications. Naresh had already survived one round of diving through burning nuptial hoops, which had left his heart singed and libido longing.

"No!.. not married," he said emphatically. "I'm envious of you. It must be easier to be free of family pressure living abroad?"

Sheila relaxed, she was happy to talk, sensing Naresh to be smart. "Family expectations are such a burden," she said, curling her lip. "It's ironic how this part of Goa is like London is for me, in reverse. Everyone here, no doubt, feels how I do when I'm in London. Something to do with breaking away from where you come from."

He basked in her frankness. It challenged and thrilled him. He'd never experienced this in an Indian woman before. His eyes became lassoes that wanted to capture the facial dance of her animated lips as they pulled on the cigarette filter—her mouth releasing the smoke through which she batted long lashes. Her jet black hair bounced on a glowing delicate collar bone, exposed through a stripe patterned V-neck top, that plunged to a plenitude of cleavage. As they chatted, he dared not let his eyes drop down further to the tight glove-like grip of her jeans containing tantalising curves, the confluence of which was a V of his wildest imagination under the heart-shaped buckle of her belt.

Undercover reporter, Naresh, was able to ply considerable information from Sheila without giving much away, except that he was from an upper caste heavy industries family in Bombay (this part was true) which brought privileges, but also weighty obligations, which like her, he was happy to escape.

"I'm here for R 'n' R," he said. Then wondered to himself what else it might stand for: *Racy and raunchy carry-on? Research and role play?*

She responded with a twist of her body and a shuffling of her feet, that were strapped into tinsel studded leather sandals with toe nails lacquered ruby red, as though she was about to break out dance moves to the music that was coming out of the speakers of Primrose. She showered him with a sweet smile. He took this to be a green light, but was riding the clutch, unsure which gear next. The situation was shockingly pleasurable, perhaps frightfully too much, which might blow his cover.

"R 'n' R," she laughed. "They call it *Rave* in the U.K., but I doubt it's the same here."

After attending some Goa parties last year, she returned to England having gotten the bug for this kind of party. She tracked down a warehouse party and a rave in a field. "It was awfully disappointing, compared to the open-air sunrise parties in Goa. There wasn't the colourful mix of global travellers and the special music they play here."

He then chanced to ask, "Have you attended a Satanic party in Goa?"

"Goodness gracious me," she said with a look of astonishment. "A Satanic party! I don't believe I have." She then asked him if he knew about a local superstition called, *The Evil Eye*.

He hadn't. She explained it had to do with a fear of the ocean.

"We Indians," he said, "we don't have a beach culture. We don't—how do you say it? We don't R 'n' R on the beach."

Sheila's plucked eyebrows shot up. "Sun bathing, swimming, public kissing—it's just not done. It's absolutely a no, no. Indians don't do that. But Goa has adapted to Western ways. The hippies have done pretty much as they have liked. Fishermen don't have issues with them naked on the beach. There's a colony of hippie cliff dwellers living in palm cabanas above the beach, here in Vagator, who are under threat. In Panjim, letters are being written to newspapers complaining that they are a plague."

"I don't suppose," he further chanced to ask, "have you heard of the *Save Goa* political party?"

"Oh, my God!" She sucked in her cheeks, her face becoming pinched like she had just bitten into a lemon. "Now you're really going to get me upset. Talk about dim wits."

CYBERELLA, **WAS THE NAME** of Asta's new fashion label, which she launched at her own flea market stall next to the *Tribes of The Moon* stall. A solo mother, Asta lived full time in Goa with her daughter, Tina, who attended Vagator Primary School, as did other *Goa kids* from hippie families who set up home there. After a fling in nineteen seventy-seven, Asta found herself pregnant. The following year, the father, a Frenchman, overdosed and died in a Delhi Hotel. Living on a Danish pension, she took out a lease on a house in Badem and hired a Hindu family for household help, a tailor and night watchmen. She had a coconut frond fence erected, planted gardens, taught her cleaning lady how to make tofu which she sold to Oxford shop and supplied Gregory's Restaurant.

In the second week of January, with the sun in the sign of Capricorn, ruled by the goat, the high season was in full swing. Asta rode her Yamaha, with Tina in front, through the dog leg bend by La Franza Restaurant in Anjuna, where she spotted Zsu having breakfast. She stopped and joined her, ordering fruit salad curd and an omelette for Tina, who ran out the back to play with local kids. They soon got talking about the last party which followers of the O.O.O. mystical cult had thrown to celebrate the birthday of their prophet, Odvar Osser. The party had been in the monkey forest back side of Chapora, near the house of the Norwegian prophet. His hypnotising oratory of a saga—a creation myth about "paradise times"—was gaining a following. The most contentious yarn he spun was the belief that humanity had sprung from a monkey and a nanny goat bonking, as well as his instruction on sexual bodily fluids. His most scathing debunkers regarding the O.O.O. "a load of wank," referring to him as "the milky balls baba."

"I actually went to one their ceremonies," Asta confessed to Zsu. "And would you believe it? Atma was there in orange sadhu threads and beads officiating in the curd-dripping-over-the-lingam ritual—"

"Oh, my God!" Zsu gasped forking one of her poached eggs, its ruptured gooeyness bleeding through the toast. "I can well believe Atma becoming ordained into Osser's cock-pulling circle."

"So, you know about it?" Asta said, spooning curd coated banana into her mouth.

"Yes darling. That wasn't curd. That was jizz they were pouring over that ceremonial phallus."

Asta choked. "Oh yeah? I was wondering. I went along out of curiosity with Johanna from Helsinki and Heidi from Austria."

Seeing Asta playing with a piece of pineapple with a spoon on her plate, Zsu said, "I bet he instructs the boys to eat plenty of pineapple, too."

"Pineapple?" Asta said with wide eyes.

Zsu licked her lips. "Hun, it makes ejaculate sweeter." She then jabbed the other poached egg and watched it run over melting butter. "Let the Odin cum cup of Osser's ouroboros runneth over." She looked up at Asta and smiled." This story is hard to swallow when it appears to be just a cock cult. There's not much in it for women—"

"Well, there is," Asta said. "Osser presented us girls with a piece of silver jewellery he calls 'a dolphin staff,' instructing us to use it to imbibe our yoni sap, saying it's a lubricant for the brain."

Zsu laughed. "I bet the boys find his shaggy goat earthiness a turn on." She winked. "Do you think his most devoted chums are—bi, or gay?"

Asta narrowed her eyes, "Um well, they say his jizz has special powers. As in these ceremonies they conduct."

"Yeah right!.. Hard-on ceremonies," Zsu smirked. "So now Atma's sucking Osser's knob?"

"Ha!—it wouldn't surprise me," Zsu said pulling a peeved, forlorn look.

"Are you OK darling?" Asta asked, reaching across the table to hold her hand.

"Sorry hun. Just some shitty feelings," Zsu said pursing her lips together and gnawing the inside of her cheeks with her molars. "I'm fine, I'm fine…" she sighed and forced a smile.

"Zsu sweetheart, you're very loved—"

"Jules didn't make it back to Bali." She said, turning to look away and sighed. "Too bad, something else happened. I met someone…got exploring a bit…got turned on with a hottie—a girl. Asta, I went to the other side. It was tender and beautiful."

"Oh… Zsu, congratulations!" her bestie said forking a piece of fleshy papaya into her mouth. I'm so happy for you, so happy you could finally go there." She stood up and put her arms around Zsu. They hugged. Then, Tina came running to the table. "Mumma, mumma, I'm hungry," she whined.

"Sweetheart," Asta said, "your omelette is getting cold, flies are trying to land on it. Please sit down and eat it."

Tina was eleven years old. Being around her stirred memories for Zsu of her own childhood. Her life in Marseille raised by her own solo mother. Her loss of innocence in the furies of an accelerated pubescence, in a home life reeking with the goings-on of her mother's licentious liaisons—not so discreet, with exposures through bedroom doors. The impressionable igniting in Zsu of an incendiary, nymphet precociousness, wrought with hostile feelings. To the extent that she set about competing with her mother and unwittingly colluded in (what could now, in hindsight, be moralised as taboo sex, or abuse), a Lolita lollipop rush seeking out a fantasist father—the longed-for banished father that she'd never had. And so, attachment and desire was laden with shameful, fractured, transgressive feelings whenever she sought closeness. Dangerous toxic feelings that left her feeling like she was a bruised and battered lab rat in experimentations of love.

JOURNAL OF NARESH KUMAR

13th February

Met Goan named, Sheila, at Primrose Restaurant. According to her, few locals are involved in drugs as police are severe on them. Locals are left alone unless they are cashed up from business with foreigners. Besides Kerala grass and charas, I'm wondering what else is available?

15th February

Overheard conversations in chai shops, LSD was mentioned. I was offered some in sugar cubes and something called Ecstasy, in powder form. Sheila said there is a party jungle drug store. Apparently, it's the shoes that are a dead give away for undercover police.

16th February

People here from all over. It's like a mecca for mysterious personalities. Everyone mostly friendly. Only seen one non-Indian black person. He spoke French. Although one unpleasant incident occurred at Orange Boom Restaurant, Anjuna. A hostile fellow, a junky from Belgium I was told, abusively lashed out at me yelling, "Chalo Pakistan!" Struck up a conversation with a Kiwi. We talked about Richard Hadlee the fast bowler, one of my heroes.

18th February

At Primrose, Sheila introduced me to some of her friends. Heard about parties. Attended a jungle party down from Chapora Fort. No sign of Satanic rituals, mostly Shiva rituals with chillums. Someone mentioned something about a Pagan cult centred around a holy man from Norway. There had been a party last month in a forest with a totem pole that included goat and monkey skulls.

Went to a party at a large mansion, known as 'The Big House.' The fellow that lives there makes movies. Exuberant dancing was happening in two large rooms. Mattresses and large cushions were in smaller rooms. Maybe for orgies? In a central court yard a naked girl maintained a sirsha-asana head stand yoga pose for over an hour. A free party potion was being offered by a Santa Claus looking fellow wearing patch work overhauls. It came in little plastic cups, I was told it was acid. Saw Sheila dancing in pink tights, her face over-flowed with joy. It was like she'd turned into a different person. She gave me a smile and yelled over the loud computer music, "It's fabulous, isn't it?" I joined in dancing. An Indian DJ was playing. Another DJ, a foreigner, took over at 2 AM, the intensity of the music increased, dancing became more frenzied and I got swept along by the ecstatic energy. No one touched on the dance floor.

Occasionally some hugged, these were mostly Pune people who wore malas with a photo of Bhagwan Shree Rajneesh.

Some passages of music drew a strong response. A wave of energy appeared to possess dancers, some raising hands in the air as if reaching for a higher power. I didn't drink the potion, but felt high from the atmosphere. Leaving at 4 AM, I felt like I was missing out on something. It's tempting to take the party potion. I want to know what Sheila was experiencing. But I must admit to being a little afraid. I might encounter Kali? I might meet the Devil? I might get the scoop and write the story. It's troubling, better I don't fall in love.

19th February

At Primrose, someone pulled a cassette out of their bag titled, 'Machine Mantra for a State of Mind.' Listening to it through the restaurant speakers, one track had a voice that repeated over and over, 'Jesus Loves Acid.' So many beautiful foreign girls there, but I fancy Sheila. She's Indian, well not exactly. I wish I could tell her that I've been in films. Maybe I can visit her in England, get acting work, sell my screen play.

Blotta Baba

POW WOW—A GATHERING OF THE TRIBES human be in, was the catch phrase of a creased, faded poster—featuring Timothy Leary, Allen Ginsberg and San Francisco rock bands—that had been pinned up on the wall above the well-worn community mail box in Joe Banana Restaurant. The central image was a noble North American Indian on a horse bearing an electric guitar. From the heavens above a claw clasped bolts of lightning.

The poster had been pinned up in Joe's at the beginning of the seventies by Blotta baba, Shazam—a brethren of *The Brotherhood of Eternal Light.* He also brought a companion poster from the same year, nineteen sixty-seven, featuring a Hindu ascetic with ash-smeared face and third eye pyramid overlaid. This he framed and suspended in a tepee he'd erected in the garden out the back of the house he rented, year by year, behind Joe Banana.

At the time, he identified as a sorcerer's apprentice. *The Brotherhood* was all about spiritual activism, pushing peace and love, riding a wave of orange sunshine acid all the way from Laguna Beach. Shazam rocked out naked on purple haze in the mud at Woodstock, attended *Haight Hashbury* be-ins, and smoked charas in the Himalayas with sadhus when Leary was sermonising his nonconformist, drop out "politics of ecstasy." This season, one of the most must-dance-to tracks, Psychic TV's, 'Tune In (Turn On The Acid House) featured the psychedelic evangelist's mesmerising voice with dissident slogans on top of wiggly, wobbly computer beats.

Merry prankster, and disrupter of straight-arrow programming, blotta babba, Shazam, could feel a renaissance revolution in "fun-to-dance-to" psychedelic techno. Having been at the epicentre of the *Orange Sunshine Revolution* during the first summer of love, he now relished playing the elder trickster, dispensing soma to neophytes embarking upon liminal journeys, telling them, "You need to lose yourself, to find yourself."

Goa, for him, was a social honey pot for which he had the goodness to tip the party. India was full of holy men and the goodness that he gave out, and sold, he regarded as serving the same purpose as what other enlightened masters were making available for seekers on the path. It was his mission to bring chemical enlightenment in a bender-blender cocktail where lifestyle biz got-it-on with dissolute shenanigans. He'd made an oath to *the Brotherhood* to spread the goodness of the solvent of the philosopher's stone, like it was an alchemical elixir from the gods put on earth to mainline circuit breakers in crown chakras. All in service to priming orbital swivel on cyber-tribal dance floors tipping—"furthur!"

Unlike his generation of the first wave of hippies at South Anjuna, who staunchly clung to jam bands, Rock and Funk and Rasta music, Shazam was an early adopter of the computer, hallucinogen generation. The thrilling fresh sounds of the silicon surf of the new electronica and medical lab quality of his blotta was an irresistible, accelerant, marriage made in heaven, in service to "furthur" more far-reaching cybernetic neuro-transmittance.

A vibe tribe high, at this point in time, could not be more better typified than the set and situation of party players, in mutual reception, synaptically lubricated on his goodness in sensual, lush, electrodelicised Asian vistas. Like all blotta babas, Shazam got off getting others off, and vouched that his was the cleanest and best. In the psychedelic circus of a party, he would illustriously garb himself out in the most glowing, vibrant, arresting threads. Blotta baba Shazam liked nothing better than bounce about luminous between speaker stacks in the hyper-spatial heat of boogie bots half his age, who'd necked his goodness in peachy beach settings. If free punch should run out, well after midnight, jump-up journeyers who arrived ill-equipped, would hit-up the acid dandy for handouts of goodness as the urgency for lift-off on a bubbling dance floor became more paramount.

The *Haight Hashbury* framed poster, with third eye pyramid sadhu, that hung on the bamboo frame in Shazam's tepee functioned as a mystic man affirmation. Zsu sat with Shazam under it, filling him in on the conspiratorial intrigue of members of Psychic TV having arrived in Goa. She was paying him a schmooze visit, detailing her arrangements for the March full moon party, which would be a twenty-four-hour affair, sunset to sunset, with all DJs playing, including a girl DJ; combined with elaborate decoration in the most magical setting where there had never been a party before. It was a grand occasion, as it coincided with the harmonic convergence of Venus and Jupiter. This is what Jules had told her when she'd run into him at Oxford shop at Nelson's Corner, a week after the Bamboo forest party, and spontaneously invited him to the secret location. All she would tell Shazam was that it was like a wilderness temple that offered shade all day and would confirm arrangements soon.

The timing was perfect, as Shazam had just received (care of his own sorcerer's apprentice) a brand-new batch of double dipped goodness. The blotter was comprised of four quarter squares, two hundred and fifty micrograms each, making up a composite image of a thousand micrograms that featured a portrait of Mikhail Gorbachev. Extolling his product's revolutionary potency, Shazam said that the quarter with the Russian president's mystical birth mark on his bald head was guaranteed to deliver the most illuminating oomph.

"Full Moon is in the sign of Virgo," Zsu told Shazam as they drank chai. "In the morning it goes into Libra, the sign ruled by Venus."

The soma sorcerer's eyes beamed. "I'm Libra."

"Aren't you just?" she said. "You're outlandish with your eye-candy outfits. Your tailor does a dapper job turning you into a lolly shop explosion." She shot him a smitten smile, like that of a groupie. "Mirror, mirror on the wall," she said, "who's the most bizarrely beautiful of them all?"

His red ruddy cheeks at the top of his snow-white beard blushed. He raised his glass of tea to his lips and toasted to, "the glory of outrageous freaksville," his wrist shimmered with a gold chain bracelet and two fingers luminous with transparent fluoro rings.

"Don't we all need some brightening up with supercalifragilisticexpialidocious," he said with a mischievous grin. "Zsu, you're a marvel," he lathered her with his golden Californian voice. "I love what you do."

"Close your eyes," he said, "hold out your hand." He reached inside his pocket and pulled out a folded sheet of coloured tickets covered in cling wrap, and tore off one full face of the President of the USSR, and put it in her hand.

"Open your eyes."

"Wow!—killer!" she said. "So, this is your revolutionary perestroika paper I've been hearing about?"

He grinned. "You know what perestroika means?"

"Um," she searched his Merlin face for an answer. "Not sure—"

"Restructuring," he said. "This batch is gonna bring down the Berlin Wall."

"I can believe it!" she said, astounded. "Yeah, unification—that's amazing, cause Jules was telling me about Uranus and the idea of emancipation and utopian technology. It seems now Uranus has got the jump on the old Devil, Saturn, who he says represents old outmoded structures. Apparently, these contrasting planets are hooking up in Capricorn, the sign of politics. Uranus is gonna zap the system. When stars connect it's new beginnings. We are in a star seed time, it's the breakdown of the old order on starship earth. We got to celebrate this cosmic convergence. We got to dance under the heavens like the ancients did."

"Right on sister!" Shazam said. "I can feel a renaissance coming on. The sound waves are refracting something which the goodness seeks to enhance in the bio magnetic field generated when we dance in nature."

"Yes! Yes!" Zus said. "Party is a unified space opening a star gate to an intergalactic centre. Shazam, you gotta hear the 'Goa Goat Head' track. It's all about this."

"Outta sight!.. can you make me a tape?" he pleaded.

"Sure," she said, "I think I can leak it to you."

The lure of an optimum occasion, with the scene aloft for an extended session on his goodness, was stoking Shazam's imagination and got the colours of his Mandelbrot fractal singlet pulsing and the spider web pattern of his leggings quivering and crawling with anticipation.

"CHARGING ABOUT IN THAT TECHNO TREACLE I thought I was gonna bust a gut," Zane told Jules as they sat in moonlight on the veranda of their house in the Vagator jungle two nights after the sick, digital, hardcore justice of the bamboo forest that mashed him into moon jelly. "I stumbled through the bamboo to take a leak. Looked down at my piss, it had turned red, I was freaking." He inhaled through the cardboard tip of a charas joint he held between his fingers.

"The first party feels like an initiation," Jules said. "Matey!—you've transitioned into another realm."

Since arriving in Goa, it was apparent to Zane that Jules was a different person. It was as though Jules had found his people, found a more fitting habitat, his expressions now peppered with a technodelic lingo. As though, not only the soma, but something esoteric in the prana vapours of the out-space of the air had permeated thought patterns and metabolisms of those who'd hyperventilated it in marathon dance sessions. As though the kicked-up clouds of red dust particles, like ancient subcontinent motes, was required to be breathed in by the collective lung, so that mother India moved through whoever danced upon her.

"The further I'm from the mainstream," Jules said, receiving the joint between his fingers, "the closer I'm to the edge. The dance floor is the dope—it sure ain't just the punch."

"Core blimey!" Zane said. "Bring on the chemical revolution. I've never gotten down with so many weirdos before. I was even feeling strangely normal compared to some mentals' goin hard-out in riotous miss-match getups all around me."

"It's a freaks' sanctuary," Jules declared. "A pilgrimage of the absurd. Man!—I'm seeing and hearing and perceiving things that were inconceivable before. It's a digital, chemical, muscular, neural interface..."

Zane laughed. "I see what you mean about the music. "

Pondering what the Berlin DJ played in the bamboo forest, Jules said, "Some kind of disco mystic vibe tapping into the universal mind. It really is theosophical techno. I heard Jung, Freud, Nietzsche, Einstein, George Orwell, William Burroughs—even Hitler. They were all inside the music. I have no idea who's making it. One track even had Gandhi's voice, and fuckhead Reagan. It makes sense to experience this existential electronica here in the land of belief systems. A mad mystical set and situation to metaphysically melt. This music ain't gonna work the same in a dark night club. It's not hard-edged rave, or abrasive warehouse techno. It's not glitzy mirror ball disco. The weirdos that show up in the wilderness here, they're out of the ordinary, they're the ones that make this place. It couldn't be any more off the dial and further from reality than here."

"Mate!" Zane said. "There I was in the bamboo with my melon mashed, and before I knew it, I'd become slime."

Jules nodded, and said nothing, and listened to insects rub their legs together filling the air with magic, and gazed wide-eyed up at the moon and said, "You know, the moon was once an asteroid that collided with the earth, back when it was prehistoric slime. Then became its satellite consort, just for us poets of the night. Ha!.." he chuckled, "makes you wonder where would the human heart be without this satellite of love." He gazed further out into deep space beyond the earth's companion, the moon, into the depths of the star-studded black velvet of night. "There's eighty billion stars out there, the same number of neurons as there are in our brains. Cosmic influences in the universe millions of years ago changed the earth's elliptical tilt, as it spun, which caused our brains to grow bigger than apes, so we could become space men. And look," he pointed to the well in the yard, "we're still pulling water by hand, and oxen are still pulling carts with wooden wheels. The technological sounds that blasted our brains in the bamboo forest is the evolution of our primitive ancestors beating animal skins with sticks."

The following night, Danilo took them to Felix's house at the back of Chapora. The Berliner applauded the 'Goa Goat Head' track and broke out the hokey cokey and incessantly jaw-jabbered music. That Zane was susceptible to white powder should have been of concern to Jules, now that his mate was in India. But it was a night of dedicated research in "technogeist music." Jules left with a bunch of Felix's cassettes at three in the morning. Zane stayed on, keeping pace with the Berliner's compulsive hoover nose, blathering till the first trace of dawn rippled through the trees.

JOURNAL OF NARESH KUMAR

22nd February

Met Sheila for a juice, told her I worked in Bollywood and talked about my screenplay ambition. Goa is firing my imagination. Heaven knows what might happen if I take the party potion like Sheila did?

23rd Feburary

Went to Shore Bar Anjuna for sunset at Sheila's invitation. Judging from accents, mostly English were there. She introduced me to an expat Indian, Amrish Sharma, an entertaining fellow who lives in London and does spice trade. He offered me his chillum to start, it was impossible to refuse. Clasping the Shiva pipe in my hands with the English Indians in Goa felt like a special moment. Getting high with the colours of sunset was magnificent.

Bollywood came up in conversation. To my consternation Amrish happened to mention the movie, Disco Dancer, in which I'd acted. Scenes had been shot on Anjuna Beach. Feeling happy, and in great company, I was on the verge of telling of my role in the film. But wisely didn't, as I became concerned that would jeopardise my current role.

There was talk about the party two nights ago at The Big House. Apparently, the Indian DJ was a Goan who grew up with the parties and married an Austrian. I learned there is another Indian who has befriended all the DJs and collects party music. He's involved in a mystical cult, known as the O.O.O.

Sheila appeared to take pleasure in seeing me high with fishbowl eyes and gave me a kindly smile. I couldn't help but wonder what it might be like to have a private smoke together? Just the two of us. Or maybe we could take something else together? Just having these thoughts is dangerous. I'm struggling to stay cool and focus on the story for The Goa Voice. But I have to admit to feeling rather troubled after Sheila's comment about the Save Goa Party.

24ᵗʰ February

At Primrose Restaurant last night, I noticed tapes passing hands. It turned out that they are dubbed copies of party music, which are exchanged like rare cards. Amrish introduced me to Remo, the fanatic Indian collector of party music. He had peculiar, matted, sadhu hair, common to the deviant Aghori sect, and golden earrings in the shape of snakes eating their own tails. Our chat was interrupted by a Chilean and a Belgian, who showed him a tape. He stopped cleaning his chillum and inspected the jotted list on the cassette, like he was a scholar.

On seeing the names on one of Remo's tapes the Chilean asked if he could play it through the Primrose speakers. The strange sadhu became displeased. "No!.. No!.. Not this tape!" he said sharply. "You don't understand!" And grabbed the tape back. He explained that the music was super special. It should only be played in the party. He then turned to me saying, "party is ceremony."

We talked about Indian classical music. I told him I had a collection of Bollywood movie sound tracks. He said he'd liked to hear them. I asked him about Satanic rituals. He stiffened with a hardened face, and said, "My God!—that sounds like a Sunday School thing. Like calling Rock 'n' Roll the Devil's music." He was happy to talk about the "oldest story which O.O.O. ancient language sounds reveal." He invited me to hear these sounds "from the horse's mouth and partake in the Norse man's pole."

IT WAS THE CATHEDRAL BANYAN tree of all trees. Its vast aerial roots hung down like a loom of electronic cables draped from the sky—some thick like the pipes of a gothic church organ. Secluded in Badem, setback off the road, which Zsu rode every day, she'd imagined a party there—a party of all parties under the sacred tree. Its vast canopy of branches radiated out like a sentient tree of life. Around it was a shaded grove with smaller banyans. The land was owned by the Headmaster of Assagao Primary School. His wife served tea and cake when Zsu visited to ask for permission to throw a birthday party there, the first weekend in March on full moon.

"Madame, your most welcome" the Headmaster said obligingly. "You and your friends enjoy yourselves." Thanking him, Zsu pressed an envelope into his hand. On top of it she'd hand drawn an OM symbol, inside was ten fifty rupee notes.

On a bright morning, in the last week of February, she sat with Jules under the grand banyan eating croissants and drinking chilled orange juice. The huge wildness of the banyan had an ancient posture reaching toward the sky, like it predated human existence. Struck by the synchronicity of bumping into each other at Oxford store, Zsu spontaneously invited him to the holy tree where she sought insight into the astrology of the occasion. But the truth be known, in her heart of hearts, what she really needed was to get insufferable, shabby feelings of remorse off her chest.

"I'm sorry I was an ice queen," she said with a disliking snicker and drew a sharp breath. "It was a pity what happened to our story."

That's right, he reminded himself. *Yes, you are unbelievably alienated from yourself. Yes, you do run hot and cold. Yes, you are a femme fatal. Yes, there's a streak of lechery laced into your frills. Yes, you are a heart breaker.*

But then, he said to her face, "It's my fault. It was a bummer I didn't visit you in Bali. But I was strapped for cash, had to buy sound gear." Privately, he wondered about Felix. Who, for Zsu, was an ex with benefits.

"In Sydney, I got distracted," Jules explained. "I fell into a hot love affair." He took pleasure in teasing her. Appearing to take the bait, her face contorted into an unkind smile.

"It was a crazy affair," he said, waving his hands about in the air like he'd spent too much time on Spaghetti Beach. "I ended up in a love triangle. I got entangled in midi leads, effects boxes and modules. I was fiddling buttons, twiddling knobs, making out in between monitor speakers, got laid waste on the mixing table. It took a lot of getting my head around. There were long nights. I was up against a lover who was a two-timing motherfucker."

Suckered in, Zsu gazed at him with a tight jaw. "What the hell?"

Seeing her distress, Jules relented and pulled a comic face. "I had a romance with my musical muse, it was a torrid love affair."

"Gosh!..you had me there," she said, taken back by his studio affair. "I can imagine you poured your heart out into the music."

"Aye. It was a wrestle at times," he said. "My musical buddy, Zane, can be a handful. And he's here now in Goa."

"So, I hear. Felix told me."

"You'd have seen him," Jules said. "He's the gangly nutter with peroxide pineapple-top hair. Dances like he's having epileptic fits."

"Oh!.. that one!" she said. "He sure cracked me up in the bamboo forest." She took a swig of orange juice. "Listen Jules," sadness filled her eyes. "I'm not what you think." She turned away from him and stared despairingly into the towering banyan, like she had something to absolve. The threads of the grand tree's vertical aerial roots had become so thick, they too, had become trunks that grew down into the earth supporting its behemoth structure. The spread of its multiple trunks, like acro props. Its thick branches, like arms that seemed to want to cuddle and comfort her. "I'm not a *vixen*," she said with a self-mocking frown, as if to acknowledge the disparity between what she gleamed to the world, and what she felt herself to be. "Ha!.." she shrugged. "Maybe I should do a fashion sub label: *Vagator Vamp?*" Feeling sickened by herself, she almost jumped into his arms.

"You should," he implored. "You'd be good at it. You know, when I got back here I had high hopes, but it soon became clear that I had to rearrange my feelings, reset expectations, move on, so I could have fun. Besides, my head is fully in the music now. Seemed like you and Felix were having fun."

Riddled with contrite her face reddened. "Look!.. Felix is a special friend. He's a player... sweet and generous. A manic depressive. Maybe he sees me as his come-back marzipan queen," she said in a trampy tone of voice. "No, I'm just kidding," she said, not wishing in her own mind to mess with Jules's head, knowing that he was getting deeper into the *Goa thing*. "Felix always brings fabulous music and makes a cracking party." Confidentially in a low voice, she divulged that he'd also brought two kilos of sniff. One kilo to share with friends, and one to pay for his play time.

Jules's face was split between a half smile of someone being entertained, and a baleful twitch of concern, as he listened to her scrappy self-admonishments and crafty disclosures. *Oh, well—its Goa*, he thought. Such is its de rigueur: the breaking of rules, not conforming to normal behaviour, normal fashion, normal music, normal parties. It's a place where nothing is normal, including concupiscence. He thought he'd done a good job tearing himself away from frayed feelings of hurtfulness since their last meaningful get together.

Secretly, she wished she could be held with all her contradictions, without judgements, and shake off shameful self-loathing. Her face in the dappled shade became overcast and doleful—she bowed her head. Raising her eyes up from the dirt of the soon-to-be dance floor, she said, "Jules, you have to understand our story last season dismantled me. I felt taken apart. As deeply touching as it was, it was destabilising. I felt upended, it opened a flood gate of emotions. I'm still processing it. I trusted you. I felt you understood me. I guess I was afraid I was gonna lose myself in you."

Thick branches at the heart of the banyan began to creak, like the ancient tree was uttering a comment on the mysteries of the heart, which, for Zsu, seemed beyond this world. As far apart as her head was from her heart in flights of fantasy. She cherished what they'd shared, and how he was able to touch her with his telepathic mind. Yet, her upended fractious self could not extinguish the hazardous flames of burning down the house, the framework of her decoratively wallpapered self, behind which lurked her most guarded secretive self, the place of solitary aloneness. When she'd made herself not available on his return to Goa, he fell pondering at the drawbridge of the fortification of her unrequited heart. It was then that he remembered something that a muso friend had once told him. *It's not wise to end either a relationship, nor a piece of music, with a deceptive cadence.* He recalled her bent over the DJ table with Felix and wondered what she really needed from a man?

Powerful forces had surged through her body on the last night with haughty Atma Blaze, which excited her and scared her, like a moth to a flame. Phoenix-like, in the form of primordial Kali, she'd risen from catastrophe, like in the kind of crisis in relationships which degenerate into power struggles exposing emotional vulnerability—leaving her suspicious of feelings that entrapped her, feelings that threatened to swallow her up in a love-hate loop.

Growing up in Marseille not knowing her father, she liked to build fantasy pictures around men. On hallucinogens, she'd become aware of how emotions attached themselves to thought patterns that imprisoned her in the past, like a trapped child. A palmist had once warned her of old karma that lies unavenged, waiting its moment. She wondered if this was what happened with Blaze? At a young age, she'd learned to be secretive about her true feelings, especially her run-ins with sex and its manipulative power. The kind of promiscuity a daughter of Hades was prone to, so as to remain emotionally unattached, and therefore in control. But this brought suffering in feeling herself paralysed by fear rooted in wounds with her relationship with her mother, which she came to realise she could heal through the mother of all mothers: the supernatural powers of mother nature.

Further to the visitation of the ghost of Donna Ferreira in Disco Valley last year, Zsu recently had another haunting visitation in which she'd been told of an *Omen*. As she shared this with Jules, he wrapped his telepathic feelers around its providence. Then, from above them, the supernature of the mighty banyan creaked and screeeched and wailed louder utterances. With eyes closed and slowed breathing, he said, "There're entities here, ineffable forces... feels like this is a place of Dionysus."

"The party's gonna be sunset to sunset," she said.

"Wow!—some session." he said. "Jupiter, the beneficent will be boosting everything Venus." He shot her a burning look. "You know— I've been collecting music like a maniac since I got here."

Her face lit up. "Excellent!.. so, you'll be ready."

"Ready?" he said, with a contrived look of ambivalence

You'll be ready to play?" she said. Her felicitous esteem disarming his tease.

"Yes.. yes.. for sure!" he said wholeheartedly.

"I want you" she blushed. "I want you to DJ!"

"Absolutely!" he fervently reassured her. "I'll be ready. You can count on me."

They gazed up into the vast canopy of the sentient banyan. It had taken on the appearance of mosaic lead light of a basilica, in which they lost themselves in its allegory of leaf and fractal forms.

Zsu turned to Jules and said, "Don't you think nature is perfect? Everything that's screwed-up in the world is caused by humans."

Hypnotised by the colossal tree and its calming beauty, he said, "Ha!— species karma."

SHIVARATRI 26th FEBRUARY

A COCONUT WAS CEREMONIALLY CRACKED over the brass head of a Shiva lingam by an acolyte with long black dreadlocks. Milk ran down over the head into a vase plinth shaped like a yoni. Fifteen devotees sat in a circle on the floor in front of it, in the house of the Norwegian prophet, Oddvar Osser, who chanted Pagan "root sounds" of the O.O.O. in a Scandinavian dialect. The incantation was delivered with a rolling of the prophet's tongue so that the ancient phonemes of his epistemological oratory tickled the brain with an enchanting, spellbinding resonance.

The house was in the middle of a monkey forest behind Chapora. Amongst those gathered were two Goans and two women. The middle-aged prophet had large feet with toes like hooves, which were tucked up as he sat in lotus position by the Shiva lingam. His chiselled visage was like that of an Easter Island head, off of which hung shoulder length grizzled hair and goatee. The phoneme "root sounds" made up a tribal saga about paradise times at the top of the world, before the earth tilted on its axis, at the third ice age of Ragnarok, 1050 AD, after which came pre-Christian times.

Undercover in counterculture, Naresh Kumar sat listening to the sounds for the first time. He'd been taken there by the maverick sadhu, Remo, whom he'd given his Bollywood tapes to check out. Looking around the ceremonial room, the actor-cum-hack reporter attempted to decipher the esoteric art it contained. A central painting featured an anagram comprised of three O rings linked together. Underneath in gothic font was written, 'The Osser Ouroboros of Oden.' Adjacent were sigil symbols and family crest with the names: Hel-Oss-I-Oden-Ra-Tor-Frey-Freya. Fixed to a wall was the head of a goat colourised with 'hundreds and thousands' minute fluoro paint dots. On a corner table, ornately carved with Norse and Pagan symbols, stood a brass statuette of the Greek god, Pan, with an elongated erection.

The dreadlocked acolyte uncorked a ceramic jar containing seed from the eye of Osser's *Norse Pole*, and poured the opaque fluid over the Shiva lingam, with it running down into the vase to mix with the coconut milk. The acolyte poured the mix back into the ceramic jar and passed it to Osser for sanctification. Holding it in his large hands, he swirled it about in a rhythmic circle as he chanted an incantation of O.O.O. 'root sounds,' dedicating its pearly contents to Odin. A tall ceremonial chillum was lit and passed around. Osser held the lip of the jug above his open mouth, poured a dribble and swallowed. The jug was then passed to the acolyte, who did the same, and passed it on around the circle. On receiving it from Remo, Naresh was seized with apprehension. *What kind of Shivaratri ceremony is this?* Holding eye contact, Remo shot him an assenting wink. Naresh imbibed.

Three rhesus monkeys with long question mark tails dropped from the trees outside and loped along the railing of the veranda. Osser leapt to his feet, fetched bananas and talked to them in triple O speak. Naresh observed that everyone was pierced with golden earrings of snakes eating their tails. Some with pierced nipples on bare chests with tattoos of dragons. The dark dreadlocked acolyte, whose forehead glared with a bright painted yellow trident tilak, was introduced to Naresh by Remo. "Meet Atma."

DJ Atma Blaze muttered, "Hi." Barely offering eye contact through matted dark tendrils of hair that hung over his face—instead, his darting eyes had seized upon a tape Remo had taken out of his Kulu bag—titled, XTRA TERRESTICLE.

"Can I see that cassette?" he requested.

As soon as it was in his hand he forensically scanned the names on the inner sleeve. "This is what I have been looking for," he said gleefully. "Well sourced Remo, these tracks I've been hunting for. Just what I need for the full moon party we're going to make on Anjuna Beach in three days' time."

DOWN ON SPAGHETTI BEACH at Nirvana chai shack, one of the regulars, Lorenzo, a sharp-shooter of checkers on the hotly contested backgammon board there, was bent over with a stomach condition. Tablets from Chapora Pharmacy brought no relief, so he went to Mapusa Pathology for stool and blood tests. Returning the following day for the results he was told to wait. Shortly after, to his alarm, a police jeep showed up and he found himself detained under a new law on contagious sexually transmitted diseases. The Doctor informed him that the results indicated the AIDS virus.

Lorenzo's backgammon buddies fumed over his predicament and were sceptical of the accuracy of the the pathology. Luchiano visited Lorenzo in a locked ward at Mapusa Hospital, bringing him some smoke. The consensus at Nirvana chai shack was that Chief Inspector Fernandese should be greased to liberate him. At Mapusa Police Station the Inspector explained to Luchiano that he couldn't assist, as the hospital was involved. A Spaghetti Beach posse decided that swift resolve was required and hatched a plan. On his next visit, Luchiano slipped Lorenzo a small crowbar. The following night with a guard at his locked ward, Lorenzo removed the window from his room and made ready escape down knotted bedsheets to a reception of two friends below, who arranged him speedy passage to Bombay.

THE DEVIL IS DANCING NAKED ON DRUGS ON ANJUNA BEACH

It was the most flagrant headline anybody in Joe Banana Restaurant could remember. Those reading the front-page story in *The Goa Voice* newspaper over breakfast at Joe's, became plagued with worry worms. Doc Silver's mango shake tasted sour, when it ought to have tasted sweet. It was as if the fire and brimstone announcement by the tabloid had turned everything acrid. Doc had seen sensationalist headlines like—DOPE VACATIONERS—coming from Panjim press before, but this was more than than a kick in the guts, this was below the belt.

Zsu was also at Joe's. She tore her troubled eyes away from the poisonous print. "It's evil propaganda!" she recoiled, glaring with clenched teeth. "It's monstrous bullshit!"

"On top of that," Doc said, his face scrunched up in disgust, "guess what, you know who, wants to do?"

Zsu shot him a fixed jaw look of disturbance.

"Shazam just told me," Doc said, "Atma, the brat, is scheming to throw a full moon party on the beach in Anjuna."

"What the hell? Jez, what a jerk!" she said harshly with a tight chest as she peered gravely at Doc's peeved face.

He shook his head. "It's not like we haven't been skewered up the arse with a hot poker of party politics before. The current situation is preposterous. Some dipshits just don't get it, do they?"

Zsu saw red. "What's he playing at?" Her face fell into a shadow of hurt. The invidious intent of sabotaging the plan for full moon at the banyan tree burned, burned, burned. The coffee shake she'd just necked was racing her jangled nerves. She visualised the goat heads and pentagrams she'd seen at Osser's January birthday party being installed in the palms by O.O.O. followers on the beach. She imagined freaks being burnt at the stake, a large wooden cross in flames on top of Anjuna hill with a full moon rising above it, accompanied to howling dogs of doom.

"Oh no!" she gasped, alarmed by the headline, it setting fire to a vat of combustible gases in her blood, making it boil with the collective memory in her DNA of burnings and witch hunts.

"It's a conspiracy! I was warned." Her eyes narrowed with scorn. "What kind of uppity, arsehole antic is this? Now I'm sure Atma is the Devil's advocate." Her now not-so-pretty face sagged from the weight of disbelief. Her chin dropped to her chest, where droplets of sweat gathered and trickled down to a silver Celtic knot pendant—at its centre, a blue lapis lazuli crescent moon appeared to weep.

"This is bloody horrendous!" she said woefully. "Did you know that Atma is into Osser's saga?"

Doc's fragile countenance of studied calm—shattered. "Oh, Gawd no!.. Now I'm maddened." He struggled to rein in his curmudgeon self. He couldn't allow a freak-out. Zsu needed shoring up. He prided himself on the buck stopping with him in such mutinous, sectarian scenarios. He was Zsu's most counted upon enabler.

"What do you make of the O.O.O.?" she asked.

"It's a fairy tale," Doc replied bluntly. "Lollyballs has sucked in a bunch of stoners. Osser thinks he's Lord of the Rings. Cults become dangerous when the story is presented as fact."

"Well, mystical mania thrives here," she said. "With all the space cases camped out, its fertile territory for extreme flights of fantasy, longing for a *paradise lost*. That's why the freaks are here." Her jaw tightened. "But this is too much." She slumped in her chair and let out a sigh like an inflatable that just had its plug pulled. "Oh, for the joy of Odin morning glory lingam suckers," she said, attempting to lighten the mood. "Oh, for the joy of dawn breakers."

"Yeah right!" Doc said. "Atma would be fully up for the sanctification of his priestly prick. He's so cock full of himself—a dickhead with knotted dread pubes."

"And according to Asta," Zsu said, "there's not much in the O.O.O. saga for women."

"It's a cock cult," Doc scoffed. "They're sitting around smoking that monster chillum. It's a Shiva lingam club for dudes' tooling with Hindu fertility rites. The Hindu's are obsessed with spunk, they see it as *Atman*, the cosmic seed. All the laws in the West about abortion, birth control, wanking, gay, oral, anal, are all to do with waste of seed."

Zsu was spurred to hear Doc beef unashamedly about flagrant sex and religious taboo. Some in the scene had been judgemental of his flirtatiousness with young chicks. Some, she could feel, spurned her, too. Her flare for risqué fashion, drawing eyes to her with gossipy, bitchy, tittle tattle, assigning her the tag—*strumpet sophisticate*. Of course, the scene was rife with delusional slippery word-of-mouth broken English, Chinese whispers and foggy information—all refracted through warped perceptions and highly-colourised projections.

Doc and Zsu were close. What they bonded over was a mutual attachment to a certain kind of unfettered party, hinging on the right people at the right place at the right time. Far from just being enshrined in a faith of Western decadent privilege, Zsu liked to believe that 'p-ART-y' (how she printed it on the tags of party wear) was co-creative and visionary—not merely a night club in nature, or entertainment—and definitely not, God forbid, commercial. Like a catalytic enzyme, trance dancing to techno was like electronic voodoo with an alternating **AC** and **DC** current—or, "the **A**nti-**C**hrist and **D**evil **C**hildren," which is what *The Goa Voice* led its readers to believe.

For a thousand rupees to make a party, Doc and Zsu got off, getting others off—just as blotta baba's did. The kick of satisfying a romantic yearning, susceptible to the belief that there might just be an allotted ration of ecstasy and joy permissible in a life time, and you ought to jump on it while you can.

"The Catholics," she complained, "did a smashing job, brain washing Goans. "Ha!—how many have been murdered in Jesus's name by dopey Popes over centuries. Here we are in Asia looking for spiritual truths and sustainable highs, escapees from what? The mind fuck of a rapacious fear-based religion. Our ancestors were infected with it. The Portuguese Inquisition here was criminal chicanery." She then was struck by the realisation that without European colonisation in Goa, it would not have been possible for freaks to spore here.

Doc rested his chin on the palm of his hand and stared out past Joe's courtyard of tables into the palms of South Anjuna. "I wonder what Darwin would make of Osser's story?.. Anyhow, Shazam gave me the ups," he said. "Jesus loves acid and Gorby is coming to the banyan tree." Doc sucked on his straw till his glass gurgled empty. The defiance in his blazing eyes was like a fuse that had been lit. "Atma can go fuck himself...and stuff those imbeciles in Panjim."

AS NARESH LAY IN BED, the mystery of the snake coiled around his mind. A track, 'Legend of the Snake' by The Bollock Brothers on a cassette that Remo had left him, played over in his head. It featured a voice that spoke about Adam and Eve being tempted by a snake to eat forbidden fruit so as to become god-like. This, he wondered, must be "dancing with the Devil."

With *The Goa Voice* deadline for his story pressing down on him, and still recoiling from the headline it ran yesterday, he was hit by a wave of worry about the assignment. The tabloid's agenda was deeply troubling. It clearly attested to the kind of story he'd been commissioned to write— which he was less and less inclined to put his name to. Writing a movie script was what he really wanted to be doing rather than fictional *facts* for a tabloid. But reality in Goa was stranger than fiction. The characters and scenes he was encountering had captured his imagination, all the more enhanced by the quality charas being generously shared around amongst outrageous company from all over the world. He'd been acting when he told the editor that he was from a Christian family. Now he found himself trapped in a mythological drama with a potentially life altering script. Was it possible that Lord Shiva, the party scene's ecstatic dancing deity, could be cast as the Devil, or Anti-Christ? Shiva wears a cobra around his neck, and the ouroboros swallows itself. What is the serpent in the garden of

Eden up to? He became seized with an overwhelming desire to eat forbidden fruit. And so, sat down and wrote a letter, sealed it in an envelope and had it delivered by motorbike pilot to the editor of *The Goa Voice*.

The next day, at Ram Dass chai shop on top of the cliff at middle Vagator Beach, Naresh met Remo for sunset. "I found a remarkable piece of music," the sadhu scholar said with a glint in his eye pointing to the title, 'Ten Ragas To a Disco Beat,' on one of Naresh's Bollywood cassettes. "It's Indian Acid," he said. "No DJ here would know of it. I'm guessing the producer, Charanjit Singh, did it as an experiment. His face beamed with the excitement of a child in soft fading amber and orange light as the sun slipped into the sea. "It was written in nineteen eighty-two, which makes it the first Acid House track. It's a special find. I doubt it's been used in any movie. It fits perfectly for party here. Ten Ragas To a Disco Beat is the musical genius of India."

"I had no idea," Naresh said, chuffed with having impressed his new Indian friend, who struck him as learned and well connected, and told him that he'd once met the sitar player, Ravi Shankar.

When Remo was not in Goa for the party season, he stayed up the mountains of Manali in Himachal Pradesh. "The cops there, where the good stuff comes from, are becoming shrewder. You gotta be ahead of the game." He handed half a tola of charas to Naresh. "Enjoy!.. a present from Shiva."

"Boom shankar... your most kind," Naresh said holding the soft piece of hash up to his nose to savour its aroma.

"Be vigilant," Remo cautioned. "You can fly high here, but you can also crash. It can happen from out of nowhere. We *alien* Indians are vulnerable. We are under suspicion, just through association. They'll even plant something on you. Now that you've met the O.O.O.—there are some individuals who might come to your aide if you find yourself stuck between a rock and a hard place."

Talk then turned to the scurrilous *Goa Voice* headline, which drew a repellent look from Remo's knowledgeable, impish face. "Bigot bastards!" he said, launching into a diatribe. "Panjim is coming out of its post independent honeymoon phase. There are some that want to accuse foreigners for all Goa's problems. Like a scapegoat. Next, they'll be declaring an inquisition. India runs on mystery and magic and corruption. The British tried for years to stop us Indians smoking hashish, but we've been smoking it for too long, that will never happen," he said with a wry smile.

After the sun had set, everything lost its edges and shape in a twilight haze. With a bulging, almost full moon rising, Naresh farewelled Remo and steered his Yezdi motorbike along narrow dusty tracks. Along the way, he encountered some goats which got him thinking about Odvar Osser's saga, and recalled Remo's opinion that nationalistic religious conservatives were seeking to frame hippies as scapegoats. Remo's understanding of the situation was unsettling and stirred further, disconsolate doubts about *The Goa Voice* assignment. Arriving at the Vagator Resort, Naresh looked up at Chapora Fort and pondered its ramparts. For what purpose had these heavy stones been hauled up there? What were Europeans defending? *Yes! Yes! The spice trade.* He turned around, walked to reception and said he wished to check out in the morning.

SLOTTING THE GEAR SHIFT INTO WARP SPEED, the rider tunnelled the rip curl board through the sound wave keeping it in the sweet spot of the party. Flying on the seat of his board shorts, his feet gripped the waxed surface made out of tessellated cassette cases with track names. Tape machines whirled, tiny spindles spun. It was a race against time. One track was running out, another needed to be loaded, cued, set in motion to tail into the one about to finish, all the while—the nose of the board must never pearl.

Can I slice 'n' dice to the next wave? Can I make the mix? What happens if I fall off? Where is the emergency tape?

Like a cassette just popped from its warm slot, where it had been snuggly rolling across a magnetic head, Jules woke up in a sweat gripped with panic, having been suddenly ejected from a dream. He found himself in an in-between world of not knowing whether what he just experienced had actually happened, or not? He'd gone to bed stoned, his head swimming with beats, melodies and technoid bleeps. After falling asleep, he saw himself dropping down into the barrel of a huge wave, instead of surfing, he was DJ-ing inside it like it was a party.

The days and nights leading up to the full moon, he wound through more and more cassettes passionately searching for techno that hotwired the zeitgeist. With a black marker pen, he wrote track times, BPM (beats per minute) and remix versions on the sleeve of his tapes. In brackets, he noted the exact time when the beats came in from ambient intros and highlighted with fluoro pens track titles: Yellow denoting morning music. Blue for night.

In hindsight, back in the sixties, when Hipster Harry and friends arrived in Goa, what everyone liked about it was the unspoilt natural beauty and freedom that was possible. The freedom to have happenings, any time, any place, with no constraints from straights. Including doozy parties where the music was bad, the drugs heavy, the sound system not up to it. Community-wise, like a family of travellers, it was most socially vivifying when all came together with—*peace, love, unity, respect*. The Asia trail became more accessible for Jetset hippies in the eighties with the Lonely Planet travel guide for India becoming brick-size, choker with traveller information. Still the cherished liberties of Goa's *freak habitats* flourished, but seething undercurrents had emerged, which threatened to undermine freedoms the scene had founded itself on.

The earth's satellite of love—the moon—exuded mesmerising stellar lust in Goa, especially at its peak every twenty-eight days, when it beckoned with a beatitude that beamed supreme blessedness, as if to say, *It's time to get on it, and dance!* The days leading up to the March full moon were highly charged. Dubious, jungle telegraph information about two parties had been going around, word of mouth, motorbike-to-motorbike, two days before full moon. Zsu was doing her darnedest not to be phased by Atma's ill-considered stratagem. With mounting opposition in Panjim, everything argued against an O.O.O. party on the beach. Doc's hammed-up approach, like a party whip ironing out sheer stupidity arising from clashing events, mostly could be relied upon. But Zsu figured it would be tactful to have Asta talk with Osser about the crazy, infuriating situation.

Asta found the Norwegian prophet at Chandrakan chai shop in Chapora. She ordered tea and pakora and sat with him. From out of a shoulder bag he took a ceramic bottle, uncorked it, and dribbled his serpent seed over his potato bhaji curry.

"I like the taste of it too," she said in a disarming tone of voice. He gazed at her and grinned. "I prefer it to mine," she said, "I can't get the hang of the dolphin staff thing on my passion fruit."

"The mun is the mouth," Odvar replied in Odin root language, as he spooned his plate. "The i mun is the immune system. Men suck seed and ladies sip sap," he said reverentially, and took a bite of his curry with a bread roll.

She raised the issue of the full moon party. "Listen Odvar, I hear Atma has ideas about an O.O.O. party down on the beach in Anjuna. This is totally uncool right now." Most concerning, they talked about the provocation of the scandalous newspaper headline.

"It's history repeating," he said, "just like when the Catholics outlawed Pagan practices."

Asta told him of arrangements Zsu had made for a longer twenty-four hour party at the Badem banyan tree. "It's handy to your house," she said. "You can slope off from the dance floor and have your own full moon ritual with goats and monkeys."

Odvar stroked his ashen goatee. "Atma didn't tell me what he had in mind. The holy banyan tree you speak of is most certainly an eminent beatific place for such an occasion. Let me talk with him."

THE DAY BEFORE FULL MOON, Jules went to the banyan tree and found Asta and friends dabbing fluoro powder paint onto its dense aerial root forms, which looked like organic wires.

"It's all go here," she greeted him. "Good news. The O.O.O. have done the sensible thing and called off their party. Everyone will gather here."

"That's a relief," Jules said, "Zsu will be happy." Standing next to Asta, he observed in detail the merged trunk structure of the mammoth banyan, and had an overwhelming urge to be swallowed up by the huge tree. He recalled the animate energies he'd detected when Zsu brought him here. He moved closer into the heart of the tree and stood in the cleft of its central trunk. He could feel currents of sap running through its sheer density and understood why it was a wish-fulfilling holy tree for Hindus and Buddhists. He imagined himself DJing, right where he stood, the spinal tap of the totemic tree, dancers spread out underneath it as he channelled sounds through the crystals that Zsu was sure to put on the table there.

"It's a magical tree," Asta said, thrilled to see him cocooned in the brush strokes she'd just applied to the contours of its fibrous skin.

"It's overwhelming," he said. "I'm feeling a bit nervous, it'll be my first time DJing."

"Really. I'm sure you'll be great."

"It's a whole new thing," he said. "The dance floor here is the most full-on I've ever known. DJing this kind of party is not like being in a band. I've found amazing new music, hopefully it does the job—"

"I really like that 'Goa Goat Head' track you made. I heard it at Zsu's."

"Oh, thanks. Hearing it in the the bamboo forest party was like it had taken on a life of its own, like an alien entity. It sounded completely different from how it sounded in the studio."

"Is it to do with the O.O.O.?"

"Interesting you ask," he recoiled with a look of intrigue. "Hm, I heard about the O.O.O. last year, but it was a mystery to me. I learned more about it after I exchanged music with Remo. He told me about this saga… Oh yeah, right!.. At Osser's birthday party there was all this goat symbolism. He's Capricorn, it's the sign of the goat ruled by Saturn, which in historical texts is regarded as the old Devil—Satan."

Asta wore thigh-length turquoise spandex, patterned with mermaid fish scales, her legs splattered with drips of dayglow, her mussed fringe matted to her brow beading with perspiration.

"I've been loving the razzle-dazzle of your party outfits," Jules praised her. "Your stall at the flea market has pizzazz. It's bodacious!"

"Wow! Thanks Jules" She shot him a quizzical look. "Bodacious?"

"Yeah," he said, "like in, bold and stylee and stunning, rather than mere—bootylicious."

She blushed and rewarded him with a wide smile. He buttered her some more. "You have taken Barbarella to another level. I bet you have a stunning creation to wear in the chroma lunar rays here tomorrow night." Referencing his horoscopic calculus, he told her about Venus. "The planet of amour is aligning with Jupiter—the romping sky god Zeus." While telling her this, his body defaulted to libidinal calculus as Asta hung on every word, like it was celestial nectar he was tonguing into her ear. His cosmic word pictures igniting mythological theatre in her mind, her imagination rampaging with visions of potential costumes with which to rise to the cosmic occasion. "Full moons reveal what has been in the dark," Jules said in a low voice, a sparkle in his eye. "What is ready to bloom since the new moon."

That night, with the moon virtually full, Jules went to Zsu's house and found her heavy hearted. Maestro Voltaire did not wish to play. Sadly she said that some arsehole had stolen his freshly recorded tapes from Sofia's house while everyone was at the beach. According to Jaeger, a bamboo stick had been poked through the metal security bars of an open window to hook a leather cassette bag and jewellery. Zsu was gutted by the theft. Her superlative DJ would not be attending the party.

"That's terrible!" Jules said, "What a shame. Can't Voltaire get that music back?"

"It was super rare," she explained. "Tracks that Jaeger doesn't have. 'Goa Goat Head' was on one of the tapes."

"Weird things happened making it," Jules said. "It was like a strange mystical force wrote itself into the music while recording that track. Contrary to what you might think, I don't want it released on any label.

Let's see what becomes of it in the underground wilderness. He shrugged and curiously raised one eye brow, as if to suggest it was an orphan child, or a mad Frankenstein experiment that escaped from the lab.

"That's some attitude," she said. "Jules, I have a special request." She lowered her eyes to his. "I want you to play at midnight."

He exhaled deeply. "My God!.. the witching hour." His mind rapidly ticked over, taking stock of the magnitude of the invitation. The honour it bestowed. The nasty twist of fate of foul play of maestro Voltaire's misfortune, which meant he, the rookie DJ, would now get to play prime time. And the expectant pressure, like committing to a date with a pack of barking rabid dogs ravenous to be fed juicy cuts.

"I trust you," Zsu said.

"No worries!" he assured her. "You can count on me." Hearing her say the word, *trust,* sympathetically fuzzed his heart, then found himself kissing her lightly on the lips and wished her a good night's rest.

Patchouli flower essence burned in her bedroom as she dropped off to sleep on the eve of midwifing the March full moon party. On the motorbike ride back to his house in the Vagator jungle, the bulging moon had turned everything chrome, its beaming brightness twenty-eight hours away from peak fullness. Jules had been lying when he told Zsu, "no worries." It being a Down Under colloquialism, which masked inescapable, cultural inheritances from the fatal shore of a so called "lucky country." (Australia's political incorrectness since its beginnings as a penal colony and subsequent near-genocide of its indigenous culture.)

Glimpsing twinkling stars through trees, while steering his Rajdoot along a jungle motorbike track, brought prescient thoughts of the beneficent hook-up of Venus and Jupiter, allowing him to push aside trepidation about stepping up to DJ. By the time, he was about to crash out—after listening to 'Fatal Error' by Fatal Error—it was Pluto, the dark Lord of The Underworld—in its ruling sign, Scorpio, and Mars, its co-ruler in the sign of the goat—that left him on edge about what was about to unfold.

Banyan Tree Party

BLACK SPEAKER BINS ON FOUR METAL STANDS stood in a semi-circle at the furtherest reach of the banyan's branches. A 125-bpm mixtape, ETHNOBOTANICAL BEATZ, compiled by Zsu, punctuated the leafy air, as Antonio, the PA owner, equalised the sound. With amplified music beckoning and the sun commencing to set and chai mummas laying down their reed mats, dancers started to arrive. Soft orange light washed through the labyrinth of branches above as Moana from Aotearoa cued a tape at the table in front of the trunk of the tree.

From out of the afterglow of twilight, the moon popped up large to the accompaniment of the DJ's first track—'Exotica' by Chris and Cosey. As dusk gave way to the shimmer of lunar rays, fluoro highlights on dangling roots and entwining vines of the totem tree commenced to glow more intensely. They were lit by UV black light tubes that Rama, the lighting man from Chapora, had fixed to branches above. In lunar and ultraviolet light, animated dancing figures moved throughout its entrancing, alchemical luminosity as local boys dampened the earthy smelling dance floor with splashes of buckets of well water.

By early evening, in the blooming radiance of the organic wonderland of the banyan grove, more and more early groovers, resplendent in shiny outfits, arrived on boogie-buggy motorbikes that looked like extensions of their own bodies. Having forsaken dinner, they bee-lined to a dhuni beneath a smaller banyan where a Ganesh statue sparkled, wreathed with Christmas lights where, nearby, blotta baba Shazam sat on an Afghan rug.

Ceremonially holding court—dressed in a vibrant, allegorical, mystical jumpsuit—a craftiness flickered in the psychedelic purveyor's face. He was assisted by two handmaidens sitting either side of him. A svelte nymph from Switzerland, in a filmy forest green tutu with peacock patterned top, served 125 mic hits of perestroika punch in small plastic cups. The other French, sprite-like, in lime hot pants with shimmering top, served 250 mic hits. Shazam's jumpsuit featured a composite collage of oriental deities that conjured the effect of a spell concocted by a megatripolis sorcerer of the East edge. From out of his pocket, he produced a sheet of double-dip 500 mic tickets which he ceremonially handed out to the most intrepid of neuronauts. Those dosing up were like pilgrims to a Ganesh Glasnost dispensary for darshan, prior to zooming off at an LSD departure lounge.

Many revellers were still at home prepping and primping and preening themselves, preparing to step out into the full moon's luminescence, that was now coating everything silver. Foot pumping Singer sewing machines of personal tailors had been busy, the days leading up to the party, making custom costumes. Three hours before midnight, Dutch DJ, Joos, had taken over and was spinning squiggly Acid House that sent the banyan grove into a world far from reality. It was fast filling up with suntan-bronzed kooky players, tribal-accessorised in a kaleidoscope of opalescent wiggy adornments. Many with face paint, some with feathers in their hair that metamorphosised them into wild feral creatures. All clad in non-conformist garb, emblematic of galactic groovers, space cowboys, interstellar sirens, cyber punks, sonic sufis and new-age spiritual wonderers. All jumping about in a techtronically tailored slipstream under the overarching span of the mother banyan, like it was a totem tree for teleportation into heightened syzgies.

It might occur to an outsider who observed the kind of dancing that was going on under the banyan—like the Headmaster who owned it, and happened to be passing on his scooter—that this was an acid head lunatic party. But most likely, the ordered chaos of the bright and joyful celebration was seen as just another religious festival in India. The Headmaster didn't care that the zaps, zonks and donks of the wobbly weird computer music was from another world beyond his, and that Zsu and her friends (many of whom proudly proclaimed themselves *freaks*), were also from another world, and were hardwired to dance to loud music in a highly-animated manner all through the night. And that the thud, thud, thud, thump of Roland 909 and 808 kick drums and clangour of cacophonous alien technoid bleeps would be heard when he went to bed. And that this pounding hot current of looney, moon juice stomping would still be thumping when he returned home from Assagao Primary School in the afternoon the next day. Another headmaster might form the opinion that such loud larking in his banyan glade was an indignity to bucolic life. A scrofulous distain of law and order and authority, which Shazam's portraits of Gorbachev were in aid of dismantling. But the outrageous, hedonistic subversiveness of such an extended off-the-hook odyssey of music and noise and dance decadence (ostensibly a birthday party), never came into question for the Headmaster. Or any other local Goan in the Bardez party triangle, as it was all just part of the permissive possibilities of a sub culture in symbiotic cohabitation with tolerant locals—assuring a felicity of mutual benefits.

Post their torrid dalliance, Zsu could only handle Atma in small doses after his serpent-seed-cup runneth over with the practices of the O.O.O. With him now imbibing himself every morning and inserting O.O.O. 'root language' mantras into every conversation.

"Odin is a ring, Odin is everything, Odin will aways be and has always been. The heart is the head of the rose at the end of the Noose pole."

Which, to Zsu's mind, amounted to the glorification of his dick. As a conciliatory gesture to him for cancelling his party, she offered him to play a late morning set at the banyan tree. This he bumptiously turned his nose up at, and imperiously demanded entitlement to impress himself upon the full moon's grandness in the night. Fed up with his tetchy invidiousness, she capitulated and agreed for him to play before Jules.

After fine tuning the arted-up dance zones around the banyan (with some paintings looking like cosmic doughnuts), Zsu went home to refresh and prepare for the night. An O.O.O. follower showed up and hung a painting of a Baphomet goat in trees just past the speakers. The esoteric creature had breasts, glowing phoenix-like wings and was seated on a burning purple plinth in the shape of a pentagram around which was coiled a snake in a figure of eight with iridescent sparkling eyes.

There was troubling speculation as to who'd stolen Voltaire's tapes. It simply couldn't just be vermin, opportunist, Indian thieves? For Zsu, it felt like sabotage. Jaeger would now play after Jules through to dawn. Word of the party was spreading like wild fire on the Goa jungle telegraph. In Calangute and Arambol, party people were brimming with excitement having heard the latest information, and readying themselves for the motorbike ride that would deliver them to the extended looney-tech session. Goa nineteen eighty-eight felt boundless. Everything possible. Everything permissible. A season in which the consistency of the brain was proven not to be cold porridge. A season in which trance-tribal-techno-transcendentalism spawned. *A second summer of love,* heralding the birth of *Rave* as a unifying, revolutionary zeitgeist. The imminent crumbling of the ideological, political divide of the wall in techno city—Berlin. The chemical euphoria of the recreational enhancer, *Ecstasy,* opening up heart chakras all over the world.

Seasoned Acid Rock trippers swore by the philosopher's stone of Leary and Hoffman as the primary axiom elixir in the experiential opening of doors. The loved-upness of the new amphetamine designer drug, MDMA, was regarded an endorphin rush mousse, and not as psychedelically expansive as dosing on hallucinogens. As horny and—*on,* as coke and E were, acid heads maintained that powder and pills did not deliver the vivid phantasmagorical worlds and outer space visions that the new electronica evoked. Richly layered with lush synths and wobbly acid bass lines from silver Roland boxes from Japan, the brand-new-better-living-through-fuzzy-logic-circuitry music was like an Italian dessert of techno tiramisu to amuse and thrill and titillate and prick neuro chemistry. A jelly head hedonism cum sabotaging of big daddy mind fuck.

This was in contrast to the strident, malevolent noire of industrial music, with its eighties, Orwellian, melancholic rage against the machine tropes. For Zane and Jules, this dystopian disaffection tapped into the spleen of a post-punk psychedelia with a DIY anarcho attitude. A new drug-tech, to hack reality myths and subvert a corporatised world. The Telepathics's gig at The Brickworks in support of SPK had been ritual performance in front of an audience. The abrasive bite of an angle grinder that spat out sparks of disenfranchisement. In the bamboo forest, Zane got that it was now about machine-rendered music made by faceless studio boffins reconstituting order and chaos, and played by would-be shaman DJs in bush huts. Not just a night club in nature at which to get shit-faced on booze and powder.

The Telepathics had sprouted out of the incendiary discontent of punk and the dark-eye-liner occultisms of Goth. In the bamboo forest, Zane heard Sisters of Mercy, Ministry, The Young Gods, Skinny Puppy and Frontline Assembly in the rawness of its digital dirt and pungent nature smells. The experience recontextualised his identification with it as urban. Further deconstructed on blotta baba punch, whilst being whiplashed by clattering-percussive electronic body blows of Front 242's high-tech theatre of the mind in 'Masterblaster' and 'Welcome to Paradise,' he was transported to a place of mystical anarchy.

Heading out to the party from their house in Vagator, Zane farewelled Jules, who was last minute checking music on his tapes. Riding his TVS moped, Zane passed Primrose where there was hardly anyone, and dropped into Felix's house where a pre-party session was in full swing. In attendance was an effulgent gaggle of freaks from around the globe. Looking like slinky lounge lizards, they sat and reclined on sumptuous cushions, their bisexual looking legs shrink-wrapped in brightly coloured stretch tights. Necks, wrists, fingers and waists were intricately adorned with silver and gold gem stone jewellery.

Zane gaped. *What kind of hippie bourgeoisie was this?* There was something about white powder for Zane Lovelock that was more than the iniquity of a nice vice. All he had to do was follow his nose, like it was a compass, and he would end up where it selectively socialised. The sybaritic seductive allure of it, the ritual chopping of it with fetish paraphernalia, the rolling up of a hundred dollar Benjamin Franklin bill, the anticipatory emboldening bonfire rush of it. The sight of its plenitude freely flowing (the likes of which he'd never encountered before), brought on, almost-gagging, palpitations. In the past, he only did it huddled in a club shitter, or grimy graffitied band room. White powder was like a palliative romance with a co-dependent OCD girlfriend. When the Columbian crystals rocketed up his nostrils turning on electrodes in neurotransmitters, delivering a snorkel-gasm to his brain, he rejoiced in the instant uplift. The smoothing out of scratchy ennui and root canal-like throb in the architecture of the corridors containing his brain chemistry. The guardian angel looking over him had already alerted him (immediately upon hitting the streets of Bombay), that mother India was an entrepreneurial cornucopia of in-ya-face, whatever you want, "special price for you." Good bhang lassi bang for black market buck, and smack, a pittance of the price of the West.

Quality non-toking non-shooting importation, pretty much was a sweet runner through Bombay customs, according to Felix. "If they catch you, just flick em some cash." Indian officialdom went weak at the knees at the sight of greenbacks. Like the prestige of charlie, the status of highly corruptible Indian Customs was prime perks of the job. Gold and hundred dollar greenbacks being the ultimate clincher of any favour requiring the turning of a blind eye.

Felix liked to live the good life and was magnanimous in doing it. Contrary to some holier-than-thou anti hokey cokey opinion, he was gregarious and not cocaine cool. He warmed to Zane's sweet and sour Northern England acerbic humour. The Berliner and the Mancunian had gotten hilariously high on a couple of jaw-chattering occasions, turning each other on with crack-up pokes at the comedy of life seen through the bumped-up theatre of their minds. Felix's thick North European eyebrows seeming to animate in synch to Zane's legs, that were in a constant state of twitch as their wise cracks drove them on rubbing powdered noses into mental seizures.

After several rounds of snorkel sniffing, Zane pondered the rare breed of characters gathered, and the copious racking-up on hard surfaces all around him in Felix's capacious Portuguese pad. Some faces he recognised from previous parties, but there were many new characters whom he guessed were only lured out by the moon's full radiance. They got about, feline-like in sleek spandex leggings resplendent in colour and jungle wild-life and reptile patterns, giving the appearance of a new sub-species, part human, part animal. The colours and fabrics gathered tonight were decoratively flashy, mind-boggling bold, freaky and flamboyant, yet did not broadcast camp. Around lithe bodies were strapped ornately crafted, studded and bejewelled, leather belts and bum bags. His eyes darted about, alighting on curvy, athletic legs above which clung garments laced and zipped like new riders of a fantasia of night. Zane felt underdressed. His only splash of colour, a pair of red Reebok runners and a tank top with a yellow flash lightening bolt across his chest with bold text stating, HIGH VOLTAGE!

Standing by the trunk of the banyan tree in the revelatory setting of the party, wearing a ceremonial orange robe, his face sadhu-ash-white, DJ Atma Blaze inhaled a lung full of nicotine and charas smoke from the chillum that had been passed to him. He eyed the dance floor at his command, evaluating its robo-motor-neurone tangential twisting and quick stepping, its chain-reaction tendons, ligaments, muscles and tattooed, pierced flesh. The party had filled up, the dance floor busy. A timely, perfect track impressed itself upon Blaze to be played as his cerebellum spun on the Himalayan head rush. He rifled through his cassettes looking for 'Join In The Chant' by Nitzer Ebb.

At the edge of the dance floor, under the canopy of the banyan, yogi Ananta swayed gently to the music. He so wanted to cut loose, full-power, with his peerless four-way-hip-swivel-assana-contortionist moves, but the stitches in his abdomen told him otherwise. Cosimo, whom he'd jumped-in to rescue at the brawl on Spaghetti Beach, spotted him and thanked him and applauded him with sympathies of endearment. Cosimo presented Ananta with a loaded chillum, which he was able to crouch down into an Asian squat, to start. The Italian ceramic artisan held two burning matches and hollered, "Boom bolenath!" Ananta ceremonially bellowed clouds of holy charas smoke that rose up into the maze of the banyan. Other Spaghetti Beach friends joined in the smoking circle, including Lorenzo, who many didn't recognise as he was in disguise, sporting thick glasses and homburg velvet hat. Happy to be back, he ebulliently reported that a medical check-up in Bombay had correctly diagnosed him with hepatitis, not AIDES.

Sheila had a burning curiosity of how Naresh would R 'n' R in the revolutionary mind theatre of Gorby, where East meets West and left and right brain mash and cultural concepts are rearranged and personality masks melt and the fountain pen ink of life scripts run in a perestroika acid rinse. She found him on a chai mat. "Tonight's the night!" she greeted him.

"Goodness, it sure is a grand occasion," he said, like he was on the set of an epic drama and about to be cued to play his part. A role that he had no script for. A role in which he was happy to surrender his trust to his leading lady.

"This is what it's all about," she said brimming with excitement, while casting wide, devouring eyes about the spreading spectacle that was unfolding beneath the banyan grove, all wondrously lit up by chia mumma lanterns. A torrent of computer beats from the central towering banyan was electrifying the air. "Shall we?" she said, motioning towards the dance floor, like there was not a minute to waste.

"Yes!—let's," he said, sucking in apprehension and jumped up. Sheila led the way out of the chai mats to the Ganesh shrine and Shazam's dhuni, where incense burned and fragrant flowers sweetened the air. They were met by hand maidens who guided them to magical potions. Naresh recalled the ceremony at Osser's house, and now found himself at the threshold of another sacrament ceremony, in the aura of another holy man from the West. An acid guru.

"Standard or double?" Blotta baba, Shazam, asked in a lofty voice with the look of a hobgoblin. Naresh recognised him as the Santa Claus character from The Big House party. Sheila shot Naresh a reassuring smile. He steeled himself, surmounting doubts that were well concealed behind the affable smile that had got him this far and brought him to this moment.

"Standard please," she keenly replied. The more petite of the two maidens raised a finely formed arm, with elegant hand and slender fingers adorned with silver rings, to offer a small plastic cup of soma. Sheila took it in her hand and fixed wicked, smouldering, moka eyes and a beguiling smile on Naresh, while he also received a standard cup.

"Cheers," she toasted, and immediately skulled hers. Hesitation not being an option, Naresh followed suite, knocking back his cup as Shazam shot him a mischievous wink. The potion was fruity and brought with it a strange nerve spasm, as though his body anticipated what he'd just embarked upon. Gazing about, the Bombay Indian was awe-struck by the abundance of comforting feminine beauty, as well as the cheerful consecrating presence of the elephant god, Ganesh, and hilarity of the guru in mystical montage attire. *So, this is the jungle dispensary*, Naresh suddenly realised.

Wearing a choker necklace made of obsidian and hip-hugging cut-off red jeans complemented with calf-length brown, swede tasselled boots, Zsu dismounted her Yamaha and parked it next to a thicket of motorbikes, the density of which she hadn't seen this early at a party before. From out of her Bali bag she took small devilish horns and clipped them firmly on her head with fingers jointed in metal talons sculpted in the shape of scorpions with sharp tails.

Not wishing to make an appearance, just yet, she made her way through small trees towards the busy dance floor and dropped to a panther-like half crouch. At the edge of the fanning banyan tree canopy she scoped the party to see who was in attendance and gauge the costume splash on the dance floor. This she did with prying cat eyes fully dilated and intensified by winged black mascara, giving her the look of a woman in total control. Another eye beamed out of her—a third eye, like a cosmic orifice. It was screen printed across her chest on a clingy lycra top.

She spotted Jules heading toward the DJ table where Atma—judging by the response to the music playing, 'The Great Divide' by Portion Control—was doing a decent job mustering players onto the dance floor. She suspected that he'd erred playing some of this season's most explosive tracks, way too early. Special tracks that worked best when their triggers were pulled much later, deeper in the night. The kind of tracks she had complete faith Jaeger would be sure to drop when the party was needing to be tipped further then it had ventured before. She wondered how many of these prized special tracks Atma had in his possession? Who he'd been swopping with? Had he acquired them by questionable means? Who stole Voltaire's tapes? She then congratulated herself on having turned the other cheek with Atma. Her glaring face then turned to shock with an alarming shiver of self-scrutiny zapping her endocrine glands, as she watched Jules and Atma standing together in conversation at the trunk of the banyan.

She shrunk lower into the undergrowth and became overwhelmed with morbid shame, like a peeping Vagator hell cat. What did these men represent for her? What did the entire some ingredients of all that had come together for this full moon mean to her? What was the scene's expectations? A scene she loved to shine in. A scene in whose moon shadows she loved to dance. A scene of transient oddballs. A scene of free thinkers not inclined to play by the rules of society and made this place—*Gonzo Goa,* their home and stomping ground. A scene residing amongst cultish goats and cheeky monkeys and holy cows and pooh-gobbling flying pigs and bent be-Jesus sticks and Shiva lingam dicks and high quality substances and spiritual freebases. A scene where the music played was the best in the world, and this party? *Well, um—Yeah!.. This party was pretty much as good as it gets.* Albeit, Voltaire not playing was an absolute bummer. *Hm, shit happens in paradise.*

And what were Atma and Jules talking about? The music? But quite likely—her? She was then seized by an arresting vision. She saw herself standing under the banyan between Atma and Jules. Together, wearing black leather gloves, they stirred a bubbling crucible with a cast iron spoon. Zsu's searing green eyes burned, and turned into a blue flame through the dark kohl around them. Her body trembled with self-recognition. Crouching lower, her skin crawled with self-loathing and feelings of detachment. It was the kind of love she experienced with men she'd let through the swinging doors of her razor wire protected heart. The heart being the most vital organ of love, which was not entirely connected to the rest of her body. She was getting insight, a new field of vision—now seeing the party as deep supernature, which she herself was made of and wanting to explore down to its most nano particle level. Way down beyond the limits of the genetics of flawed, fractured love. The blue flame wildness of her supernature that represented a triumph over genes rooted in an excommunicated father she'd fantasised about. The animus of an inner partner who invisibly exposed vulnerabilities to the black-market fluctuation of ever changing currencies of the world around her heart.

Adding to her confessional discomfort, Felix joined Jules and Atma at the DJ table that she'd adorned with fresh flowers, crystals and miniature Shiva Nataraja. Disgust pinched her tummy as she got further peep hole glimpses of herself, her capacity for self-deception and the pain it brought. How she'd learnt the power of sex at a young age, and how it could easily end up having nothing to do with feelings of love. At the DJ table, she saw Atma and Felix lower their heads to snorkel sniff. She had a love hate relationship with it, regarding it a dominator substance. She hoped Jules wouldn't succumb. In all honesty, she didn't get-off dancing to DJs coked off their tits. Then she was struck by a vision of distorted images of these three ex-lovers breaking into pieces. Or was it the adorable illusion of her heart of glass? From these splintered fragments of her heart she found herself attempting to only piece Jules back together again. There was a circle of energy which he'd described to her as the four cardinal points which come together at the centre of magic. Taking a deep breath, she stood up and switched on small LCD lights inside the plastic horns on her head, which made them glow red. She stepped out of the bushes and into the hermetic circle of the party.

Loaded, Zane arrived to find the chai mats full-up with a carnivalesque tableau of journeyers—many with faces highlighted with stardust glitter and paint. The paths between the mats were a procession of multitudinous ad-hoc styles of the Asia trail. With open-mouth amazement, he gawked like he'd stepped into a deviant freak show. He wandered about until he found a bar and gulped down a shot of whisky to smooth out the charlie charging through his arteries.

Sometime later, convinced that what he was seeing was not a chimera, he saw a large pulsating, gooey, pink, pod sack (elongated like a huge bubble gum ball), hovering over the banyan tree. Pouring out of it, insectoid extraterrestrials with translucent skin emitting limey glowing light, descended into the maze of the branches of the banyan grove and transformed into humanoids that dropped down onto the dance floor to jack and mingle.

This all happened after he'd prostrated himself at Shazam's feet and earnestly requested a thousand microgram portrait of Gorbachev's head. It didn't take long before he found himself lolling around in the melting gob-stopper idiocy of an absurd jello psychedelic circus. Hallucinations wrapped themselves around sounds in the music, some becoming voices that spoke to him as he shat slabs of mental blocks. Optic nerve pixelating-pictogram panoramas teased his inner eye. Inside his skin, he screamed like a child as he danced on air above a cesspit of feuding feelings that sought to suck him under like a devouring abyss. Looking up, seeing that the moon had turned green, he transformed into a wolf and howled at it. With eyes wide, he stared down the barrel of his mind and met his future self in a world of cyborgs wearing ultra-thin techno gizmos. Cybererotic bodies with fibre optic skin writhed all around in a quaking cochlea-gasm under the ancient banyan tree. Its canopy became St Peters with everyone dancing on the skeletons of dead Popes. Naked nuns wearing only their coif headpieces were being buggered by extraterrestial devils. Micro mini-skirt teenage burka babes rode hogs.

The ancient tree of life told Zane that it had been here since the Holy Himilayas had heaved up cataclysmically and exploded skyward to the heavens, when the subcontinent gave birth to itself. Every epistemological emblem and religious symbol and mythological glyph was dangling down from the banyan on silvery strings, like Godhead wind chimes through the eternity of time, which the mother tree had sprouted from. Sir Edmond Hillary appeared before him (or was it Om Tom?), saying "Do you realise laddie, you've knocked the bastards off. What was Ed referring to? The bane of Zane's beleaguered, unshakable barnacles on his brain? Or the incorrigible cheeky monkeys on his back? Zane gasped the dusty digital air of the party like a scuba pearl diver whose tank had run out in the depths, necessitating the abandoning of his aqualung and belt weights for a hasty ascent to the surface, clutching shiny treasures on one last breath.

Pounding like a kick drum, his heart clocked double time of that of the music. The cuckoo bird of the master clock in his hypothalamus flew the coop. If brain cells were marbles, his had fallen from a great height and bounced about on acute angled musical surfaces that sent him ricocheting in all directions, until chanting Tibetan monk-like humanoids ushered him to a gravity-free zone that was like a sacred space. One of them jabbed him with a hypodermic needle to suck out the amniotic toxicity of all that was sick in the womb of the world, which he experienced inseparable to himself. Weirdo, paranormal paramedics gathered around him, hugging him back into his body. (Later he would find out that it was Agar and Kirsten whom he'd met at Shanti Hotel.) From a state of speechless, shapeless, insolubleness, he jumped up back into his body which then got sucked into the fantastical-spastical whirligig dancing of the banyan tree party.

PRANCING, SHIMMERING, COSTUMED GODS and goddesses, with fluoro-glow highlights, cast dancing moon shadows in the luminescence of the lunar light. The most astral of all, had silver spiral armlets that were like asteroids wound around her arm. She romped about in a metallic outfit emanating chroma radiance with blonde hair streaked green and gleamed lustrous like an android from planet Claire.

Hunched over cassettes and mixer, the DJ from out of the corner of his eye snatched glances of the astral goddess. The lustre of her mane flickered and glowed phosphorescent in the black light as her spring-loaded body bounced and pivoted omnidirectional. 'Black Planet' by Two Frenchmen was playing and it occurred to the DJ whilst preparing the next track that Asta's Cyberella aura was like that of a new celestial goddess in his metaverse.

It was the DJ's debut playing tapes at a Goa party. His nerves were on edge. He'd expected his mate to join him, at least share a joint. He suspected Zane had gotten *glasnost* loosened on double dip Gorbachev. Ceremonial chillums had been offered to the DJ, one he touched to his forehead and took a couple of puffs, then locked into DJ chores of singly manning multiple spinning tape decks, retrieving tracks, and keeping an eye on the playing time and cueing the next cassette. A sangfroid grip on the machines with steadfast precision mixing, tape to tape, was required for a hysteric dance floor gagging for appetising audio. DJ Jules was on a constant conveyor belt of in-the-moment on-the-spot decision making. A pressured stretching of gut instinct, flying on the seat of his spandex. There were momentary rushes of rewarding satisfaction in the energetic response to the segueing of tracks that connectively flowed with smooth mixes. The thrill of having his foot on the throttle of the party and reading its flaring delight. Judging from the dance floor action—all was groovy, hunky dory.

But a sharp corner was turned when something urged him to select a wild card track called, The Tingler. Leaping out of the speakers, the contorting acid riff of The Tingler tore up the dance floor like pounding teeth of a heavy earth works front end loader. Bodies tipped upside down. Some dancing on hands with feet in the air and heads bouncing on a pulverised dance floor. Others with limbs flailing from disconnected torsos. Piercing electronic body blows guillotined heads, that rolled like a coconut shy gone amok. Dancer participation with The Tingler became polarised, like metal iron filings in a magnetic field. The head strong ate it up like a rotary hoe with rapid twisting feet churning up the dance floor into a maniacal frenzy, akin to piranha feeding on sonic sirloin. Whilst others were seriously flattened by the gnashing caterpillar wheels of the ferocious, futuristic techno of The Tingler. Not content to be just a hallucination, The Tingler became a decapitating, towering, technosaurus, dump truck laden with ballistic, basalt boulders that threatened to crush skulls and pommel bodies into pulp.

Stricken with consternation and filled with dread, Jules shook at the knees. *What the fuck is going on?* Had he collapsed the party? Hang the DJ. A lynching mob must be on their way? He understood music, had identified the right tracks, played get-on-it grooves. His piloting had been transporting. He'd hooked dancers, built connective continuity to engage and invigorate. He'd risen to the occasion. He'd incrementally nudged up intensity thresholds according to the body heat he was reading. He knew he could do it—besides there were plenty of shambolic would-be DJs in Goa who fumbled around off their faces with no idea. But this was prime time full moon. He was indebted to Zsu for her trust in him and whom he'd been bewitched by with green eyes that held a universe of secrets. Many music collectors didn't want to DJ, it was too stressful, they just obsessed about finding the music and possessing it and exchanging it with other collectors and DJs, like a fungible currency. They just wanted to dance to it in the party without the pressure of putting it together. Better let others put their neck on the party chopping block and aspire to DJ it, and appease high expectations.

Jules figured that the dropping of The Tingler might be risky. It being one of the more piquant of the avant-rave acid tunes. Its never-heard-before gnarly frequencies put it in the category of—risque game changer.

The electrickery of what came out of the PA was not what he was expecting. Desperately he needed to play something friendly. A soothing, sonic smoothie. A yogurt and cucumber track. An antidote to the burning chilly rush of The Tingler. The perfect track sprung to mind in a split second, like a spirit guide was assisting him with hidden hands. Urgently, he scrambled to find a cassette he'd compiled and labelled—RESCUE REMEDY. Plucking it from its case he became distressed to discover that the perfect track was at the end of the tape and required fast forwarding. Anxiously he wondered whether he could cue it on time before The Tingler ran out?

After checking the numbers on the tape meter of the Sony, and comparing the track time he'd written next to The Tingler's title on the inner sleeve of the cassette, he had to make a crucial make-or-break decision. The fall-back option was to slot into the empty player the emergency RESCUE REMEDY tape cued with a less appropriate track. One minute of The Tingler remained. The smashed dance floor was in disarray, those still on it were wildly entangled in its mangled, machine musicology. Jules's mind raced. *What to do?* A DJ's worst nightmare? The silence of dead air not permitted. The DJ hit the rewind of the cueing JVC boogie box to rapidly retrieve yogurt and cucumber. The nether world ferocity of The Tingler's flammable frequencies were inflicting collateral damage—nearly clearing the dance floor. Had he delivered a fatal error? What was coming out of the PA was not the music he'd been expecting. Had he been set up to be the Devil's advocate? There was no escaping horrified looks directed at him.

Mysteriously, The Tingler played longer than the track time he'd written on the sleeve. What was playing? Was it a special *Razor Maid* stretch mix? An unknown alternative hex mix? Had he miscued? What the hell was playing? The music had turned into a horrendous version of itself, with a mind of its own. A hair-raising version that was a bloodcurdling turbo-charged ride that was battering bodies and lacerating heads, with some jumping out of their skins and clinging to a jagged-ridge dance floor, sharply dropping away to plunging escapements at its serrated edge.

Panicking, clutching the DJ table with clammy hands, Jules was desperate to load the RESCUE REMEDY tape to urgently play the yogurt and cucumber track to salvage the escalating emergency that was seemingly beyond his control. Alarmed, he felt an invisible force preventing him from sliding down the channel fader on the mixer playing The Tingler. It was as if everything had jammed. He attempted to press the stop button on the Walkman, but got a severe jolting electric shock that shot through his arm and down his legs. It felt unearthly, and left him in a state of paralysis and powerless to do anything about the mayhem on the dance floor. The Tingler's impact was like a ghost train careering off its rails. Thunderous kettle drums poured out of the PA. Netherworld sounds riding staccato violins, screeched with rapid bow strokes that sought to draw blood. Bombastic brass stabs hailed from speaker stacks like clattering machine gun turrets. The music had literally gone hysterically mad.

Up until eight minutes ago, prior to The Tingler tipping the party on its bleeding ear lugs, Zsu had been rollicking to Jules's tasty selection. All pieces seeming to fit, which got her moving in new ways and loving him all over again. But The Tingler was an out-of-the-theme-park shocker. It threw her into a vertigo spin, reminiscent of the first visitation from the ghost of Donna Ferreira in Disco Valley on the same full moon a year ago. In the first two bars of The Tingler, she thought she'd heard melancholic guitar of Portuguese Fado folk music, which struck a chord in her heart. But then the music skewed obliquely into a maelstrom of sounds that threw her into a fit of mortal terror, with the ghost of Donna Ferreira appearing as a wispy nebula. Zsu trembled with creepy necromantic feelings running through her panting body. The ghostly figure moved closer to her and spoke into her ear about the *Omen*. Other disembodied spirits appeared and sang in chorus, "We are the dead. We are the dead. Watch your behind."

Zsu felt her flesh fall off, and became a skeleton with her devil horns continuing to glow red as she danced with the dead. Her flesh returned to her bones and her eyes bulged bug-like. She freaked and bolted from the dance floor. Stumbling over herself, she desperately sought secluded bush behind the goat painting to relieve excruciating tension in her colon and bladder. With nickers pulled down to her boots she squatted. Feeling precariously vulnerable on the edge of the party, that the marauding, technosauraus claws of The Tingler had traumatised, she teetered on her boots desperately wanting to expunge horrid sensations that seized her body like she was being devoured by an alien incubus. A chill ran through her body. Visceral. Primal.

All of a sudden, a dark figure sprung up out of the bushes toppling her violently sideways. For a split second, she went numb with shock. Then came the terror. She shrieked a shrilled scream, like a pig having its throat cut. Adrenalin pumped through her struggling, twisting body. Crazed, black eyes with porcelain white around them fixed upon her with raging lust. Arms grappled with her twisting body and groped her chest. An erect black lingam lunged at her from out of polyester pants. Its heat-seeking spear head aimed at her exposed fan above her thighs. Hands pressed down attempting to spread them. She yelled raw-throated, but no one could hear her as her scream was swallowed by the tumultuous thump and growl of The Tingler. The black spear head missile thrust at the nub of her delta. Missing its mark, it skidded north off of her pubis up her midriff. She head-butted the assailant, clawed his frenzied face with the sharp edges of her finger talons, slicing strips of flesh away like bacon rind, and yelled at the top of her voice like a banshee. A forceful hand, now covered in blood, smothered her mouth and another gripped her throat. Gasping sharply, she desperately reached for the deadly pee needle that was in the lining of her boot but the weight of the body on top of her pinned her down. Struggling, choking, panicking—on the verge of blacking out—a goat-headed Baphomet hermaphrodite appeared holding a black obsidian dagger and placed it in her hand. She gripped it tight, and lunged at the belly of the assailant.

The PA died. All that could be heard was the screeching yell of the attacker in pain, fleeing into surrounding bush. Haywire-stricken psychonauts, whose space ships had spun out of control and crashed landed, stumbled about picking up pieces of their costume. All eyes were on the DJ. Bewildered dancers gathered at the mammoth trunk of the banyan. Irate, dishevelled revellers hurled expletives. Jules shook like he had just been cut out a horrendous car crash by jaws of life. Chaos whirled around him like the scene of a catastrophic accident site. Mortified, he held his chin up. He couldn't impress enough upon those distressed dancers gathered about him that he hadn't fucked up. The Tingler was inexplicable, off the clock, a ferocious force beyond comprehension. A paranormal nightmare in the form of a heinous, techno trickster that unleashed something unimaginable. He was adamant that he'd done nothing wrong. What came out of the PA had been beyond his control. Zikos and Asta stood close by shielding him from the abuse of pissed-off dancers. But where was Zsu?

Doc Silver shouldered through to Jules. "Hey dude—what the hell was that?"

Jules's face was white as a ghost, he felt ghastly. "It wasn't my fault. It was weirder than weird. Man-o-man…I have no fucking idea." He clenched his jaw to stop his teeth chattering. "I got electrocuted by the Walkman. It was untouchable. I have no idea what happened. I couldn't change the music. It had a mind of its own. It was freaky shit—"

"What on earth were you playing?" demanded Doc. "It sent me into an infernal abyss—"

"The Tingler," Jules said. "It turned into a nightmare. I swear to God, that sound wasn't on my tape."

Doc's face was shell shocked. "Whatever it was, it goddam hammered the bejesus out of me," he said in a disturbed voice. "It was technological terror."

Jules threw his hands up in the air. "It beats me. Maybe it's the psy-core sound of the future. Maybe its music we aren't ready for yet. Maybe our brains are not evolved enough to handle it, decipher it. Maybe its invisible entities residing in this huge tree. Maybe extraterrestials were tinkering with the magnetic information on my tape and messing with the micro circuitry of Sony. Fuck knows!" He shook his head. "I'm sorry!.. I'm so sorry!.. I really am."

Jules attempted once more to press play on the Walkman. This time, to his relief, the tape played. The yogurt and cucumber track pulsed the strip level lights of the mixer. The resuscitated PA lurched the dance floor back into life. Asta stood at Jules side like an archangel. Her cute, celestial prettiness had the effect of a coolant on the hot flabbergasted air around the DJ.

"Your play was fabulous," she said leaning into his ear. "Don't be phased by those twisted trippers. Partying here is a wild ride. It ain't jukebox cheese disco. It's Goa histrionics. It gets so crazy. I love it when the music takes the dance floor into the unknown." She cast her glitter-clad eyes around the party. "Where is Zsu?" she anxiously quizzed everyone standing around. "Has anyone seen Zsu?"

Sheila and Naresh had not been dancing when The Tingler hit. Coming up on the perestroika had brought on woozy turbulence for the Bollywood hack as his mind became vast and required skydiver courage. Seasoned flight attendant, Sheila, suggested they retreat to some small trees away from the belting action under the banyan with the beaming moon reigning over it from above. She'd warmed to Naresh's urbane Bombay charm, zany humour and sweet mocha eyes. Realising he was green in the world of high-end party potions, she kept tabs on him. She'd already voyaged on Gorby at a small party thrown by Shazam at his teepee, where the acid guru was in fine form tickling his fancy, canoodling with girls under the influence who had eaten his ice cream infused with boundary-dissolving glasnost. This semi-private affair he'd called, 'Ganesh's door mouse party.'

Sitting under small trees, Sheila and Naresh had witnessed The Tingler's havoc upon the dance floor and its screeching culmination with a stabbing yell. Immediately after, they'd seen an Indian with bleeding face run hastily past them clutching his waist with his shirt soaked in blood. They questioned each other about what they saw. Had it been a hallucination? Just prior, Naresh reckoned he'd seen a flying feathered serpent ridden by Indra. And Sheila believed she'd seen crocodile skinned creatures on two legs engaging in interspecies sex.

Three tracks into his resumed set, Zsu snuck up behind Jules and pressed her bruised body into the banyan's trunk, as if to draw solace from the supernature of the mighty mother of all trees. Sensing someone was behind him, he stood up straight from hunching over punching buttons on the JVC boogie box and looked behind him. Astounded by her appearance, he peeled off his headphones, narrowed his eyes and surveyed her from head to foot. *My God!.. What the hell happened?*

Zsu appeared bedraggled, her T-shirt ripped, as though savaged by a wild animal. With teary eyes squeezed shut and mascara trailing down pale wretched cheeks she said, "Don't worry about me." Her lips trembled on a blotched, reddened face that was pure torment. "I'm OK! I'm OK!"

"Are you sure?" He said anguished to see her in such a state.

"Yes," she said, a hand clutching her bruised throat.

"You look dreadful? For God's sake what happened?"

"I'm fine, really, I'm fine. Please keep doing what your doing. I love the music," she said with dreadnought valiance, while shivering inside her skin feeling violated and terrorised, her strangulated scream still reverberating inside her head.

Jules mind whirled with worry all over again. The worst possible DJ nightmare really had occurred. He was under extreme pressure attending to tape decks that demanded his full attention. He wanted Zsu to enjoy the music, but she looked like she had come back from the dead. Talk was impossible, she didn't wish to tell him and bum him out. Her ravaged face registered something horrific, something grotesque, something traumatic resulting from a malefic force. He turned away to monitor the dance floor, but then snuck another troubling glance at her. What he was seeing made him wince, he'd glimpsed it before. The tape decks required his undivided attention, but he couldn't help but wonder if perhaps he'd been set up to play the role of a mad scientist in an acid techno test tube experiment, in which the head fuck of The Tingler had exploded in his face, unleashing a laboratory, nut house, shock treatment of horrors on the party.

Zsu picked up a large amethyst crystal off the DJ table and held it behind Jules, channelling reiki energy to purify them both. He considered playing 'Liquefaction' by The Telepathics. His mind was in a squeeze. The resuscitated dance floor demanded his concentration. Tapes were winding. There was no dropping the ball. He couldn't afford to legitimately fuck-up. He peered at the track list of the cassette case of the tape being cued. On top of its inner sleeve he'd written in thick black marker pen— DANCING MOSAIC OF VIBRATIONS—and stuck reflective, holographic foil on its reverse side. He fixed a dutiful eye on the time counter of the Walkman playing as well as the cueing JVC and hit its stop button. He listened with headphones for the first beat of the track by toggling the rewind and forward buttons. He snatched a glance back at Zsu. Her pained face of a moment ago, had completely changed like quicksilver. He thought of alchemy, and how quicksilver was associated with Mercury, messenger of the gods, a metal of enormous density, yet so liquid. For a moment, he experienced himself levitating above the humble wooden DJ table. But the synaptic jolt of seeing highly energised dancers in his immediate field of vision snapped him into—*get a grip!* Fingers manipulated the buttons on the portable Jap tech as though he was a slight of hand conjuror. He was totally at one with these devices as he had been sleeping with his Walkmans since he arrived in Goa this season.

There were other forces at play that his horoscope calculus hadn't revealed about this full moon. Powerful hidden forces bound up in arcane magic, forces that had been locked up for centuries, a place where genies could quite easily leap out of an alchemist's glass bottles under heat. Had he rubbed the genie bottle of the dance floor too hard in playing the hell raiser Tingler? Had this unheard-of version resurrected the dead? Was this the kind of *Thelema Magick*, Aliester Crowley practiced? His mind raced a thousand things at once. He recalled how his heart had been shredded to bits by Zsu. He wondered what pseudo reality she lived in with men? Was playing this party some kind of test?

Whilst shuffling through cassettes searching for a track, he reflected on playing after Atma Blaze. How it was like having been passed a fiery torch from a hip-priest at an induction ceremony whose uppity megaphone voice left him feeling mentally mauled. After loading a cassette, he looked over his shoulder toward the banyan trunk, but Zsu had slipped away. He recalled what she'd told him about her story with Atma. The overdosing on his smarmy gift of self significance. The ruthless competitiveness wrapped up in flowery spiritual platitudes. The rudraksha bead shtick of sadhu cosplay. The impotence of not moving his arse to dance. Just another freak in India under the spell of holy man rhapsodic diatribe—like all of us. And for her—well, she'd alchemically transmuted her base resentments into the gold of longing and remorse.

Releasing the pause button on the cued track he'd loaded, Jules was hit by the realisation: *You can be whoever you want to be, and here, the most alpha smoking god of all—is Shiva.* He felt a warm glow of empowering satisfaction as the track he'd just set in motion, with an *Om Namah Shiva* mantra inside it, was triggering brand new responses, like it was an electronic elevator to starry heavens above upon which was pasted a glittering phantasmagoria in high sheen moonlight. Under the banyan tree, the dancing mosaic of bodies surged, bringing a smile to Jules's face.

The intensity level had gone up considerably, post the stoppage, which brought the realisation, that other than when the music stopped, no one looked at the DJ. There was no stage. The DJ was not there to put on a show, was not there to entertain, was not there to be centre of attention. The humble DJ table was not a temple with lots of lights illuminating it and eye catching art. It was a private place shrouded in secrecy where cassette tarot cards were shuffled. Where special sequence spreads were laid out, tracks selected like magical cards that the dance circle of the party had evoked, and the DJ had picked up on and channelled like a feedback loop. DJ-ing in Goa, in nineteen eighty-eight, was a new experience, totally unlike singing and playing keyboard in a band on a stage performing a show flanked by a PA. The more out of the picture the DJ, the more individualistic and self-expressive the dancing. No one facing a stage. If there was a show, it was on the dance floor. The DJ stood barefoot in moon shadows on the same level. The sound spread around the open-air play space of the supernature. Dancers moving freely throughout it in three hundred and sixty degree directions.

The fluidity of group emotion in motion on soma, other than booze and powders, was liberating, compared to a stage and cubic night club, with business centred around a bar. The essence of the experience was what was happening on the dance floor. An existential, emancipatory, euphoria inhabited by a spectacle of inimitable characters and entities made up of time travellers, humanoids, occultists, wizards, prophets, would-be gurus, sprites, seekers, devotees, blue-eyed sadhus and dance dissidents of all ages from all over the world whooping it up in digital dust. Coming into the last half hour of his set, Jules considered which of his high priority tracks hadn't been played before Jaeger was due to show up.

Asta found Zsu draped in a sarong that covered her ripped T-shirt. She looked wretched and crumpled like a refugee in a war zone, and was sipping a steaming glass of chai on her mumma's mat at the periphery of the party. Zsu's account of the horrific attack in the bushes was shocking and disturbing. It stirred frightful feelings for Asta, bringing back a horrid incident two seasons ago on the isolated coastal hill trail between Spaghetti Beach and North Anjuna. It was where predators and viper snakes lurked. It had been siesta, unsuspectingly Asta was strolling alone there, and jumped-on, and violently thrown to the ground by an Indian. She too, struggled and screamed, as he attempted to have his way with her. But she could feel that the more she struggled, the worse it was going to get. Then she went into a counter instinctive lapse of reality. She thought, *Just stop, don't do anything. Cause he won't know what to do.* She realised, the more she fought, the more the violence would escalate.

"What saved me was my gran's ring." Asta told Zsu.

"Oh!—so your gran's ring had magical powers?"

"Well, it was gold with big opals and Egyptian rubies and diamonds worth heaps of rupees. It definitely saved my arse. I pleaded with him. 'Here, take my ring… take my ring.' Fortunately, he then fixated on the gold and sparkling jewels. My gran's ring put a spell on him, got him frothing at the mouth, allowed me to escape," Asta let out deep breath and put her arm around her bestie and said, "India sure ain't just doe-eyed holy cows."

Then the distinctive opening riff of 'Goa Goat Head' by The Telepathic's could be heard from the direction of the banyan tree. Jules was playing his last track.

"Oh, my God!" gasped Zsu, a creepy shiver ran up her spine. "Would you believe it? I was saved by a goat-headed god."

Asta gasped in amazement. "Do you mean Satan?"

"That's right! The Baphomet god, Satan. It was hermaphrodite, it appeared in the nick of time just before I felt like I was going to choke, black-out and die. It all happened after Donna's ghost spoke to me," Zsu tilted her head and gazed up at the moon as though lunar was her testifying witness to what she'd survived. "Donna appeared on the dance floor, informing me of an *Omen*. Then the music went completely berserk. My colon locked up, it was excruciating, painful. I desperately bolted to the bushes, there was no time to find someone to accompany me. It was foolish, but I was on the verge of shitting myself. Asta, it was hell…" Zsu sighed deeply. "Come!..let's hit the dance floor," she said, needing to cheer herself up. "We have to dance to the 'Goa Goat Head.' There's profound magic in this music."

Nearby, in monkey valley, sun rays on the other side of the world were being reflected off the fullness of lunar's face and coating the roof of Odvar Osser's house silver. In the lounge, gold painted antlers of a Himalayan stag had been fixed to a wall and a totem staff had been positioned, standing-upright, in the middle of a circle painted on the floor. Around it stood Osser and his followers, that included Atma Blaze and Remo, who'd given Jules The Tingler. At the top of the staff was a monkey's skull (or was it human?) with horns. Everyone was naked from the waist down in a trance with erect willies chanting O.O.O. root language sounds to offer up moon juice spume for the revealing of an underground Pagan temple. Odvar predicted it would be discovered in Norway this year, pending funds being raised to excavate a stone entrance of a cave leading down to it.

THE SOUND SPREAD OF THE SPEAKERS, placed at the edge of the far-reaching span of the ancient banyan, created spacious sub-zones. This is where some of the more highly expressive dancers, who liked to move free-form in multiple directions, cut loose, getting-off like headless chooks. While others took to orbiting and spinning like rotor blades, moving in concentric circles throughout the entire dance space, synergistically engaging with the movements of others.

Then there were the hardcore addicts of banging techno who loved to sound abuse themselves with more intense, up close and personal, loud dosages. This maniac lot would subject themselves to the physical battering of blistering, kicking beats at point blank range for maximum frequency saturation. Not just content to bury their heads in PA speaker cabinets, they became speaker hogs, attempting to crawl inside the mouth of bass bins, as though Techgnosis gods required human sacrifice. Everyone who got to do time on such a dance floor, had a hundred psychotherapeutic deaths and rebirths in its polyphonic spree.

There was a new look in Naresh's eyes, as if he was seeing the real nature of existence at a godhead where time ceased to exist. This look in his child-like mocha eyes thrilled Sheila, who lived by the manifesto: *acid keeps you honest*. She figured her curiosity about the dashing Bombay chap in harem pants was sure to be answered by the personality paint stripper of Shazam's Gorby. For Naresh, she was an intoxicating blend of East and West. His heart had over ridden his head, the enamel of his actor mask was in danger of bubbling and peeling off as he found himself (with eyes closed and pineal gland popping) in a colourful, spectral state of disembodied consciousness. With eyes open, he saw that he'd stepped out of himself, left his purple and black striped harem pants standing where he'd been dancing.

Then, with trailing white hair, Shazam streaked through Naresh's vision and commanded space around an adjacent speaker stack. The soma sorcerer's hair turned into a nimbus halo with him becoming Krishna, playing a flute—gathered around him were boogie-bot milkmaids. Outrageous thoughts filled Naresh's head. He experienced himself as a leaping lizard in a groovy new habitat. A place that was pre-karma. A place that was antediluvian. A place where everyone belonged. He locked-in on Sheila. She was the only Indian woman on the dance floor. His eyes feasted on hotties from all over the world getting down all around him, as rivets popped on his stitched-up Indian male, cultural conditioning. The Gorby in his brain cleaved the casing of formative traditional Indian society from the housing of the furnace in which burned uncontainable, ignited desire. Rampant, racy feelings coursed through his body. Maddening thoughts ran riot in his head. The head gasket of family pressure was blowing. Snooty caste privilege was cracking. Bollywood bitchiness puking.

At the threshold of—*out of control,* both his lingam, coiled in his jocks, and his spinning-wheel heart, hitched their hopes on an on-the-job romance in a chaotic psychedelic circus. Was what he was head-over-heels succumbing to worth sacrificing a job for? What kind of job did the inhabitants of this crazy happy habitat do? He recalled the Indian with bloody clothes, he'd seen earlier fleeing the party. What kind of fight had he got himself into? The party appeared so friendly and inviting and safe? The thought that troubled him the most was that he had not discovered tabloid dirt, but rather—pure pleasure and flirtatious fun, in what Sheila referred to as—*naughty playtime.* What he dared most not to think about was the now-overdue scoop he'd signed up for with the *Goa Voice.*

Zane had been abducted by aliens. Felix found him up a tree clinging on like a koala bear, and managed to coax him back down to administer dopamine reinforcements. Like mental floss, Felix presented his Enfield key dipped in Columbian crystals to Zane's nostrils, which were gunked-up with dust kicked up from the dance floor. Eyeing the pick-me-up, he cleared his nose with a snot rocket.

"Hear me for God's sake! Help me! Help me!" Came a damsel's voice in the music out of the speakers. Jaeger was playing 'Bastion In-D Stress' by In-D. It had a hang-on-tight-here-we-go urgent pounding bass line. After a couple of zings up the sinuses, Zane felt antithetical chemical forces splitting the hemispheres of his brain apart. Cocaine and acid were having a tug of war inside him.

"Is this a piece of your brain," came another voice in the music. All at once, he found himself bent in competing directions. Yet motor neurone functionality had him snap-locked to the suspense-laden beat that was hurtling and whip-lashing him in a thrilling drama. He experienced flashbacks of twisting torment that The Tingler had purgatoried him in. "Hear me for God's sake. Help me! Help me!" came the voice again, followed by a frightful scream. He recalled that he'd heard similar distressed cries inside The Tingler. His heart pounded. There was no getting off the dance floor. The urgent building tension of the drama in the music demanded more stomping action, as though it might save the poor damsel in peril. The suspense on the dance floor was like a locomotive was puffing full speed toward the damsel in distress bound over the tracks ahead. With a contorted gait, Zane galloped about the dance floor until he got to the edge of it, where his flaring nostrils were slammed by the cloying smell of eggs being fried in foul oil by a local man on a kerosene cooker. The sickening, oily egg olfactory sent him into a head-spin on the verge of toppling over and wanting to toss.

Seeing him put a finger down his throat, Felix came rushing. "Zane!.. Zane!.. Are you OK, man?"

"I'll be right," he spluttered and dry-retched trying to throw-up, but there was nothing to bring up.

"Let me get you water," shouted Felix in an alarmed voice over the music, and headed to a bar. When he returned with cold mineral water, he found Zane sitting on the edge of the dance floor. Felix rolled a joint. Half way through smoking it together, Zane leaped to his feet and threw himself at the music.

"I'm convinced that our time is desperately short," came a voice out of the speakers. It was one of his favourite industrial dub tracks. "This has been an age of Freud, an age of pragmatism, behaviourism, secularism, materialism, nihilism, an age when all the emphasis has been on ingenuity of science…" It was as though the voice in the music had summoned him to dance floor drill. His Reebok runners ground and twisted so vigorously in dirt and fragments of stone that sparks could be seen in the clouds of dust he churned up.

"Judgement and destruction!.. Judgement and destruction!.." ranted the preacher's voice in the music, as Zane's head swivelled like the knob on the end of a jiggling gear stick. "Morally our nation is on the skids. Our nation is on the way down. I'm convinced that our time is desperately short. Our time is now!.. Our time is now!.. There is no way out!...."

Sweat sodden and soiled, Zane's HIGH VOLTAGE! printed T-shirt crackled and steamed with smoke, like overdriven circuitry with no fuse box. A neurochemistry hotwired on eccentric electricity reshaping a reality that he regarded as untrustworthy. The rat-ta-tat-tat stutter gun of the staccato electro got him footloose dancing the plasticity of his brain— normally encased in cranky emotions—now pharmacologically over-ridden in a synaesthesia. Jumping for joy, he heard a voice inside of him say. "To hell with balance. I want to crash. I want to burn. I want to break myself. I want to live only for ecstasy. I'm neurotic, perverted, destructive, fiery, dangerous, an inferno, unrestrained." The track that Jaeger was playing, 'Mind at The End of Its Tether' by Tack Head, was off a tape he'd recorded and titled, SPARK PLUG.

Zsu had left the party to her home nearby. Pulling off her ripped top and looking at it discarded on the floor, it really did look like an *evil eye*. She was desperately in need of cleansing herself of the desolate wretchedness of the violence. She needed to purge herself of the terror of the knife edge of coming close to being savagely raped and left for dead. She needed to lick her wounds, do a water purification ritual with crystals that she'd left out in the moon light and don a new outfit that would be like a new skin, so as to re-embody herself for a brand-new day—like she was Joan of Arc.

Returning to the party wearing gold leggings, she suddenly braked her Yamaha to a screeching stop, after coming around a bend. Looking down, her body went into a cold sweat. A long khaki coloured cobra lay across the road—*dead*. Seized by a spooky unease that chilled her, the symbolism of the snake was disturbing. It did not appear to have been run over. With a stick, she dragged the lifeless reptile to the side of the road. Putting her hands together, she took a moment, bowed, and offered a prayer. Continuing, she rode toward the music and became entranced by the full moon as it dipped low in the west silhouetting, flickering, animated branches in trees that rushed by. She could not shake the snake off her mind, and slowed down and stopped and gazed at the earth's consort— the moon—the enchantress of the night, the castor of moon shadow spells which would soon lose its silvery powers to the sun's golden rays at dawn. Gazing intently, like the lunar light was an all-knowing oracle orb in the sky, Zsu yearned to piece together what Donna had told her just prior to the vicious attack. And now a dead Shiva serpent across her path.

Cantering back into the party with new, bold, gold bounce, she shored herself up to shine, which belied underlying wounds of hurt and brokenness. She found Jules and hosed him with a hosanna of praise for his DJ-ing—but The Tingler had been a terrorising shocker.

"That fucking track," he said, clearing his throat like there was a foul taste in his mouth and needed to spit. "I got so much grief for that," he lamented. I didn't mean to freak out the party with heavy music."

She told him about her horrific experience. Jules's breath constricted, his thoughts scrambled to believe what she was telling him. Distressingly, he recalled her horrid state and pained face when she'd come up behind him at the trunk of the banyan.

"You poor thing," he said kindly. "You looked like you'd been dragged through hell last night. Can you identify the bastard that did this?"

Her eyes glowered fiercely. "I'll cut off his balls if I see him."

"You gotto believe me," Jules pleaded. "That sound was like the PA had been hi-jacked by some ungodly marauding terror. Jeez, I was totally freaked, was powerless to do anything."

"Jules, I believe you. Where did you get that music?"

"The Tingler—Remo gave me."

"Aha!" Her brow knotted. "Hmm… I see."

"How well do you know Remo?" Jules asked with a suspicious upturn of his lip.

"I have misgivings," she said with guarded concern. "He's a bastard child of a Portuguese missionary and a Goan. He's slippery. It's uncanny how he ferrets out music. Pounces on every cassette he can get his hands on, winds through tape obsessively."

"He's a strange cat," Jules said. "He laid some outstanding music on me. The version of The Tingler that I thought I'd cued and played was for sure, exceptionally far out! But what came out of the speakers wasn't what I expected…" Massaging the temple of his forehead bewildered, "it definitely wasn't the version that was on my tape."

"Don't worry Jules I truly believe you," Zsu said. "I'm a hardened tripper. What I experienced nearly killed me. Something is going on and it ain't the drugs."

"The music here is not regular," he said. "It's not mainstream. It's left field. It's underground. It's experimental. It's like nothing heard before. And now…is it possible, it's supernatural?

"Jules, something beyond belief happened to me," she said like she'd been abducted and possessed by an unearthly force and saved by another one. "There's much, much, more going on here than meets the eye, or we

230

think we are hearing. Something in the frequency, something in the supernature of this tree, something from another dimension. Music wise, you found the balance of new weird and easy handrail tracks. Believe me, you played well," she reassured him batting her eye lids and could feel emotion threatening to burst out of her chest. "You can't imagine what happened to me in the bushes while The Tingler was playing."

"Fucking hell," he said, upset. "How horrible…you poor thing." Jules held her hand. "Zsu I'm so sorry for you, but you know what? This is the most epic fucking party!—"

"Listen Jules," she said with her brow in a puzzled frown, "I have to make sense of the *Omen* Donna was telling me. It's like I combusted, had a near death experience for a reason."

JUST BEFORE DAWN, WONDERSTRUCK, Asta found Jules and pointed to the bright morning star, Venus, low on the horizon. Putting his mouth to her ear he said, "See the big bright one next to it, that's Jupiter. Do you know about the pentagonal cycle of Venus?"

"No."

"Every eight years Venus traces the shape of a five-pointed star in the sky, the same shape as a pentagram."

"Wow!" she gasped. "That's amazing!"

At dawn, when the first trace of light filtered through the stain glass of the banyan cathedral, everyone fell in love. A chorus of bird calls could be heard in a quiet passage of the music when the beats dropped out of the track Jaeger was playing. Light-to-sound transcendent tech-knowledgy in ascending arpeggios delivered group teleportation. The rapture of a dancing congregation in the glistening light of a brand new day.

No one spoke. Smiles said everything. Those that had ridden through the full course of the night were feeling like they had been trekking on a razors edge of dark and light, which they experienced as both coexisting inside of them. 'Changing Minds' by 16 Bit, pulsed the airspace of the banyan grove. Second and third rounds were being necked at blotta babba Shazam's dhuni dispensary, whilst others imbibed mushroom extract. Stepping into glorious sunshine, Zane felt much lighter, his predisposed back-up-against-the-wall, Sheffield-steel self, having been sand blasted by top shelf Gorby, his body techno-tenderised like a tandoori roast. It was chipper to be in a Nirvanarama place beyond all that was sick in the world. It was comforting to be in a place where it was normal to be not normal, where the inalienable right to be contented could be had.

"Fancy an E?" Sheila said in a seductive voice to Naresh. He smiled and nodded like she knew best. Placing an MDMA bomb in his hand and offering him her bottle of mineral water, she said. "You'll need this, it tastes foul."

Naresh recalled 'The Legend of The Snake,' the track on the cassette that Remo had given him. Had Sheila become Eve, tempting him with forbidden fruit in the garden of Eden?

For raver, Sheila, the E was a loved-up lollie with a bitter taste, which, unlike the woozy unpredictability of the mind-warp of acid, never failed to deliver maximum joy. Swallowing unquestioningly, Naresh surrendered to the moment like an avid virgin.

The two Walkman Professionals—one owned by Zsu, the other Jaeger—that had driven the party since sunset were now coated in dust. At eight o'clock Danilo arrived with replacements and a six-pack leather case of cassettes from which he would select the best of his morning music. Sweet melodic techno that was guaranteed to caress the opening of hearts and give wings to the soul with the rising sun. Toward mid-morning, the sun beat down blazing tropical heat, yet the dance floor remained cool in dappled shade from the banyan's sprawling canopy of branches.

After the tumble-rinse cerebellum spin of the over bloody flood of the night, it was as if Nareesh's X factor had been put through the ringer by Sheila. Her dawn, dopamine booster—a lolly reward. But disturbing thoughts of the world beyond the bouncing blissfulness of the banyan threatened to gate crash. Like, what was he going to tell the editor of the Goa Voice? And, how was he going to pay the advance back? Besotted, he couldn't resist stealing glances at Sheila as she danced with a huge smile resplendent in the sunshine of all the love that he was feeling. *Was there a future with her? Was all this just an X dream?*

Knowing the party would go on all day, some dancers dashed off on motorbikes back to rented rooms and houses to refresh with bucket showers and don new outfits and refuel on fruit salad breakfast. Most though, could not tear themselves from the fun being had on the rising high of the morning dance floor, which was having its dust dampened by local boys sprinkling well water and was being rhythmically massaged by Danilo's uplifting, melodic, Electro, Italo House and fun-filled Acid Techno.

In her golden outfit, Zsu danced glorious and triumphant like the sun vanquishing the darkness of night. She moved further out from the banyan's canopy where, like photosynthesis, solar rays penetrated the cells of her dermis, recharging, energising and purging knotted moon shadow emotion. Dancing to the sound of the sun, its rays impregnated frequencies into her body like musical tattoos. Turning to face the colossal, mother of all trees, its multiple trunks, branches and roots turned into a vision of a Kabbalah tree of life reaching up to father sky and down through the red soil to mother earth's magna core.

In the proximity of a speaker stack, sub zone, Jules and Asta danced. Their post sublunar chemistries subliminally coalesced like drum fish. With techno-cogs telekinetically driving limbs, Jules closed his eyes and spiralled up his vagus into quantum physics contemplation of whether he'd gone beyond the brain. Then, opening his eyes to silver, spiral, entwined arms and wiggling hips and sweat beading brow of Asta's face, brought a swelling to the Y of his geometric patterned spandex, signalling he was very much inhabiting a hot-blooded body hardwired to a brainstem. Streaks of green in her hair turned into serpents like the head of a medusa. As he wondered what Zeus and Aphrodite were up to in the heavens above, a dirty appealing possibility occurred to Asta. And so, late in the morning with their reflexes revved and minds hypnotised, they left the party together for a fruit shake in nearby Chapora.

The village was in its normal daily routine of women in sari selling fish and vegetables, while local men in thread-bare singlets and white button down short sleeve shirts played cards at the big tree. No motorbike taxi wallahs hanging about, as all were shuttling dancers to and from the banyan tree. Revellers in loud eye-blistering garb scooted through the village like a circus troupe on lunch break.

Sitting together at a table at Scarlet Juice Bar sipping papaya and lime shakes Asta said to Jules, "I have a special present for you."

"Aw... shucks!—Asta—really?"

"It's from Cyberella."

His mind went into free fall with speculation, a curl of blond hair falling over one eye as his pleasure centre was hit with a sweet rush from the iced shake. "I adored how you glowed in the lunar rays and ultra violet last night." Sitting with her he found himself bedazzled by the splintering flashes of sunlight reflecting off the silver sequin of her space-age outfit.

"You're an astral goddess."

She blushed. "Thank you, Jules. It's true, I've become Cyberella."

"There were cosmic serpents in your hair this morning."

She wrapped him in a melting smile and beamed lustrous eyes at him. Her daughter, Tina, was away for a few days. She released the straw from her lips and said, "Cyberella asks that you come to her place and receive your present." Her wet lips were right there, her mouth with the aftertaste of sweet fruit was right there. He reached over and held her hand. They gazed into each other's eyes. Hers were telling him, "Kiss me! Kiss me! Kiss me!" But he resisted the burning urge.

They whizzed on their Yamahas along the narrow road that hugged Chapora River, picturesque with canoes and birdlife. Riding behind Asta, Jules delighted in the play of the streaming air upon her medusa hair twisting and snaking around her neck, until his eyes where disturbingly averted by large chunks of raw meat hanging at a road side butcher, thick with flies. A flock of goats greeted them when they came to the end of a dirt track that led to Asta's house nestled in trees.

Stepping inside, Jules found himself in a sci-fi cosmology of peculiar dolls. "Wow!—the world of Cyberella!" Asta relished the glee on his face as he visually feasted on her collection of "far out" fetishes. On shelves were strange figure dolls and miniature robots, the most grotesque, a replica of the *Alien*, the creature from the movie of the same name. Walls featured posters of Star Trek, Blade Runner and anime, Sailor Moon and Ghost In The Shell.

Perplexed, Jules peered at the dolls up close. "They're from Japan," Asta said. "The Japanese are into animism, ghosts and ancestor spirits. Extraterrestrials thrive there."

"They're amazing," he said, casting his eyes around Cyberella's pad.

"It's animist voodoo," she said. "Japan is not just a robot kingdom of technocrats. It's full of weirdness. It's another planet."

"This one is trippy," he said, picking up a strange looking doll.

"It's special," she said, "comes from the hunter and gatherer Jomon period before Buddhism. All throughout Japan there are references to aliens, UFOs, creatures from other worlds. She fetched chilled lemon water from the kitchen and they sat together on a couch.

"Check out this one," she said playing with a robot on a low table next to them. It had a praying mantis looking head with animatronic parts. "I made it from a kit set. It's called a *Transformer*... Hey Jules, welcome to the world of transforming alien robots," Asta said, delighted to have him in Cyberella's world. "In Japan, you'll find one in every home. It's the place of aliens. Did you notice there's lots of Japanese here this season?"

"I've met some," Jules said. "They invited me to shrimp cook-ups at their house. They love techno. Gave me some great tracks. It makes sense, the machines to make it come from there."

"It's a UFO friendly place," she said. "So many sightings there. I have a pet theory that aliens have mated with Japanese to produce zen robot droids."

Jules picked up the *Transformer*, made it walk on the table by moving its legs and played with its mechanical arms.

"Now for Cyberella's present," she said beckoningly. "You have to close your eyes." Jules obeyed. Asta went to her bedroom. Returning, she stood in front of him and said, "You can open them now."

"Wow!" he said gaping at a pair of midnight blue leggings that she held in front of his face printed with a deep space vista of planets, comets and flying saucers.

"They're stunning!.. so astral!.." he said in awe of Cyberella's gift. She dropped the feather light leggings into his hands. He held them, feeling the smooth micro weave and gazed into her eyes. "They're so silky, stretchy, spacey—just like you."

Asta's pulse leaped. Her eyes widened. "Oh, thanks Jules. It's next generation lycra, an ultra-high-tech fabric, just like the music." She shot him a comely grin. "When you dance in these you'll feel like you are flying off into space—totally naked."

"Hm...amazing! Where did you get 'em?"

"Tokyo, of course. It's the most cyber city. Please put them on."

"But I'm so filthy from the party."

She threw him a towel. "Jules, please take a shower, I want to see you in them."

Whilst splashing and soaping himself from a large urn of well water in her bathroom he saw a wild picture on the wall. A poster of a woodblock image of a nude Japanese woman reclining across a mountain range being suckered by two octopus. One performing cunnilingus, the other a tentacle in her mouth and one around a nipple of a breast. With his gourd still awash with Gorby, the more he gaped at the exotic picture, the more turned-on he became.

By the time, he'd finished rinsing himself off he found himself with a throbbing erection. He looked down at his boing, boing lingam pointing up at him. It told him that it was now in charge, alerting him to a burning, tingling desire. Having no clean jocks, Cyberella's gift of brand new lycra hanging on a towel rack took on the appearance of galactic condoms into which he was now required to insert his clean loins and horned-up arousal. He imagined himself walking back into her lounge, his enflamed desire, lycra gift wrapped. *What kind of Venus fly trap is this?* He thought of Dionysus and pondered Zeus and how timing is everything.

To complete the Venus fly trap whilst he was showering, she'd racked up two fat lines of MDMA crystals on a cassette case titled, HORSE PLAY, and placed it on the table next to the *Transformer* robot. What he'd told her under the banyan tree about Venus and Jupiter had fuelled her imagination. So, when he appeared in his brand new stretchy galactic-groover wear at the lounge door, the embodiment of romping Zeus, with a stonking hard-on, her eyes popped out.

"Oh, my God!" she gasped. "Rocket man!—holy shit!—take me now!"

In bright body-sock lycra, blood raced through his body as he walked boldly up to Asta with his pronounced horned glory pointing one o'clock, afternoon delight, and planted a firm kiss on her lips. She replied by poking her tongue in his mouth, which was like turning a key to a treasure chest of raging desire. His comet rocket pressed up against her midriff landing pad. They embraced and caressed—lips and mouths wet together. Tips of tongues teasing each other. The curve of infinity dived and spiralled, their heads giddy in a spin like the upswing of a ferris wheel. They necked, petted, swooned—became awash in desire and soon found themselves entangled in a warm pool, like they'd just plunged down a spiralling wet and wild dream park ride.

After subsiding sighs, Asta said, "Let me take a shower." She turned her head toward the HORSE PLAY cassette on the table. "I've prepared lunch." She untangled her Cyberella body from his and put a cassette titled, ROBOTICO, into one of the slots of a double deck Hitachi ghetto blaster. Jules kicked back on the couch and surveyed the florid decorum of Asta's Cyberella planetarium pad. Hypnotised, he gazed at the strange figure dolls and transformer robot. *What kind of world did these bizarre characters inhabit?* The music that played he recognised from the parties. But this was an unfamiliar mix with a transfixing alien robot voice.

People of earth please allow me to introduce myself, I'm robotico, a digital replicant of yourself. I function beyond the bounds of your physics and can travel instantly to any point in the universe. I am antimatter, a mirror image of matter, existing in the past, the present, and the future. I exist as clusters of digital chromosomes generated from a gene pool of algorithmic shareware. Superconductive, I am quantum state within particles of light synthesised into sound of an extraterrestrial nature. I am a bit stream conductor of electromagnetic fields containing source code synchronised to stellar rhythms. The matrix of my mainframe is clocked to the beat of the galaxy and cyclically adjusted to oscillations and movements of stars and planets in your solar system. The binary tree of the bass I emit was bitmapped from the big bang that created your universe thirteen billion years ago.

Asta returned, her tussled blonde hair wet, her curviliciousness wrapped in a sarong. And then, an android voice announced, "Humanoid!" from out of the ghetto blaster, as the Acid House hit by Stakker powered out of the Hitachi. Holding the cassette case in his hand, Jules said, "My God!—that Robotiko Rejekto track is some trip. The voice sounded like it was an entity from another world. Listening to it made a lot of things click in my head, I realised why I'm at home with this music. It's all about parallel universes, isn't it? Cosmic intelligences inside sound waves?"

"Absolutely!" Asta said, sitting down on the couch next to him, her almond butter moisturised skin impressing perfumed persuasion on his olfactory receptors. "Alien intelligences sure are making this music."

Jules's twitched. "Perhaps extraterrestrials had something to do with that berserker track—The Tingler. Man!—it sure laid waste to the dance floor. It was like it was coming from another dimension."

"It was crazy… totally earth shattering," she said holding his hand. "It felt paranormal, not human… like something from another world."

He glared at the transformer robot on the table. "Is it possible that dark matter…a kind of astral wildlife was messing around with us at the party?"

Asta nodded. "Yes!—very possible. We are interdimensional beings."

Jules rolled his eyes wondering if Asta might be an implant android? But his animal self knew better, having just tasted her in his mouth and now feeling the creamy softness of her skin on his. Taking orders from the engorged Y of his galactic, condom lycra, he nuzzled his cheek to the nape of her neck—breathing her in until they became awash in desire. Kissing opened-mouthed with darting tongues, they ardently embraced. Secretions of sweat appeared around her breast bone. They spun light headed, like they were on laughing gas. From out of a pocket of a leather bum bag on the floor, she pulled out a hundred rupee note rolled it up and picked up the HORSE PLAY cassette case from off the table. Holding it in her hand, she presented the note to him. Taking it between his fingers, he thought—*naked lunch.* Lowering his head, he nostrilled a line of endorphin exciters. This was followed by a sharp burning sensation, like wasabi up his nose. Then, he dissolved into the couch like it was devouring lips. She handed him the HORSE PLAY cassette case and snorkelled it clean. The ghetto blaster played the instrumental version of 'Lick It' by Karen Finley. Their infatuated bumped-up-ness had them spilling into each other on the couch, their porous perimeters unbounded like two bodies of water flowing into each other, melting in mutual exigency of erotic pleasure. They canoodled, cuddled and caressed as 'Bryllyant' by Boytronic purred out of the speakers. They became soluble, merging as one body, quivering and squirming in liquid love, then slithered onto a rug on the floor like a palpitating jellyfish.

Asta slipped away. Returning, she wore scant silver sequin tassel beads and goat horn head dress, and placed a plate with a peeled mango on the floor. Kneeling over him she dangled beads and breasts and gently dabbed and brushed and swung them along his out-stretched body. She peeled off the lycra from Jules's loins to release his lingam which shot upright. There was no getting around it, it wanted to be in her and she wanted it there, too. She teased it with her dangling delights, and swept firm nanny goat nipples across his face, and pressed them into his open mouth. With an octopus tentacle tongue he twirled her buds and nibbled softly with his lips until she buckled and collapsed upon him.

She took the pulpy naked mango and slid it in and out of his mouth. He gnawed and sucked its soft, sweet, pulpy flesh from around its curvy pip. She instructed him not to swallow, then mounted his mango mouth with her moist lower lips and he slurped them both to ecstasy. She got on her hands and knees and butted him and turned around. With the flat of his hand he spanked the cheeks of her cute arse red. She then insisted that he mount her from behind like an ape.

In the afternoon, shaded from the beating heat of the sun, never less than a hundred fifty dancers under the banyan, tranced-out. The red dirt and brown landscape, all around, was bleached and baked dry. Returnee dancers bolstered the dance floor as cassette jockeys kept the music pumping. Ox-cart replenished bottles of mineral water and blocks of ice, and chai mummas maintained their posts. Late afternoon, everyone was back on the dance floor heading for final touch down with the banyan aflame in the second sunset. Inexhaustible superhuman reserves of energy fuelled the boundlessness of the marathon occasion with glasnost spandex expansion taking participants 'furthur' than they'd ever been before.

Thrilled astonishment rippled through everyone dancing at sunset, when bush telegraph lip service was saying that the music would continue a second night, further buoyed by rumour that Voltaire would play. His tapes had been mysteriously returned, left at Sofia's door. After the second sunset and moon rise, the pan-psychism of the transpersonal experience under the banyan was viscerally palpable—way, way beyond the brain.

Subsequent dosages had less zap to boost mental masonry, as hammered tolerances became saturated. It now becoming a journey where faces became mashed like pulpy, paper mâché, with running eye lids straining not to shut. A journey beyond, beyond, beyond—as if, should the dancing stop, the sun would not appear again, as though the aerial roots of the banyan had fed encoded unearthly signals through the new language of the music into the earth—only interpretable by moving to it.

By the time the second midnight came around, with Voltaire shuffling his cassettes under the holy tree, the frequencies had infused with the supernature and turned the experience into an outworlder faith—the dance floor becoming a place of subatomic edgecore. By the time, unflagging legs superhumanly delivered dancers to the third sunset, those that had forsaken sleep over the two days—which was well over half the four hundred who attended the first night—became exotic matter in chi energy transporting spirit beyond the physics of the body and wiring of the brain—turning la dolce vita into chthonian rhizome.

AFTER WAKING FROM A LONG SLEEP, Naresh had no idea what day it was. He could not recall exactly when he'd left the party and returned to it. Though there was no doubt about the affectionate kiss he received from Sheila, or was it several kisses? Which must have happened after he confessed to working in Bollywood, which sent her into hysterics; and later, further divulging that he'd acted in the movie *Disco Dancer*, which she was totally charmed by and applauded him with gushy endearments.

Laying on a coconut fibre mattress in a rented room out the back of Day And Night Restaurant, where he'd moved to after Vagator Resort, he pensively recalled her questions and his disclosures about his life in Bombay. Most worrying, in his cross examination of what he remembered saying, was the extent that he'd spilled the beans on his fraudulent gig for the *Goa Voice* under the influence of Shazam's Gorbachov, in which his role play unravelled.

That morning at the Francisco Bar while eating an omelette, Naresh's stomach churned as he read the front page of *The Goa Voice*.

HIPPIES SPREAD AIDS EPIDEMIC
Infected Patient Escapes Lock Up Ward

The days after the banyan tree party, for Zsu, was like she was resurfacing out of a Phil Spector wall-of-sound reverb chamber with atomised emotions and in need of taking stock of its echoing ocean deep, mountain high refrain. Then, another headline appeared.

A THREE-DAY ORGY OF SEX AND DRUGS AND SATANIC DANCING

Reading the scurrilous story, she heard the ghostly voice of Donna Ferreira's foreboding *Omen* in her head. Her mind then fell upon the dallying between Jules and Asta that was impossible to ignore in the later stages of the banyan tree bash. She knew in her deepest, dissociated, sound-proofed self that goings-on had come to pass, which stirred in her a longing that her capacity for self-deception kept her from feeling. And so, there came a reckoning and she went to Asta's house to come clean about the unreasoning of her gut instinct.

Sitting crossed legged on a pillow opposite Asta on her veranda, Zsu—with closed eyes and the sour taste of her feelings in her mouth—took a fortifying deep breath and declared, "I love him."

Asta shifted uncomfortably. Zsu sat upright in a lotus position tucking her feet up onto her thighs like she was straightening more than just her spine. She was straightening out something in her head. Most pressing of all, she was straightening out something in her secret heart. She opened weepy eyes and fixed them on her bestie. "Well," she took another deep breath. "I just have to tell you…" She sighed. "It's a pity you had to go and fuck him," she said in an injured tone of voice with crippling sadness in her face.

"Oh Zsu!" Asta said, shocked and mortified. "I really had no idea." A horrid flame of shame made her sweat. "I was under the impression—"

"I know! I know! I know! It's so sick and twisted," Zsu sighed dramatically, her heart heavy in her chest. "In all honesty, I have no right to blame you. It hurts so much, I'm so disgusted with myself." Every feeling in her body screamed betrayal! Betrayal to herself, betrayal to her most private feelings rancid with desolate loneliness.

"I'm so sorry," Asta said contritely. "Jules and I were so spaced out. We just started fooling around. But I really thought you two weren't an item anymore. And you mentioned the fling in Bali."

"Right!" Zsu said, "It's true. I really don't have an emotional life jacket at all. I have no right to be angry with you. I was in denial. I realised I was unexpectedly mad for him," she said with teary eyes, feeling gutted. "You must know me by now. Romance is almost a utopian concept." Her voice trembling. "When I'm in love, on some level, it's like being in a war with myself."

Asta reached out and held her hand. "Zsu hun, I didn't wish to hurt you. I really thought it was over between you two. That's the impression he gave me. It's not like you and I haven't been there before, you know... stories with guys—"

"Yes, I know, I know. The banyan tree party was beyond imagination. Bloody hell!—I nearly died."

Asta squeezed Zsu's hand. "Zsu darling it's not fair. Its terrible what that mother fucking arsehole Indian did to you, and there's nothing we can do about it. The cops are useless."

"Yeahhh..." Zsu shrugged. "It goes with the mercenary territory we now find ourselves in. And now," she sighed heavily, "these horrendous stories by that evil Catholic funded propaganda rag and..." she sighed again. "You and Jules... and me being in absolute denial of my feelings." Her voice choked with self-pity. "It's just too much. I'm livid with myself. I feel loathsome. It's all my own making. I don't know why?.. Well, I do know... I took my eye off the ball. I just couldn't deal with it—"

"Zsu please don't feel like that. I love you, Jules loves you, everyone who made it through those two days and nights had an experience of a lifetime."

An upwelling of jealousy avalanched the betrayal she was feeling. The love that she didn't let in. The love that she felt unworthy of.

Asta looked Zsu in the eye. "So, you really do have strong feelings for him, don't you?"

Zsu sucked in her cheeks and pursed her lips, her face fell into a shadow of sadness.

"Yes!—It's hurtful," she said, her green eyes intensifying. "The pain of not allowing myself to move closer to him. It'a a betrayal to myself, really...I've built walls so high inside myself, walls that I was afraid to tear down to let him in. I felt trapped by difficult feelings. Feelings I was protecting myself from. Perhaps this pain of jealousy has a purpose of bringing me closer to myself?"

"Zsu listen—the truth be known," Asta confessed. "Jules and I took ecstasy—we didn't go all the way, his lingam wilted sometime after I turned into a nanny goat."

The front gate swung open and Asta's daughter raced up the steps to the veranda. "Tina sweetheart," Asta said, "what have you been up to? You're all dirty."

"Playing mumma."

"Let's go take a shower." Asta went into the house with her daughter leaving Zsu to sit alone swamped in sulphuric feelings. Seeing Tina, stirred ingrained, cellular level emotion that Zsu wished she could purge. Feelings embedded in the undercurrents of love triangles, like the one she'd found herself in with one of her mother's boyfriends when she'd been not much older than Tina's age. Back when she was in need of filling the daddy hole in her heart. Back when she'd been allowed into adult conversations where dope was smoked and run-ins with sex occurred. Back when affections were subsumed with carnal infatuation.

In Tina, Zsu saw innocence, the essence of something she longed to return to, something not entwined in complexities of desire bound up in the power play of seeking closeness with men. Zsu could never imagine herself being a mother, having survived her own. Vicariously, through Asta, she got a taste of what it might be like to be a mother. She didn't regard herself together enough to bring a child into the world. "Tina saved my life," Asta had told Zsu. "No matter how fucked-up I might feel, I had to get it together enough to provide for another. Tina has given me the gift of selflessness, the closest I imagine that is unconditional love, a kind of love I've never experienced in romance."

Asta had once fallen in love with a wandering Indian sadhu, who'd been hanging around the parties. He charmed her with his "special kind of *otherness*, like being with a wild animal." They never went further then kissing. She got flak from her posse of friends for bringing him into their social circle. "What are you doing? We don't want him here. We don't trust him," they had said.

Then, one night riding together on her motorbike, they were stopped by cops, who jumped out in front of them when they slowed down for speed bumps on the notorious late night Vagator Road heading towards Starco Corner. Asta immediately threw the piece of charas away she'd taken precaution to clasp in her hand whilst holding the throttle handle. But the cops grabbed him, accusing him of having ganja and roughed him up and threw him in jail. She tried to help, got a lawyer, went back and forth to Fort Aguada bringing him food. But he sat and sat and sat, which broke her heart.

NARESH RODE HIS YEZDI MOTORBIKE along a trail through palm trees and local village houses at the back of Anjuna. After crossing over the bridge to Baga and passing Three Sisters shop, he pulled into Tito's Restaurant. Sitting at a table, Sheila greeted him with a warm smile. A sea breeze from the river mouth rustled palm fronds and whiffed shiny jet-black hair around her bare shoulders to which was fastened a bikini top. They drank Kingfisher beer with dark mocha eyes gazing into each other, their mouths incapable of articulating the ineffableness of what happened at the banyan tree. Mutual feelings reached out into the air between them, like insect feelers finding a way through amorphous emotions in the afterglow of the evanescent alembic of the visionary world they'd journeyed through.

Yet, Naresh felt shame about how he came to be in Goa, and the extent of his disclosures under the influence of Gorbachev at the banyan tree. As they lunched on fish curry looking out on the sunniness of Baga Beach, where bodies in g-strings baked and bounced about swinging beach rackets, Sheila said that he'd told her on the first night at the banyan that he was in Goa to write a script. On the second night, he revealed to her that he'd acted in the blockbuster movie, *Disco Dancer*. On the last sunset, he disclosed that he'd been commissioned to write a story about hippies for a Bombay magazine. After lunch, and into a second bottle of Kingfisher, his tipsiness and affection toward Sheila dared him to spill all about *The Goa Voice* assignment. At first, she was outraged that he could take on such a job for an unscrupulous newspaper and vehemently detested the paper's agenda supporting the contemptuous *Save Goa Party*. But after he'd told her how he'd deceived the editor and became hooked on the parties and had no choice but to quit and declared his infatuation for her, her amazement turned to hilarious laughter and she kissed him.

His suave charm, she'd initially been suspicious of, but somehow his bravado in embarking upon such an audacious assignment and becoming seduced by its subject matter, turned out to be an absolute enamouring clincher. The hilarity of it turning into an infatuation, the likes of which she didn't think possible with an Indian man. So off-beat was the attraction, it took her by surprise. So unsuspecting was she, that in the course of the craziness and his psychedelic christening at Shazam's dhuni, her heart became the only guide that truly knew where it was going, whilst her head was in a fata morgana. Faced with the problem of having to pay back the advance from *The Goa Voice* Sheila offered to help out by proposing that they go to Bombay and sell Ecstasy to his Bollywood connections.

Lithium batteries of the bio-musculature and neurochemistry of trance dancers at the full moon banyan blow-out required several days to recharge. The party that followed was at the monkey forest near Odvar Osser's house and finished at ten in the morning. Shortly after, plain clothes heat visited the houses of the DJ and party organiser. Charas was found and cash coughed up. A villainous stench of suspicion pervaded the tropical air. More houses searched. Paranoia spiked jangling nerves. Not just a crackdown, it felt like a dragnet. Chillums were now smoked behind locked doors. Large stashes buried. Many took to living nocturnally when plain clothes and jeeps were not around. Those preparing to export, wrapped swallowable product in the wee hours. Then, SAY NO TO DRUGS signs appeared at beaches.

By mid-March, many felt like sitting ducks about to be popped and shortened their seasonal stay in Goa. Rumour was rife that there was a new broom higher up the ranks of the cops. With nerves fried, Jaeger was holed-up and needing to attend to packages for Europe and consulted inside trader, law enforcement double agent, Alfonso, about the situation. It turned out that the plain clothes knocking on doors were a Narcotics Squad from Delhi. Maggie Thatcher, the PM of Britain, had come out with a broadsword statement: "The dregs of Western society are living in Goa." Interpol advised the Indian Government that it had become a hub for drug outlaws.

The presence of Delhi Narcotics getting about in mufti put Alfonso and Chief Inspector Fernandese on edge. They'd recycled up to fifty kilo of seized smoke and other goodies this season, their people took to burying stockpiles and got shiftier in laundering black market cash. And besides, everything was on the way up. Goa was becoming more popular with foreigners, but the wrong kind of tourists according to loud slanderous voices in Panjim. Party tourists and lifestyle hash smugglers up till now, cohabited just fine with locals and accommodating cops on the make. Happy high hippies that rented houses and motorbikes and ate at restaurants and made parties were golden gooses, prime pickings for eliciting bribes for the illicit flaunting of the law.

CYBERELLA'S TRYST WITH JULES had stirred deep longing in Zsu and forced her to feel her heart's true conviction behind a wall of cold play entrapment. As in show poker, Zsu was compelled to reveal to Asta her royal flush spread of hearts, her true feelings that she'd been in denial of. And so, desire rose up like a phoenix out of the smouldering ashes of a rekindled flame that had not been extinguished and now heated by the searing March sun in Aries as it commenced a new solar cycle.

Jules got to play another party before the season wound down earlier than usual. After which he and Zsu taxied to Arambol for a togetherness binge and hung out at the dhuni by the Shiva tree near the lake where they spent a couple of nights in a jungle hut. When they locked lips, Dolphins ducked and dived in waves curling by the shore. They caked themselves in mud in the lake and later lay together in candle light tracing fingers over the shifting contours of their bodies, as if they didn't belong to the outside world any longer.

Their embrace spoke unspoken feelings since their intimacy last year. Jules heart had suffered, it had become duped into wanting her as much as he believed she wanted him. Merging for her meant facing her murkiest doubts that she was unlovable. She was now seeing pain as proof of love. It was as though the sunshine of his love was terrifying until it became the safest place. A sunshine that made petals uncurl from buds deep within her. She offered an apology, a recompense for having to protect herself, for having to insulate herself from feelings: the fear of losing herself in him, the despair of destructive paths love had taken in the past, the sinkhole of memories of her roots. She wanted him now more than ever, as though only he was capable of deciphering the aches of her heart. Only his lips capable of kissing away every doubt.

"I adored what we experienced together," she said. "It took me to a new place, but it was scary. I freaked. I had to pull away. But you know what? The banyan tree confirmed many things and especially when you were playing."

Jules looked into Zsu's glistening green eyes like she was a clairvoyant. "DJ-ing there shook the shit out of me," he said. "What the hell was inside that music?"

Zsu stared into the distance with faraway eyes. "That first night was fucking horrific." She then turned to Jules. "Oh, my God!—The Tingler!.. I was dancing with the dead. The ghost of Donna Ferreira appeared and then I nearly died. The whole shocking experience put me in touch with something. A psychomancy. It also happened the last time I was at Atma's house."

"Like what?"

Zsu's eyes narrowed. "It was as though I was looking into the evil eye of fear, some kind of dark astral wildlife. A mediumistic force appeared in the form of Kali. Just came right through me."

Jules gave her a penetrating look. "Paranormal!.. Yeah, I can believe it. Zane reckoned he got-it-on with aliens at the banyan—"

"I felt them there, too," she said. "Invisible forces were present in every dimension. Goa is full of them. I believe every hallucination that has every happened here is pooling into a psychometric hive mind. Like the music and dancing is not solid state, but rather an altered state ozone community of electro-beings that reside in the ether here. Not just living souls, but also disembodied ones. Invisible forces… all kinds of weird phenomena are present here. Whilst The Tingler was playing, Donna's ghost appeared. It was as though I was downloading through the depths of time a universal cry. The struggle of life and death. Light and dark. Love and fear. Freedom and oppression. The *Omen* forewarns of the dark religion in Panjim hell-bent on a hippie witch hunt and police crackdown. Did you see what *The Goa Voice* has been printing?"

"Unfortunately, yeah—It sucks!" he said. "That story about Satanic dancing. Who's writing this crap?"

"Some sicko," Zsu said, scrunching up her nose. "They must have a spy, probably paying someone to snoop about. They're funded by the same dark religion that killed Pagans in ancient Europe and by conquistadors in America and here in India and now the persecution of heathen hippies as 'Evil Satanists'—just like when I'd been burnt at the stake in another life."

"Wow!.. so that really happened to you?"

"Yes…in rebirth therapy and hypnotic regression I was taken back there. Jules, just think about it, all the magic potions with herbs and mushrooms and ayurvedic medicine and mind expansion with psychedelics since the sixties has seen a renaissance in witchcraft. Acid has opened up a whole world of psychic sorcery. Osser talks about a pre-Christian Pagan paradise at the top of the world in Scandinavia. It's a big part of the ponder-head appeal of his Nordic shamanic saga. A mythic romanticism for a natural way of being before the fall from paradise into power lust and rape of Gaia and oppression of women."

Hearing this threw a switch in Jules's head and brought a flood of feelings. "The Tingler at the banyan tree was insanely intense," he said. "Man, that's some download you got—"

"It felt like a battle," she said, "of everything that ever had a will to live. Like the universe giving birth to itself."

He kissed her. Hidden parts of themselves sprung to life like electrical circuits being plugged in, only possible through the unique inter-wiring of the synastry of their personality componentry—the vagaries of a combined voltage that made their dynamos hum. It was now occurring to her that a romantic relationship thrives on mutual vulnerability. *Love is risky.*

"Jules, don't you think all the signs indicate something big is building?"

His heart was emitting a fuzzy warmth all through his chest, the heart being the most vital gauge of what really mattered. "I'm really feeling it," he said, and kissed her.

"Whew!" she gasped. "I'm happy for us. But hey—Mr Celestial Mechanic what are the stars saying about the bigger picture?"

He took a deep contemplative breath. "Well, with the dark Lord—Pluto, in your sign, Scorpio, until the middle of the nineties it looks like its gonna be a ride of intense metamorphosis."

"Whoa!—that sounds huge."

"Yeap—no half measures, I'd say. And then there's Saturn—the cosmic cop, Lord of karma. The ringed, old Devil planet went into Capricorn, ruled by the goat, during the banyan tree party."

She recalled the goat-headed Baphomet."Tell me more."

"Politics, for sure—"

"Oh, Gawd!" Her brow creased. "That sounds heavy." Then flashed upon the dead snake across her path when she returned to the party. *Had Saturn assumed the form of a serpent?* "There is an election here next year," she said. "The *Save Goa* political party want to stamp us out with their bullshit campaign, it's their platform ticket. We are portrayed as low life, we are to blame for all their problems. It's a backlash, a hang up about Western colonialism, all to do with nationalism since Goa's independence. They reckon if they kick us out they'll attract up-market short term Club Med tourists to Anjuna and Vagator. The beaches here are not flash, facilities are basic, it's not luxurious like Bali and Thailand. But hey, the local villagers love us, they are thriving off selling us food, drinks, renting us houses and motorbikes and do alright at the flea market and protect us from cops and robbers."

"All is not lost," Jules said in an upbeat tone of voice. "I'm sure magical times are afoot. It was a harmonic convergence on the full moon at the banyan tree. Uranus and Neptune conjoined in Capricorn. This is revolutionary—like in…waking up starship earth... get inspired…a technological revolution is happening, it's gonna impact a collective movement."

"I like the sound of that," she said

"Neptune is Shiva's planet," he said. "Neptune is dreamy and artistic. Neptune rules metaphysics, music and dancing and alternated states. Neptune's trident is Shiva's sacred weapon."

"We're Shaolin warriors," aren't we?" she said. "We're Techno mystics."

"Yes! Yes!" he said. "We're trans-Neptunians of the dawning digerati."

"I believe it."

They hugged and kissed. Electricity pulsed through their combined bodies inciting inflamed desire.

ON THE APRIL NEW MOON, just prior to leaving Goa, with only the hardcore monsooners remaining, Jules and Zsu returned to the mighty banyan for a purification ritual. Sitting together with sage burning, they engaged in tantric breathing under the sentient tree's vast aerial root structure that poured down from above. With eyes closed they imagined they were seeds sprouting, growing roots down from the base of their spine, reaching down through the soil of the earth, down to the bedrock beneath. Holding hands, they kept breathing and felt their roots reaching further down and down and down until they wrapped around the core of the earth—like it was a giant magnet. Feeling deeply rooted in the earth and inhaling more fully into their bellies, they felt a vital life force flow through them. Then a channel open up through the crown of their heads, like they had grown branches up above the banyan through the earth's atmosphere all the way up so that their branches reached into a star gate. Then a dancing celestial entity appeared informing them that it was from the seed star cluster—*The Pleiades*, and that they were eternal, immortal, not trapped in the skeleton of time.

Before leaving India, they travelled to the tantric temples of Khajuraho in Madhya Pradesh where every imaginable sex act, including threesomes and bestiality, was chiselled in stone. Zsu turned to Jules and said, "Can you believe it? These erotic figures were sculpted more than a thousand years ago—and the Kamasutra is even older."

Jules gaped in amazement. "What happened? Why did India become so puritanical?"

She shook her head. "You have to thank Islamic dynasties, Christian overlords and the Brahmin priestly caste. Religion—the great oppressor of the body."

Returning to Bali, they immersed themselves in the conjugal chemistry of their togetherness amidst the animistic vapours of the island of the gods. Jules was spellbound by its lush tropical sensuality, refined crafts and trippy animal gods with engorged eyes. His imagination became ignited and charmed with mystical allure, yet further to Zsu's warning the antennae of his sixth sense was alerting him to hidden treachery that belied its spiritual intoxication and aesthetic deduction.

Whilst sipping a Bloody Mary in a luxuriant swimming pool with Jules wrapped around her, Zsu realised that pain had shaped her as much as love and laughter and play and creating and dancing had. Jules made himself her dedicated understander, as though his deep empathy might scald her awake. A hungry, wild tenderness consumed them on the volcanic island. Their groaning couplings generated an energy field, unlike they'd felt between them in the astral static of Goa, in which her vulnerabilities became his vulnerabilities until all personality boundaries where shattered in transfiguring abandon. The laminates of moulded sub personalities shearing off, reconstituting into the coalescence of a merged shadow dance.

Zsu became aware of how an intimate relationship was an opportunity to get in touch with hidden, split-off parts of herself. The buried feelings she was prone to being mired in. The pain and pleasure entanglements that had driven the furnace of her passions and the need to feel special— to feel loved. And so, a new kind of commitment to trust allowed her to let go in ways she'd never known before. She became braver and braver holding eye contact longer and longer when every part of her body begged to look away. Whereupon her banished secret *self,* came back from dungeons of denial, like the stealth bats with sonar frequency vision that flapped their wings in the languid banana leaves that hung over the concrete wall of their Legian compound—on top of which were cemented pieces of broken glass. Their coupling brought a deeper connection and release from the vitriol of the past. Where before there had been a numbness, she now trusted him with her secrets, and explored ways that they could turn each other on. At times, the feeling was so intense they felt as though they would implode into a gazillion particles. When inner obstacles arose, they would lose themselves kissing until every doubt was dissolved, all perimeters of flesh merged. While making love at a jungle retreat near Ubud a rainbow serpent appeared.

Freakquency Metanoia

Tribeadelic was the name of a new label Zsu launched in Bali. She employed Javanese batik artists to make large fluoro, décor, party banners featuring sacred geometry, oriental mandalas, celtic and extraterrestial themed motifs. Jules DJ-ed at warehouse parties Down Under, but there was mixed reception from the urban crowd to the weird spacey sounds of the astral Asia techno on his tapes. Zane landed back in Sydney with a belly full of charas. The Telepathic's made two tracks, then Jules went to Bali where he and Zsu threw a Goa style party. But high flying trippy techno was way too-over the heads of the chichi poolside set there. Only seasoned Goa heads, who did fashion business in Bali, could fully jump on it.

By Christmas, Zsu and Jules had returned to Goa with him moving into her house. Kicking like a mule, the nineteen-eighty-nine season got off to a rip-roaring start with oodles of romper stomper parties through January. New music belted torrential, every cassette arriving in backpacks loaded with freshly milled, never heard before, sounds. The scene was on the up with parties being made by a miscellany of organisers and DJs and décor artists with no shortage of blotta babas dispensing lysergic *Lucy love*.

In February, the sun returned to where it was the day Jules was born. Dancing to the new musical science between Antonio's speakers under palms on middle Vagator Beach, it occurred to him that spirituality through technology was where it was at. That this music was the sound track of the mystique of the metaverse. That trance, tribal, techno had become a belief system of a freakquency fraternity. That the parties were an unstoppable intellecto-techno tsunami. That he should aspire to be a maven of metaphysical, machine music. That he should apply it to the psycho-acoustic space of dance floor communion. That the Indo tribe, disco in the sky was on the verge of hysteria. That redemption through rave was possible.

The *Save Goa* party only managed to get one seat in last year's election. According to Alfonso, the Delhi plain clothes operation was over. But police permission was now required for parties and none during school exams. The season was bouncing boundlessly until, for no apparent reason, at the end of March it came to a deadening halt. It was assumed that various factions within the police had not been adequately greased. Nonetheless defiant, a bunch of Dutch friends who lived in Arambol put together a party. Antonio trucked his PA from Mapusa and speakers were carried on the heads of labourers around the seashore rocks and set-up in a circle next to Arambol lake. Shazam arrived staking-out a *Lucy love* dhuni who, together with pretty pixies, dispensed his goodness. All DJs played, the music went sunset to sunset finishing with everyone caked in mud in the lake. One last party was pulled off before the end of the season, which entailed everyone convoying on motorbikes and taxis down south to the white sands of Palolem Beach, where Antonio's speakers were erected for the very last time under palms for unfettered trance dancing to outlawed, quirky, psychedelic techno.

Redemption Through Rave

THE NINETEEN-EIGHTY-NINE Christmas party and new year party celebrating the beginning of the naughty nineties (the decade in which electronic dance music would resuscitate the music industry), heralded a promising new season. Word got out fast. "The season is on again!" Rave tourists arrived in their droves to Goa's Dabolim Airport with tickets that included an E. Every available house, including refurbished pig styes, got rented out. Everyone telling friends, "Come to Goa, it's going off!" By the end of January, all houses, rooms, and beach cabanas were full-up with pale skin new arrivals. Restaurants, bars and chai shops were rammed. Chapora spewed over at night, as did Primrose and other hitching posts with milling punters priming themselves in billowing plumes of chillum smoke.

Through-out the mid to late eighties, party makers mostly relied on Antonio from Mapusa to set up his four stack PA for a modest price, but with hordes of rave tourists arriving the scene had rapidly swelled and a bigger sound system was required. A new PA wallah, Vijay Prabhu, from Assagao impressed himself on the scene with a brand new more powerful system sourced from Panjim. Its large black speaker cabinets came with the name, OMSONIC, stencilled on them in orange dayglow. His brother ran a bar and claimed to have a connection to the cops. Many would-be party makers gave him the benefit of the doubt. But Doc and Jaeger, long in the tooth, were suspicious. *Which cops?*

Seasonally, Atma Blaze and his pals spread their rupees generously around Anjuna. He'd bought his Enfield off Sebastian, one of the Starco Corner boys, and rented his house from another family member. With two to three parties a week in January, the nineteen ninety season boomed and brought an increased demand for motorbike rentals. Sebastian and his brother bought two new Enfields, a Yamaha and two TVS's, plus rented out older model Rajdoot and Yezdi motorbikes. The new bikes would easily be paid off by the end of the season. Other members of the family owned restaurants and houses which were leased out yearly to freaks. During monsoon, freaks would store their stuff with Goan families. By the beginning of the season, Sebastian's brother had half-finished building a new house financed from rents and restaurant business of the previous season.

The family of the wife of the Panchayat of Anjuna, Sylvester de Souza, ran the Anjuna bakery near Nelson's corner. It stocked "gourmet" (for Indian standards) munchies that stoned motorbike riders would avidly drop in to score. The yummiest being chocolate brownies, croissants, cheese and mango ice cream.

Blaze, together with the O.O.O. and Anjuna pals, was the first to throw a party with the new Omsonic sound system at the beach. He managed to persuade Voltaire to play and sat next to him winding tapes. Everyone was happy that Voltaire was playing, but those in his inner circle were surprised, as Voltaire had previously suspected Atma of being a beneficiary of the music that was on his stolen tapes prior to the banyan party. A music mafia collector had trainspotted Atma DJ-ing exclusive special tracks on the first night of the banyan party, which were only obtainable from him and alleging that Atma paid an Indian to poke the bamboo stick through Sofia's window.

This season Voltaire was recording his collection on DAT tapes and was keen to hear the higher fidelity sound through the Omsonic PA. The party was setup in middle Anjuna close to the beach. The O.O.O. installed a totem sculpture with the skull of a monkey and horns of a goat that was painted fluoro. The party raved ravenously to a bumper crop of fresh psychedelic electronica. Voltaire's Goa-nuanced selection was not *Rave* music by definition of what was trending in clubs and warehouses in Europe. E heads, first time in Goa, without having been broken into India, soon found out that Goa was not Ibiza. Fluffy, handbag, cheesy House Music and bland Techno didn't cut it in—*mystery school,* Goa. What was heard on Voltaire's high fidelity DAT tapes through the voluminous, brand-new spanking system, intensified by the pharmacopoeia of blotta baba Shazam's latest batch (given out by him in signature mind-boggling garb), sent sky divers warp speed, arching and bending new choreographies of wild dance under star spangled palms.

By February, the most socially prime-time of the season, a rising cloud nine euphoria bloomed with Goa brimming mile-wide smiles. Accommodation was full up. Circles of friends took to throwing dinner party feasts in compounds of rented houses and the flea market expanded onto the adjacent rice paddy, as more stalls began selling party fashion. The cop connection of Vijay, the Omsonic PA wallah, seemed to be working, but the PA rental had more than doubled and the baksheesh to the cops had skyrocketed. It was not entirely clear who else, besides Chief Inspector Fernandese, was giving the nod and pocketing wads of cash.

At the flea market Danilo spotted a Goa party tape—'Anjuna Sunrise Mix'—being sold at a local stall amongst bootlegs of commercial releases, such as Deep Forest. Curious, he asked the stall wallah if he could hear it. A low noise BASF cassette was removed from its case and played on a battery powered tape player. The first track Des recognised and fast forwarded to the next, and then to the next. Astonished, he was seized with shock to realise that this was a recording of Voltaire's set through the Omsonic sound system at the Anjuna party.

"Where did you get this tape?" Danilo interrogated in a hostile voice.

"My friend," the cowering Indian replied.

"You can't sell this music," he scolded the Indian. "Who made these tapes?"

The stall wallah replied with a blank face. Danilo began to boil.

"Who recorded this?" The wallah averted his shifty eyes.

"This is a bootleg. Your pirating the party. The music is not for sale!"

The stall wallah shuffled nervously on his feet saying nothing. Danilo's outrage at the recording of the mix of the special Goa music then flipped to irony. *Ha!.. we are making free pirate parties with shared, pirated copyright music. Well, a handful of collectors are scoring vinyl. Dancers want a mixtape at the end of the season, like a musica momento. But selling tapes? No!.. No!.. No!..*

The Italian DJ more than ever was now feeling like a pirate in a rip tide of a black economy that had gotten bigger and so desperately needy, it was rife for extortion. He shook his head and pondered the price of *paradise tax*.

"Give me all these illegal tapes," Danilo demanded with a spurning look that shook the stall wallah. "Here, I'll even pay you." He threw down three twenty rupee notes. "Tell whoever is stealing this music, we'll track them down."

On a Monday the last week of February at sunset, Vijay and his assistants were setting up Omsonic speaker stacks above middle Vagator. Zsu supervised the placement of bamboo poles to which she fixed her bright Bali batik banners comprised of mandalas and sacred geometry. By evening, chai mummas were camped out along the top of the cliff overlooking the beach. By nine o'clock, dancers began pulling-up on motorbikes. At ten, the cliff top was amassed with party people. After eleven, with no sound coming from the large speakers, doubt descended upon Vagator cliff and the stars ceased twinkling. At midnight the sky turned inky black and the air became foul with bad news. Bitter disappointment bit hard as anguished jaws spread the disheartening, crushing words— "NO PARTY!"

The scene sunk into despair: "Oh no!.. Fucking hell!.. Unreal!.. Your joking!.. I don't believe it!.. This is too much!.. I'm gutted!.. I just wanna cry!..

Doc chewed Vijay's ear off about his "guaranteed arrangements." Then two police jeeps arrived which had Vijay feeling like he was about to be road kill in headlights. In shock, and not wishing to encounter cops, many sat down on the dance floor gazing wishfully at the assembled speaker stacks hoping somehow there was a chance that the music might start. But alas, the non-negotiable devastating presence of uniformed cops confirmed that this was to be a *funeral party*. (The funeral of the Goa party season that everyone had high hopes for.)

Zsu's eyes filled with tears, she rested them bleakly on her strung-up banners now unlit as the generator had been switched off. Hearts sank like the dance floor was the Titanic, no one wishing to abandon it. Sitting by a speaker stake with shoulders slumped, Zsu bowed her head clutching it with both hands and sobbed with disappointment.

The next day, grief sunk in when it was learnt that it was not just an issue of school exams, but that Panjim had ordered a crackdown on parties. The Panchayat, Sylvester De Souzer, was saying that some influential Catholic families, who had returned from the Gulf States in the Middle East all cashed-up, now regarded themselves as middle class and did not care much for foreign tourists and weren't pleased about the increased loudness of all night parties. After two weeks of no parties, die hard groovers, fly-in ravers and frustrated party makers wallowed in misery. The mood of despair was like riding an Enfield around Goa with flat tyres.

Donna Ferreira's *Omen* gnawed on Zsu's mind. Jules brought his telepathic powers to bear on the situation and peered into his ephemeris looking for a way through hurdles with authorities, which grim reaper Saturn in Capricorn appeared to be a harbinger of. He looked at phases of the moon in which spiritual agencies might be summoned to assist with the abomination that the scene now found itself beset with. After three weeks of no parties, frustration spewed over. Rookie, Asia traveller ravers and seasoned freaks defiantly attempted parties in back yards of rented houses, but all got shut down. "There will be a showdown," Donna informed Zsu in a necromancy ritual.

Soon after, Vijay came to Jules bristling with renewed hope saying his brother had negotiated a day party which could go through to the next day if it was held down on Spaghetti Beach where the sound did not travel. Throwing caution to the wind and desperate to dance, Jules and Zsu jumped on Vijay's proposal. Besides Shiva's drum and Ganesh's protection, other deities were evoked by Zsu to assist in rebooting the disco in the sky, which now had become a contentious, political, hot potato. The mobilising potency of loud *special Goa music,* for the scene, now felt like contraband. Jules struck on the idea that there was a *freakquency* inside the music that triggered a chemical response in the brain—like a drug. And that the *freakquency* was highly addictive and the ground swell popularity of the parties—an electrodelic epidemic. The *freakquency* was being shared, tape to tape, by a subversive underground that thrived in an underworld that came out at night and craved to dance to it through to sunrise. Yet, the no-face, no-brand, free-style of the *Goa freakquency* was beyond genre. The experience of the *freakquency* in the parties, beyond commerce, and now impossible to extricate from the quick sand of corruption feeding off punitive politics that was intent on exterminating the scene. A scene which now did not have a leg to stand on, let alone dance.

On the full moon in February, nineteen ninety, when Chief Inspector Fernandes had been notified that a party was happening on Vagator beach in the afternoon, he told his boys to let it be. But a couple of hours later, Calangute police became aware of the party. Under guidelines of a decree from Panjim, two jeeps were dispatched with officers, one armed with .303 Lee-Enfield rifle.

After a shot rang out over Spaghetti Beach day party—at which Zsu, possessed by the dark, mother goddess Kali, was wailing and confronting baton wielding cops like a Shaolin shadow boxing master at the centre of the dance floor—Odvar Osser joined her wearing only an orange sadhu g-string and holding a holy totem staff on top of which was the skull of his grandfather with goat horns attached. Joining in with Zsu, he chanted incantations in Odin root language sounds and pointedly motioned with his head at the cops like a rampaging billy goat and thrust his staff into the centre of the dance floor like a Maori warrior laying down a challenge. The combined witchcraft forces emanating from the new occult coalition of Zsu and Osser was spellbinding. It was the shamanarchy of spiritual activism, just like that of Tibetan priests facing off with the Chinese army.

The Goa cops shuddered. Their training told them to hold their position, but their Indian reverence for mystical possession urged them to move to the edge of the dance floor. But then a second warning shot was fired from the cliff top above and more khaki uniformed cops with bamboo batons filed down to the party. Doc met with the officer in charge. Beseechingly he attempted to offer cash for the party to continue, but it could not be bought. Instead, two officers arrested Vijay. It was not going to proceed without Bardez turning into a civil war between the seasonal colony of party freaks and Goa Government forces. Hopes of salvaging the promised nineteen-ninety redemption through rave season, at any cost, were dashed with the wheels having come completely off the collective space buggy.

Those who'd dosed-up were distraught—like they'd suddenly been wrenched into a military war zone. The once seemingly permanent Vagator blue sky above was now dark and stormy. The late afternoon sun—a black disk descending toward a bloodshot sea of sorrow. Blotter baba Shazam pulled hard on his long white beard, the psychedelic beach opera that thirty minutes ago was in full swing, now dopamine derailed in tatters around him. A flock of acid heads stupefied in post-traumatic shock. Zane, totally wired, tore off his clothes and threw himself into the tide.

Under Siege

A LARGE EFFIGY HEAD OF SHIVA had been sculpted by Lazzaro out of rock at the end of Spaghetti Beach. Next to it stood a wooden carved trident, off of which hung a marigold garland and small bongo drum. When the Italian artist wasn't painting T-shirts, frescoes on walls, and party decor, his *happy place* was the beach. Making art was an obsessive, compulsive necessity as he had an over active imagination, which was both a blessing and a curse. As a child brought up in a devout family in Florence, he'd been prone to visions, some torturous—as in purgatory. So troubling had these been as a teenager, his parents took him to a priest for sacrament penance hoping confession would relieve their son of an affliction of "sinful alienation." But this did not bring absolution from his imagined sentence in purgatory, so a psychiatrist was consulted who gave him electroshock treatment and put him on Xanax. It wasn't until Lazzaro arrived in India and discovered Buddhist and Yogi practices that he gained better management of his highly impressionable imagination and vulnerability to tormenting thoughts.

Like everyone on Spaghetti Beach, Lazzaro enjoyed the social ritual of a chillum circle—it being not dissimilar to the sacrament of Catholic holy communion. Kneeling in an Asian squat he received the ceremonial pipe from the left and passed it on to the right in a counter clockwise direction. It was the cannabinoids in Malana cream (a premium quality high-end hand-rubbed jungle hash from Parvati Valley) he discovered worked best for modulating brain chemistry for peace of mind and art making.

Irksome thoughts would still occasionally arise, but Malana cream quickly dispatched them, like they were benign brain farts.

Besides Lazzaro's muse, Lord Shiva, he also took inspiration from salamanders, devas, dragon serpents and other entities residing in Jungle Palace behind the chai shacks on Spaghettti Beach. They all came to life in his emotion-tossed visionary art. An irritable bowel would sometimes get him into dire straits, but jungle pigs took care of that with him never caught short. Although a pang of anxiety hitting his colon could quickly escalate to full-blown panic attacks if he let his high-strung nervous system get the better of him. This condition, he believed, was a religious malady. A pact he'd made with God when he'd taken Confirmation. Having lapsed, he'd become afflicted with a persecution complex about law and punishment and repentance. Police had locked him up once. The incarceration was unbearable.

So when police entered the flea market on Wednesday the first week of February in nineteen-ninety-one with two officers heading his direction, he became tense. They were armed with rifles as earlier in the day there had been an alarming, ruinous incident and were searching for the culprit. Lazzaro had a piece of charas on him and not made enough rupees in sales to pay them off if subject to a search. With his chest tightening and heart racing and police heading his direction, his adrenals spiked sending a frightful nerve spasm down to the pit of his stomach squirming his bowel and pinching his sphincter.

"I need to go to the toilet," he urgently said to Asta, his neighbour stall holder. "Please keep an eye on my stuff." He briskly walked to towards the edge of the market and snuck a glance over his shoulder and saw the police approach Asta. A voice in his head urged him to "get the fuck out of here!" He started to run. A policeman pointed at him. "YOU!.. STOP!"

Caught in the grip of unnerving dread, the voice in his head screamed—"FLEE!" Lazzaro kept running. A policeman raised a rifle, as if to shoot. At that moment, a gasping on-looking flea market of freaks, freaked-out. They screamed and yelled abuse at the police and then started angrily throwing stones.

The next day *The Navhind Times* ran a story saying that the Anjuna flea market had been shut down after a pistol had been seen waved about over three kilos of charas by a foreigner who fled. When Police attempted to apprehend the culprit they were set upon by stall holders. The Chief Minister of Goa said that the Anjuna Flea Market was run by a "syndicate of armed drug gangsters."

Jaeger was outraged. He'd witnessed the heedless incident earlier in the day when an errant "gangster" dealer made a show of the hash with a pistol at the flea market. Guns were strictly prohibited in India and charas regarded a sacrament to Shiva. The reckless stupidity of the act was tantamount to disrespectful blasphemy. The "gangster" outsider left the market on a rented scooter before police arrived later and mistakenly pursued Lazzaro. The Nelson's Corner Boys, who'd rented the scooter to the culprit, knew where he was staying and told Jaeger that he had not left Goa.

Immediately, Jaeger went to Mapsua to do a deal with Chief Inspector Fernandese. He informed him that no one knew this "lone wolf idiot outsider" that brought the flea market into disrepute and would give the troublemaker's location if permission could be granted for a party. Fernandese was sympathetic but couldn't guarantee anything as he was under orders from Panjim.

Deceptively, the nineteen-ninety-one season had gotten off to an encouraging start with a Christmas and New Year party. But, like the previous season in which high flying party people had expected sustained lift-off, once again no further permission was being granted for parties and the scene grounded with wings clipped. But then, out of the blue, a one-off party did happen on January seventeen, the same day the U.S. invaded Iraq just across the Arabian Sea. The mood of the party had a strange parallel reality, like that of a cavalry charge of renegade rave revolutionaries who'd been set free to dance through the night and out of their bodies into the rising morning sun. One of the most poignant tracks played was 'Wardance' by Peyote. The feeling on the dance floor was like tarred fallen angels who'd been excommunicated, but teasingly for just one night and one morning, repetitive-beat communion was sanctioned for sacramental moon juice magic in homage to Sun God Ra—thus assuring holy ascension.

The season had seen the arrival of traveller circus freaks intent on spicing up the parties with juggling, fire spitting and balancing on tight wires between palms. But with the psychedelic circus coming to a halt, they took to the main streets of Panjim and staged performances in which they waved placards protesting the banning of dance parties.

By February, with the shutting down of the flea market, as well as the parties, the life blood of the scene was totally cut off. The sultry tropical air of Goa turned oppressive, its oxygen coated in rank despair. Lungs choked on short breaths of gloom. Chillums could only safely be smoked behind bolted doors. The boom shankar high had now become a defiant act, yet much-needed palliative for the dispiriting angst and doom that rained down on the scene like a bursting bladder with intolerable levels of paranoia that hung heavy in the sticky tropical heat like the foul fumes from plastic bags and bottles that the locals burned in their rubbish.

As well as a music curfew, houses were searched and road blocks setup. The sight of a jeep sent smokers scampering like hunted animals. Trees wept, palms dolefully hung their coconut laden heads. With no amplified music permitted, the once-paradise playground languished in discontent. Bodies and minds, that once bounced playfully to uplifting, eclectic, electronic music in brightly painted décor in tropical nature under beckoning starscapes, became despondent and took up yoga to calm frayed nervous systems and frazzled heads. While others thrashed out frustration whacking balls with beach rackets. It was not the first time the flea market had been shut down. It had also happened in the late seventies. Back then, the freaks outwitted the cops by having it not regularly on a Wednesday, but running every six days on an irregular cycle.

Not to be entirely snookered, some intrepid party pirates took to hiring large boats and sailing out to sea with speakers strapped to the rigging. But for most, the torment of being sitting ducks with paranoia of smoking hash had turned funtopia into a nightmare and were forced to evacuate for peace of mind. The police did manage to arrest the idiot "gangster" with information forwarded by Jaeger. The outsider, first time in India, was the son of a tycoon from the Balkans. A fat, kickback, wad of foreign cash would later have him released, but Goa continued to labour under siege. With its survival at stake the severe crackdown that the scene felt unjustly inflicted with brought fractious divisions within it together. Some believing that its shady core creeds had been compromised and misrepresented beyond all repair and that the forbearance now required was like that of a remote Amazon tribe under threat of extinction.

In the third week of March, Jaeger and Doc returned to Mapusa Police Station to parley with Chief Inspector Fernandese, telling him sadly that pretty much everyone had packed their bags and left Goa. This nearly brought a tear to the Chief Inspector's eye. He rubbed his chin, leaned forward over his desk and whispered, "You have your party. Must be in a private compound, small sound."

Powerful metaphysical forces had come together on the dance floor of the Spaghetti Beach party when police came down the cliff. The ghost of Osser's Nordic shaman grandfather and the powers of the avatar of Kali, channelled through Zsu, joined forces. Their combined holding of the sacred space of the dance floor created a new underworld, supernatural coalition. It was an underworld that the predominantly Catholic Goa Police and *Free Goa Party* of Panjim had no idea about, but which local Goans, believers of *The Evil Eye*, had deep respect for. Whilst Zsu was possessed by Kali, she heard the lizard king Jim Morrison screaming raw-throated in her head. "You cannot petition the law with prayer!"

The "unofficial" last party of the season happened in Zsu's garden behind the walls of her compound that crawled with bougainvillea, off of which she draped flouro, batik party banners. Atma got involved providing a smaller sound system and even didn't wish to DJ and arranged for sugar cane juice and fruit salad in the morning. The O.O.O. coordinated a vegetarian feast early in the evening before computer beats started. The DJ table was set up on the veranda next to a sewing machine. Asian, Jomonesque, alien dolls with translucent skin, belonging to Asta, were pulsing with coloured light powered by sensory circuitry plugged into the sound mixing board.

Escape from Paradise

THE NEXT SEASON STARTED WITH THE TEASE of a Christmas and New Year party, but no further permission was given, which left Zsu feeling like she was living under a wet sack. Unable to rid herself of the tetchiness of not being able to dance to all the exciting, fresh sounds of the new technodelica pouring into Goa on tapes, she felt like she was going through cold turkey. She couldn't even enjoy getting stoned. All she could do was cling onto the wings of hope like she was on a hope overdose. An acrid cloud hung over the place she called—*home*. Life did not feel lush. It was like a nightmare she wished she could wake up from. Her paranoia became tap roots feeding on the oppressiveness of the festering situation. She took to medicating on Valium and drank vodka at the Prassad Bar down in Chapora at night to ease the grief of the flattened party scene. If the previous two seasons felt like riding the motorbike around with flat tyres, this one, with no parties and no flea market, felt like a bike with no wheels. The *Goa state of mind* was so down in the dumps, rankled, and exasperated, that only a miracle or extreme action could fix it.

Concerned about the local economy, Panchayat of Anjuna, Sylvestor De Souza, went to Panjim to negotiate the return of the flea market. It being the only place, without party, where everyone gathered, not only to buy and sell, but exchange information. A minor concession of allowing music in restaurants and bars till ten o'clock was granted, which was like dangling carrots in front of fenced-in starving wild horses that just wanted to cut loose, lope, gallop and pace. Then a week later, to everyone's relief, the flea market resumed, but regulated with stalls required to pay a fee and a police presence.

"Where've you been?" Doc said to Jaeger at the flea market, having not seen him down on the beach lately.

"Recording new music," Jaeger said, pulling out a long leather DAT bag from his day pack. "The underground never sleeps. The music matters. Killer tracks just keep coming, even if there ain't nowhere here to dance to it, besides the secret parties that happen inside houses."

"The situation is grim," Doc said with a pinched look of the snookered. We sure ain't gonna take this lying down. His eyes rolled over the freshly recorded titles Jaeger had written on the sleeves of his DAT tapes which he'd named: AURAL ORACLE, BODY ANTENNA, TECHNARCHY, SONIC SHRAPNEL, HIGH VAULT HEXER, THE AGE OF SHIT, SUPERSATURATED, HYSTERIC ODYSSEY, FREAKY CHAKRA, TANTRIC TELEGRAPH, MOVE THE COLOURS, IDEAS AND IMITATORS, PROPHET OF TRIBAL TEKNO

"Man!—you sure have been busy—"

"It used to be dis," Jaeger said pulling a C90 cassette out of his pack, "and now it's DAT. The quality has gotten better, and look how small these suckers are. I can now cue tracks quicker by searching ID numbers. But it's the pits!" he moaned. "There ain't no full-power proper parties to play all this crunchy new music."

The Goa traveller, *DAT Mafia*, thrived on the new format high-resolution digital tapes on which lossless DAT to DAT copies were made with the micro-circuitry of the new portable recorders, that were much smaller than their predecessor—the Walkman Professional WM-D3. New, difficult to find underground dance music released on vinyl and CD—and most sort after of all, unreleased tracks sourced directly from master tapes of producers—were selectively shared via a traveller DJ/collector network. The computer revolution of the eighties freed up music making with Do-It-Yourself home studios. New technology ushered in a quest for future music and facilitated alternative networking to propagate it. Yet, the most psychonaut place, championing and road testing cutting edge dance music, had been shut down.

With a collective sigh of relief, like their survival depended upon it, Zsu, Asta, Lazzaro, and everyone making art, craft, clothes, jewellery, and any kind of party fashion wear, were relieved to be back displaying their creations on their patch at the Anjuna flea market.

Late in the afternoon, the sun hovered an intense orange about to drop to the horizon. It's rapturous flaming rays unable to rid Zsu of an inconsolable desolation: a crisis of freedom, a crisis of entitlement. It made her need a drink, which came to her in the form of a worm in a bottle. She'd been sitting with Doc on a reed mat at her stall, when a freak offered them shots of mescal. Gazing out to the ocean through the vibrant colours of the psychedelic party wear and fluoro sarong art hanging from strings in the palms, she could feel the tequila worm over-ride diazepam and cannabinoids to internally, warmly, wrap her in sozzled, compensatory contentment.

The flea market truly did feel like a tribeadelic encampment of nomadic, wandering travellers that had communally come together as a subculture, within somebody else's culture, which had once been under the thumb of a colonising Euro tribe—not far removed from her own distant ancestors. *What's our right to party here? What's our right to live the way we want to here? What are the terms and conditions of freedom here?*

It hurt that the scene was being stigmatised as "drop out scrub druggies." What about all the depression and unwellness in the world, and all the legal consumption of alcohol and pharmaceuticals? She thought about spirituality and enlightenment and sacred substances and how many in the scene signed off their, 'Love Me In Goa,' post cards with the valediction: "Love and light xxx." She thought about the resourceful ways many in the scene had devised to live outside of the system, and the reckless malcontents who took pleasure in ripping it off, and the extreme ones with chronic compulsions that dangerously careered them to the verge of self-destruction, and the fatal overdoses that were hardly accidental. Yes, freedom was more possible before, at a time when Goa was more primitive, off the map, no rules and regulations. Yes, India has been the place tolerant to weirdo-beardo waywardness, the place of non-ordinary states of consciousness. She thought of Osho, his teachings and what went terribly wrong at the Rajineeshpuram community in Oregon?

And now, big surprise (or was it big embarrassment?), mystical hedonism, the likes of which started with trance dancing to computer music in Goa, had bloomed into mass hysteria. She considered her namesake. *Tribes*—that most noble and romantic of fashion branding, conferring a subgroup sphere of association and identification. *Tribe*, as in a subfamily, yet, made up of fierce individuals—free spirits coming together on a world techno beat on a beach in Asia, fated to spawn a proliferating, unifying vibe tribe experience. Even with no parties in Goa, the magic had not left, it burned ardently inside everyone who had experienced it here. Surely, it's the people that make a scene? So why not just move the scene?

The sun floated on the Arabian Sea. A discrete, small chillum got passed her way, followed by another swig of the worm. The combination sent fiery heat through her body and wrapped her brain in happification. With mescal-infused blood roaring through diazepam coated arteries her face blazed a full-bore burning look. But what fuelled her engine most was music and dancing.

The orange disk of the sun dissolved into the ocean like a huge palliative tablet. In an altered state of *otherness*, she temporarily shed the dread of the most disappointing and prohibitive of seasons, in the most under-duress conditions, in the place she'd once escaped to, to set up home, establish a business and fall in love multiple times. The place that now had become more repressive than where she'd escaped from. With a fanatical blaze in her eyes, she looked around at all the freaks gathered on the beach. It was packed. Everyone standing around in loud-lycra action wear—busting to dance. She heard Jules's voice in her head. *Man!—you are just pushing shit up hill. Nothing can stick in the current situation.* It was what he'd said to friends who showed up at their house conniving a secret party in Morjim, across the river from Chapora, imploring her and him to get involved.

The freak offered another round of shots, which sent Zsu tipsy-topsy-turvy as the worm rode the diazepam and Manali cannabinoids. She looked at Doc, his glazed face and glassy eyes primed for mischief. She loved this look. She identified with it. She loved that Doc didn't act his age. She loved that he would unashamedly self-dramatise with an air of infantile entitlement. It was India, bent beyond belief—the place where you could get away with it. Then the brainstorm caprice—*GETAWAY!* exploded in her head. With echo delay and sustain the notion bounced around inside her skull. It was what she'd heard the ghost of Donna Ferreira tell her in a dream last night.

"We gotta escape!" she said to Doc, her lip turned up at a tragic angle. "We gotta get out of here! We gotta get out of Goa!"

Doc Silver's face lit up—his aluminium hair became electrified, as if in the seizure of a eureka moment on hearing what came out of her mouth. "BINGO!.." Doc yelled. "Silver bullet!.. now your talkin' Zsu, best god damned idea I've heard all season. Right on, right on, let's do it. Let's haul arse. Let's get the hell out of Dodge. I'm all in—"

"But is it possible?" Zsu wondered. "It would be like evacuating the entire scene."

"As it stands, right now, we're screwed," Doc scowled. "Everyone here is a traveller. I'm fed up feeling like an illegal, alien detainee in an immigrant camp. I need to escape this *war on drugs*. This war on fun. We gotta get out of here so we can have some play time. Fuck it!—we're here to go. I was just talking to Luchiano. He's fed up, too, and is prepared to do whatever it takes to make a proper party. The music is in desperate need of being heard and danced to. Party is our life blood—"

"But where?" Zsu said.

"Across the border."

"Maharashtra?"

"You got it sista," Doc confirmed. "It's a sweet runner. Totally doable. It's insanely beautiful up there. The locals are unspoilt."

The resolve in his voice buoyed Zsu's heart. The plan they'd just hatched filled her with rebellious defiance. She was pumped.

Doc skipped along the beach to pow-wow the plan with Luchiano, who was in a huddle of Italians finishing up a sundown smoking ritual. In the fading light, he found Zsu packing up the *Tribes of The Moon* stall to inform her in a hushed, conspiratorial voice that Luchiano wants to do a Shivaratri party, Monday, first week of March. And he'd lead a reconnaissance mission north tomorrow to suss out a party spot. On hearing confirmation of the plot, Zsu's hand went to the Lilith, talisman pendent on her chest.

North Goa and South Maharashtra was one of Doc's secret getaways with pretty playmates who were up for adventure on his chopper, which involved hair-raising road trips on the back of his chopper belting through gears, hurtling through bucolic countryside dropping in on local villages. Having explored all the back roads, he knew well the remote coastline, its beaches and historical ruins and was upbeat about convoying the party scene across the border on a magical mystery tour.

The next day, as soon as the Siolim ferry had delivered Doc and his pirate, party scouts across Chapora River, the heavy miasma of the psychosis that the scene was afflicted with, evaporated. Everyone felt lighter, the further away they got from Vagator and Anjuna. Doc lead the way North to Terekhol Fort at the border of Maharashtra on his hotted-up Enfield 500 with Asta on the back, clinging onto him, followed by Luciano and Savina on a Royal Enfield and Jules and Zsu on a Yamaha.

Slicing through radiant green patchwork of rice fields, Zsu felt like she was back in Bali. They stopped on the side of the road where there was flowering hibiscus to eat wild berries and cashew fruit and smoke a chillum. It was the first time in quite a while that they were fully relaxed smoking charas in Goa, without looking over their shoulder, or having to lock their door like they were living in a cat and mouse lockdown zone. Pulling into a village, where men spat betel nut and women in saris ground coconut masala in stone pestle and mortar, they were served bhaji, dhal, curry and rice for lunch. Doc recounted a hilarious, just deserts story, in which Zikos, the other night was being chased on his bike by police in a jeep. Doc took great pleasure in describing how Zikos deftly out manoeuvred them on a tight side road turn, "flipping the jeep arse over tit... poor bastards," he scoffed.

The North Goa flora was verdant. Wayside shrines and crosses whisked past them as they motored along narrow backwater roads sparsely inhabited, the locals not used to foreigners. Once the motorbikes crossed Terekhol River, the air and nature felt different. They were now in Maharashtra. The landscape was similar, but different, as though imprinted with its own unique history that had nothing to do with Portugal. Doc turned his chopper into a road that headed to the Coast, north of Terekhol Fort. When they hit the sea, they were greeted by a pristine beach that was idyllic with nobody on it.

They pulled over and marvelled at its unspoilt natural beauty with two fishing canoes on the sand. Asta flashed on what Hipster Harry must have felt in sixty-six, when he and the original freaks laid eyes on South Anjuna for the first time after crossing Baga river. Zsu took off her sunglasses, as though she couldn't believe what she was seeing through them. She'd seen this part of the Konkan Coast from a distance on many ferry trips from Bombay, but now up close, its simple sublime beauty with no buildings and people in sight took her breath away. "Oh, my God!.. It's paradise reborn!" She then stopped short of mouthing what next came into her head: *So, is this the new Goa?*

Doc radiated a satisfied smile, chuffed that his road trip of secret treasures was alleviating the agonies of a downtrodden Goa. "Let's press on to Redi Fort," he said with the enthusiasm of a wilderness tour guide. They headed north on a local road that narrowed to a dead end where there were ancient looking stone ruins embedded amongst trees and overgrown with vines. High walls with arching doorways led into a maze of cavernous spaces that once had been a 16th century Mughal fort and Maharaja's palace. In the centre was a palatial "ball room" where trees sprouted up through its stony floor and spidery thick vines had clamped themselves to its towering weedy walls.

"Absolutamente fantastico!" bellowed Luchiano. It's faded grandeur thrilling his Mediterranean imagination like the Mughal ruin was a relic of Roman times. The erosion of the brick and mortar, the crumbled abraded surfaces, the stained, decayed, derelict historical grittiness of its architecture stirred archaic emotions. Its neglected, overgrown isolation from the world, most fitting for such an outcast occasion. A freak feast of friends ostracised and banished from the place they once called, "home." It brought to mind, 'Time of The Gathering' by Time Modem, one of Luchiano's favourite tracks from two seasons back.

They drove back to the pristine beach that Zsu had fallen in love with. Doc led them down a side road which became a bike track down to a flat area with palms and low sea wall that dropped to golden sand. They dismounted and wandered in awe, envisioning the party circus transplanted there. The golden sand was warm from the sun's heat. They shed clothes and dived into the clean, blue-green Arabian sea and smoked a sunset chillum. They crossed back over the border at night fall. By the time they hit the Bardez beach strip, Goa was languishing under a curfew, shrouded in attrition.

A few days later, Luchiano and a posse of pals from Spaghetti Beach, including Lazzaro, headed back to Redi Fort with Doc to meet with locals and prepare the site for the Shivaratri party. Large woven flax mats were bought from a local village and laid down on the spacious "ballroom" floor inside the palace within the fort. Everyone pitched in with fluoro paint to highlight crow's feet-like branches that crawled over the interior walls. Lazzaro supervised the hanging of his paintings, a new one featured a pegasus horse, its outstretched wings symbolic of wild horses airborne, no longer fenced in by party prohibition in paradise.

Local boys pulled weeds and cleared areas inside and around the fort where party trekkers would camp and chai mummas set-up and locals provide food and drinks—but no alcohol, as it was strictly controlled in Maharashtra.

In negotiations for hire of the Omsonic PA, Vijay haggled hard for his brother to set up a bar, but Luchiano and Doc were not happy. "Everything must be kept top secret," declared Luchiano. "No cops!.. No bars!.. We don't want to upset the locals."

Luchiano had been in Goa since the mid-seventies, when it was rare to see a cop anywhere near Vagator or Anjuna, except maybe when a junkie had OD-ed. Which tragically happened to someone he knew, who'd shot up through the vein of his lingam.

"Smack was everywhere, back then," he recounted. "Everyone thought powder was cool. So many were nodding off. It was too easy to overdose on that shit, man. Now we're accused of being armed drug outlaws. But alcohol is the big problem. Shivaratri is about boom shankar, not booze. Now gambling thugs and bars are calling the shots. Before the parties were stopped, we couldn't even make them without doing deals with cops, by way of a bar mafiosi to get permission. Fuck that!.. That's like being back in school being told what to do by the headmaster. Now we have to be more underground than ever, we've been pushed out of Goa and the cops aren't even able to make black money from us, except from searching our houses and setting up surprise road blocks to catch us with a piece of charas. Now those dumb arse bars can't even make money from us, except when we're sitting around hitting the bottle needing to drown our sorrows."

A faint rumour that a tearaway party might be possible, started to circulate on Sunday. By Monday morning, rapid word of mouth was saying, "Party in Maharashtra tonight, North of Terekhol Fort." The news of a renegade party couldn't come soon enough as mounting frustration and tension had everyone feeling like they were about to explode. Many took to colonics for relief. But what was most sorely needed was a loud psychic flush on an unbounded pumping dance floor.

Motorbikes were tanked up with gas, overnight backpacks filled up with necessities and hammocks packed. Charas and substances were stashed down underwear and hidden in sneaky, secretive places. Ambassador taxis were booked for overnight return trips to an undisclosed destination north of the border. By late afternoon, motorbikes of all descriptions were descending on the Siolim ferry, their riders convoying on local roads north, hell-bent on dancing into the dawn like their lives depended on it. Hipster Harry was one of the last to leave Anjuna. Gregories Restaurant, where he'd dined, was empty. He couldn't remember a night, early March, ever so empty in Goa. Zikos picked him up on his Enfield and they raced to the ferry. Only some mothers with babies remained in Goa.

Across the border in Maharashtra, locals directed Goa escapees to Redi Fort. Local Goa chai mummas also did the trip north to set up their mats around the walls of the Maharaja's palace, inside which the Omsonic PA was installed. A notorious pushy Goa bar owner also showed up. Luchiano got hot under the collar, telling him he was not welcome. When the bar owner persisted in setting up, party whip, Doc Silver, who knew the barman, stepped in with slap stick humour to diffuse the situation. But then another Goa bar arrived. Luchiano overheated and spat the dummy, waving his hands irately about in the air. Dramatic discussions ensued, with him acquiescing, agreeing to allow the Goa bar to set up, but outside the fort, not by the entrance to the dance floor in the palace.

Wave upon wave of bikes arrived, parking up, handlebars and headlights all knitted into each other around the entirety of the ruin of the Mughal fort. Inside was a maze of broken walls, grottos and turrets where Goa escapee camps were setup and hammocks strung. Everyone was elated to be in a new magical setting, to dance in a palace highlighted with fluoro colours and art works and blasting with banned computer beats.

Voltaire was seated at a table sifting through DAT tapes, like a chef conjuring never-tasted-before recipes. Each sleeve of his micro sized tapes with hand written lists of new ingredients—i.e., all the music that had poured into Goa in the past four months which no one had danced to, except maybe a few pieces heard at the Christmas and New Year party.

The derelict grandeur of the Maharaja's palace ball room became a banquet smorgasbord of technodelica that ignited highly-charged dancing freaks. The dance floor was jumped upon with abandon. Loud-music-deprived-bodies thrashed about in torrents of fresh sounds coming out of the Omsonic speaker stacks, like it was a gourmet genre meal. Lazzaro's emancipatory flying horse, hanging on a central wall, reminding them what it was all about.

Shivaratri in the palace ball room became an occasion of elation, as opposed to the besieged, oppressiveness of Goa. Some dance-to-trance devotees had their heads shaved by an elven looking creature wielding a battery powered electric razor on the dance floor, next to a Shiva tree of life that had grown up through a crack in the stone floor. Others sprinkled themselves in Holi powder colours like they were members of a Naga sect at a Kumbh Mela festival. One dancer, dressed like Tarzan with a leather loin cloth, climbed a thick vine that hung down from a wall and perched on it like a temple monkey.

A hullabaloo broke out between Luchiano and the pushy Goa barman when he positioned his bar at the entrance to the palace ball room, closer than the local chai laddies. Luchiano was off his chops and got rattled and commenced to wrangle with the barman when friends came to the rescue. The friends set about helping themselves to water and beverages without paying until the barman retreated back into the fort. But by morning, with Voltaire playing, 'We Came in Peace' by Dance 2 Trance, the pesky barman was back.

The dance-or-die adventure to the Maharaja's palace, fitted-out with the Omsonic system and garnished with dayglow art, delivered a much-needed sonic tonic for dancing feet to rejoice once again. The music stopped in the afternoon with everyone satisfied, floating on air, and in no hurry to return to Goa. Many lingered in Maharashtra to explore the unspoilt natural beauty of its coast. Zsu, Jules and friends returned to the pristine fishermen's beach they had been shown by Doc Silver.

Unanimously, they decided it should be the location for the full moon party on the eighteenth of March. They envisioned the dance floor in a palm grove and positioning of speaker stacks and the DJ place and artwork. There was concern about the large turnout that was expected. Local fishermen, hauling in a net, told them it would be a full king tide at midnight retreating to low tide by dawn.

The success of the Maharashtra pirate party in Redi Fort brought relief for the scene, but stirred chagrin in Goa bars who were feeling the pinch from no parties. In the past, as long as there were parties made by freaks, rupees flowed in an unregulated, haphazard, blackmarket economy from which locals thrived. It was crushing that the scene—with its ecstatic dancing deity, Nataraja Shiva—was prohibited from getting down, the way it liked, brain-chip-wired to computer music. For diehard 'Goa head' travellers, it was disastrous. For rave tourists, the crackdown curfew was intolerable. They up and split to Koh Phangan, Thailand.

Last year, when the gangster put the revolver on the charas in the flea market, in the eyes of Panjim politicians, the flea market and dance parties were seen as a front for an armed drug cartel. Previously, bars weren't selling much alcohol, but sold large quantities of bottled mineral water and lemon soda. Turnover for drinks at parties increased considerably with swelling new arrivals in the early nineties. When some bars heard later of the Redi Fort party, and that rival local bars had attended, bitter jealousies became inflamed.

In Mapusa, Chief Inspector Fernandes secretly bemoaned his overlords at Panjim Police HQ, but he was still on top with the amount of protection baksheesh he was able to extract from freaks willing to pay into his paranoia-free hedge fund protection scheme. Their houses, supposedly immune to being searched by officers under his command. Although, opportunist cops from other parts of Goa might appear, marauding baksheesh backhanders, especially from rookie, rave tourists and green, unassuming party makers who didn't know which slippery rope to pull on.

All up, Zsu and Doc would splash a thousand bucks to set-up the March full moon in Maharashtra. A discounted price for the hire of the PA was agreed if Vijay's brother could run his bar together with a bar by locals—but no alcohol. The owners of the coconut palms climbed them to hang party decor banners and constructed a DJ hut. In the afternoon, Vijay delivered the Omsonic PA on a truck from Panjim to the Maharastra coast where labourers carried speaker boxes down a cliff and assembled them into two high stacks. Those who arrived early for sunset were stunned by the beauty of the beach. A local store by the turnoff was cleaned out of bottles of petrol, fruit, water, tobacco and mats.

With lunar rising large over Chapora River, once again the Siliom car ferry ran through the night packed with convoying motorbikes, the scene desperate, mobilising on a road trip of swashbuckling high adventure to dance on a virginal beach across the border. Accompanied by hand maidens, blotter baba Shazam arrived in a pink Ambassador, run by *Karma Cabs*, its dash decorated with stickers of Indian sages. His entourage made their way down the narrow path to set up a ceremonial soma dhuni, away from the dance floor and chai mumma area.

There was immense feeling of collective release and deliverance when the towering Omsonic PA powered up at nine o'clock with the melodic techno of 'Frogs in Space' by Komakino. Jaeger and Jules were DJ-ing with Sony TCD-D3 DAT players. They'd brought back up players, as the micro technology (a condensed sandwich video player mechanism) was prone to glitching from dust.

Yogi Ananta led the charge, breaking in the new dance floor with a fluid synthesis of his signature four-way-hip asana-swivel moves, including somersaults. Others joined him, cutting loose in an outpouring of ecstatic dancing—the release of pent-up tension from party prohibition in Goa. The palm grove soon packed out with dancers going mental. The DJs fuelled the flaring contagion with an arsenal of fresh explosive tracks as the peaking full moon exerted a magnetic pull upon a rising king tide, that would soon flood the beach like oceanic gravy at midnight.

At around eleven o'clock, Doc Silver's second worst nightmare occurred (the first being a visit from the cops). An uninvited Goa bar started setting up at the party close to the dance floor, which sparked a quarrel with Vijay's brother running a bar. Doc had weathered more bar squabbles than he cared to remember and now the border-hopping arrival of a cretin Goa bar was threatening to push a red button in his head.

After a long day, the tooter-upper that he'd just sniffed to bolster his stretched faculties, telescoped the moment just enough for him to step back and laugh at the ridiculousness of the slapstick sitcom of it all. But then a spike in blood pressure flicked the now flashing red button, setting off a tempestuous hair-trigger barrage of prickly neural sensations, like hot squash balls ricocheting off cranial walls from all directions at once, leaving him no other option except, default circuit breaker, scatter-gun Doc Sargent Major mode.

"Hey listen up!" he lambasted in a terse voice to the errant barmen. "Your out of state. No one invited you here. It's invite only. Chalo Pakistan!... You really want to be here? Give me a couple of hundred bucks. Now!"

Zsu arrived adopting a conciliatory approach, explaining the deal with the local bar and Vijay's brother. "Please be considerate," she pleaded and directed the bar to the chai mumma area. Doc bristled and rocked, shifting his weight from one boot to the other and crossed his arms and dug in the heel of his cowboy boot on the edge of the dance floor. Then, a must-dance-to track ('Psychopath' by Confidential) sprung out of the PA. "Do what she says," he ordered, kicking off his boots, "I'll be back." He then leaped onto the dance floor and broke-out apeshit moves.

Followers of the O.O.O. gathered down the end of the beach in amongst large rocks around which swirled the rising king tide that was exerting a pull on menstrual cycles, seed sacks and central nervous systems. They shook like Quakers, the eccentric electricity of the acid music triggering convulsions like the catharsis of a Rajineesh dynamic meditation. Bare foot, they twisted toes into warm sand as frothy spume lapped up to their loins. The dancing became like a voodoo stomp in which they sought to heal a dissonant hex of spirit through star seed sounds in the music.

Approaching midnight, the edge of the dance floor was preyed upon by another opportunist bar from Goa. Three Indians set up a table with drinks. Doc and Zikos spotted them. Not wishing to put himself through another round of wrangling Doc asked the tall, barrel-chested Greek, "Do me a favour. Give 'em the short shift, will ya?"

After Zikos alerted them to the error of their ways, one of the Indians became argumentative. Zikos moved closer and eye-balled him, then picked up the table and attempted to move it away and was immediately set upon by all three Indians. Doc raced to help him and managed to push one Indian to the ground. Onlookers yelled, "HEY!—HEY!—HEY!—STOP!—STOP!—STOP!" Some jumping in to dissipate the brawl. Zikos got a punch in before another Indian pulled a knife. Everyone stood back. In a terrifying moment, Doc flashed on the Indian's face and was hit by the realisation that it was the same lowlife who'd threatened him with a long blade at his house a few season's back.

All of a sudden, from out of nowhere, Ananta, bare chested, jumped between Doc and the knife wielding Indian. With swift movements, Ananta agilely circled the Indian and taunted him by rapidly sucking in and out his stab-wound-scarred abdomen, inviting the Indian to stab him a second time. On seeing the scar, which he'd been the perpetrator of, and the fearlessness in Ananta's eyes and surrounded by peeved party heads, the Indian turned and scurried off. His friends collected their table and cartons of bottles and retreated up the cliff.

Well after midnight, with the tide high up to the sea wall, motorbikes and Ambassador taxis continued arriving with Goa escapee, party people. They immediately descended to the palm tree grove packed with dance-music-starved-bodies surrounded by speaker stacks piled high like black pyramids. By two o'clock, with the king tide retreating, full power dancers, desperate for space, took to dancing calf-deep in the Arabian Sea.

Just before the faint aurora of dawn outlined the cliff above, 'Wir Schicken Dich Ins All' by LDC, purred out of the PA. The music had an eerie, floating, astral, translucent melody with a whispering voice, like that of a sprite of the night taking flight before the first rays of light. This was followed by the celestial crowning glory of 'My God the Sky is Full of Stars' (Rising Star Mix) by General Base, which sonically surged the collective pineal gland swarming the beach, injecting it with stellar lust ascension. The kind of unified communal rapture everyone had been dearly missing and hankering for, with everyone riding a cosmic frequency, as one body of emotion.

On this groovilicious morning of restored glory, a graced paradise had returned. It required winged feet on wheels. The emergency dash of renegade, techno tribalists border-hopping the margins of law and order in pursuit of a promethean quest to engage in ritual rites of technodelic trance dancing under the heavens. Then, 'Organic' by The Overlords pelted out of speaker stacks, its groove propulsion igniting jugglers and ballet-like dancers to cavort like gymnasts trailing aerobatic moves upon the wet sand on which crop circle pictograms had mysteriously been etched.

Down by the ocean a divine light entered Ananta's body. The life throb of ages danced in his blood sending him aerial. One word—"*Organic*"— was vocalised in the music, which otherwise was non-verbal, prenatal, like early memories of the amniotic altered state of his mother's flotation tank womb, from which he'd been delivered by a blade to her tummy—

caesarean airlifted into the world. He looked down at the scar on his tummy, it seemed to hark back in time before he'd ever stepped foot on an Indian beach. An attachment wound inflicted by forces beyond his control. A shadow wound, the plight of love jumping into conflict. An emergency. A rescue. What was his mother feeling? She'd been awash on opiates. What had the assailant been feeling? He was drunk and enraged. What was at stake on Spaghetti Beach with incursions into its cul-de-sac *paradise?*

Ananta healed. The wound to his gut taught him special powers? His gut deepened an instinct: a calling to the role of teacher. At birth, he'd been put in an incubator. His first breathes in a high-tech container, in which he experienced a split-off solid state separateness, while his body yearned for fusion.

Jaeger fed a tape he'd titled, ANGELIC POSSESSION, into a DAT player and fast forwarded it to the fifth track and cued it on the first beat and pressed the pause button. Two local fishermen leaning on their outrigger canoes, nonchalantly beheld the emancipatory outpouring of dancers frolicking, rollicking, rejoicing—one cartwheeling the full sweep of their beach. Young children, who'd arrived with their mothers in the morning, joined in with the play. Just when the fiery disk of the newborn sun appeared at the edge of the cliff, Jaeger released the pause button. 'Music For The Life' by Electroheart, let rip out of the Omsonic speaker stacks, sending bouncing bodies ballistic. Later, the fishermen would offer rides out past the waves in their canoes.

In light of the success of the Maharashtra pirate parties circumventing Goan authorities, one last renegade party was plotted the last week of March. Once again, Redi Fort was setup, but this time the Maharaja's Palace was installed with Baphomet goats and art with esoteric motifs by members of the O.O.O. But at ten o'clock in the evening the troubling appearance of a police jeep sent shudders through those that saw it arrive. Atma met Maharashtra Police and hastened to negotiate. Five hundred dollars was the sticking point for the party to proceed.

Atma implored the cops to take three hundred bucks, which he immediately produced from a Kulu bag hanging off his shoulder. The Chief Constable in charge smiled, then shook his head. Atma returned to a fretting O.O.O. gaggle to explain the grubstake. Heated discussion broke out. Some were willing to cough up another couple of US big notes to party, but others were against it, particularly Vijay, who wore a dismal face, as he'd ran the gauntlet with police before and didn't want to risk the sound system out of state.

Many freaks, oblivious to the cops showing up, had gathered on the dance floor inside the fort on large reed mats in front of the Omsonic PA with keen anticipation of it, once again, filling the palace ball room with loud contraband computer beats. But the anxiety inducing words, "Cops are here!" was inflicting a bitter blow of fear and loathing, followed by the disquieting appearance of eight Maharashtra policemen wearing blue berets. The scene just froze, everyone sat down where they stood. The party was over before it had even started. All hopes of dancing one more time were dashed with the last of the Redi Fort plots foiled.

Later, it was learnt that an aggrieved dumb arse Goa bar had steeped so low with rupee jealousy to snitch to Goa cops, who then alerted Maharashtra cops of the current black market rate for sly party permission. Something which Mapusa and Anjuna cops secretly wished they could continue to be beneficiaries of, but "Satanic" and "Gangster Drug Parties" were unequivocally banned. The Goa Minister of Tourism, Julio Silva, maintaining that "The hippie lowlife party scene was a menace. Upmarket Club Med resort tourists was what Goa needed."

Besides this season's New Year party, the O. O. O. had somehow obtained permission for Odvar Osser's annual birthday party, the second week of January in monkey valley. Confidentially, the go ahead had only been possible by Asta accompanying Atma to Chief Inspector Fernandez's office in Mapusa. After Atma left, with her alone with the Chief Inspector and the door locked, she glowingly set upon Fernandez casting a seductive spell, culminating in a deal breaker whereby she popped the head cop's Odin seed.

Waveforms of reality began to warp in the haze of the heavy April heat. The naked body of a male foreigner was discovered on rocks below Chapora Fort by fishermen, reported the *Goa Voice,* the first week of April. What police investigating the apparent suicide were not aware of, was that there had been an attempted murder the same night. It happened prior to the fatal leap. A piercing scream was heard from Osser's house at three in the morning. The local family, whom he rented from, lived nearby and found him writhing on the floor in a pool of blood. He was rushed to the Badem doctor, bandaged, and sent to Mapusa Hospital.

The police only became aware of the attempted murder after the Norwegian consulate got involved flying Osser to Oslo for emergency specialist surgery. He said he couldn't identify who'd stabbed him in the back. The body found on the rocks beneath Chapora Fort with a fractured skull had been identified as Ragnar Groop from Finland—a member of the O.O.O. His clothes had been discarded on a rampart of Chapora Fort.

Drug Tech Transcendentalism

FOR NO APPARENT REASON, other than black market forces and unfathomable quirks of Goan politics, permission was being given for parties in January nineteen-ninety-three. Electronic dance music was trending. It had become hugely fashionable and was reviving the music industry globally. But with no face, and no vocal, was tricky to market—especially the left field kind that Goa thrived on. The kind of special purpose maverick music that had been propagated in the undergrowth of alt-Asia by a traveller fraternity—curated by anti-commercial, anti-establishment DJs and party makers who didn't wish to be walled-in and regulated.

With the arrival of the first modem at Starco Corner last year, there was nothing underground about Goa any more. The bush telegraph was now plugged into the World Wide Web and the latest speed-of-light-mojo-wire information on computer screens was that parties were once again thumping in Disco Valley, which drove waves of rave tourists and budding career DJs to book flights to Goa. The largest horde lured by the mythos of religious-like rapture to transcendental, trance techno in a promised land were Israelis. They arrived like pilgrims on a crusade—including many with post-traumatic stress disorder. A kibbutz was even set up on middle Vagator Beach and became known as *Tel Aviv Beach*.

Previously, Israelis had not been permitted a visa for India, in sympathy of Arabs. Straight out of military service, they landed on the beatific head land of Vagator Beach like a battle-fatigued deserting army hankering for R 'n' R to let off steam in pounding kick drum decompression. Camped out in fluoro-patterned palms, amidst bright powder paint-smudged cows, it was like the promised land: A 24/7—"Boom shankar!"—dance or die, party-playtime paradise. A redemptive, recreational, escape on tap from the pressure drop of the festering, geopolitical, religious abscess that they were born into and conscripted to do service for.

Transcendent trance dancing was the ultimate therapy for the stress of the Israel Defence Force. Regular Goa dance floor freaks under the palms had to step aside, least they got sideswiped by crazed Jews jumping on kick-arse triumphant, thumping, trance techno, like packs of dogs let off a chain of tank duty. Many not returning. ("Last seen gonzo AWOL on a dusty dance floor in India.")

Camo wear was shed for fluoro, stretch, party wear. At the flea market, Zsu and Asta and freak-fashionista friends made a killing, kitting them out in trippy threads to get loose in. Relieved to be out of combat boots, they all took to wearing Japanese jika-tabi footwear with a split toe. These gave them the appearance of having insect feet with special powers to grip and dance horizontal up bending palm trees. Many sported razored heads, as if having converted to a sonic sect. Jewish cash was abundant. AWOL was written all over faces gagging for emotional release. "We want party!.. We want it now!.. Go for broke!.." AWOL didn't mean, Away With Out Leave, it had fast become, A Way Of Life.

The Omsonic PA blasted every second night. More party makers and DJs and alt-Asia travellers arrived. Goa raged louder and harder than ever before. Ecstatic dancing to a drug-tech-futurism of revolutionary music became a life-altering metanoia. The rapture of a Goa party was like that of a spiritual conversion. The bliss felt on the dance floor was such a contagion that it was destined to spread around the world. From out of this collective euphoria, a fountainhead of inspiration appeared—like a *scenius*. (A communal genius of a cultural scene spored from individual and collaborative creativity.)

Travellers, tokers, spice exporters, party makers, collectors and DJs started making Goa music, as though having been taken possession by a rhythmystec apotheosis, like star seeds within a dawning OS. An astral projection Operating System capable of algorithmic bitmapping of binary beats and bleeps and frequencies into zeros and ones cybernetically translating the vapours, vibes, highs, hallucinations and angelic particles of the Goa experience into a rave signal. Its distinct sound signatures destined to resonate and replicate, like rhizome fractal wavelengths into the future.

The prediction that Celeste Star had told Jules in Byron Bay, and the prophecy of the *Omen* alluding to the fate of Goa, which Donna had revealed to Zsu, was coming to pass. A *scenius* was getting its head around the new maths of conjuring midi devices with the head land of Goa having now become a proselytising drug-tech belief system. Initiated, inspired DJs—cum music producers—dedicated themselves to a mythical, transcendent disco in the sky deified by Lord Shiva.

Returning to where they came from—California, Europe, Japan, Australia, Israel—Goa heads, with the assistance of tech-savvy buddies, set up DIY home studios and camped out around Atari computers that functioned like creatrix cyber wombs into which were plugged synths, samplers, drum machines and effects boxes, all patched into mixers decorated with OM stickers from Mapusa Market. Midi equipment was expensive. Boom shankar export and trustafarian resources funded sound gear and the launching of record labels. Drawing from epiphanies had flying in the red dust of Goa's dance floors, and summoning assistance from machine elves and Hindu animal god muses, hidden hands were evoked in the channelling, writing, and producing of psychedelic techno music which magically took shape on monochromatic Atari screens.

Disappointing for Jules, The Telepathics no longer got together to make music. Zane had gotten in with a nose funk posse, and become too fast to live. He'd become a border runner, which was not strictly smoke. This deeply troubled Jules. In Amsterdam, the previous summer, Zikos had given Zane connections, with him quickly graduating in its blackmarket finishing school, and gotten in with the big boys. Pissed off, Jules took Zane aside and eye-balled him and said, "Hey man!—it's breaking my heart seeing wasted talent. Ya can't be an artist and a drug dealer at the same time."

This season, things came to a head when Zane had been caught out with an Israeli friend. They'd been nabbed and couldn't pay off the heat, and taken to Anjuna cop shop. Typical negotiations to obtain their release had broken down in a comedy of errors, so an Israeli tank platoon of party mates took matters into their own hands. They overwhelmed two local cops in a surprise raid to liberate their friend and Zane from a cell, after which, he and his new business chum fled Goa.

Late in February, Danilo met with Zsu at Nirvana chai shack at Spaghetti Beach to discuss concerns about a party he and friends were planning for Jungle Palace. "There's a problem," he complained. "I just heard a celebrity DJ from Europe—known as the Techno Pope— is in Goa and wants to make a party the same night as ours. This hotshot DJ is sweetening the Chapora boys to make arrangements. He's brought flight cases of vinyl and two Technics turntables. It must be a big-splash promotion party? I don't think he understands how things work here."

"Actually, he's a nice guy," she assured Danilo. "I met him at the flea market, he shopped at my stall and commissioned me to paint a backdrop for his club. He fully respects our scene, in fact, he made some tracks in the eighties that were popular here. Don't worry, I know where he's staying, I'll talk to him."

Visiting the house of the Techno Pope, in Gumal Vaddo, where he stayed with his producer, Zsu was told that they had secured permission for a party, and could the Italians kindly do their party later? But then, no sooner had he spoken, one of the Chapora boys appeared at his door telling him, "Party now not possible."

"What the fuck!" the Techno Pope said, furious. "What's happened? I thought everything was fixed?"

"No guarantee," the Chapora boy said with a blank face.

Hearing this, Zsu's heart sank. "Oh, for God's sake, not again." Up until moments ago, the season had been bouncing bonhomie. Despairingly, she recounted to the Techno Pope the trials and tribulations of running the gauntlet with local authorities, which he had no idea of.

That night, enraged support was rallied for an illegal renegade party in Morjim for the Techno Pope to spin vinyl, which would be a first in Goa. At one o'clock in the morning with the dance floor in full swing, just as the celebrity DJ took to the decks putting the needle on his first record, a police jeep pulled up on the road. Some revellers went to meet it. The Techno Pope cued the record, adjusting the pitch control slider. Stomping on the dance floor was fierce. Frantic, desperate appeals to the police were going nowhere.

"THE MUSIC MUST STOP!"

On the dance floor, someone shouted "POLICE!.."

The Techno Pope reluctantly slid the slider down to minus eight and pressed the stop button, bringing the record to a startling halt. A loud cracking, warning gun shot rang out. The dance floor panicked helter skelter. Dancers bolted in the dark, many stumbling into irrigation trenches injuring themselves. A girl fell down a well and broke her leg. The twelve-inch vinyl that had just started to spin was 'Accident in Paradise.'

A party ban, once again, was being enforced, apparently as a result of Mossad, the Israeli Military Intelligence having met with the Goa Police Commissioner expressing concern that R 'n' R (rest and recreation) for its AWOL service men and women had gotten out of hand, depleting its army reserve. Outrageously, it was learned that Mossad were paying Goa police more foreign cash to stop the parties than its army were paying to make them.

With the sun in boundary, dissolving, Pisces (the most space case, spiritually receptive, prone to habitual indulgence, and most prodigiously represented of all signs in Goa) in the third week of March, the stars colluded in dissolving the hard edges of restrictive reality with authorities yielding. To everyone's relief, permission was granted for a party. The much-needed respite eased irritabilities that had become unbearable in the stifling end-of-season heat. The Italians immediately set about pimping the spaghetti maze of tropical flora of Jungle Palace with dripping fluoro colour. Turning it into a snaky, voodoo, plantopia of bewildering forms to enchant UV lunar-tech creatures of the night.

The night before, Zsu and Jules embarked upon a twin flame extrasensory ritual with *Demetri* (code name for DMT crystals). With the alembic bulb of a glass pipe held over a candle flame, spirit molecules of *Demetri* swirled into a vapourous presence that filled the air with an otherworldly smell. Heroic lungfuls hurtled them down a rabbit hole that tore a hole in the fabric of reality, which felt like a near death experience. Laying down together, they found themselves in a spherical, vibrantly patterned reception lounge with shifting lattices of form inhabited by shape-shifting elf-like entities that implied that they were bodiless souls vying for reincarnation.

Ten minutes later, Zsu and Jules emerged from the rabbit hole of *Demetri*. Back in their bodies, they shed sarongs with her sitting on his lap and wrapping her legs around him. Kissing and caressing and maintaining eye contact with their breath synchronised, an ecstatic current ran through them as they became one heartbeat. Interior openings occurred in their embrace with him inside her beckoning spirit molecules to constellate the future. The mutual reception and attraction, so great that an entity did, indeed, jump in and set about crocheting a membrane web of darting gametes determined to DNA-mosh-pit an egg in the quest of conceiving itself into a future cell dividing zygote.

Inside the fluoro, flora drippings of the mutant, psychotropic plantopia of Jungle Palace, the music Voltaire was playing induced a lollapalooza afflatus with magic mirror doors opening. (Best understood by imagining all this while dancing to 'Smoke My Dang-A-Long' by E-Rection, in which the Lizard King announces, "Out here we are stoned immaculate."

Into this, at two in the morning, Zsu and Jules swanned. It felt like the chaotic abandon of group Eros, or the fuzzy logic of a communal mother board where oscillating XY dancing cells got it on in a milky way. Jungle Palace had become an orgasmatron of converging hermaphrodite bodies emitting phosphorescent light trails with androgynous, bubbling flesh, egg sacks, ball sacks, orifices, phalluses, nipples—all orbiting a central jellyfish-like ovum. The BPM was clocking 140, the fastest ever heard. A Gaian, genetic mitosis of X and Y chromosomes was rotating faster and faster, binary spinning a platter spindle of DRAM (dramatic random access memory) in hard trance. Ecstatic groans and high pitched screams could be heard as the dance floor spiralled up like a collective double helix of nucleic acid. Then, out of all this, a space frog zygote leaped so high it found itself in the galactic centre.

"I can't go through with it," came the distressed voice of Zsu down a phone line from Bali to Jules in Amsterdam, in early May.

"Please Zsu!" he anxiously pleaded, pushing the earpiece of the phone hard up to his head. This child is a star seed from the Pleiades."

"I thought I could do it, but now I'm feeling repulsed by the thought of it. I've never felt so off balance in my life. I'm feeling physically ill. I'm sick with dread. I'm losing it, Jules. I don't want to be a mother."

She was in the grip of crippling, cold, dejecting feelings. She felt alienated from her body: the conviction that love hurts.

"Zsu!—this child is a gift from the universe. You're a matrix—"

"Jules, you have no fucking idea. My body is freaking out. I can't go through with it. It's like an alien has taken over my body. I'm ending it."

"Your what?"

"I'm terminating—"

"Oh, no!.. please, please, Zsu—don't. I'm coming to be with you. I'm catching a plane to Bali. I really want us to have this baby."

"I'm not going through with it. I'm going to Bangkok. I'm aborting."

Jules sighed heavily across the time zones. "No!.. no!.. no!.. Zsu, you can't do that, please, please—for God's sake!"

"I'm gonna hang up now, Jules, I love you, I'm so sorry, I just can't do this, please understand..."

The line went dead. Mortified, Jules fell through the floor. His heart pounded his chest. What to do? He tried calling Zsu again on the number she'd called from. An Indonesian travel agent answered saying she'd left the shop.

"Do you know a Danish girl with a young daughter?" Jules anxiously asked. "Her name is Asta, she's a friend of Zsu, who just called me."

"Yes, I know her," the agent said.

"It's urgent. Can you tell either Asta, or Zsu, to call me back." Jules left a Dutch phone number. To his relief, a few hours later, the phone rang at the apartment he was staying. It was Asta saying she was doing her utmost to convince Zsu that being pregnant was a marvellous thing. Zsu had not bought a ticket to Bangkok yet, but her visa was due to run out.

It was after one more white-label vinyl hunt at Music Man shop, in Ghent, Belgium, and recording his last find of freshly minted booty of tracks onto a DAT tape, and about to set off to Schiphol Airport to fly to Denpasar that Jules heard that Zikos had "disappeared." No one had seen the Greek in over two weeks. Some at the chillum circle in Vondelpark were concerned that he'd been busted out of Holland, or a more sinister scenario (the perils of dicey dealings with the maw of Amsterdam's black market underbelly), which no one wished to believe could've happened.

When Jules rocked-up by taxi to Zsu's house at Canggu Beach, Bali, it was locked up with no one home. He got back in the taxi and tried to remember how to find Asta's house, recalling that it was at the end of a narrow road through rice paddies. The taxi driver said he knew the villa and delivered him to a Ganesh guarded gate of a walled property with a multi-pavilion villa.

Pushing the gate open, Jules was met by a barking dog. It cowered away when he stepped inside to a verdant garden of frangipani, off of which hung staghorn ferns. A path led to a swimming pool surrounded by colourful tropical plants and large stone sculptures of the child-eating demon Queen, Rangda—Kali of Bali. The black, mother, warrior goddesses took on a horrifying form with pendulous breasts, claws, fangs, and gargoyle-like goggle eyes and protruding tongues.

"Asta!..Asta!.. he called out.

Her daughter, Tina, came running out of one of the pavilions followed by her Balinese pembantu nanny. Tina was happy to see Jules and said that her mum had gone shopping. Jules dropped his backpack in the lounge, peeled off sweaty clothes and dived into the pool. Resurfacing, he breathed deep sighs of relief at having arrived. Not long after, Asta came through the Ganesh gate, her face distraught, but snapped on a mask of animated joy upon seeing him and they hugged. But distressed worry poured out of her, and she began to sob.

"Jules… something horrible has happened."

"Oh shit!..did she kill the baby?"

"No!.. No!..Zsu is at Denpasar police station with Shane and a couple of others."

"What the fuck happened?"

"Two nights ago," Asta said distraughtly, "Shane had a party, it got raided by undercovers. Everyone threw their illicits, but the Aussie DJ and Shane were caught with MDMA, and Zsu with a few grams of hash, and were taken away. Zsu is coping, but it's a pretty screwed-up situation."

"This is terrible," Jules said, his face furrowed, his mind racing.

"Seems they were after Massimo, a reckless dealer," Asta said. "He bolted, jumped the fence, managed to get out of Bali the next day."

Wrung out from the long flight, and now wired with worry—Jules collapsed into a beanbag.

"When can I see her?"

"This afternoon I'm taking them food."

At the watchtower of Denpasar Police station Zsu and Jules kissed through cell bars.

"God!—I'm glad to see you," she said with a haggard face. "This is all so crazy—"

"It's insane," he said, strung out, his frazzled emotions and distressed mind over-riding time-warped jet lag. "We've gotta get you out of here," he held her hand, she broke down in tears.

Asta had hired a lawyer and provided a doctor's certificate of Zsu's pregnancy. Discussing her case with the prosecutor, the lawyer was able to negotiate a backhander to secure her release without charge or deportation. The others would spend three months in Kerobokan Prison and make big time payments to judiciary to have their charges changed to possession of cocaine, a more addictive drug which would allow for article 88 of Indonesian law to apply: The failure to report a drug addiction to authorities. Which had a maximum sentence of six months, not ten years if charged as a user with possession of 0.3 grams of MDMA. Shane, who ran a surf apparel franchise, and the DJ, would also have to weather the political storm that media whipped up about the bust, fanning an ongoing beef about Aussies falling fowl of Indonesia's strict drug laws that included the death penalty.

Returning to her Bali home, wrung out from the ordeal, Zsu suffered severe cramps and abdominal pain, and started bleeding heavily worsted than any period. After a medical examination, it was confirmed that the spirit of the star seed from the Pleiades had exited her body. Sadly, with mixed blessings, she'd suffered a miscarriage.

Shortly after, Jules and Zsu visited a temple spa in Ubud for a healing ritual and consulted a witch doctor. By a trickling stream in the jungle they had massages, ate raw food and did yoga. On the last day, Zsu sat in a vegan restaurant sipping coconut juice looking out on terraced rice paddies sprouting green seedlings. She had a vision of herself as a container for life, too, but in which there'd been conflicting feelings. Yet, her own extraordinary life had been hard earned out of formative struggles, like in the rejecting womb of her own mother, which zygote Zsu experienced as hostile. Within the container of the cell of Denpasar Police Station, she confronted and exorcised a demon in the form of dangerous vulnerable feelings, which the gift of the ordeal of the unsuspecting, shocking experience starkly confronted her with. Feelings bound up in the struggle of everything that had ever strived to give form to itself. Like what she felt on the full moon at the banyan tree. And what she'd felt with the star seed spirit molecules in her womb. After her release from the cramped police cell, she felt freer than she'd ever felt, something deep inside her had been shed.

By the time, Jules and her left Bali for Japan, she would be pregnant again. Arriving in Tokyo for a party in the mountains, they learned that Zane had been popped at Narita airport. Jules visited him in custody, he looked gaunt in the throes of cold turkey. Harrowingly, Jules realised that if this had not happened, his edgy, at risk, talented mate was on course for checking out.

charas.com

TRAVELLING ON INDIAN ROADS WAS HAZARDOUS. An obstacle course dodging cows, bullock carts, random pedestrians and higgledy-piggledy opposing, overtaking traffic. Tata interstate tourist buses were not much more premium in comfort than local buses between Chapora and Mapusa. In nineteen-ninety-four a new overnight Tata bus service had commenced between Goa and Pune, and offered improved comfort and privacy by way of bunks with curtains.

In the second week of February, Jules found himself lying on one, looking out the window, watching Maharashtra countryside whiz by as he headed to Pune to play at a two-day party on a farm run by the Osho ashram. He'd already done the trip once before, having DJ-ed at a party by the river that ran next to the ashram. On this occasion, extra lie-down buses were chartered to accommodate the exodus of virtually the whole Goa scene which, once again, was languishing under a music curfew.

At the German Bakery in Pune, Jules breakfasted with Felix, who would also be playing. Over muesli, the Berliner dropped bad news. "Zane got five years."

Jules's jaw locked up, he stopped eating. "Oh fuck!"

"He might get out in three," Felix said in a consoling voice, like he knew the score of the predicament.

"It's bloody tragic!" Jules sighed. "Well, at least he's still alive."

Zsu was happy to stay at home in Goa, as she had a new love. Like the gift of a pearl from the depths of her miraculous self—for which the Balinese witch doctor's malediction had given her courage—she'd given birth to a promised star seed baby in January, the same day as Odvar Osser's birthday. The O.O.O. prophet was back in Goa—but in a wheel chair. The violent assault had left Odvar a paraplegic living off a disability pension. He returned to his house in monkey valley and employed locals for household help. Zsu paid him a visit with her new born son, Starco. On meeting baby Starco, Odvar immediately identified him as a spirit from the Pleiades and became enamoured by the star seed child. "He's a matariki," he declared. "An Odin spirit." The maimed prophet could not take his eyes off Starco. Zsu's baby emanated a mystical tranquillity, like the sentient transference of a spirit dolphin with oracular eyes radiating a purity that was from the beginning of time.

Oh, to live in the now, Zsu thought. *Without memory. Without future-anxiety.* "This is how we all started," she said. "It's like Goa has been all about getting back to—*baby*. Tell me Osser, where does evil come from? Does it exist outside of humankind?"

The paralysed prophet stiffened from the waist-up in his wheelchair. "The extraterrestials I've encountered have been friendly," he said drolly.

"Well," she said gravely, "someone tried to kill you."

Osser averted his eyes, his lips firmly closed and gazed at Starco.

"Someone tried to kill me, too," she said. "You were attacked from behind. How gutless, how treacherous is that? Osser shifted in his wheelchair and grimaced. *Who betrayed who?* Zsu wondered.

Opinion in the scene was split as to whether Ragnar Groop—whose body had been found on the rocks below Chapora Fort—had been the psychopath within the O.O.O. who'd violently attacked Osser. If the cult leader knew, and many believed he did, he wasn't saying. Goa Police had not closed the case. It made you wonder, what kind of sway he had over his followers. What kind of cock brotherhood was it? Hearsay about Osser's family tree had it that his grandfather was a sorcerer of Norwegian Wicca arts. Norway being one of the last countries in Scandinavia to convert to Catholicism. The auto fellatio asana and mystical O.O.O. phonemes had been passed on to Osser by his mother, who received the knowledge from her father. Zsu supposed he must have been a magus of transgressive magic. "Was there abuse in your family?" Zsu pointedly asked. "I've heard talk that your grandfather bonked your mother?"

Osser's craggy face tightened like stretched old leather. The word, *abuse,* having lacerated his goat head stoicism. He didn't reply, as if silence was an admission, and stared with set jaw straight ahead at baby Starco. According to the O.O.O., incest was common in the early breeding lines of paradise days at the top of the world before the ice age. Zsu's skin crawled. She recalled her first sexual experience with her mother's boyfriend, with whom she'd avidly competed for attention. A pubescent sexualisation, so loaded with overwhelming feelings, that for her precocious Lolita self, it offered empowerment in the form of undifferentiated, wanton, hormonal desire to inflict carnal retaliation on her hurtful mother. The abuse of being dragged by the hair and locked in her room. The abuse of being photographed nude by her mother's lesbian friend. The resentment of being stymied in attempts to know her father.

"What kind of genetic inheritance is that?" she said to Odvar. "Isn't that patriarchal abuse?"

The O.O.O. prophet turned to Zsu, his face stony, emotionless, the look of a goat head authority figure, his body now reduced to half a man. His deep set rigid eyes fixed upon her, the same kind that she imagined his Devil cock ancestor must have possessed.

"You are correct in some regards," he said. "But in ancient times of Frey and Freya, the first man and woman before the ice age, it was natural evolution."

Zsu considered the sexual mangroves of her own family, muddy with an Electra complex. The first sex with her mother's boyfriend. Was it revenge? Had she wild child colluded in the secret teen, tease tryst—like a taboo love triangle? Was this hand of fate the ultimate agency of a code of the soul? A predestined formative, precociousness, precipitous to a pattern of promiscuity and emotional cut-outs in intimacy. Like the first sex with Jules, when she'd imagined another yoni, other than the one he'd entered, because hers housed conflicting feelings.

In light of her quest for an absent father, was it right to make Osser uncomfortable now with her biting reproach about his grandfather, how he'd come to be, and how he became the prophet of a cum imbibing cult in which a bad seed nearly ended his life. What kind of karma was this? How dangerous is an ancestral gene? Was this manipulative power tripping? Was he using his voice and O.O.O. root language sounds like hypnosis to tinker with impressionable stoners' minds? Was she venting anger at her own father who'd fucked her mother in the most aggressive and reckless of circumstances. (This was Zsu's mother's account of her conception, which in her mind, was rape.) Were Zsu's feelings of rejection and abandonment and betrayal rooted in coercive control games from the get go? How successful was her mother's cloak and dagger snubbing out of her father? Was it really rape? Was her conception the product of a collision of all of this feuding inside of her? She looked at Starco, he appeared so pure and oblivious to all of this. How would the nascent, inherited genes of his star seed way-of-being play out? What strands of family curse were constellated in him? Especially the generational strings that bind grand children to grandparents.

Zsu felt sorry for Osser. They had bonded in the most extreme of paranormal circumstances. The show down with cops at Spaghetti Beach defending the sacred space of the dance floor. The O.O.O. boys' club was not her cup of seed. To behold Osser crushingly paralysed from the waist down by a murderous act, never to dance again, was deeply sad and disturbing. What pernicious forces had the sorcerer unwittingly, or perhaps consciously, whipped up in someone's head? And so, she stood up out of her chair on his porch and bowed her head to his in the wheelchair, and kissed him on each of his cheeks.

"Odvar it's nice to have you back in Goa, even though its dreadfully empty as everyone has gone to Pune to party."

During Osser's absence from Goa last season, Atma continued with O.O.O. semen sessions and reciting of root language sounds and disseminating Osser's saga on tapes. Atma did not go to Pune. He was an absolutist. "A Goa party was not a Goa party unless it was in Goa." Against all odds, he was burning to pull off a party in homage to Osser's return, together with even more pressing reasons.

It seemed like the entire Goa party scene had uprooted to Pune to get high on Osho's farm. According to accounts of those that attended, the atmosphere was fun-filled and liberating with non-stop dancing to a variety of DJs playing the right music. But after everyone left, the local Indian organisers were raided and arrested by Pune Police for dealing charas, which had been at the behest of the inner circle controlling the Osho Foundation. Some of whom, Jules had been told by disenfranchised sanyassins, were the same faction that kept the foundation's finances close to their chest and armed themselves with automatic weapons when everything unravelled disastrously for the Rolls Royce collecting Guru in Oregon—where he nearly died in prison having been arrested for immigration fraud.

After the cult guru passed away in Pune, January, nineteen-ninety, many lost sanyassins set-up in Goa, which became a second home. So that when Goa did come to Pune—at the invitation of rave revelling sanyassins, and partied hard on Osho's farm—it galled the inner controlling circle. It wasn't as if bending the law was not something they didn't already prescribe to.

"Osho was a holy scoundrel," Zsu said to Jules, recalling her stay at the ashram in the early eighties. "He even referred to himself as a cheat. What I liked about him was that he was a disrupter. A dismantler of human programming. An illuminator of family dysfunction. His amassing of all those Rolls Royces at his Rancho Rajneesh commune in Oregon was about tipping values upside down, he wanted to provoke anger and envy in others by possessing so many. The absurdity outraged so many. Materialistic Americans flocked to him like ironic, spiritual nectar. He was a holy trickster. There sure ain't no flies on shrewd Osho people when it came to business. The Osho Foundation accrued millions. But that's India for you—the dualism of mystery and materialism and rituals of life and incessant rupee haggle in a deeply moving drama of survival."

By the time everyone had returned to Goa from Pune, a whole new wave of dance-to-trance backpackers, label hounds and ambitious, marketer DJs had landed on its legendary beatific beaches wanting to experience its mad party magic. It was the middle of the nineties—*Rave* had become a raging revolution. Goa was trending on the World Wide Web as a higher transmission style of party. A transporting, transcendental music meme customised for a trance-techno-tribal traveller lifestyle. To rave, Goa style, in India, was hip. Weird computer dance music was resuscitating the evil music industry. It was like Sargent Pepper had returned to India to fast forward to the future. Whereupon Sargent Pepper ditched the band and reworked **L**—ucy in the **S**—kies with **D**—iamonds using new tech midi devices enhanced by designer blotters and pills.

Where once it had been a lonely heart club band on stage entertaining an audience, it was now bliss-bomb dance floors with kaleidoscope eyes. Newly established labels promoted the *Goa Experience.* DJ proselytisers espoused the *Goa state of mind.* An underground sprouted like hybridised flowers with variegated leaves propagating out of a subculture underworld. One which had no face, having thrived on faceless, obscure, hard-to-find music funded by a black economy in which cameras were banned and was now being marketed by new branded labels like, *charas.com*, with alpha smoking god—Lord Shiva—licking a Rizla as its logo. Goa was being championed as a party vibe, and from a multitude of stylistic tributaries coalescing into an identifiable trippy genre, still not bound by the rubric of rigid, fashion formula. It being more about a mystical context, purporting to be open-minded and non-conformist. Music labels vibrantly packaged psychedelic Goa music in Asia-nuanced cyber-hippie sleeve designs. Ostensibly, party sound tracks inspired by the *Goa experience.* All increasingly made by artists who'd been turned on there, and aspired to translate the experience musically, and producers who'd gotten the bug by proxy, after hearing Goa mixtapes passed onto them by DJ traveller brethren who'd done time on dance floors there.

Boom shankar biz had been funding the collecting and collating of *Goa music* and commenced to fund its production. Charas and psychedelic trance techno was a match made in heaven. Record label, *charas.com*, was established in the early nineties. Its manifesto was to move as much vinyl and CDs as hash with their take on *Goa music.* Other chillum wallah music fanatics in the scene, like-wise, started record labels. A cottage industry mushroomed. Many got their heads into midi tech and DIY-ed themselves into making tracks. Studio gear was expensive. Boom shankar biz sponsored the making of *Goa music.* Goa DJs, for the first time, got paid playing parties in Europe, Japan, Australia and America. Acid disco, curated by freaks in the red Goan dust, was going commercial and careers launched. Yet, the core, original, traveller scene fiercely identified with its underground *outsiderness*. Especially, now that a bevy of new fashion, trance-techno tribalists were camping out this season in its palms, cabanas, rooms, houses and selling at Anjuna flea market. The new arrivals were hungry to experience first-hand, the *Goa experience*, in the frenzied international body heat of a full-tilt acid party, which they'd read about on the net.

Ironically, as the world was becoming hip to Goa, Goa—the wild party paradise—had become imperilled by its trumpeted, trending popularity. It now having become, less and less a level playing field, and more and more a slippery slope minefield of, on-again, off-again, in dealing with the shifting goal posts of authorities. Quite frankly, for the Goa Government, it was embarrassing for rave tourists to be arriving on mass to glaringly flaunt the law in such open-air hedonistic displays of dancing decadence. When there ought to be more regular tourists coming, who respectfully retired to bed by ten o'clock.

But undeterred—swept up in the hysteria of exotic raving in Asia—aspiring DJs, dance floor initiates, and die-hard regulars, kept showing up expecting a psychedelic techno utopia in troppo India. The word—*megalomania*—had been popping up in conversations about cult gurus at Goa dinner parties. And now it was popping up in chai shop discussions about Goa parties becoming a profession. And how the music industry grappled with faceless trance techno made by boffins. And how it was now trending and being marketed as a brand, fronted by the face of highly paid superstar DJs pushing a label, adhering to a prescribed style of music. As opposed to novel, unbranded, free style, random eclecticism of taste—which was how dance data had previously percolated through the underground of the *Goa DAT mafia*, for purposes of free parties in Goa. The most idealistic maintaining the belief that the Goa was not a product, and still the domain of the unbranded, outsider, black sheep.

At the beginning of nineteen ninety-four, grisly news befell those close to Zikos. Their gravest fears confirmed. Identified by dentistry records, his remains had been discovered in the Amsterdam sewer. The gruesomeness of it all shook everyone to the core. A ceremony was held for him on South Anjuna Beach.

By the second week of February, the season was off again, and the hunger for the *Goa experience* had become so agonising and unbearable that something had to be done. The scene felt persecuted and vilified and suffered from psychosis, paranoia and victimisation. Like the party belief system of a religion, the *Goa state of mind* was worth upholding. Someone had to have the gumption to relieve themselves, and the scene, of the burning need and frustration of the intolerable situation. It made sense that Atma should be the prime contender, considering what was at stake for him. After all, he knew the ropes with locals and had been in Anjuna since the beginning when the music was just candles in the sand with acoustic guitars. He'd weathered two and a half decades of fraternal politics from within, and without. There was no getting around it, no matter how many peace pipes were smoked, feuding and insidious deceit were inextricable to some measure of super loose, communal consensus of brother love and the cult of the unstraight.

Atma was miffed. All the upstart DJs arriving, seeking to claim their stake on the *Goa experience*, were stealing his fire. The Shiva sponsored *Goa state of mind,* sacramental to charas, was trending on the World Wide Web—and up for grabs. Its *state of mind*—enshrined in rituals with metaphysical machine music, a dancing deity, and holy pipe circles—was one that he self-righteously believed he had entitlement to ordain over like a protective guardian. A scene in which he'd erected a virtuous identity as a holy man. But after Osser's stabbing, which everyone assumed had been by a delusional member of the O.O.O., Atma's reputation had become tainted by association. Not that anyone in their right mind might believe that it was he, holier-than-thou, who was the back stabber.

The situation had now become Machiavellian, such that Atma turned to Voltaire to assist in saving Goa. Not just from it being shut down by the authorities, but to keep it truly underground, to make just one last party that authentically defined, in the purest of terms, what the *Goa experience* truly was all about, rather than a party by some come-lately outsiders riding Goa hype on the World Wide Web, and what European music magazines, like *Jockey Slut,* were hailing as the latest craze.

Atma normally didn't hang at Spaghetti Beach, but went there looking for Voltaire, who was every day at Nirvana chai shack this season. Which indicated one thing—which everyone was in denial of—as it was just too bad to fully accept. Atma prepared a chillum and offered it to Voltaire to start. It circled their table, and just as the maestro DJ was taking a second toke, Atma told him in a hushed voice the asking price from cops for party permission. Voltaire suddenly, violently choked. His lungs convulsed with savage coughing that sounded painful. He gasped for air with his hand fumbling the ceramic chillum and dropping it on the table where it broke in two. Everyone in Nirvana chai shack gasped and froze, alarmed with shock.

The maestro's face was contorted, his eyes bulged like a hung person. Luchiano rushed to give him water. "Voltaire!.. Are you OK?.. Are you

OK?..." Rejecting the water, Voltaire rose to his feet and dashed out of the chai shack coughing up thick phlegm, spitting it out onto his beloved patch—Spaghetti Beach. Looking up, he turned to gaze at Jungle Palace—the last place he'd DJ-ed at the end of last season. Now plastic detritus floated on the stagnant pool of water surrounding it. He then gazed toward the end of the beach at the rock from which Lazzaro had sculpted the head of Shiva. He wondered how much longer he and his friends would be protected by the smoking deity on their cherished beach head. He returned to Nirvana chai shack and gave Atma an answer that was so sad to hear, it brought a tear that rolled down his cheek.

The next day, Atma visited Zsu and Jules's house. Zsu greeted him with baby Starco wrapped in a sarong close to her breast, her face radiant like an angel. Atma wondered if this was the same person who'd once fried his balls so severely he wanted to kill her?

She led him into the lounge about which was scattered the bright new *Tribes of The Moon* collection, which was a big hit with the new party people thronging through the flea market.

Atma sat down on a cushion on the floor and crumbled charas. Jules appeared from the back of the house.

"Boom!" Atma said.

"G'day." Jules greeted him.

"I heard the Pune party went well?" Atma said.

"It was awesome," Jules reported. "Everybody happy—great to get full lift-off again—hear all the new music over two days and nights. A choice setting—but man!..it was a fucking bummer that the ashram put the cops onto the locals who organised it."

"That's appalling!" Atma said disgusted. "How could they do that? There must have been lots of Rajaneesh party freaks there."

"I guess it's not surprising," Jules said in a dour tone of voice, "considering that inner circle mob of sanyassins got pretty ruthless in Oregon, like poisoning the local town's water." Jules sighed. "The situation here is really the pits. It's more expensive and stressful to pull off a party in Goa than anywhere. Four times the price it costs in the West. What to do?"

"We're getting shafted," Atma said, heavy hearted, furrows creasing his brow over which hung dangling clumps of dreadlocks. "I don't suppose you know?"

"What?" Jules's eyes widened.

"Voltaire has stopped recording," Atma said in a dispirited tone of voice. "He has no feeling to play."

"That's terrible," Jules said. A death knell rung in his head, his face fell pensive filled with despair.

"Oh, no!" Zsu gasped, visibly shaken and stricken with sadness. "Surely not?" She said plaintively, not wishing to believe it. "No, it can't be true?"

"I'm afraid so," Atma said.

"I can understand why he's fed up," Jules said. "I can see why he's lost heart to play."

Atma's disappointed face was long like a fiddle. "Voltaire told me he was finished when I asked him to play." Atma hung his head down to the polished coconut mull bowl into which had dropped tiny charas pickings from the piece in his fingers, like he was now a beggar longing for one more full blast party to make everything better.

"Atma, you really think you can pull off a party?" Jules said with a look of disbelief. "A proper open air sunrise party, like we used to have here that goes the full course."

"We have to!" Atma snapped sharply, like his whole life depended upon it. "That new night club that's opened at North Anjuna is not what it's about. Newbie ravers don't understand. We gotto preserve the essence of a Goa party. The cops are giving permission again. For sure, they want to rake some cash before the season is over. It's now set off a bribe bidding war between the Starco boys, Nelson Corner boys and Chapora boys. The worst are the underhanded bars in cahoots with the gambling mafia. They'll all busting to broker a deal for whoever coughs up the bucks to make a party. But I'm going direct to Chief Inspector Fernandes in Mapusa."

Atma passed Jules a loaded chillum. "Do you want to play?"

"Um… just a moment," Jules said, giving the chillum back, and got up and walked down the hall to check that the front door was locked. Slowly returning to the lounge he pondered Atma's invitation. It conferred a graduation and respect, but then he reproachfully frowned, as other motives tore through his mind, a mind not yet stoned, but after smoking Atma's pipe he knew he'd be rendered permeable, his defences porous to infiltration, susceptible to seditious suggestions that would surely suck him back into the fractious fray of Goa party politics.

Sitting back down on the cushion facing Atma, he said, "Hey, thanks Atma for the invitation, but let's talk after you get the permission. I wish you luck, man. I'm really glad we got the chance to trance dance in Pune, the way we used to here."

"Boom bolenath!" The chillum was fired up, and just as Jules was about to take a toke, the sound of a jeep could be heard. Everyone panicked. Zsu hastily took the smoking chillum and baby Starco to the back of the house where her tailor was working. Atma stuffed his stash down his underpants. Jules went to the window, but the jeep must have parked at the side of the house. He cautiously opened the front door, then from around the corner of the house appeared Doc Silver.

"It's you!" Jules said surprised. "My God! I thought I heard a jeep."

"Come look," Doc said excitedly.

"Jules walked towards him, then turned his head in amazement when he saw a green coloured Mahindra jeep exactly the same as Goa Police.

"I picked it up in Pune," Doc said. "It was a fun drive down with the girls."

"Girls?" Jules chuckled.

"Canucks," Doc grinned. "Toronto… They hitched a lift after the party."

"Doc, you sure put the shits up us," Jules said. "Atma is here, we'd just fired up a chillum and heard a jeep. Man!—we freaked big time."

Doc cracked up with laughter. "Jeez, I'm gonna have some sick fun now, ain't I? Reckon I'll get myself a Goa cop uniform to go with it."

Back inside the house, the chillum was fired up again, and Doc put in a special order for Zsu to make him a new outfit.

DEEJAYS JOSTLED to succeed in making a party. Rumours were rife, whipping up hope: "Party Disco Valley…Party Bamboo Forest…Party Monkey Forest…Party Chapora Fort…" But all amounted to nothing, only "funeral parties." Partial relief did come when the Bombay owner of the newly constructed Paradiso Night Club on North Anjuna Beach clinched a deal with police allowing one party a week. But true believers were disparaging of an Ibiza style club party, it was not the real deal of an unfettered, freer-than-free Goa rave in raw nature, not bounded by walls with the music making an allegorical story, crowning with sunrise.

At Mapusa Police station Atma sat down with Chief Inspector Fernandes, who told him that party permissions were no longer his sole jurisdiction and bars must first apply to the Anjuna Police Station. Atma then set about marshalling support from backers in South Anjuna, cash was pooled, and it was decided to take a punt with the Starco boys. Competing DJs went to other bar cartels who convinced them they could seal a deal. Anjuna cops were treating the needy, splintered, party scene like a market in which they fielded backhander bids for permission, like it was an auction. On top of that, Calangute cops now wanted a cut of the action. Desperate party organisers were being strung along, one hand not knowing what the other was concurrently negotiating, with the going party permission price gouged.

Party wear at the flea market became more racy and sleek in hi-res trippy, zappy, hi-tech fabrics. New fashion labels exploded on the scene with stalls selling hallucinogenic patterned lycra. Asta launched a sub label—*Planet X*—featuring designs she made in Bali. The flashiest label of all, its eye-blistering lycra party wear screaming the loudest, was—*Supernova*. Its hyper patterned leggings and tops were like luminescent alien skins. Its intense ultra-violet colour frequencies seemingly empowering its wearers like a new species of radioactive cyborg.

An androgynous looking humanoid entity with purple hair, going by the name of, Cipher, fronted the *Supernova* stall. It was assisted by another entity, with insect-like legs and green razor-streaked hair, known as, Gothos, who'd just spun extraterrestrial music at the Paradiso Night Club.

One of the Starco boys came to Atma's house in the morning, the day after the flea market, with good news. Permission had been granted. Atma was thrilled. Word spread that there would be a party on South Anjuna Beach. But by evening, there was uncertainty as, apparently, the cops had reneged. It was off. Then word quickly spread of another party. "Bamboo forest back of Anjuna tomorrow night".

The next day, Atma woke up feeling pipped, and belted over to the bamboo forest on his thunderous Royal Enfield where he encountered a tribe of *Supernovas*, all vividly clad in UV fluoro-stretch wear. Far from being regular freaks, they radiated electromagnetic auras, which, to Atma's disdainful eyes, gave him the impression that invading humanoids were taking over. They were attaching the largest party banners he'd ever seen to bamboo poles. Marching up to a couple of Supernovas, Atma threw his hands up in the air. "Who's making this party?" he remonstrated in an authoritarian voice.

The Supernovas turned and gazed at him with an expression of cool indifference, and gave no reply. It was as though they didn't understand a word he was saying and continued positioning banners. With his dreadlocks piled high on top of his head, more than just feeling like he had a bee in his bonnet, his overheated head now felt like a beehive with his scalp being stung to death.

"Who gave you permission to make this party?" he said in a stern voice. Once again, he got no response. Pacing about the dance floor, he barked the same questions to other Supernovas raising banners, and received the same impervious response to his bluster. Fuming, he straddled his Enfield, angrily kicked it over and gunned it to Joe Banana.

By late afternoon, the biggest sound system Anjuna had ever seen (double that of the Omsonic PA), comprising four matte-black speaker stacks, had been assembled throughout the maze of the bamboo forest. After sunset, large banners saturated in black light pulsated with penetrating cosmic eyes. Two hours before midnight—bouncing with chutzpah, and glowing bright like a jump-up harlequin humanoid wearing retina-piercing skin-tight fluoro wear—DJ Gothos pressed the play button to power up the music. Gyrating from the knees up from behind a console, upon which were micro devices, Gothos's movements in front of matching artwork behind were like the lego extension of an animatronic fluoro stick-insect. Gargantuan, supersonic frequencies blasted out of the massive speaker stacks rattling rib cages. The bass and kick drum thumped Anjuna so loud it could be heard in Vagator and Chapora. *Supernovas* were the first to swarm the UV drenched dance floors. Luminously bright, they hopped about like radioactive fire flies.

Two hours past the witching hour, the virtual reality of the screaming colour and holophonic sound of the bamboo maze was full with bodies bouncing hyperspatial. Zsu bumped into Remo on a chai mat, who'd been seen at the Pune party and not shown his face in Goa since the horrid attack on Osser two seasons ago. When the incident came up in conversation, Remo became shifty, giving Zsu creepy feelings that sent a violent chill running down her spine. It was her first party since becoming a mum, she was feeling highly sensitive, yet it was great to be back in the the maze of the bamboo forest. This time, the cyclorama ultra-ness of the *Supernovas*' intense, entrancing, installation of art and mega sound felt overwhelming. She returned home to Badem to appease a burning need for a divination session.

An hour later, an unearthly phenomenon occurred deep in the night, like an interstellar force inside frequencies of light and sound, as though direct from the galactic centre. It took the form of an android voice inside the music.

> *I'm Robotico, I come from an omnidimensional realm of quark filaments warped through dark matter in a time space continuum. I'm a particle waveform of artificial intelligence from an omniverse mathematically created at the beginning of time. I'm the neuromorphic atomology of the quantum computation quickening the techtopia of your planet.*

More than the obscenely loud yammering of a psychedelic rave, the party in the bamboo forest turned into a cosmosis. Its blast—immune to earplugs, sleeping pills and disgruntled protest—impacted every life form in a vast radius. Starco had been sleeping next to his babysitter when Zsu returned home. She lit incense and candles at her courtyard alter of deities and sacred objects, sat down and commenced to chant a mantra whilst gazing into a large quartz crystal. An invisible presence soon could be felt, its source, the epicentre of sound coming from Anjuna. The presence was that of the android *Robotico*, which—at the same moment—was being transmitted through the party. Zsu felt an electrical current course through her body, the same sensation as The Tingler at the banyan party. Her body tightened, as if on the verge of a panic attack, then the reassuring spectre of Donna Ferreira appeared.

"The time I told you of has come to pass," Donna said. "Goa is unworldly, like me. The joy that was experienced went out into the world and it brought the world back here." Zsu relaxed, found composure, breathed slowly and listened intently. She was longing for guidance and hoping this ritual would provide it as much as other rituals, like the parties she used to make—which served as a form of ritual resistance to that which she didn't like in the world. The resistance now was in accepting how much Goa had changed. She too, had changed, having been in her longest committed relationship. Starco's arrival stirred deep seated feelings about the broken world of the family she'd been bequeathed. *Tribes of the Moon* had become popular. And more and more, she felt like a phoenix.

"Everything seeds, sprouts, blooms, brings joy," Donna said. "Everything that is born, is born to die, be transformed. The evolution of your DNA and nervous system has wisdom. Nothing exists in a vacuum. Your circle has become something else. What was hidden is now on show for a price, the gift that was, has gone. Players will become an audience seduced by ringmasters and the spectacle of a show. What was experienced isn't forgotten. There will be an eternal return."

Zsu felt sad, she wished Donna had a body, she wanted to reach out and touch her. Then, was struck by the realisation that Donna was Dionysius, and that Dionysius was ecstatic Shiva and Shakti, and that

Dionysius was the Devil and the Goat. It was Dionysus that was alive and kicking in the irrational mad ecstasy of a Goa party where substances (in the form of divine sacraments) brought visions of God and reconnection with her most core self. Happiness was an ephemeral experience, and that trapping it leads to despair, and that Dionysus and Donna suffer in the rational world of rules and limitations.

The clairaudience of the space Zsu was holding around the altar turned to static. In the distance, the thump of technological drums in the bamboo forest was whipping up electromagnetic, explosive forces into higher spin states. Suffering was being transmuted. Time and space transcended. Dancers were getting outside of themselves, experiencing something greater then themselves. From a distance, the call to subversive psychic adventure, that *party* had once been for Zsu, now seemed like a teleportation mania, or the repetitive beat drum roll of a religious rally, or the insatiable addiction to a fix beyond this world.

Gazing deeply into a large quartz crystal she heard Donna's voice say, "The goat head man is in danger."

"Oh, no!—Osser!.." Zsu gasped in distress. Starco started crying and she rushed inside. On returning to the altar with Starco in her arms, Donna had vanished.

The psycho-combustive charge of the group electronic Eros in the bamboo forest had been scorching. Not merely myosin proteins rapidly shunting endorphins along streaming filaments of dancing brain cells, registering—*joy*. But a subatomic, metanoia signal transmitted from deep space to reprogram life on earth. Within it, an exotic dark matter from a subsonic blast had triggered a collective cathexis of extreme digerati proportions—in the form of a meccanoid megalomania riding fractal frequencies of transcendent light, seized upon by avatar humanoids to induce a psychedelic hypnosis tagged with the label—*Supernova*.

It was as though all those wearing it had been branded into a cult of alien beings via the shape shifting sound DJ Gothos was wielding, like inking the bodies of dancers with musical fluoro tattoos. All looking like visitors from another world. The eye-blistering visuals and electron bending bamboo and liquid elixirs an escape velocity. As if a formidable force, posing as extraterrestrial fashion, had taken control of Goa's beatific head land in its darkest hour. The proliferation of the Supernova's screaming, patterned, colour blitz on the dance floor was like an overwhelming shoal of deceptive predator fish in a bamboo forest lagoon, which once had been the habitat of creatures in a multitude of styles.

Nelson Corner boys had set up two bars at entrances leading into the bamboo forest. Chai shop mumma mats were chock-a-block. Dancers, with pulverised bodies, clad in soiled neon-glowing stretch wear coated in digital dust, got spat out of the molten intensity of the bamboo maze's multiple dance floors—their brain cells having turned into dewdrop globules.

Hardly surprising, Goa Police showed up at dawn. They were from Calangute. It was assumed that everyone had been paid off. Doc Silver met them dressed in a khaki uniform, matching theirs, his silver mane tucked up under a faux Goa cop peaked-cap. "Good morning sir," he said like a beat constable to his senior. "I can report everything is under control."

The head cop, stony faced, shrugged at Doc's temerity, then became amused. Which was a good thing, but the charade of officialdom became a downer when the cop said, "Party must stop."

Doc levelled his dreamy blue eyes at the cop and shot him a shrewd grin, and winked, as if to say, *Sir, you must be joking!* And said, "No, not now, too much fun is being had, it's in the interests of everyone that the party continue."

Looking anxious, Cipher and a couple of Supernovas arrived and stood at Doc's side. The cop gaped at the dense bamboo from out of which seriously loud sound blasted with vibrant coloured figures ducking and diving through-out it. "Party can continue," he said with an oily smirk. "Payment required."

Doc consulted with the Nelson Corner boys, went back to the cop and haggled. It didn't take long until, with a disgusted look on his face, Doc went to Cipher telling them to fetch ten thousand rupees, or else the plug has to be pulled. The party continued, but by seven o'clock, Margoa Police arrived. Doc Silver met them, and the same deal went down. Finally, at eight o'clock Panjim Police arrived. Doc, relishing his hammed-up beat policeman act, was about to greet them when one of the Nelson Corner boys grabbed his shoulder and said, "Enough!" Doc turned to consult with other Nelson Corner boys. "No more pay," they adamantly instructed.

When Gothos reluctantly stopped the music, the silence was deafening. After a while, the daily rural morning sounds of Anjuna: roosters, cows, crows, dogs, bicycle bells, motorbikes…emerged from the post blast that left ears ringing. The collective shock of cessation of the intense hyperspace descended on the packed-out bamboo forest. It was like suddenly all the water had been sucked out of a swimming pool, leaving ravers high and dry like colourful tropical fish flapping about gasping for party oxygen.

Cipher, standing next to Doc, said, "Wow!—that really was something. I wish we could have kept going."

Doc took off the cop cap, releasing silver hair that fell down around his shoulders and wiped sweat from his brow. "I've never known a party to pull so much heat. All with their hand out. It's not a free market economy, it's monkey business. Supply and demand. It used to be all about love, not product, not money. What you paid to the cops was for the privilege of putting on a party. It used to be a secretive utopia—off the map. A gift for those that found it."

The "excessive volume" of the large PA in the bamboo forest drew many complaints from Goans. *The Navhind Times* blared a headline: LOUD DRUG PARTY BLASTED TOURIST BEACH STRIP. After a report from police, the Goa Chief Minister decried dance parties and declared a total ban. Fed up, backpack ravers packed their bags and headed to Koh Phangan.

The day after the bamboo party, perturbed by her necromancy with Donna, Zsu visited Osser warning him. He immediately pointed to his grandfather's skull with goat horns saying, "I've also been in touch."

She looked him square in the eye. "Listen Odvar, I know you know who tried to kill you." Her eyes narrowed. "We both know it wasn't Ragnar Groop. My spirit guide has told me something which you should be concerned about." Osser held her gaze not blinking an eyelid.

"Odvar, beware, you are in danger. I ran into Remo at the Bamboo Forest, he really creeped me out. He's totally out."

Osser appeared undeterred. "Thank you Zsu for your concern," he said unflinchingly. "Please don't worry. If something should happen, Atma knows what to do."

Naresh and Sheila were back in Goa, but not together. Both were sporting *Supernova* lycra and ran into each other in the bamboo forest where they complimented each other on their chic cyber-hippie stretch wear. Nostalgically, they later caught up again at Primrose for old time's sake, as they hadn't been in touch since their dalliance ended at the end of the eighties. Sheila spoke of how Goa had become "a movement," and her exciting career in the music industry. "Goa is taking off," she said, like she was pitching a campaign slogan. "I work for two record labels—*charas.com* and the *Safi Connection*. Her business degree had come in handy, she was responsible for marketing and distribution and got to meet producers and

DJs, many of whom were original Goa freaks who'd gotten out of monkey business of the spice trade and established professional careers. Now they got paid to DJ and make tracks for the many labels that were popping up all over the world—all thanks to Goa.

"Parties are booming," she said. "It's a whole cottage industry with decor artists, performers, graphic artists and party fashion. Those that were turned on in Goa now make parties and have started labels and put on annual festivals. Goa is all the rage, yet it's so sad," she said with a heaviness in her heart. "So, sad…" her voice faltering, "the situation here on the ground—in Goa, itself. It's terrible now how restrictive and expensive it is to make a party here in Goa. It's now become more costly than the West. The only place possible is the Paradiso. That's not Goa. It's Bombay money turning Goa into an Ibiza night club. "Surely this is not going to be the Goa of the future?"

But then, Sheila brightened and she invited Naresh to Germany for a summer festival where he could party with Goa people. A place in the countryside, that was previously communist East Germany where he could experience Goa with the same kind of freedom they'd had at the banyan tree party, back in the eighties before the Berlin Wall came down. Sheila's outrageous account of her exciting career in London, and invitation to visit Europe, exploded Naresh's imagination. Life in Bombay had been dreary after what she'd introduced him to. Although, he'd had some success with one screen play that he'd co-written. He puffed on the joint she shared with him, which exploded his imagination even more, with him flashing on the idea of a remake of the blockbuster hit, *Disco Dancer*, set in the current craze of a Goa party. Passing the joint back to her, he told her his vision. She cracked up and animatedly glowed. "Oh yeah!.. an acid disco movie. It has to be an absolute hit."

The April heat ripened mangoes and baked dendrites in noggins. Those that stayed, languished, dispirited under siege conditions. Members of the O.O.O. remained, pleased that Osser was back. He got around Chapora in a wheelchair and was always under the chillum tree after sunset. When not eating out, one of his home aides, a young local Goan man, would prepare meals.

Early in the second week of April, a full moon rose over the monkey forest coating everything silver. Osser sat on his porch gazing at bats that flew across the face of lunar's radiant disk, their screeching sounds piercing the loaded lunacy of the night. The usual bark and response of dogs could also be heard, but also foreboding wolf howls, which he'd never heard before. Candles burned inside the house, as there was a power outage. Spooked, he turned suddenly to peer through a window to behold animated long shadows on the interior walls of the house, which looked like shadowy characters of a Javanese puppet play. Then, frightfully he saw one of the shadowy figures produce a sharp object and heard alarming, shrieking cries from monkeys that dropped from a mango tree onto the roof of the porch. He turned his head and looked up at the full moon in Scorpio. Suddenly there loomed a figure that lunged at him, sticking a kitchen knife into his chest.

ON TOP OF MAPUSA HILL, a week later, on a Hindu pyre, Osser's body was cremated, as requested in a hand-written note sealed in an envelope with foreign cash he'd handed to Atma Blaze. O.O.O. members and those from the scene still remaining, gathered to farewell Osser, including Hipster Harry who remarked, "Odvar was an odd dude. But man, he sure did put on a stomping, hell fire birthday hoot." Wrapped in a white shroud, the rigour mortis body of the Ouroboros prophet appeared to dance one more time in the hissing heat of blazing, chopped wood that was incinerating it. Placed above his body on the pyre, according to Osser's wishes, was the skull and goat horns of his grandfather.

The Norwegian prophet's home aide told police he thought Odvar was the Devil. A psychiatric report concluded that he'd suffered a psychotic episode after allegedly being brainwashed by Remo Chandra, now wanted for questioning. The Goan would later be found guilty of involuntary manslaughter, insane at the time, and set free.

With no proper parties possible, it was agonising for Doc Silver to be in Goa, but he did return the following season to hang out with friends who still roosted there out of the Northern winter. And besides, bottom line, he figured he could still get some kicks road tripping on his Enfield chopper. But a final straw came when he heard that an off-shore casino had been permitted to anchor permanently in the waters of Mandovi River, and given an all-night license by the Goa Chief Minister. If that wasn't disappointing enough, it was even more clobbering and personal to learn, on his return to New York, that family business associates in Las Vagus were involved with the Indian consortium setting up the casino in Panjim harbour.

Like a dirge for a paradise lost, the absolute final toll of the bell came when Doc heard it from the Anjuna Basilica on a Sunday morning whilst stopped at the intersection by Bobby's Bar. From out of the blue, Voltaire pulled up behind him with sad news. Hipster Harry had left his body at dawn. The lead-like thud of the news was such that Doc laid his darling chopper down flat on the side of the road riddled with plastic bag rubbish, and went to Bobby and ordered stiff drinks for him and the retired maestro.

Naresh did accept Sheila's invitation to the German Goa festival, and was astounded by its scale, production, atmosphere, art decor and music. He then went to London with her and attended another Goa style party which had an image of Buddha as its logo. It was held at an indoor venue which had elaborate installations with crystals, fluoro art and ritual performances. As well as its popularity moving hips, *Goa Psy Trance* were the buzz words on everyone's lips. Sheila and Naresh agreed it was timely to pitch a screenplay to a movie production house in Bombay. The story, they figured, should be about a disco in the sky, set in Goa, featuring *Goa Psy Trance*. Naresh setup a meeting in Bombay with Prasad Kapoor, the owner of a film production house.

"Sci-fi Bollywood," was how Sheila described what she had in mind. Kapoor's eye brows shot up above his tinted glasses. Sitting in his office with Naresh, from out of a shoulder bag branded with *Safi Connection Records,* she pulled out CDs and spread them on the film mogul's oak desk, like a spread of colourful Hindu cards featuring gods and goddesses. He picked up one which featured a Warholish graphic of Lord Shiva with dreamy eyes. Others featured OM symbols and yantras and mandalas.

Naresh drew Kapoor's attention to the nineteen eighty-two blockbuster, *Disco Dancer,* which he'd acted in. "It put Bollywood on the map, globally," he said.

"Sure did," Kapoor agreed.

"It used to be Disco," Sheila explained, "then became Electro and New Wave and House and Techno. Now it's Shiva Shakti Trance."

"Really!" Kapoor said, surprised, and picked up another CD and opened its fold out cover, his eyes widening behind the gold frames of his glasses.

"This music was inspired by Goa." Naresh chimed in. "It's now a fashion craze."

From out of its pearl case, Sheila removed a CD disk with ornate cosmic design and handed it to Kapoor. Holding it, he was impressed by the artistic symmetry of its space-age computer graphics, the central image a mirrored temple, not dissimilar to the sacred geometrical architecture of the Taj Mahal. He rotated in his swivel chair and slotted the disk into a CD player and pushed the play button. A blizzard of twisting 148 BPM electronic sounds filled the office. After three minute's worth, he lowered the volume. "You say this started in India?"

"Indeed," Naresh said. "Right here in Bombay in nineteen eighty-two with 'Ten Ragas to A Disco Beat' by Bollywood composer, Charanjit Singh."

"Prasad, can you believe it?" Sheila said. "Disco became Acid House right here." Charanjit Singh was the first to use a mystical silver box from Japan—the *Roland TB 303*, which became the revolutionary acid sound of cosmic dance music that is now *Goa Psy Trance*."

"'Ten Ragas to A Disco Beat,'" Naresh proudly pointed out, "was made the same year *Disco Dancer* was released."

Kapoor rubbed his trim beard, leaned back in his leather, executive chair and pondered what he was hearing. "Do you think this will catch on in India? "I thought Goa was for hippies?"

"It's changed," Sheila said. "Hippies are getting the short shift, chillums are not allowed, sunrise raves have been banned."

Kapoor tapped his fingers on his desk. "Hmm…Goa does have a reputation for criminal behaviour—"

"No worse," Naresh said, "than the underworld of Bombay and the black market laundering that funds most movies made here." Kapoor averted his eyes and peered down at the dazzling artwork of the CD jackets.

"Like the music and parties," Sheila said, "market forces are dictating change. New night clubs are popping up in Goa. The government wants more tourists. Local tourist numbers are up. It's becoming hip with Indian yuppies. Of course, our label DJs and producers love the free spirit that the Goa brand identifies with. They'll keep coming back, no matter what. It's good for promotion and music business and DJ bookings worldwide."

"Look Prasad," Naresh said with a beaming, dream weaver Bollywood smile, "don't you see a glorious rags-to-riches story in all this?"

This was Sheila's cue to pitch for gold. "It will have it all," she said with upbeat conviction. "A musical with outrageous dancing and complicated lusty romance. But what would be most novel, is that the lead could be an extraterrestrial disk jockey, or crack-pot comedian, like a character in the *Muppets* show, or mystical philosopher, or guru—like Timothy Leary or Osho."

Kapoor's jaw fell to the drawer of his oak desk. "Oh!.. now I get it. That's what '*Psy*' stands for." He reached for a packet of Gold Flake from the pocket of his button-down pinstripe, silk shirt.

"Please Prasad," Sheila said, plucking a gold packet of Benson & Hedges from out of her handbag. "Have one of mine." Everyone lit up.

"Drugs are a problem," Kapoor said taking a puff, concerned about censorship.

"Don't worry," Sheila said. "The bars in Goa have taken control. It's all about alcohol now. It's cheap and accessible for out of state Indians. It's middle class, good for business. Sadly, for the original Goa scene, charas is illegal, its regarded as subversive, but it gives our label underground cred, which everyone in the broader global market respects."

"We have to be careful about sex," Kapoor said, with an embarrassed voice. "It's forbidden in Bollywood."

"Yes!.. Sex is a really big problem in India," Sheila complained. "I can assure you there's no dirty dancing at a Goa party, although there used to be lots of dancing in red dust. Now come on Prasad!.. don't tell me Indians aren't hedonists, they love trends like anyone else, and like always, unofficially, you can still score any nice vice you like in Goa. The domestic Indian market will be hungry for this, as its coming from overseas, but there's the added appeal and pride of it having started here, and in Goa. Just like Bollywood, which now has a broader global market, as do the clever start-ups of Silicon Valley in Bangalore, the story of this high-tech music fits perfectly."

Sheila had empowering lips, and especially when combined with a B & H cigarette and the symphony of her persuasive voice. "Isn't it always the case, just like Goa," she continued on a compelling roll, "something starts off so strange, on the edge, then there comes a time when it moves to the centre. The artists in our stable have smoothed out the formula for tracks that work best on the dance floor, making *Goa Psy Trance* more accessible for a guaranteed fun party. The success of a fashion genre requires that it fulfil predictable expectations, not vary too much from the program—adhere to a formula. Software presets allow for dependable live shows. We'll present our DJs and producers on a stage, turn a Goa party into a show. Make it entertainment. The market audience will be happy to pay for an imported talent with the same expectation they have of attending a concert with real live musicians. There'll be sets and lights and projections and puppet masters on a stage, which we'll design like a temple. You know what we are talking about Prasad, just as in the smoke and mirrors of your business. *Goa Psy Trance* is so sci-fi paranormal we could just as well fake it with a virtual reality extraterrestrial disk jockey. It's not about disco dancers any more, it's about who is on show, on stage, pushing buttons—like a-jack-in-the-box."

In Sheila's highly excited mind's eye, what she really wanted was for Bollywood's *Disco Dancer* to go Bollyweird at an acid disco, where romance loses the plot and *true love* is discovered. Kapoor reached for his packet of Gold Flake and monkeyed another cigarette, lighting it from the B & H that was down to the butt and about to burn his shaking fingers.

By and by, Jaeger would only briefly pop into Goa during February. He bumped into Atma, now getting about in an Ambassador *Karma Cab*, who moaned, "They took our religion and turned it into a money making machine." He met with Zsu, who now supplied shops there. Speaking in a whisper, he told her of a new place that was "paradise on earth," totally unspoiled with lovely locals. It was vital that it remain a secret for as long as possible so that—like the gift that Goa had once been (which now seemed another lifetime, and nostalgically yearned for)—it might last.

www.raycastle.com

Made in the USA
San Bernardino, CA
12 February 2019